What was it about her that attracted such evil men? And why was there never a decent man around when she needed one?

Hannah, angry as well as afraid, struggled to escape him. Her boots lay far away on the grass as she twisted away from his grasp. Getting to her feet, she ran toward Fancy with blood dripping down her leg from his filthy fingernails.

"Naw you don't, little missy. I got you now an' there's nobody aroun' to cry to." Leaping to his feet, he grabbed her around the waist and pulled her against his sweat-stained shirt.

She felt his course, work-hardened hands grasp her breast and squeeze. She cried out in pain and fought her faintness from his assault on her body. She kicked at his lower torso and clawed his face, leaving long bloody trails of torn flesh. His bleeding face quickly became a wild mask of insanity, as he clutched her tighter.

If he felt the clawing of his flesh, he gave no sign. She realized he was intent on something else.

"Now jest let me have some of the same as thet baby gits. You got a'plenty thar. I can see that much!"

He yanked her dress open, making the fine little buttons fly into the grass, and bent his protruding lips to her full aching breasts. Her mad struggling only made him more inflamed.

In horror, Hannah screamed, "Please don't! Oh, please don't do this!"

Unable to escape his heavy grip on her body, she raked his face again with her nails. His strength easily overpowered her, and Hannah felt the darkness overtake her as his foul lips closed over her breast.

She went west to marry a stranger…

In 1892, Hannah Carlson, an innocent young farm girl from Iowa, arrives in Flagstaff, Arizona, as a mail-order bride. She marries Jacob Moore and soon finds herself isolated on his ranch with a sadistic monster. After months of physical and mental brutality, Hannah—nearly dead from her injuries—fights back, striking a fatal blow, and flees into the night. Now she's on the run from the law with her infant son…

Now he's the only one who can save her…

When lonely surveyor Brice Fowler discovers the battered woman who has taken refuge in his cabin, he tends her wounds, takes care of her, and finds her sanctuary on the Jesse Bidwell Ranch, caring for the rancher's ailing wife. Brice falls deeply in love with Hannah and wants to marry her, but she fears the intimacy of marriage. After running afoul of an over-zealous cowboy, Hannah is arrested, tried, and sentenced to hang for the murder of her husband. Knowing she has only one chance, Brice combs the deserts of Arizona for an unlikely witness whose testimony could save her life. But will he make it in time?

KUDOS for *Hannah*

"A good Western requires certain characteristics. It needs to have suspense and drama, plenty of action, heroes and villains, be based on a real time in history, and include geographically accurate depictions of the gorgeous and dangerous landscapes of the rugged west. The ending must be satisfying, as the good guys win and the villains are punished. *Hannah* has all of those things and more. A good romance also requires certain characteristics, including a sympathetic heroine who is strong yet vulnerable, a dashing masculine hero who also has vulnerabilities, plot twists, and the underlying fear that things won't work out. Then it must end with a 'Happily Ever After' ending. Again, *Hannah* fits the bill perfectly." ~ *JJ Riever, Kayenta Mountain Media*

"The story is charming, filled with interesting characters and fast-paced action. The author's vivid descriptions and knowledge of life in the Old West give the book a strong feeling of authenticity." ~ *Taylor Jones, Reviewer*

"Hannah is another jewel in the crown of this accomplished author. Well written, intriguing, and thought-provoking, *Hannah* is the story of one woman's fight to save herself and her child from the vicious things that some men can do. It's a heart-warming and heart-breaking tale of courage, sacrifice, and second chances." ~ *Regan Murphy, Reviewer*

HANNAH

Ramona Forrest

A Black Opal Books Publication

Black Opal Books

BECAUSE SOME STORIES JUST HAVE TO BE TOLD

GENRE: WESTERN/HISTORICAL ROMANCE/ROMANTIC SUSPENSE

HANNAH
Copyright © 2010 by Ramona Forrest
Cover Design by Jackson Cover Designs
All cover art copyright © 2016
All Rights Reserved
Print ISBN: 978-1-626945-31-9

First published as A Mail Order Bride

Published by Black Opal Books http://www.blackopalbooks.com

DEDICATION

I dedicate this book to all those unsuspecting brides who happily embark on the marriage journey where all those hopes and dreams may come true—or not.

CHAPTER 1

Northern Arizona, early spring, 1892:

In the early morning, after long tedious miles through country wild and unfamiliar, Hannah Carlson stepped off the train and caught the first glimpse of her final destination. She'd arrived in the roughly hewn mountain town of Flagstaff, Arizona. Small, rustic, and crude in appearance, the town wound its way slowly and haphazardly upward. It appeared as though the small gathering of shacks, stores, and stone buildings rested in the shadows of the far mountains that held bits of snow glistening in the sun.

Clusters of weathered, clapboard buildings, in various states of repair, sat snugly side by side and, beyond them, the landscape was covered with conifers. There were other trees she did not recognize scattered about amidst the buildings. The outlying homes appeared nestled in a green, tree-covered park.

One peak in particular, the highest of them, rose bare and stark above the tree line. *How different from Iowa. Those wild and rugged mountains are glorious!* The air felt thin to her, cool and pine-scented. Icy-tinged, it nipped at her nose.

Standing alone, her possessions beside her, Hannah waited for the person who would meet her. Seeing no one about, she took in her new surroundings. The town and buildings were about what she'd expected. The wild frontier town of Flagstaff, sprawled before her, upward over low foothills, edging toward the soaring San Francisco Peaks.

She'd read that Flagstaff was the center of commerce for northern Arizona and, in 1892, it was young and raw. Though a small place, the community bustled with early morning activity. In addition to the fumes of railroad machinery, dusty streets, and the occasional sharp assault of animal dung, she caught the clean, sharp scent of pine trees in the cold, dry air.

She glanced frequently about. The man she was to meet hadn't shown himself. Would he fulfil a good part of her maidenly expectations?

Her hands trembled as she paced about on the railway platform, waiting for a man she'd never laid eyes on. *Would the man she was to marry be here to meet her? Would she like him—at all. Would he be a good man?*

She shivered. *Get hold of yourself, girl.* With increasing trepidation, since no welcoming voice had met her, she grappled with visions of herself, a young woman of eighteen, stranded alone in a land completely unfamiliar. Looking about, she realized it hardly seemed a part of the country she knew.

Hannah felt prepared to be a frontier wife. Readying for this journey into a new life, she'd studied the sort of life her prospective bride-groom offered. She awaited seeing new lands, meeting new faces, and riding horseback about this beautiful, wild land.

She'd read all she could find about the West, and the agency had said she had the option of refusing the marriage if the prospective husband didn't satisfy her expectations.

Hannah squared her shoulders and looked about again. It was early spring and those tall, majestic peaks just beyond Flagstaff gleamed with small remaining bits of glistening snow. Was that why the breeze seemed so cool—

"Miss, might you be Hannah Carlson?"

She startled at the sound of a voice, deep and soft, resonating from a broad chest. A solidly built man approached, looming tall over her small person.

"Yes, I am. Are you Jacob Moore?"

"Yes, ma'am, I am."

The man appeared friendly, soft spoken and, to her delight, quite handsome with his square jaw and darkly tanned skin. His features bore the deep vertical lines of a man who spent much time outdoors.

Now that he stood before her, the mere size of him made her feel off center. Taken aback by his great stature and those deep, dark eyes, a small shiver passed through her. Why, she wasn't sure.

His clothing looked strange, as well. He wore rough corded pants stuffed into strange appearing high-heeled boots, a leather vest, and a checkered shirt of some coarsely woven material. Clean and neatly dressed, his hair had been newly barbered.

But she gasped at the sight of the gun holstered about his hips. "Oh, God!"

She got herself in hand and remembered what she'd read. *This is the West—they carry guns here.*

"Care for a bite to eat, miss? You must be worn out from your long journey." He'd paid no mind to her reaction to his gun, other than a slight smile as he held out a well-muscled arm. "They're servin' breakfast at the hotel right across there." He nodded toward the other side of the street, rutted with dried mud.

The masculine scent of him sent a thrill of apprehension through her body, but Hannah shyly placed her hand on the crook of his arm. They set out, walking side by side, to enter, sit down, and order a meal—a solid, though plain, meal of ham, potatoes, coffee, and a huge stack of flapjacks.

She acquainted herself with Jacob Moore as well as possible in the short time he allowed. "How far away is your place?" She couldn't think of anything else at the moment, since the entire situation seemed so bizarre.

They chatted a bit, until the breakfast was consumed. He turned in his chair to face her. "Well, Hannah, would you want to marry me, now you've had a look?" He grinned at her with a wide mouth and slightly squinting eyes. His face bore the markings of his outdoor life, deeply tanned, seamed, toughened skin, and a squint that could be from working in the brightness of a semi-desert sun. "We could make it to the ranch before sundown, then."

She had to decide, and now. He appeared to be a big bear of a man who exuded gentleness, confidence, and manly grace. Nothing about him gave a clue as to what her future held. Ready to begin the life of a rancher's wife, she acquiesced readily to their union.

Jacob smiled down at her as he escorted her down the boardwalk and along the side of the rutted street to a small weathered cottage. "This here's where the parson lives, Hannah. I believe he'll marry us right away, bein' you're willin'."

The parson's home, small and poorly furnished, rather matched the couple within. His plainly dressed, thin little wife served as the only witness, and the marriage took place without fanfare. No man stood with Jacob Moore, and Hannah, used to a lot of joyous hoop-la at weddings, thought it rather unusual. *Has this man no friend to stand with him on his wedding day?* She questioned it, said nothing, and shrugged away negative thoughts in her eagerness to begin life as a married woman and rancher's wife.

The stodgy older parson, Will Elkins, appeared nearsighted and slightly confused. His frail, wispy-haired wife, Martha, attended the wedding and helped him with the paperwork required to complete it.

After the hasty nuptials, Martha offered Hannah and Jacob a drink of sarsaparilla water as they waited until the parson recorded the marriage in his log book. Curiosity in the wife's probing eyes was obvious as she observed them.

"New out here, are you?" Her eyes squinted with the question.

Hannah nodded, her head held high. "Yes, ma'am, I arrived here just today."

Men in this country were lonely and isolated. Finding a bride in this manner was an accepted practice. The interest gleaming in Martha's eyes made Hannah wonder how many of these marriages they'd seen, if any.

The marriage completed, she and Jacob set out on a long, rough ride over rock-strewn, rutted roads in a buckboard filled with supplies. She clung to Jacob's arm as she took in the strange, wild scenery. Passing wonderful huge pines covered with rough reddish bark, Hannah inhaled the scent of them. Miles of chaparral, scrub oak, and piñon pine delighted her senses as the team made its way to lower, more open, grasslands.

Completely strange and new to her, she waited for him to name all she was seeing and instruct her in the ways life was conducted in the wilds of Arizona. Jacob, delighted to answer her questions, cast heated glances into her eyes. Those looks sent wild tremors racing through her body. Sitting close enough to catch his male scent, she trembled inwardly, trying to imagine her wedding night. Anticipation and fear coursed through her small, slender body. *Would he be gentle with her?* She'd married him, and her happiness now lay in this man's huge, work-worn hands. *Had she done the right thing in marrying a total stranger?*

Evening descended rapidly over the wild escarpment that lay on all sides, and she thrilled at the vivid colors across the western sky. Nothing she'd read had prepared her for the incredible beauty of this country. In the deepening dusk they arrived at a large ranch yard. The horses were sweating and blowing from the last hill they'd climbed to enter the wide area between the ranch house and outbuildings. Other horses whinnied to the tired team, and dust rose from their corral as they stamped about and hung their heads over the rails in welcome.

Her excitement grew as Jacob pulled the team to a halt and turned to her. "This is it, Hannah, my ranch."

She heard the pride in his voice as he waved his long arm about, encompassing the house, barns, corrals, and the vastness that surrounded it. The glorious purples and mauves of the fading light threw long shadows over the distant mountains and the sight of it struck a chord of wonder in her heart. This ranch was hers now, too.

Looking away from the glowing sky, she saw a long, low-roofed house of rough timbers and stonework. A wide covered porch held up by poles ran across the front. Bales of hides, shovels, and equipment lay stacked across it and strange-looking items hung on the walls.

Jacob helped her down, took her bags, and led her into his

home. Setting her possessions in the only bedroom, he looked into her eyes. "I won't be long, my wife."

His deep, hushed tones set her heart a flutter as he left her to put his tired, sweating horses, to feed and rest.

His words filled her with anticipation. She awaited him with timidity and eagerness. She busied herself putting things away, guessing where they might belong, though it was dark inside and she couldn't see the layout of the house. She didn't know where the lamps might be and fumbling about gave her a feeling of unease, even of trespassing. "This is my house now, but—"

Heavy-treaded footfalls sounded on the wooden floor when Jacob reentered the low-slung home. He came to her, said no words of love and longing, but swept her into his strong arms and held her so tightly she could scarcely catch her breath.

His grip crushed the breath from her lungs, until she cried out, "Jacob, you're hurting me!"

Told there might be pain, she was instantly ashamed for complaining. But his roughness frightened her, and she found it difficult to comply with him.

"Come on, now. It's not so bad." He grabbed her close, pulled her blouse open, ripped away the tiny buttons, and squeezed her tender young breasts. She tried to hold her fear in check, but when he threw her on the bed and fell roughly onto her, she cried out. He stopped her mouth with heavy kisses, grinding into her lips. She felt his teeth and, in fear, struggled to escape.

He was big and very strong. Unable to stop him or reason with him, she tried her best to believe this was the normal course of events on a wedding night, but when he pulled up her skirts, tore away her underclothing, and plunged deep into her tender flesh, she screamed. His hard mouth stopped her cries and the pain she endured was heightened by her rising fear.

His rough and painful assault continued on and on. Her agony and despair was such that she prayed inside her mind she'd live until morning!

This is my wedding night! When it was finally over, she was fearful, filled with pain and bitter disappointment from her new husband's brutal assault. She clung to the side of the bed, keeping her body as far from him as she could. Listening to Jacob's heavy, deep snoring, she felt the horror of her situation settle insidiously and permanently over her. *Oh, God, help me. What have I done?*

She'd long planned to meet her new husband's embrace fully, excited at being a wife, eager to find the fulfillment of wedded life. She'd never heard of a wedding night like this, filled with pain and desolation. No one had ever told her it could be this way. Terror of her new husband claimed her. It struck deep.

ᏟᎠᏟᎠ

Awakening, she scanned her surroundings. With a sigh of relief, she saw her new husband was gone. Bruised inside and out and exhausted, she fought her terrible disappointment, trying to accept what he had done to her as the lot of the married woman.

In his absence, she limped slowly through the house, blood smeared on her legs, as she acquainted herself with her new home. The stove looked ancient, but she stuffed a few shreds of paper in and chucked a few sticks of wood on top. Finding a half box of matches, she lit the fire. Enjoying the warmth it gave off, she hunted about for what foodstuffs were available. She managed a cup of coffee and sat at the table, contemplating her future.

CHAPTER 2

Hannah tried to face her lot in life. Adjusting to living with a rough and secretive man, trying to understand what made him the way he was, proved nearly fruitless. He was rough with his riding stock, freely using his spurs and whip, and she never met any ranch hands, if indeed the man had any.

Life in the isolated and wild Arizona high country, went along peacefully, if painfully, for nearly three months. No neighbors had come to visit, and she wondered about that. Did they know he'd married? Did anyone?

When Jacob came, in she asked, "Jacob, I haven't met any of our neighbors. When will we see them?"

She longed for another female to share thoughts, recipes, tips on living in this country, but she'd met no one. More than that, she desperately wondered how other marriages were conducted and if anyone would enlighten her.

"In a while, Hannah, we'll be workin' the roundup right soon. Then we'll see about a get together."

Two more months passed and no one came to pay them a friendly social visit. She wondered, but knowing his taciturn nature, decided it would be best not question him. She settled to wait patiently for the day she'd meet his fellow ranchers and their wives.

"After a while, darlin'," Jacob replied, when she got up the courage to ask the question again.

Loneliness and isolation seeped slowly into her thoughts.

Why have no neighbors come to call? It went against all she knew of rural people and added to her feelings of unease. In time, Hannah felt fatigue, nausea, and with the sensation of dizziness, believed she was pregnant. "Oh, how I wish one of our neighbors would come by. I need a woman's advice right now." Her voice echoed in an empty house.

Trying to sort out her feelings, fighting nausea, and wondering how to tell her husband the happy news, she burned the cuts of beef while making his dinner. The smoke of it drifted all through the house while she salvaged what she could.

When he discovered the ruined food, she watched in amazement as Jacob's face turned a fiery, dark red, accompanied with a towering anger worse than anything she'd ever seen in her inexperienced life, "Jacob, what's wrong? It's only a bit of meat, for heaven's sake!"

"Well, now, ain't that just fine! You're wastin' the good food I provide and you think it's nothin'!"

In disbelief, and more than a physical blow, the scathing words he'd flung into the air between them caused shock and pain.

As his clenched fist rose up before her, she shrank away. "You ugly, useless bitch! Can't even fry up a little meat? God dammit, woman, you're careless and wasteful as hell! I'll teach you to be more careful! Come here, you filthy slut!" His big hands reached out for her.

Her world, already lonely, crashed to bits about her. "Jacob, what have I done wrong?" she cried. "No amount of meat is worth your laying blame on me like this!"

His utter disdain for her, and any of the attributes she'd thought so important in their marriage, sent her dissolving into bitter tears.

"I'm sorry, I didn't mean to burn the meat, and all those other things you said. I don't know what you want me to do."

Hannah sank to her knees, trembling in fear and the added agony of utter disappointment. Her shock at this sudden change in her husband made her physically ill. She staggered to the door and vomited in the yard.

Jacob changed suddenly. "Aw, honey, I didn't mean it.

Can you ever forgive me? My temper gets the best of me sometimes."

He reached out to pull her into his arms, soothing her, kissing, and uttering soft words. She was amazed by his sudden tenderness as he held her in an unusually gentle embrace.

She apologized again for her mistakes, but couldn't find the courage to tell him about the forthcoming child. *It might set him off again!*

Within the next week, he struck the first blow, knocking her head against the door lintels. She screamed in fear and sank to the floor. He aimed a hard kick into her ribs. "Now get the hell out of this house, you god damned, miserable, useless bitch! I never want to lay eyes on you again!"

Later, cowering in the barn, sobbing her heart out, she saw him coming. He looked for her, and she shrank away in terror at his approach.

"Honey, I don't know how my temper got the best of me. You know I love you. I promise, this temper-rage of mine won't let loose no more and do anything like that again. I'll never hurt you anymore. You have my promise on that."

His soft, conciliatory words as he gathered her into his arms belied the deeper truths she'd unhappily learned. But she became his again. She had no other choice.

By then, Hannah was certain she was pregnant. Since he was being kind at the moment, she found the courage to tell him, but watched fearfully for his reaction. "Jacob, I believe we are to have a child."

"Why that's just fine, Hannah." His look and words, soft and caring, made Hannah believe giving him a child would change him, make him a happy man, and maybe even a gentler one.

The relief she hoped for was short lived. The beatings never stopped. Careful not to hit her in the abdomen, he spared nothing else. Desperate to know the reason for his sudden changes in behavior, she had no one to turn to. At odds with all she knew of rural people in Iowa, she was totally alone in her misery. Hannah feared for her child's comfort. Having no clothes for an infant, she unraveled old socks to knit booties, and cut up some of her softer things to make a few clothes for the new infant.

She knew better than to ask about other ranch folks. "He wouldn't want his fellow ranchers to see what his nice new wife looks like these days, would he?" She bit back a bitter laugh. "Do they even know he's married?"

He kept his distance from his neighbors. Certainly, he wouldn't want anyone to know the kind of man he really was. No matter what face he presented to fellow ranchers when he met with them, he'd become a monster in her eyes. He worked with them for roundup and branding, if at no other time, but they never came to the house.

Hannah's life, a deepening hell of utter loneliness and desolation, now became one of excruciating pain and fear. Looking in an old cracked mirror, she cried out, "Oh God! I don't even recognize myself! I've cuts and bruises everywhere. All I see now is an ugly swollen creature I don't even know." She sobbed quietly. "I'm trapped out here. No friends, no family, and my poor little baby waits to come into this hell on earth!"

Desperately fearful, angry, and alone, with her greatly swollen belly, she had no place to go.

When her time came, he brought a Navajo woman in to help her with the birth. Showing no signs of interest or delight in his forthcoming child, he merely told her. "This is Neebah. She knows about bringing babies. She'll do what's needed. You just do what she tells you now," he admonished her sternly, then he turned and stalked out without a word of comfort or concern for his pain-wracked, frightened wife.

Hannah looked into the glittering black eyes of this total stranger, and managed a tremulous, "Hello, Neebah." A feeling of helplessness overcame her as another hard, tearing contraction struck her. "God, help me!"

She gritted her teeth and moaned softly while waves of deep, ripping pain encompassed her.

Her words were answered with a soft grunt. "I help you, missus."

The Indian woman's hands felt cool and soothing as she

gently rubbed Hannah's distended belly. Hannah noted how extraordinarily soft the woman's hands felt.

Neebah approached middle age. Hannah saw deepening lines in her face and silver streaks coursing through her thick black hair. Her blouse was of deep magenta-hued velvet, trimmed with bits of silver and turquoise. The skirt was a gathered non-descript and worn print. She kept her eyes cast away as much as possible, as though afraid to converse with Hannah, other than telling her what to do concerning the delivery of her baby.

She made no comment about the numerous bruises in all shades of yellow, green, and purple, scattered about her body. The woman's last name was not given and Hannah never saw her again after her baby boy lay clean and nestled in her arms. Neebah had said little and, with a few words of instruction, faded quickly away, her task done.

Hannah felt inadequate and confused with this tiny new human. She'd heard instructions came naturally with babies, and for her, that was the way it had to be. By instinct, she nursed him, washed him, and cradled him. In a very short time, her infant son took possession of her lonely heart, bringing a clandestine happiness to her beleaguered and terrified soul.

For a month, there were no beatings, but a small incident began it again and the brutality continued. And on one fatal night, he'd beaten her back, arms, and legs to the point she wasn't sure she could walk. But this time, she knew instinctively, that her tiny infant boy, Thomas, was in mortal danger.

Terrified, she waited. When his furor had at last died down and he lay snoring in a deep, drunken stupor, she saw her chance. Spittle drained from the side of the lax mouth that had said such evil, foul words that Hannah could scarcely credit to a civilized human being.

In one terrifying moment, her heart beating like a trip hammer, Hannah grasped the nearest weapon at hand. Clutching a heavy cast iron skillet, and with all the strength her weakened arms could muster, she bashed it down heavily against the side of his head.

"There, you devil, you'll not beat me again, and you'll

never lay a hand on my boy!" She struck again for good measure.

She barely looked at her husband's bloodied head, terrified he'd rise up and take deadly revenge on her and her baby. She quickly gathered what few supplies she had for her baby, packed saddle bags, and limped to the corral. She caught up Concho, a horse, she knew to be gentle.

From that moment, she began her escape from cruelty and torture at the savage hands of her enraged husband. Tears of pain escaped Hannah's swollen, blackened eyes as she hunched over her saddle. She'd wrapped a heavy woolen blanket about her tortured body to hold the cold night wind at bay.

"Please, God," she cried aloud, "I'm cold and I hurt so much!" Pain surged up from her knees, into her tender, bruised abdomen, while she nudged her horse along in the darkness of an unfamiliar trail. Guilt at striking her husband haunted her. "That monster was going to kill me and my baby. If I killed him—I had to do it!" She grew terribly tired. "I can't fall. I'll never get back on old Concho."

Falling in her weakened state would be a disaster for both her and child. She clung desperately to the saddle. The gentle paint horse walked slowly, but even that much jostled her battered body, causing additional torment. Moans of pain escaped through the bloody froth dried on her lacerated, swollen lips. The horse found his way by some inborn instinct and the dim light from the emerging sliver of moon.

Hannah held her baby snuggled against her breast, held securely in a sling lest he fall from her weakened arms. Frequently, she glanced backward over the faintly visible trail. Each movement caused fresh waves of agony to wash over her, but the terror of being followed kept her frequently nudging the horse, urging him onward in the deepening gloom. Her arms and body ached with fatigue, and newer pain from the last brutal beating.

Hannah kept seeing the dreadful events in her mind. The sounds of that skillet crushing his skull sickened and haunted her very soul.

"I guess I'm not the nice, meek little wife anymore, and

God help me, if I live through this, I'll never be one again."

The infant squirmed against Hannah's chest and his muffled cry told her he was hungry. She pulled the horse to a halt. That small effort made her moan with pain. The reins lay slack across the saddle horn. "Whoa, Concho, time for a rest."

A quiet, gentle horse, he'd stand if she pulled him up.

She rearranged her son so that his seeking lips found her breast, and he began suckling noisily, making the soft, pulling sounds of contentment while he filled his tiny stomach. Again Hannah experienced the familiar sensation of wildness that the baby's eager sucking sent arching intently through her body. She wondered at the kinship, so acutely felt, with other mammalian creatures during this most intimate of moments. Only at these times, had she known contentment in her hell-on-earth life with Moore.

Was he mad? She'd had frequent thoughts about it, didn't know, but she certainly knew the consequences of life with a man like that. Stroking the baby's fine pale hair as he fed, Hannah glanced back into the darkness that covered the trail and wondered. *Could he be dead?*

She had no answer, only remembered her fear for their lives, and her utter desperation. She'd struck those heavy blows and, haunted by the sounds they'd made, she shuddered.

Have I done murder now? She questioned the fate that lay before her if her husband had died from her onslaught. *They'll hang me or put me in prison. I'll be free of him, but what will become of my child?* She shook off the worry. More pressing needs faced her. She refused the feelings of guilt. She'd be dead by now and her baby son with her, had she stayed at Moore's ranch.

He'd hunt her down, kill her and their child now that she'd taken action against him. "How could a man want to kill his own flesh and blood?" When his hideous temper took hold, and his boiling point was exceedingly low, the merest error on her part, real or imagined, sent him into towering rages.

He'd managed to destroy her sense of self-worth. He'd made her feel inadequate as a wife and homemaker. She'd felt more than equal to the rigors of making a home anywhere, even in this wild unsettled place. How useless her skills had seemed under constant criticism and cruelty.

Finished feeding her infant, Hannah changed his soiled cloth as best she could on horseback and nudged the horse into action. Her arms were heavy with fatigue, and her back ached from sitting in the saddle for many hours. Fortunately, the child slept continually as she rode, comforted by the constant jostling and warmth of his mother's body.

Knowing she must find shelter, and praying she'd ridden far enough for safety, she sought a safe spot where they could rest. Against her fear of the night in a strange country, she dwelt continually on her husband's evil wrath. She shuddered with memory, knowing if he found her, she'd suffer another onslaught at those thick, heavy hands and puzzling over a man like Moore. "May I never see his bloated and reddened face again—never!"

Hannah had to rest. Both body and spirit were done in. About to fall from the horse in desperate fatigue, she turned him onto a faint sort of trail just off the road she'd followed. She guided him into a passage through the blackness of thick underbrush. Cruel bushes with long curved thorns, much the same as cat's claws, tore at her jacket and the thin stuff of her worn-out dress as the horse pushed through. She sought a soft patch of grass to rest her aching body.

The light of the slowly enlarging sliver of moon aided her search for a thicket deep enough to hide herself and the horse. Concho stopped and tossed his head before a large solid blackness then reached down for a pull at grass.

Adjusting her eyes, she realized it was a cabin of some kind. "Thank God, it's shelter. Oh, let it be a place where we can rest!" Praying no one was home, she slowly and, careful of her baby, painfully dismounted. Her legs and feet stung as they adjusted to standing, after long hours in the saddle. Nearly fainting, she waited while the feeling returned to her feet.

She secured the horse to a tether so he wouldn't return to the ranch and leave her stranded. Carrying her baby in one arm and the saddlebags over the other, she felt around the sides of the cabin seeking a way to enter.

When she found the door, she tapped softly. Hearing no response, she pushed it open and cautiously stepped in. The warmth in the room reached out to welcome her.

The darkness inside was complete. She had no glow from the fading moon to light her way in the stygian darkness. She let her bags slide onto a wooden floor. That spoke of the cabin's solid permanence and gave Hannah a comforting sensation of security.

She moved carefully, feeling her way. The edge of a table caught against her hip and, searching about for any contents that might be laying there, her fingers came against a lamp. Shaking it gently, she knew it had fuel enough to light.

"Oh, thank you, God!" A prayer escaped her swollen lips. If there was a lamp, she might find something to eat as well. Her stomach rumbled with hunger now that her other terrors were assuaged for the moment.

Her fumbling fingers touched the solid, papery feel of a box of matches. The squeaking, scratching sound of metal on glass while raising the globe made the only noise in the silent cabin. She turned the screw to release kerosene up the wick, struck a match and held it to the singed and blackened edge. When the lighted lamp flickered into illumination, she lowered the smoke-streaked globe and picked it up. She turned to take in her surroundings.

Her eyes slowly accommodated to the dim interior while she moved, holding the glowing lamp higher to shed light on the furnishings, and acquainted herself with whatever she might find that would be useful.

Turning farther, she stopped. Her mouth gaped open, and her wildly beating heart stopped cold. She found herself staring directly into a deadly pair of black eyes! The lamp wobbled dangerously in her hands to send wild flickering shadows about the cabin walls.

"Howdy, ma'am, care to explain your presence in my cabin?" a deep, masculine voice bellowed out of the darkness and froze Hannah as the solid figure of a man rose toward her.

"Oh, my God! I'm sorry if I disturbed you, I was so very tired, I couldn't go farther." Her voice, weakened with fright and fatigue, faltered. "P—please—would you allow me to rest just a while until I—"

With that, her knees weakened, and she sank toward the floor, gasping in pain and curling her body sideways to protect her infant. The burning lamp slipped from her grasp as she met the floor.

"What the hell?" the man cursed and leaped quickly, in time to catch the lamp from crashing to the floor and setting the place on fire. Holding it aloft, he bent down to look at his intruder. Even in the dimness of the lamplight, he saw her battered condition, the cuts, and bruises of many shades, spread over her lips, jaw, and the crusted blood matted in her hair.

CHAPTER 3

My holy God!" he uttered in disbelief. "What in hell's happened to this poor woman?"

The man set the lamp on the table and reached for the frightened and crying baby bound to her breast. Extracting him from the sling that held him, the man took the warm little body into his arms. Without thought, he jostled the child gently while taking in the baby's face. "Hey there, little feller, don't take on so. You'll be right enough. You're a wee mite of a young'un, aren't you? What in thunder brought you two out in the middle of the night like this? Your mother's all cut up, looks like she tangled with a bear, or maybe not."

He softly whistled through his teeth as he contemplated the battered state of the young woman lying crumpled on the floor before him.

The man gently tucked the baby into his own warm bedding and turned to the limp form on the floor. Taking closer scrutiny, he gasped in shock. "God almighty, lady, who did this to a little thing like you?"

He scooped her into his arms, laid her on the low bunk beside the now sleeping baby, and covered her with his bedding. He turned away from the woman and child, walked over, grabbed a poker, and nudged the coals in the fireplace into life. He shook his head at what had just taken place and sat there his hands splayed out. "Now what the hell am I supposed to do about this?"

Keeping himself busy while figuring what to do with the

woman, he fed pine knots and twigs of dry pine onto the coals and watched them quickly burst into flames.

He laid more wood close by and sat in a chair to await daylight as the flare of light from the newly burning wood caught against the walls of his cabin, revealing wall hangings of colorful blankets, baskets, and trapping gear. In one corner sat a wide table, a tripod, and various pieces of equipment, well used and maintained. Long rolls of paper lay propped against the wall.

Casting his eyes on the slight figure of the woman in his bed, he knew by her heavy, slow breathing, she had fallen into deeper slumber, rather than a faint. He wondered what her story would reveal. Had she escaped some fiend?

Someone had beaten the poor woman within an inch of her life, and anger at that rose mightily, roiling within his chest. Poor soul and her wee baby. He spent the rest of the dark hours before dawn wondering.

Sitting before the fire, deep in thought, he heard a wailing cry of hunger from the infant filling the cabin. Rising to attend the child, he bent over the low narrow bunk, to take up the babe and comfort him. As he bent near, the woman's eyes opened, staring into his. Alarm rose in her swollen and blackened eyes, and dark shadows of fear blanched across her face.

His protective nature aroused, he hesitated and stopped his reach. "Hold on now, lady, I just wanted to see if your little mite was sick or just a tad hungry. No harm intended."

"Who are you, and where is this?" she asked in a fearful whisper.

"My name is Brice Fowler, and this is my cabin you've wandered into."

"We've intruded on you, but I couldn't manage things any further." She hesitated. "Thanks, Mr. Fowler, for letting us rest here awhile. We'll be going as soon as it's daylight." She indicated her fretting infant and turned away, moaning through her teeth from the effort. "Please, I must feed him now." She moved the infant's bobbing head and seeking mouth to her breast, careful to hide herself from a stranger who'd been kind enough to let her rest awhile.

Brice appreciated that, even in her battered condition, she was able to hang onto a shred of modesty. She drew part of her heavy shawl over them both and settled to feed her baby.

He withdrew from mother and child, feeling awkward in the presence of the intimate scene of a nursing mother and her babe. Outside, the first light of dawn sent dim rays into the little cabin. Shrugging his shoulders, he went to the fireplace, set a large black frying pan over the coals, and cut thick slices of bacon to fry. He put a pot of coffee on to boil, then set about making biscuits on the table's surface.

What the hell's happening here? He pondered what to do next, hoping the woman wasn't too fearful of a stranger to enlighten him about her hellishly savaged state. *She has a terrible story to tell, must have.*

With the smell of cooking food wafting through the small cabin, the woman seemed to gain enough strength to rise from the bedding. Finished feeding her child, she changed his soiled clothes. Brice heard a low moan escape her battered lips as she rose from the low bunk. Glancing at him before limping out the door, she left her infant lying on the bunk. That action alone told him she'd gained a small amount of trust in him.

Hannah checked on her horse, who was pulling at his tether, trying for grass just out of reach. She re-tethered him, and splashed icy water over her face from a pail near the door and, after a time, re-entered the cabin.

"Horse still out there, is he?" Brice asked.

"Yes, thank God, he's still there." She looked at him as she limped to the bunk. "I heard sounds of rushing water. A stream must be nearby. Before we leave, maybe we could get washed up, if that's all right."

"You're welcome here as long as you need, ma'am."

Outside the birds began their chatter, high in the pines. It was coming into a bright sunny morning. She appreciated the light of day, but had too much on her mind for anything but survival. Fear and worry consumed her every thought. How could she let herself enjoy the sounds of birds outside when the desperation of her situation weighed heavily upon her? She had no place to go.

She faced Brice, her swollen lips tight and painful. "Now that I have time to think, how will I ever care for my child in this wild place? You've been very kind to me and my son. I don't know what to say." She sighed. "I'm grateful for your hospitality, thank you."

Her baby lay on the narrow bunk gurgling and kicking his tiny feet in the air. Of course, the man was curious about her situation, yet he'd set tin plates on the table and kept to his tasks without overtly noticing her. Her disfigured face, and terrible bruising, expressed her situation more than words.

"Care for a bite of breakfast, ma'am?" He nodded at the rudely built table and set the hot food out in the heavy iron skillet.

Drawn by aching hunger, she moved near the steaming breakfast, desperate to eat something, anything, and found the courage she needed to tell him her story. "Your food smells delicious. You're very kind to put yourself out this way." She reached for a fluffy biscuit. "I haven't eaten since sometime yesterday, before all hell broke loose at the ranch." Flushing, she admitted. "You have a right to know about me. It's not pretty."

"You go right on ahead, ma'am. Anyone can see you've had a tough time of it somewhere along the way." He dreaded to hear her story but opened the way for her to tell it.

"Yesterday, I knew my husband would kill me and our little son, too. After beating me nearly unconscious, he went to sleep." She shuddered. "I struck him over the head with a heavy iron skillet, about like the one setting here." She choked back a sob, her voice barely above a whisper. "I packed what I could and left on horseback. I didn't know where to go or what to do. But to save our lives, I had to run from that dreadful place. I hurt so much I barely kept to the saddle. Now you know what I've done, maybe you won't let me stay any longer but I had to save my son." Emphatic, she stood her ground.

Her story roused a deep anger at any man who'd do that to a woman. "We'll talk more after we eat, dig in now, it's gettin' cold."

She blotted her brimming eyes. The tears made him uneasy. "We can wait until after breakfast to sort that out," he said. "I hate cookin' and don't want the stuff wasted. I scrambled the eggs, not knowing how you liked them."

He shoveled a generous pile on her plate. The bacon and more biscuits lay before her. Steam and a tantalizing odor from them spiraled lazily into the air.

Hannah blotted her eyes on a tattered sleeve. "I don't know what to say, you've been so kind. You know nothing about me except what I've told you."

Tears still glimmered in her eyes, and Brice was quick to get her settled. "Here, ma'am, set yourself down."

She sat on the proffered stool, handmade, and poorly done at that. Her stomach rumbled at the smell of food. Her mouth, swollen and sore, made eating painful, but she managed good amounts of the eggs, even the crusty biscuits.

The bacon was too hard for her to chew. Brice rose quickly to cut it in small bits with a huge hunting knife. "Guess this bacon's a mite too tough, you're mouth bein' so swollen an' all."

She drew back in fear at the sight of his knife. Seeing that, he told her. "Don't be afraid of me, ma'am. I'm just a lonely surveyor out here working for the Land Banks. They're settin' up places for farms and ranches in this area with more people settling here every year. That's my job, laying it out. I'm near done around here. We'll be moving on to the open rangeland, south and west of Flagstaff, hopin' to get it done before it gets too hot out there."

"Sorry, I'm frightened about everything." She tried to smile. "I hate feeling afraid. I never used to be this way."

He settled back in the one chair. "I reckon things haven't been so good for you, all hammered up the way you are."

By the time the meal was finished, she felt more relaxed with his words and continued on with her story. "Last night I believed—I knew—my husband would kill both me and our baby. I just knew it! Everything I did set him off. I burned the meat some and he went clean out of his head with rage. He wasn't that way when I met him—or I didn't know he was. I'd never heard of a man being like that or what made him turn mean and ugly like he did." Tears escaped and coursed down her bruised cheeks as she talked.

"Young women were offered the position of wife and marital partner in the West, and it seemed so exciting. I'm from central Iowa, and not the prettiest of women. It all sounded so adventurous—becoming a rancher's wife."

She swallowed hard. "My father's disapproval still rings in my ears. Throwing my life away, going to some far off God-forsaken no-mans-land to marry a man I'd never met. I can still see his face. He was so angry. But I told him hundreds of women have done the same, why not me? What is there in Iowa for me? Nothing! There was no man in Iowa I saw fit to marry. Jacob was a ranch owner, a man of substance."

She stopped for a while and sipped the coffee he'd made. Tears made their way down her battered cheeks as she went on. "I was slim and strong, and had nice hair. I wanted more than being another farmer's wife."

She laughed bitterly at her youthful ideas. "So I took the train and, after a long trip through country so amazingly wonderful and unfamiliar, I came to Flagstaff. It was all so different from Iowa, those wonderful mountains!" She told him about meeting and marrying Moore. "He looked like a good man to me. His face was tanned from his outdoor life. He said we could get married and make it back to the ranch before dark."

Brice listened carefully to her story, wondering what went wrong. She relaxed considerably while unburdening herself of pain, fear, and guilt, while his own anger grew into a devilish, raging inferno at the horrors she laid out for him.

With the freeing of her soul, she felt lighter somehow, yet questioned, "What will happen to me if they find him dead?"

"You don't know if he's dead? The son-of-a-bitch oughta' be, sure as God made little green apples. Pardon my swearin', ma'am, but I wouldn't mind a lick or two at the bastard myself. You sure as hell can't go back there now, we both know that. Nobody knows for sure where you've got to, and I reckon I can throw him off the track for you." He rose to head for the door.

"What are you going to do?" The fear in her voice choked her.

"Don't you bother your head about anything, ma'am, I reckon I know what to do. You just rest yourself now." He went out and closed the door. In a few moments, she heard the slap of leather, and the sound of horse's hooves pounding away from the cabin.

Hannah rushed to open the heavy wooden door as fast as her painful body allowed. "What have you done? That's my horse! What am I to do now? I need that horse to get away before he finds us!"

She sank to her knees in the grass beside the door, tears of hopelessness filled her eyes.

"Don't take on so, ma'am. If the horse makes it home, the bastard won't be able to find you that way. I have a horse or two, myself."

He strode over to assist her to her feet. She flinched automatically as he neared her, which only intensified his anger at her situation.

His angry face frightened her. Struggling to her feet on her own, she avoided his offer of help. Mopping tears carefully from her bruised face with her sleeve, she raised her eyes. "What are you saying?"

"I'm moving west in a couple of weeks, and I keep a wagon for the surveyin' equipment. You and your young'un can ride along as far as you need. There's a few ranches down that way, before the worst of the open country starts. It's good ranching country around there, set up before surveying by earlier cattlemen. You might find work, cookin' or something, with one of them. Think about it, anyway. You haven't much of a choice either way, as I see it."

Hannah felt gratitude welling within her. This man offered her a place of safety and help. Somewhere inside her heart, where Jacob hadn't been able to reach, she found the ability to trust again. For the first time in many weeks, her spirits lifted. She'd found a reason to hope. Looking at Brice Fowler, amazed at his kindness, Hannah considered his idea. "You'd do that for us?"

"Hell, yes, and if that bastard husband comes looking here, I'll do a damn site more than that." He grinned slowly down at her. "Man like that sure don't deserve a fine little woman like you, ma'am."

"You don't know anything about me. I might be a murdering woman, like I told you." She took in his big frame, and rangy, loose way of moving. He wasn't really handsome, but with his thick dark hair, dark blue eyes, slightly hooked nose, and wide mouth, he looked like a mighty solid sort. Trusting any man would come hard for her after what she'd suffered, but with her horse gone, she had no other choice.

"Ma'am, everyone's got the right to fight for his life, and in your case, there was the two of you. You haven't said your name either, that I can remember." His voice held a note of curiosity as he stood before her, and to her surprise, his soft drawl affected her in some deep, strange way.

"My name is Hannah—Hannah Carlson. As I mentioned, my folks have a farm in Iowa. I left there to come out here and get married. The worst mistake of my life, except for Thomas. I'd give up my life for that boy." She murmured under her breath, "I almost did."

"Good to meet you, Hannah. As I said, my name is Brice Fowler, surveyor for the Land Banks. If you won't be afraid of me, would you want to go along on the trail when I leave here?" His brows, large and dark, furrowed toward the middle, as he looked down at her. "What about it? I'll look out for you and your baby boy too, while you're along with me."

"Looks like I will. I don't have my horse anymore. I'll take your help and thank you for it." Lack of trust lay edged in her voice. How could she trust him or any man? But what other choice did she have?

"You lay low here in the cabin until we leave this area. That'll be in a week or two after we finish the last section we're surveyin'. It's broken country and takes longer. Nobody ever comes here, but if they would, you keep out of sight and make sure your young'un doesn't cry out."

"We can do that. I'm a good cook, or thought I was until I married Moore. I'd be glad to make vittles while we're here.

I'll do what I can to repay you. I have no money." Hannah declared, reluctant about depending on a stranger. "I want to pay my way."

"I reckon I'd be mighty pleased for that, ma'am. I'm not much at fixin' vittles anyway. Never was much good at it. No need to talk of payin'; I'm not one for cookin' and dishes, and such."

"I can't agree with that after the wonderful breakfast you fixed."

A faint ruddiness crept over his neck and face with her words of praise. She turned away to enter the cabin and look after her child. She feared being generous in her praise, not wanting him to think her forward in any way.

Brice stood alone outside, pondering just what in hell he was letting himself in for, taking on a woman—and a baby. He could do nothing else, not the way her husband had savaged the poor soul. She'd quickly perish out in this wilderness without help. The fact that she might be wanted for murder never entered his thoughts.

CHAPTER 4

The baby slept. Brice re-entered the cabin and, immediately, the fascination of watching a woman moving about, attending to things, took hold of him. She cleaned the breakfast utensils and skillet. Painful though her movements were, she held her head a bit higher, knowing she earned her keep while putting distance between herself and the disaster she'd left behind.

Forced to trust him, she frequently cast her eyes his way. The whites of his eyes were more than prominent, giving him a stare-like appearance at times. He wasn't handsome, but solid, strong, and a good man.

Brice surmised she was grateful but helpless, hated that and the feeling of always having to be on guard. He wanted to ease her worries. "Have you thought what you might want to do if you don't go along with me?"

"Going home won't do and there's no ticket money. They wouldn't want a murderer either, if Jacob is dead." She shuddered at her thoughts. "My parents thought I was crazy to go so far from home to find a husband." She shrugged, and continued. "Settling for life as an old maid spinster seemed like a waste of my life—that, or settling for the leftover men around there." She laughed, but it held no humor. "How ignorant are the thoughts of a young girl. Any one of those cast offs would have been better than Jacob Moore." She looked at him. "I'll face whatever comes."

Brice stopped at the door. "You're about the bravest woman I've ever seen, I'll say that."

He went out to finish caring for his livestock, a team of mules, and a saddle horse, a large well-muscled dappled gray gelding called Romer. His livestock were confined in a pole corral, one that had been put up before he'd moved into the place. The land company either owned it or had the use of it.

The sun was well up. A soft breeze rustled through scrub oaks clustered haphazardly about. He enjoyed the soft sigh of pine needles from the mixed conifers high above, the majority being the slightly orange-barked ponderosas. *Nice country hereabouts.* He'd often thought about settling somewhere around here when this present job was finished.

Brice returned to the cabin. He had an unfamiliar eagerness regarding the woman. Females were a rarity in his solitary life, and this woman, in her plight, had touched him deeply. He felt protective of her, any decent man would. There wasn't anything unusual in that, maybe it was the fact of her womanhood.

Battered and swollen as she was, he couldn't get a picture of her in a normal sense. "She's a feisty one, standin' up against a devil like her husband," he murmured. "But for her child, a woman might do just about anything. Best keep an ear out before I finish work in this area. Maybe I can find out what happened to the dirty bastard!" His anger soared, remembering her battered condition.

He noticed her quick look of apprehension as he entered the dimness of the cabin. Seeing him, she sighed in relief, *At least she's not afraid of me now, if I mind my manners, at any rate.* "Say, ma'am, this place looks mighty fine, now you've tidied things up in here."

She flushed, acknowledging the compliment, and a faint blush rose up among the distorted shades of bruising scattered about her features. She'd washed her face but dark, dried blood remained crusted into her hairline, probably imbedded in her hair as well. He wanted to offer his assistance in cleaning the cuts around her hair but thought better of it. *She'd never stand for that sort of closeness.*

"Thanks, I hope to be helpful—you've certainly helped me. I don't know how I can possibly ever repay you." She turned to her baby, struggling to kick off his blanket. "Oh, Thomas, you need a bath, let me see about it." Riffling through her saddlebags, she pulled out fresh clothing for him and turned to look for a pan to warm bath-water. With a sudden start of fear, she came face to face with Brice's steady gaze and looming form, holding out a flat pan.

"Here's a pan ma'am," he said with a grin coming over his face, "an' I'll go out an' fill it for you."

With that, he left the cabin, chuckling to himself with the joy he felt in watching the young woman with her child.

He had work to do, writing down his field notes from yesterday's work, creating usable plats, making them ready to mail in by the last day before he left the area. The woman had interfered with his work, but he'd had his nose to the grindstone for so long with this job, he welcomed the diversion. He had that much time and more coming to him. He dipped the pan into the running creek filling it with clear icy water and returned to the cabin.

Walking to the fireplace, he kicked some of the coals into a nest and set the pan to heat. "Shouldn't take long to heat up."

Hannah had baby Thomas undressed. His fat little body wiggled and kicked on the bunk as he gurgled at his mother. She busied herself readying his clothes and hipping cloths. "May I bathe him on your table? I don't want to get your bedding wet." She awaited his reply, apprehension in her eyes.

"Why sure, ma'am. I'll help if you like. I reckon it's been a long time since I've seen a little fella like this one. He's something, all right."

Together, they washed the soft infant body and oiled his skin with her preparation. Brice's big hands gently smoothed the oil over the baby's tender skin and, by the softness in her battered eyes, he knew she no longer feared him. Instead, he saw a warmth of feeling toward him that she couldn't hide. He went easy with his huge hands.

"You must love children very much to be so gentle with them." She dressed the wriggly boy with fresh clothes and looked at Brice with tears in her eyes. "You know, his father never took a close look at Thomas, his own son—not in all the time we were in that house. I guess that's why I knew he'd kill him right along with me—I knew he would. I've wondered if the man had any normal feelings, even toward his own flesh and blood," she sobbed. "Why would a man like that want a wife? Why, in God's name?"

"I don't know about things like that, ma'am, never heard of anything like a man not having feelin's for his own child, but I guess there's lots I don't know about."

"I don't know either, Mr. Fowler. It all went bad for me. I'd never heard of people being like that man. Something terrible must have happened to him somewhere in his life, and I walked right into it." Hannah shook her head at memories of a brutal man and shivered at the unspeakable cruelties suffered at his hands. She'd developed a feeling of trust toward Brice, if she could tell him so much. Her eyes bore testimony to secrets that would stay within her soul till the day of her death. He'd never want to know those things.

Her son asleep on the bunk, Hannah gathered her soiled clothing and headed for the door, "I'll just wash this outside in the stream I heard running out past the corral."

"Want soap?" He handed her an irregular hunk of brownish soap. It looked handmade.

"Thanks." She turned it in her hand. "What is this?"

"Some stuff I picked up from a ranch back near Flagstaff. Rough on the hands but does a good job."

Saying no more, she went out, carrying the bundle, and Brice followed. The air felt crisp under the shade of the ponderosas and oaks, and the grass grew thick beneath scraggly bushes along the mossy banks of the small stream. She got busy using the chunky brown stuff. It irritated her hands, but if her baby's soiled clothing came clean, she'd be happy for that. She rinsed the harsh soap out, and spread the stuff over nearby bushes to dry.

Entering the cabin, Brice saw she was near exhaustion from her efforts of the morning. "Ma'am, rest yourself a while. You aren't up to much work, feelin' poorly the way you are."

Dark circles had deepened beneath her eyes. She sank down beside her child, murmuring, "Thanks" Within minutes, she slept.

Brice watched in fascination as her chest rose and fell and the soft mound of her hips were outlined as she lay there. Her womanhood, her gentleness, yet her fighting instinct, were wonders to his lonely bachelor soul. He felt stirrings deep within his body, and a heat spread through him just looking at her. That feeling, new to him, was pleasantly disturbing.

Watching a sleeping woman was a rare and pleasurable thing, and he hoped the rest would heal the unfortunate soul. Her hair, a dark wavy blonde color had been fixed in a thick braid down her back, unkempt, but clean, except for the blood around her scalp. He thought her eyes were blue, but the swollen, bruised flesh around them distracted his observations to the point he wasn't sure.

Shaking off the thoughts of how his crew would handle his taking on a woman and a baby, he knew there was no help for it. He'd take her with him soon, hoping her injuries would fade enough before the men met her.

The colors had faded long ago from the torn and drab dress she wore. Considering the sort Moore was, maybe he'd never brought her any material to make new clothes, and her things from Iowa had worn out. He figured she'd been afraid to ask him for anything in the later months of her marriage.

The crew was camped a long ways off these days. He'd handle that when he had to. Party chief of the outfit, he'd see the work done. But he'd also not abandon this young woman in her present condition. He didn't want to be shut of her. Alone in the world, she needed a man's protection, but he wondered if she'd ever let a man near her again. Couldn't blame her for that either!

∽∾∽

Hannah lay, as though asleep, wrestling with worry while contemplating her situation. What kind of man was this Fowler? As kind and caring as he appeared, was he? How could she know? With her horse gone, she had no choice. *I must go along with him and his idea of finding me a place to stay. It's my only option.*

Grappling with the horror she'd escaped from and worrying over the safety of her son, she found herself in another situation. Again, she was forced to place her trust in a man she didn't know, a total stranger. He appeared to be a kind, trustworthy, even rather handsome in some ways. Was he what he said? Could she be sure, and after what she'd suffered, dared she trust any man ever again?

She sat on the edge of the bunk. When Brice entered the cabin, she told him, "I can't stop thinking about things, Mr. Fowler." Tears escaped as she spoke. In frustration, she rose from the bunk, wiping her eyes on her dress sleeve. Seeing her tears, Brice rose from his chair and moved toward her, offering his neckpiece for her use.

"Now, now, ma'am, what is it? No need worryin' your head for naught. I'll find out about your husband when I see my men in the morning. Two of them went in to Flagstaff yesterday to get supplies and send off our drawn-up plats. They might've heard something about it. I'll be careful askin' around. They'll know about you, though, when we start down the trail. Will you be ready to stand that?"

"I have to face things. You've made me feel safe here, and I've had time to think. But things keep coming to my mind. If they hang me for murder, what happens to my child?" Wide-eyed, she looked directly into his eyes, voicing her deepest fear.

They're bright cornflower blue! Distracting thoughts about the color of her eyes burst over him while she made her brave declaration. Though a stranger, she looked for mercy at his hands.

"A woman with a child needs protection and care," he replied, "not what happened to you. I can't answer that for you, but try not to worry about it just yet. You've got some healin' to do, and we don't know anything yet about your husband, do we now?"

He saw her relax. A slight trace of a smile pulled at her

lips. She turned to gaze lovingly upon her sleeping child. "Oh, Thomas, we're all right for now, thanks to Mr. Fowler here."

"Well, I've got things to attend to. There's venison meat hung up high, outside. I'll bring in some. If you'd cook it up, I'd take it kindly, ma'am." He turned and left the cabin, knife in hand. After bringing in a hank of the dark meat, laced with whitish tissue and streaks of fat, he went out to work on a project he'd decided on, and striking his thumb with the hammer, he said under his breath, "Hope she don't mind a bit of cussin'."

Hannah heard the pounding and occasional expletives while she went about preparing a meal of stewed venison, potatoes, and a few dried up carrots she'd found in a bag beside the potatoes. She mixed a batch of biscuits and set them aside to rise near the warmth of the coals. Feeling flushed from the heat of the fireplace, part of her glow came from feelings of accomplishment and appreciation. Her child lay on the bunk, alternately sleeping, gurgling, and kicking his tiny feet against his blanket. Balmy outside, it was warm enough inside as well. Overwhelmed by this unexpected bit of security, she dropped a tear or two and wiped her eyes with her ragged sleeve.

Carefully she raked just enough coals under the stew to keep it cooking and saw the savory mix bubble merrily. When Brice entered the cabin, she turned toward him. She supposed she presented a disheveled sight, with her uncombed hair and battered face, but she'd lost enough fear of him to seek his company. He'd helped her forget the horrific reason she'd fled into the night, if only for a little while.

Hannah reached down, picked Thomas off the bunk, and turned to Brice. "What were you working on out there?" She was curious, even eager to be in his company. He seemed such a solid sort with his quiet ways.

He opened the door. "Come outside with me."

She walked outside the cabin with him. The air was cool and the slight breeze carried the clean scent of dry air and pine. She crunched across dry twigs as she walked, carrying Thomas against her shoulder. Her lips brushed the baby's soft cheek as she walked beside Brice. He hadn't answered her question and she repeated, "What are you making out here, Mr. Fowler?"

"Nothing, ma'am, putting a few sticks together, whiling away time." He drew her attention to the corral. "Come meet the livestock, if you'd like. They're just plain stock, but do all I need."

They moved toward the corral side by side. His nearness was comforting, even pleasant as Hannah took him in. The sun glinted off his dark, glossy hair and, with his sleeves rolled up, the fine dark hairs on his arms as well. Why she noticed things like that puzzled her, but what she saw struck a chord deep within. Some inborn sense compelled her close observation of this kind, gentle man.

Forgetting her dire situation for the moment, she reveled in this very fine experience. Having known few such in her life, she clung to the feeling. It'd been a lifetime since she'd been a carefree, unsuspecting girl.

"Now here's Romer. He's my saddle horse. These two are my driving mules, Hank and Jeb."

She saw a big dappled gray horse and two brown mules.

"They'll pull the wagon when we move out," he said, "and carry equipment and supplies sometimes, too."

The mules and Romer came to the pole fence, vying for a chance to nuzzle her outstretched hand. She shied back as one of mules reached out his velvety nose to catch the baby's scent. She uttered a nervous laugh. "Are they safe? Maybe they never saw a baby before."

"Likely, they never did see a baby before, ma'am. I've hardly seen any myself. Not many little ones in my line of work. It's pretty lonely out where we are."

She heard his soft chuckle at her interaction with his animals.

Hannah let one of the mules reach out to snuffle her baby's cheek. Thomas's tiny hand reached for the furry nose, and he gurgled in delight. Brice seemed transfixed, watching the scene before him.

Maybe it tugged at a child hunger deep within him. She didn't know. The other two animals shoved closer, and she hastily drew away in caution.

Brice laughed. "They just want to nose him a little, ma'am."

"Not so close. I don't know what they might do." Hannah's protective instincts were too strong. She turned away from the animals to return to the cabin. "I'd best see to supper, it's almost ready."

Conscious of his eyes on her as she walked away, she wondered. Was it that he saw so few females? Even beaten and cut up as she was, she instinctively straightened her back and held her head a bit higher as she moved, reveling in how it felt to be noticed by a man.

Walking still caused a great amount of pain. She had a lot of healing ahead of her, but happy to be useful, she made no complaint and went to work inside the cabin. Having a woman cook for him might be a delightful change for him, and she worked to make it so.

Having the meal well in hand, Hannah went out to gather the clothing she'd spread over the bushes to dry. Feeling the cloth, she gathered it, sniffed the cleanliness, and laid it over her arm while she collected it. Brice watched her every move, forgetting the tasks he worked on. With a sense of joy, she re-entered the cabin again. What was it about that man? Was it merely seeing a woman going about her work that enthralled him?

From the cabin door, she saw the sun lowering into a fiery, blazing, ball that set the sky ablaze. She thrilled again at the vivid colors flaming across the western sky. Nothing had prepared her for the incredible beauty of Arizona. It set her heart afire every time she saw it. She'd hidden those stirring thoughts from her husband. *You never took this away from me! You never knew how I loved the colors of sunset.*

CHAPTER 5

Evening descended rapidly over the wild escarpment and, with a full heart, Hannah called Brice to come eat. She served the food in its steaming pot, setting it on the table. Baby Thomas lay sleeping on the bunk as they sat down. Fowler dug in with enthusiasm, taking a big helping of stew and some of the fluffy biscuits piled before him.

"Say now! This is mighty fine eatin'. I reckon these biscuits just might float right out the window if I didn't hold on to 'em." He was effusive with his praise, and the hearing of it sent a blush stealing through the discolored areas of her cheeks.

He dug into the stew heaped on a battered tin plate and set to eating. Sopped biscuits from the juice of the stew went into his wide mouth. Hannah forgot everything for the moment, watching the man enjoy the food she'd prepared. The sight of Brice eating with enjoyment gave Hannah a deep satisfaction in this very normal activity. She smiled the best she could, as he mopped the drops of stew off his lips and chin with his scruffy neck scarf.

"How'd you come to be a surveyor?" she asked. Her questioning was more for conversation than curiosity—that, and longing to hear more of his deep, comforting voice.

"I was always good with figures, and one of my teachers suggested the need for surveyors with the West opening up after the Civil War. There was considerable need for them. I had to go up to Boston for the training. They ragged on me about my Texas way of talkin' but I was near the head of my class and that toned 'em down a bit." He smiled at her, obviously pleased at her interest in his work.

"That's important work. Do you like it?"

"I do, but my folks were ranch people and I think about taking enough land to start a ranch. I haven't decided on anything, but it's on my mind. I've taken quite a special liking to the country just south of here."

"There's an incredible beauty in this country. It's wild and isolated. It made me feel small and lost at first, but the far distances are familiar to me now. In fact, I'd feel closed in living in Iowa. Why is that, do you suppose?" She gazed into his dark blue eyes and didn't want to look away.

"A lot of the West is that way, ma'am. Everything is too far away for close neighbors. I guess you get used to seeing fifty to a hundred miles because the air is thin and dry. You don't feel closed in that way—takes gettin' used to."

"That was true for me. I feel at home now with the wide, far distances, even though they frightened me at first." She nodded agreement with his comment about wide spaces.

Hannah noticed his well-used neck scarf and gave thought to washing it for him, but couldn't say anything so intimate. She determined to wash whatever clothes he might leave behind when he left in the morning.

The meal over, she moved to clean up, but he bade her to the chair. "I'll do these things up, Hannah, it's the least thing I can do. Just you rest yourself."

In astonishment, she took the only chair, and watched him deftly set about cleaning the utensils. *What sort of man is this? Not even at home does a man do woman's work.* She couldn't stop watching his rangy body and broad shoulders. Comforted at the sight of him going about his work, warm tremors overcame her and an unbelievable streak of heat shot through her body. Puzzled, she wanted to cry at how kind, he was, and how thoughtful. Hannah turned her attentions to Thomas when his fretting cry told her she needed to feed him again. Brice left the cabin to give her privacy, but returned later carrying a crudely built crib in his big hands.

|

She stared in surprise at it, realizing he'd worked and cussed out there to make it for her baby. "Oh, how kind you are!" she cried. "Is that what you were working on when we heard you cussing?" Tears of delight lay in her eyes and she had as near a smile on her lips as she could manage.

She inspected his handicraft. "It's wonderful. His own father never did that or anything else for him. I used an old box, and he was fast growing out of it." She shook her head in wonder, fighting to hold back tears of gratitude that would make her look weak. Mentally, she refused the thought of it.

Together they used old bedding to pad the crib, and after changing her baby's cloth again, she laid him in his new bed. "He fits just fine, Mr. Fowler, just fine, even has room to grow."

"Ma'am, you might want to call me Brice, now we kind of know each other." His dark eyes met hers directly, reinforcing his sincerity. "You take the bunk. I'll just sleep over here on this pallet. I use it when we camp along the trail." He indicated his bedroll resting in a corner.

"Thank you, Brice. I appreciate that. I hate to put you out, but I do thank you. You'd best call me Hannah, then. That's what I'm used to."

"No need trying to repay anybody, ma'am, glad to be of help, and I'll be damned happy to help string up the bastard who beat hell out of you, if I ever get the chance." He added slowly, "Hannah."

She smiled at him. Seeing her baby asleep in his new bed, she groaned with fatigue and, once again, sought the comfort of Brice's bunk.

"Ma'am, I've got some healin' salve. I'd like to work on some of your cuts and bruises if you'd allow it."

She heard his deep whisper across the cabin. Amazed at his kindness, she hesitated. "Well…ah, I guess it might help some. I hurt all over, B—Brice." The familiarity of using his given name came haltingly from her lips. She started to rise from the bunk and moans escaped her swollen mouth.

"Stay there, ma'am, I'll tend your injuries right there." He moved the flickering lamp close and knelt down beside her.

She heard the flick of a tin lid as he opened the ointment, and knew when he reached out to her. His body had a good male scent. She'd never given thought to anything like that before. She couldn't remember if Moore had any scent that didn't conjure up fear.

"Just a little and rubbin' it in might do your wounds some good. It's real healin', got sheep's oil in it. Maybe you might get some extra sleep, that's good medicine too." He turned her onto her back, patted salve on her facial bruises, and gently rubbed it in. "When that cut into the hair heals a bit more, you could maybe wash your hair. It's got a real nice color."

Hannah reveled in the glowing warmth his touch aroused in her, something she'd never known, except from her mother. This was different somehow. Was it his gentleness, his kindness? She only knew she wished it would never stop. Her love-starved soul grasped onto this small bit of kindness.

When he finished caring for her wounds, Hannah heard him take to his bedroll. *He's a man. Does he wonder what other parts of my body bear the same terrible bruises he's seen over my arms and face?* She'd never allow him to check her over that way, but smiled painfully into the darkness, thinking about his big firm hands, recalling vividly how he smelled, how her skin felt from his hands touching her face and the few un-bruised areas. "Whewww," she whistled beneath her breath. "What have I got myself and my child into? Please God. I had no choice. Take care of my baby and me," she whispered in the darkness of the silent cabin.

For a short while she knew Fowler lay awake on his hard pallet. Did he think about this unforeseen change in his life? The last she heard was his soft snoring as he'd finally drifted off to sleep in the hush of the dark cabin.

ↄ⁊ↄ⁊

When the faint blush of sunrise crept over the tips of the trees, Hannah sat on the narrow bed rubbing her eyes carefully. She smiled. "I believe I slept all night, and I haven't done that for a very long time, Thomas slept too."

"I reckon I'll be leaving soon's I eat and get my wagon loaded," Brice told her. "You'll be right enough in my cabin. There's a mite of food around and plenty of firewood just outside of the door. I'll be gone a week or more. After that we'll be moving southwest of here."

He put the skillet over the few coals and started breakfast.

Hannah knew she should be making the breakfast, but his impending departure caused a sense of loss and emptiness. Worried at being alone in this isolated cabin, she made no move to assist him. Watching him at the business of making breakfast, she saw that he was handy at it, whether he liked cooking or not.

Hannah had come to rely on Brice in a very short time, and dreaded being on her own without his protecting presence. She said, "I'm afraid to be alone in this wild place. Moore might find us. I know what he'd do to me and I can't bear thinking of it."

"Don't fret about it ma'am. If you hit him as hard as you say, he won't be going anywhere for a while, and this cabin is hard to find from the road."

After they shared a hasty breakfast, he left to harness his mules while Hannah tended the baby, and put the cabin in order. Her bruises had deepened, changing into paler shades of blue, green and yellow. Stiff and uncomfortable as she was, she smiled and said to her baby in a soft whisper, "Thomas, we're safe here, thanks to Mr. Fowler."

She went out to enjoy the sight of the man hitching his mules and settling his gear in the wagon. He loaded his bedroll and equipment into it and turned to face her. His eyes were a darker blue as she met his gaze. "You know for certain we'll be safe here while you're gone?"

"Nothin's ever for certain, ma'am, but I've been using this cabin for more than a couple of months off and on and never had any callers up here. Just keep watch and be extra quiet if someone comes pokin' around. It's not likely though, so don't be afraid, just rest and heal yourself. Those bruises will fade, and that'll be better when you meet the crew," he said with a half smile.

His eyes crinkled in the corners and deep thrills passed through her body, making her legs feel weak.

"There'll be questions enough when I bring a woman and baby along with me."

His voice came deep and quiet, and she took comfort from it, in spite of knowing he planned to take her from this haven.

She helped him prepare for departure. Brice tied Romer to the back of his wagon, climbed aboard, and, with a cluck of the tongue and slap of the reins across their rumps, drove the mules forward. Her heart skipped a beat as he flashed a broad smile her way before passing under the big pines and out of sight. Thrills shot through her at his broad, white-toothed smile.

Hannah felt the loss of his solid presence, but got herself in hand and turned to the cabin. It was solely hers for a time and that gave her a small sense of ownership. He'd taken the folding table and instruments she'd seen in the corner. She was alone. Brice had saved her and her baby, almost against her will and she'd quickly come to rely on him. He'd shown her kindness and certainly a greater measure of security than she'd ever received from Jacob Moore.

"My life as a rancher's wife is in ruins and I've likely committed murder. Thank God, my father won't know about this after he begged me not to come so far from home. Now I'm beholden to another man for my life." Hannah spoke aloud to break the silence that surrounded her. Repaying Brice set heavily on her mind. She hated being obligated to anyone, not anymore. Determined to find a way to square things, she set her jaw firmly and went into the cabin.

ఴఴఴ

Brice was deep in thought as he drove away. He'd be seeing his crew this morning, and Hannah had nearly two weeks to rest and heal her wounds. Maybe some of the men had heard something. After seeing the condition of Hannah, he was eager to hear anything that would enlighten him on the condition of the husband. He'd sent men into Flagstaff to mail his prepared surveys to the head office. They'd hear if there was any news when they bought supplies and heard town gossip. If her husband was dead, Brice would soon know about it.

CHAPTER 6

Caring for her child kept Hannah's days filled, but her nights were rife with frightening dreams and memories. Looking into the pool of still water where the small stream gathered before meandering its way downstream, she smiled. "My bruises are fading, that's something." Brice's healing salve had helped. "I'm near back to myself—in looks, leastways."

She thought of Brice many times during the day, remembering his kindness, white teeth flashing against his darkly tanned face, and how he handled Thomas with those big hands, gentle and sure. He'd touched her lonely heart enough to help her realize that all men were not evil fiends. They couldn't be.

"My father wasn't," she recalled.

Hannah's thoughts roiled constantly. Trying to understand the ways of men, what had happened to her, left her mentally tired and confused.

The next morning, she took all of the clothes she had and, wearing only her barest under things, went to the stream. She added Thomas's and the few items of Brice's she'd found. It had rained heavily during the night, and the stream ran full. She washed the clothes in the swift current, seeing her hands became reddened and numb from the icy water.

She spread the clothing over a few handy bushes to dry in the sun. Thomas lay on a blanket kicking and giggling in the dappled shade while she sat beside him completely relaxed in dreamy reverie. "Oh, Thomas, it's so quiet here—so safe."

In that quiet moment, her hideous memories were forgotten until she startled in alarm at the sound of horse hooves clip-clopping toward the cabin. Filled with icy dread and fear of discovery, she grabbed the baby and ran into the cabin. Attempting to hide the evidence of her presence, she rushed hurriedly out to collect her newly washed clothing, fearing it might be Jacob riding into the clearing. Her heart froze with terror. She could scarcely breathe.

Brice drove his team into the clearing next to the cabin and, seeing him, she wanted to faint in relief. Remembering her half-clothed state, she gasped and clutched the bundle of clean clothes against her body.

"Howdy, ma'am, hope I didn't scare you comin' in this way."

"Yes, some, I tried to get everything hidden away but you came too fast." She held the clothing close, trying to hide herself from his eyes. Though embarrassed by her state of undress, she was greatly relieved to see it was him.

"I've just been to Flagstaff and reckoned you'd want to know what things I've heard." Concern in his eyes, he dismounted and turned to untie a large pack off the back of the saddle.

"Yes, I want to know whatever you found out. I've lived a nightmare of fear, worrying," Hannah responded, backing carefully into the cabin. "I need to put on a few things. I won't be a minute, Brice." It was easy for her to say his name now.

He laughed softly. He'd caught her unawares and saw her embarrassment. He followed her into the cabin, pretending he didn't see her state of undress. "I thought I might just bring you a few things while I had the chance."

Hannah caught the twinkle in his eyes. He'd caught a few glimpses of shoulder and leg and tried to hide his amusement. Rather bold of him. She might fault him for looking, in spite of being overjoyed to see him.

Hastily throwing her torn dress over her head, she turned to face him, waiting for his news, afraid to hear what he had to say. Her heart pounded. She forgot her momentary embarrassment, worried what news he might bring.

"First of all, they found your husband's body after he didn't show up for the calf brandin'. It'd been a few days, and things were kind of bad out there. I didn't hear any talk about him having a wife or child, but I didn't hear everything. I guess the parson who married you, and his wife, may be the only ones who knew Moore had married." His eyes twinkled at her, and she remembered the hasty act of throwing on freshly washed and wrinkled clothes.

Dismissing his humor, she couldn't care either way after hearing the dreaded news. "He's dead—oh, God! I've done murder!" Hannah felt her head spinning. She contemplated what lay before her. "What'll happen to my baby if they arrest me?" Tears started down her cheeks as she slumped onto the bunk.

"Don't fret, Hannah, maybe no one will ever know about you or how Moore died, unless they find out from that minister. Of course, there might be a few female articles lying about, maybe some of the baby's things."

Hannah sat in shock, looking at Brice, not knowing how to voice her fear of the future. "The only clothes the baby had were made from my old things," she said around the lump in her throat. "I wonder what to do now, where I could be safe and away from all this."

He smiled at her and sought to take her mind off her fears. "I could sure use a bite to eat. It's been a while." He reached for the large bundle he'd just taken off the saddle. It was tied with string, and he handed it to her. "Maybe this will put your worries to rest for a while."

Hannah opened it to see piece goods for a dress, a hat with flowers on it, a comb, and cotton under garments. "Oh, where did you find this? How would you know what a woman needs?" Tears formed in her eyes while a burning flush crept up her cheeks.

"Now, ma'am, the lady at the store made up this pack. I just told her she was about your size and near had your hair color. She put this together for me. I never saw what she put in there."

"Oh, it's a dress! I haven't had anything new since I came

to Arizona and my clothes were wearing thin. After Moore
became violent, I dared not ask for anything." She held a blue,
flower-sprigged dress in front of her, and slowly pirouetted
about in her delight. "You shouldn't have done this!"

"Why shouldn't I? It's nothin', ma'am. I'd have done the
same for any woman in trouble," he added. "Another thing,
you'll look better when you meet my crew. It'll be tough
enough explaining a woman and child along with me, without
you dressed in rags and all beat up. You're lookin' much better, but it looks like another week or so might help your looks
even more." He still wore that amused look across his lips.

She'd washed her hair, and it had taken on a mellow, dark
gold color. When she saw he'd brought a comb and sewing
needles, she could have hugged him. "Oh, you've brought so
much!"

Her fears lay forgotten for the moment in her excitement
over things desperately needed and long denied.

"I brought some new vittles, too," Brice said. "Figured
you'd be needin' somethin' more to fix."

He left to bring in the rest of his packs. Hannah caught the
shine in his eyes and the look on his face of a man who'd
pleased and provided for his woman.

Her thoughts spun wildly at his kindness. "I wish I knew
what to do. I must wait for him to take me far away from here.
Maybe we'll be safe then, Thomas, maybe we will," she murmured to her child as she dug through the things Brice had
brought. Shaking her head in disbelief, she felt a small flicker
of hope for her future take hold amidst her worries.

Brice brought in another pack containing dried fruit, coffee, tinned milk, canned tomatoes, bacon, fresh carrots, and
potatoes. "There you are, Hannah. This should hold you for
another week or so."

"Oh, how wonderful! I'd best get a meal on, if you can
stay a while." Cooking was all she had to offer and she was
eager to make him a nice feed. She didn't miss seeing the
pleasure he'd gained at her delight over the few simple things
he'd provided.

"I'll leave here in the morning. There's not much I can

get done at camp anymore this late. We're pretty far down from here now. The country there is open for the most part, grassy, antelope runnin' about, and good cattle grazin'."

"This fruit will make a nice pie, I'll get busy." Her mind raced, full of conflicting thoughts. On the one hand, she was safe from Moore, but if she was arrested for murder, then what?

She busied herself with food preparations, reveling in the precious time she had left. "There's time enough to spend on worrying," she told herself aloud and set about fixing a good dinner for Brice.

He left the cabin to tend his horse and, later, carried in a large load of chopped wood for the fireplace. "I'll kick up the fire a bit. It'll help get your cookin' started."

Thomas gurgled and Brice reached out to take up his wiggling little body in his huge hands. She watched him and smiled her assent. He dwarfed the tiny boy he held out before him, *vis au vis,* as they gazed into each other's face. Hannah formed the idea that it was man to man between the two. *My baby boy is a man in his own way!* Deeply touched to see it, she wondered at the male gender, knowing she'd never fully understand that mysterious chasm of difference created between men and women.

She heard Brice talking softly to her baby, his deep tones comforting. Thomas cooed and gurgled in delight. Hannah, though near to tears at the sight of them together, busied herself making a pie from the dried apples. Her heart sang with a happiness she hadn't felt for too long.

Brice's very presence gave her courage, safety, and hope. Somehow fate had brought her to this cabin, and that good, strong man inside.

When the pie was ready, he showed her how to bake it in the huge cast iron Dutch oven. "Just rake enough coals to sit it on, then place that heavy high-rimmed lid over it, and cover it with more coals. Ought to bake just right."

She blinked in amazement. Brice made everything right, even baking a pie. "I've never seen a pie made that way, only biscuits," she told him.

"You can cook about everything in one of these. It comes in handy way out like we are."

He laughed softly and the deepness of it went right through her. Flushing with warmth, she turned away. It was too much. She wanted to cry.

She set venison on to cook, made a savory stew of it with potatoes, a few onions, and the vegetables he'd brought. When she said, "The biscuits will have to wait." She hesitated, waiting with icy chills for his rising temper. It didn't happen and she breathed a sigh of relief.

"We have lots of time, ma'am. It'll be worth the wait." Turning to Thomas, Brice took him up again to jostle him gently in his big arms.

Hannah sighed. She'd learned a great deal of fear toward men. *Is he being kind now, only to go into a towering rage after I learn to trust him?* She fought these thoughts, remembering her father, a fine, gentle man. Yet, lurking deep in her soul burned sad memories of sadistic cruelty.

৩৵৩

Brice left again in the early morning. Hannah went about cleaning the cabin, tending her baby, and healing daily the multi-colored areas scattered about her head, face, and arms. Most of the minor injuries had healed, and she no longer hurt while moving about. She washed her hair often and plied the comb through the shinning locks. Usually keeping it in a braid, she let it flow out some of the time. It felt good to toss her shining hair about in the sun. She no longer worried about Moore finding her and thought no further, unwilling to dwell on darker issues.

With no one about to watch, Hannah relaxed, healing emotional pain along with her body. She'd not been at fault in her marriage, only terribly unfortunate in her choice. Perhaps coming to a strange land and marrying a man she'd just met had been a foolish thing, but many others had done the same and knew success in having done such. There was no going back, she knew that.

She was safe for the time being in Brice's company, but he planned to place her somewhere and ride away, leaving her among strangers. Shaking her head at these thoughts, she heaved a sigh, shrugged her shoulders, and re-entered the rustic cabin to bide her time until he rode in again.

CHAPTER 7

After ten lonely, yet peaceful days, Brice drove his team of mules into the cabin yard and, seeing him, Hannah felt her blood run cold. The time had come. She would go along with him on the trail and leave this friendly haven where her long process of healing, within and without, had begun.

Watching his tall, spare form as he put the mules and Romer into the corral, she relaxed just a bit in the security of his presence. Still a multitude of worrisome doubts regarding the new situation she faced troubled her thoughts. "Won't your crew wonder why a woman and child appeared out of nowhere? What will you tell them?"

"Don't you worry over it, Hannah. I gave them an idea about your coming along with us for a spell. We'll be near a ranch on down the line. The Jesse Bidwell Ranch might be the right spot for you two. I've talked with Jesse, and he'll consider it. Man's in a dilemma about his wife."

"What's wrong that he needs help?" She twisted her hands then sighed. "But I'd be more than glad to help them out if you think it'd be a safe place for me."

"I don't rightly know her trouble, Hannah, but it'd be a good spot for a lone woman," Brice answered. Jesse's getting on in years, lost all his sons one way or another. Now his wife's ailing and he needs a woman's help caring for her. He's a good sort. A bit gruff and rough around the edges, but he cares a great deal for his wife, I know that. The ranch house looks to be good sized." He paused a bit, his brow wrinkled. "It's an old ranch, put together long before Jesse bought it, or any kind of surveyin', yet surveyin's as old as people having property. A man needs to know what's his, I suppose," he went on, smiling in her direction. "Mexican people work the gardens, fields, and do the housework and cookin'. The Mex folks keep a small village right near. Even have a padre some of the time. It just might do for you and Thomas." He looked at her. "I'll take you to see him if you'll consider it."

"I'd appreciate a chance to earn my way. If this place is far enough from Flagstaff, maybe they wouldn't have heard about Moore."

"Maybe so, can't be sure, though." He noticed her cuts had healed and the bruising had faded. Her hair, all clean and combed, looked buttery soft and gleaming. With a bonnet on, the injuries would be hard to detect unless someone was intent on close examination. The blue flower-sprigged dress fit her well, too. Not a raving beauty, maybe, but Hannah was a totally feminine woman.

His outside things in order, he sat quietly in the cabin, following her every move as she prepared his supper. A warm glow swept over him as her nimble fingers sliced apples for a pie. A new feeling for him and one he enjoyed. He'd missed the sight of her while surveying the vast, untracked lands southwest of Flagstaff.

Hannah had healed in her body. Her movements, sure and smooth these days, gave no hint of the pain-wracked creature he'd seen that first night. His heart filled, knowing he'd helped her and seen a gentle strength returning in her body and mind. He liked everything about her, and doing for her, like he had, was natural and right. New to him, he found satisfaction in all of it.

She put the food on the table. "It's ready now...uh... Brice." She hated feeling hesitant at using his name. Familiarity with him was hard for her, yet he'd given no evidence of a violent nature and had shown only kindness. Still, trust in any man was not easily earned. Fascinated as she was by his masculine ways, she remained wary of closeness. Safe, now that he was with her, she shrugged off her conflicting thoughts and finished putting supper on the table.

Brice sat, groaning with delight at the food before him. He dug in and helped himself to stew, biscuits, and, after that, a hefty slice of apple pie. "Hannah, my dear, I reckon you are one damned fine cook!"

She flushed at his compliment. "I'm glad you like it. Moore never said one good thing about my cooking. He hated everything I set before him. I only had the things he brought me and it wasn't much. He never got an apple pie. I never saw an apple—ever!" She grinned at that.

"Well, he was a damned fool, now wasn't he? I'll clean up. You'd best pack up your things. We'll be leavin' early an' be sure to wear that bonnet, keeps the sun off and it'll hide any leftover bruises."

He finished cleaning in short order and went out. After tending to Thomas, she picked him up and went outside. Brice had made a crude set of arches over the wagon and was pulling canvas over the front portion of it.

Seeing Hannah, he explained, "We can fit the baby's bed in here among the rest of my things and yours."

He waggled his bushy eyebrows at her and grunted as he finished pulling the canvas over the hoops. Hannah tried to help one-handed, but holding Thomas in her arms, she wasn't really effective.

By the time it grew dark, the wagon was packed and ready. She followed him into the cabin, frowning. "How well do you know the Bidwell people?"

"Not so well, passed that way a few times. I've the idea they're real good folks an' have a mighty nice place for ranchin' with trees, grass, and some far mountains. A good stream of water runs through it, too." Brice sighed. "He's a sad old man these days, though, with his sons gone and wife ailin'."

He relaxed in his poorly made chair. "The way I see it, the Bidwell place is about all there is for a long while. Traveling in this wagon might be hard on a baby, and for you, washin' out his clothes and all. Of course, there might be other ranches farther back from where we'll be. Don't know that yet."

"I'll do the best I can, and thank you for your help. I pray they'll want me." She looked up at him. "Will you come by to see us after you leave us off?"

"I'll be headin' in to Flagstaff from time to time to send off plats and buyin' supplies. Sure do plan to stop in and see how you and your young'un are making out. I know for sure if they ask for your cookin', you'll do just fine."

She felt a hot flush rise over her face, knowing Brice enjoyed handing her a moment of pleasure.

"I'll be turnin' in. Hannah, you need your rest too. We've a long drive ahead tomorrow." He threw his bedroll in the corner and knelt down to it.

☙❧☙

Morning's light had them up and ready. After a hasty meal, they left the familiar cabin. Brice handed her up to the seat beside him and put Thomas in his crib. He'd left a place for it right behind the seat so she could reach the baby easy enough. With a slap of the reins over the mules' rumps, they began the journey. She felt the jerk and pull of the wagon when the mules started, taking her away from the comfortable aura of the friendly cabin.

Hannah faced moving into strange surroundings, remembering the poor, creature she'd been when Brice had taken her in. She'd never be able to repay him. He'd proven to be a good man, and thank God, he'd been there that night. But, for her, learning real trust of a man proved elusive.

She sat next to Brice, his male scent filling her senses and lulling her fears. Safe in his company, she knew contentment. Thomas slept in his bed just behind her. The rounded rumps of the mules moved rhythmically pulling the loaded wagon and Romer plodded along behind. Puffs of powdery dust rose from their hooves as they walked, and the wheels made tracks over part of the hoof prints.

Hannah found it mesmerizing to watch. Only the creaking

wagon wheels, jingling harness, and clopping hoof beats, broke the silence.

"It's very beautiful around here, isn't it?" she asked after long moments of quiet.

"Yes, its mighty fine hereabout, the best I've seen. Moving all the time, like we do, gets old after a while." He shrugged and gently slapped the reins across the mules. "I'm more of a rancher than a surveyor, anyway."

She didn't say anything, there was nothing to add. The thoughts of a ranch sounded idyllic with Brice a part of it. *Is it always this way, a woman's life tied to a man's?*

The landscape gradually changed as they followed a rough, little-used track that trailed downhill for the most part. The huge pines had left off, replaced by shaggy piñons and bushes with shining red bark. She asked Brice about them.

"Those are manzanita, always liked the looks of them myself. Usually grow at the four to five thousand feet levels so you can pretty much tell how high you are by seeing them."

He smiled down at her and her heart beat faster. Something in his dark blue eyes made her shake her head to clear her errant thoughts. His smile changed his looks into one of handsomeness. He almost looked like someone else then. The whites around his eyes grew nearly invisible by crinkling when he smiled. His teeth were strong and white and his lips went wide.

The jostling of the wagon fascinated and comforted Thomas. He alternately slept or made his baby sounds. They stopped by a small stream to eat biscuits and bacon left from breakfast. Hannah fed and changed him.

The sun had grown low in the sky by the time they pulled up to a campsite with several white tents. Campfire smoke spiraled lazily skyward, and a man bent over the coals, working his magic on several huge Dutch ovens. Her apprehension, which was already monumental, grew even higher. She was about to enter a new situation and hated the fear it engendered.

Eight or ten men stood awaiting their boss. Their curiosity regarding the woman was obvious, but subdued. They crowded around the wagon, their faces uplifted toward her.

Brice greeted the men then turned to help Hannah down. "Here, come meet my crew." He drew her forth and introduced her around one by one.

"Gentlemen, meet Hannah Carlson from Iowa." Surprised at his use of her maiden name, she knew he was right to do it. It would do her no good to bear the name of a man found with his head bashed in. She appreciated his wisdom in the matter.

He added the information. "She'll be travelin' along with us a while."

Hannah shook the men's hands as they were presented, her heart beating wildly. "Pleased to meet you."

She contemplated the new deception of belying her married name, but it had to be. She could never be Hannah Moore again if she was to escape the consequences of her husband's death. She trembled. For her, that name held only horrors.

"This is John Bates," Brice said, indicating a thin be-whiskered man of medium height.

His clothes were reasonably clean, though slightly tattered. Then she met a dark-eyed man with vaguely sinister good looks, Hank Watkins. Something in his eyes caused an unsettled chill to pass through her body. *I'm fearful of certain men. He seems too much like my husband.*

Hannah shook his rough, moist hand. "Pleased to meet you."

His touch increased her feeling of unease. His look was hard and piercing.

Brice led her to another man. "This is Jim Emory, my assistant party chief. He does my work when I'm not around."

She instantly liked the tall, sandy-haired, neatly dressed young man with a friendly look in his pale blue eyes.

One by one, the men came forth to meet her. They seemed a friendly group, educated and well spoken, except for Hank and the cook, Campy. She remembered Brice had said Hank did some of the chaining work. His eyes were shifty, unlike the rest of them. He continued to make her feel uneasy. His overt interest in her, excessive and downright nosey, compared poorly to the accepting attitudes of the others. Chainwork? She wondered about that, too.

From the wagon, Thomas set up a howl, breaking off further conversation until Hannah fetched him. "This is my son, Thomas."

She held the child out for inspection. The men eagerly gathered around to look at this little human. It had been a long time since any of them had laid eyes on a tiny babe and expressions of delight were written across their faces. These lonely men, deprived of home and family while working on this assignment or some other, always in a far-off place, saw little of family life. If they wondered that she appeared in this camp with a man not her husband, it wasn't mentioned.

Needing privacy to feed her fretting infant, she excused herself. Taking him, she entered the wagon. While she nursed him, she heard murmurings from the men. She hadn't counted, but thought there were about eight, and wondered if there might be one among them who'd put two and two together? She tried not to think of that as she settled to feed her hungry child.

Later, she met the rest of the crew. They were accepting and friendly, allaying much of her worry. Only the man called Hank, with an appraising sort of familiarity in his eyes, made her uncomfortable. She'd seen that look on Moore a few times after the marriage. Hank would bear watching.

Thomas giggled and cooed, being handed about and jostled from one set of arms to another, and Hannah relaxed. These men were hungry for the sight of a little one. Her baby was in safe hands with any of them, yet she noticed Hank never touched Thomas or asked to hold him.

"Come eat now, ma'am," the cook, Campy, called.

She sat next to Brice while they ate. The table was broad and set in a tent full of paper-like material and tubes of metal scattered in the corner. The baby lay asleep in his bed nearby. Brice had taken it out of the wagon.

Given her own tent, she found relief from the close company of the men and greatly appreciated the privacy. Living in the midst of male eyes who watched her every move, she accepted as normal in men who rarely saw a woman. Brice watched her, too, but from him it was right somehow.

She also watched him at every opportunity.

Meeting the crew, she observed them for signs of suspicion and, seeing none, stopped worrying. Settled for the night, she slept on a pallet that felt nearly as hard as stone. Questions about the Bidwell Ranch filled her mind. "Will they want me, or have the need to hire me?"

Praying for answers, she went to sleep and, extremely tired from the long uneven wagon ride, rested well in the comfort and safety of this camp.

Thomas slept next to her in his crib, crafted by Brice's big hands.

CHAPTER 8

Hannah helped Campy with the cooking. The men, effusive in praise of her biscuits, and cooking enough for their voracious appetites, kept her hopping.

"I'll wash clothes for anyone if you'd like," Hannah offered, making herself useful where she could. Washing the men's clothes whenever a stream lay nearby, proved unusually difficult in a rustic location. The work kept her busy and her efforts, gratefully received, brought her a few dollars, the only personal money Hannah had seen since coming west.

The men happily enjoyed her cooking as well.

Campy worked with her and praised her often. "Say, ma'am, this here's about the best venison stew I ever tasted, and them fluffy biscuits too."

The men watched her, likely starved for the sight of a decent young woman. They made no advances, nor any remark to set her worrying.

The safety and slow pace of camp life gave Hannah a feeling of security until one day at a nearby creek, while drawing a pail of water, Hank approached. He came quietly, until a twig snapped under his boots.

Sensing a stealthy advance upon her person, she whirled about to face him.

"Say, Hannah, you seem like a nice enough woman." He grinned. "Tell me, you married, widowed, or what? A woman with sech a little'n must have a story behind her." He moved too close and Hannah drew back. "I don't see a husband no wheres, just Fowler hanging about, watchin' you every chance he gits. Somethin' goin' on there—that it?"

His leering grin spoke volumes, and his disgusting suggestions made her blood boil. Her jaw set firm and her face flushed hot, responding to her inner fury and his filthy implications.

"That'd be my business and certainly none of yours." Hannah bit off the words, as she faced his leering grin.

He edged closer. Until now, he'd never been unfriendly to her. Yet something about him made her think of Moore. That had jogged her senses more than once, and she felt threatened by him.

She edged back, his presence set her on edge. Her heart pounded with anger and a touch of fear. "I keep my affairs private. I'll be leaving here soon to go back east."

She kept her voice even, trying to control the situation. His black eyes bored into hers and she winced as his inquiring gaze passed over her body.

His suspicions sent shivers of anxiety racing through her. Hannah realized he wouldn't want the rest of the men to know he'd accosted her, or the fury he'd caused her. Ignoring him, she turned to the stream to fill her bucket.

"Hold on jest a minute. I know it's none of my business, but you got no need to get uppity with me, neither. Looks like you'd be needin' a good man to help you along, a woman alone like you are, unless Fowler's thick with you."

She saw his rising anger at her silence on the subject. A ruddy flush crept up his neck. Seeing it, Hannah knew all about rage and violence at the hands of an angry man. She wanted no part of this man or his sinister questions. He made her feel threatened, and she wanted to get away from him. She filled the water pail and turned to leave. "Excuse me, please. I must see to my baby."

"I'll find out all I need to know about you, ma'am. There's something not square about this here deal. Fowler's being tight-lipped about somethin', now ain't he?" His hard eyes squinted as his gaze drifted over her person again. "Peers he's a keepin' you all to hisself."

Shaking with apprehension, she carried the bucket of water to the cook and went to her tent. *Oh God, he'll find me out! But if I tell Brice about this, it'll cause trouble in his crew.* She couldn't help the cook as usual, because she lay on her pallet shaking with anger and ominous dread over her ugly encounter with Hank.

ℰↄℰↄ

Days passed. Thomas appeared to thrive on this outdoor life, but she worried how long he'd tolerate the rugged conditions of a men's camp. As they passed southwestward through the wilds of Arizona, the days became steadily warmer and his baby cheeks were often flushed with heat.

The Bidwell Ranch lay close, Brice had said, and soon she'd be leaving to go there. Since the encounter with Hank, the man openly stared at her with barely concealed animosity burning in his eyes. If he was in the camp, she felt unsettled, knowing he'd make trouble for her if he found a way. Because of him, she'd be glad to leave this company of men, and Hank's ugly, leering glances no one else seemed to notice.

She did not confide her worries to Brice. He'd helped her too much to ever repay and she refused to cause trouble with a crew member. His days were kept busy, lining out the chain men and all those mysterious orders related to his work. He spent long hours on horseback or in the charting tent, making the plats from the field notes, readying them to send off to the government. He didn't need more of her troubles.

Part of the crew made ready to take the long rolled tubes of finished plats into Flagstaff. They'd be gone for several days and bring back a long list of badly needed supplies. The surveying party had advanced much farther toward the southwest and ready supplies were non-existent in the area. Everything but fresh game had to be brought in by wagon or pack horses.

The men left for Flagstaff, Hank among them. They had two pack mules as well as a wagon for supplies. Relieved by his absence, she worried what he might learn during their stay in Flagstaff. *Would he think to ask questions about a strange woman and her baby?* Those worries muted her pleasure in working for the other men in camp.

Brice approached her and spoke in confidence. "Today, I reckon we'll visit the Bidwell Ranch to see about findin' a good place for you. We're close enough. It's a short ride and the country hereabouts is real pretty."

She enjoyed the new found closeness with him, but the situation with Hank had clouded that pleasure as well.

Hannah knew this day was coming. Seeing Hank leave camp, she relaxed with the rest of the men. They'd been more than friendly, like big brothers. She regretted parting with them and the security she'd felt among them. Keeping her personal matters secret often hampered exchanges, yet reticence about personal affairs was an unwritten law in the West.

No one had made anything over her situation except Hank. Western culture never hampered his curiosity about her, how well she knew. He also remained angry. His innate vicious streak and temper had made her edgy. After her ordeal with Moore, Hannah looked for signs of rage in every man.

Her things, along with those of baby Thomas, were loaded into a small buckboard and she said a reluctant goodbye to the men. "Thank you for your kindness to me and my son." While addressing the crew, she again felt relief that Hank was absent, lest he feel included in her gratitude.

"Thanks, ma'am, for the good cookin' and letting us play with the little feller," she heard someone call out as they drove away.

"Brice, it's like leaving home after so many weeks. They're the grandest bunch."

She didn't mention Hank. Later on she might, if the time seemed right. She sat near Brice on the narrow wagon seat and felt at peace in his presence. A growing need to be near him had taken on a life of its own. *Am I falling in love with this good man, only to have him leave me off among strangers?* Hannah wondered that she could look favorably on any man again, though Brice was no ordinary man in her eyes.

She'd have to say goodbye to her only friend. He knew

everything about her, had taken care of her, and enjoyed the sight of her. He'd watched her much of the time around the camp, and she never saw it as threatening, only caring. He always caught her eye if he could, and his deep, probing glances never failed to send thrills coursing through her. She wondered what his thoughts were. *Does he care for me?*

"I hope they'll want me, Brice."

"You'll do fine, Hannah. It might be strange at first. Just be the brave girl I know you are. They need you real bad from what I hear, and women like you are scarce as hen's teeth around these parts."

She took notice of the country as they passed through, part waving grasslands and distant mountains with dark fringes of pines on the upper levels, all put together the way God made it. The wild beauty before her took hold in her soul, thrilled her senses, and she reveled in it.

The air felt warmer here than at the cabin, yet Brice had told her the heat hadn't really begun at this lower altitude. That made her wonder all the more about this country called Arizona. The sun beat down on them, but a slight breeze kept them cool enough as they traveled. When they stopped for a quick meal and rested the mules, Hannah tended to Thomas. She'd kept him on her lap part of the way, and Brice chucked him under the chin at times, making him shriek with joy.

"I'll sure miss this boy. He's a right handsome little tyke. I plan to drop around at times if I'm close enough. I'll want to check on you and Thomas. Need to be sure this is a good place for you both."

"Oh, Brice, yes, I'd like it if you'd come by whenever you can. You've been…I don't know what to say. I only hope somehow—"

Tears slipped down her cheeks, and she daubed at them with the hankie Brice had bought her. He didn't need any more gratitude from her. "Hannah, you never need to be repayin' anything to me. I've come to enjoy the sight of you, and that young'un too."

Hannah couldn't find words to reply to his statement, but happy to hear it, she felt that way about Brice, too. His presence had become very dear to her and soon she wouldn't have it. Being dependent on anyone made her feel uncomfortable. She had no right to put a hold on him with a man's death hanging over her.

They rode in silence for a long while. Hannah sat beside Brice, deep in thought about her future. They came over a rise on the trail and he pointed to a large group of gray, weathered, structures. "There she is. Can you make out the ranch house? It's long and low, looked plenty roomy, from what I saw of it. Only been in it a time or two, ought to be there in another hour or so."

Hannah shaded her eyes, peering down at their destination. Her inner turmoil rose. She faced a new challenge, and looking into the tiny face of her son, knew she must. "Got lots of green around, must be plenty of water, looks real homey from here, Brice." Trying to sound fearless, she knew she had usable skills. "If they really need me, I'll do my best."

She reminded herself she was capable and could handle most situations. She'd relearned that from Brice. During her time with Moore, she'd lost confidence. His constant disapproval, cruelty, and disdain had been devastating. She'd had no one to speak to or who would provide support.

As they neared the ranch, she saw corrals with horses, barns, and out buildings built around the perimeter of the large green treed area that looked to be an orchard. Chickens and geese scratched and picked for tidbits on the ground, and that touch of home gave her a feeling of warmth and welcoming familiarity. Something about the place soothed her uneasiness and she silently prayed this would be a place of refuge.

CHAPTER 9

They passed under high wide gates. The crossbeam bore a huge B within an iron circle. To Hannah, it named the owner and had the appearance of solidity and grandeur.

"Didn't I say it looked to be a good place to stay?" Brice encouraged, and Hannah tried to smile as he clucked the tired mules up to the ranch house.

It was built of strong thick logs chinked with some sort of daubing. Long, low, and spacious, it boasted a wide porch across the front that held chairs, swings, and huge water jugs hanging from the rafters. They were wrapped with roughly woven burlap. Water dripped from some of them.

From the door, a Mexican girl approached, calling out in rapid-fire Spanish for a boy to take the mules. She waited for them to climb down. After Brice reached in to retrieve Thomas, the girl exclaimed in unfeigned delight, "*Oh, senora, esta nino!*" She reached to take Thomas from Brice, clucked to him, and gently rocked him in her arms. "Come een, they weel wish to see you." She pointed toward the door and started off with Thomas in her arms.

Hannah's legs and back, stiff from the long ride on a hard wagon seat, slowed her exit from the wagon. Brice spanned her small waist with his large hands and lifted her to the ground. "Oh, thanks, Brice."

She felt a heated flush rise to her cheeks at his touch. How gently and easily he handled her. His touch had warmed more than her waist, and the knowledge shocked her.

They entered the ranch house through a heavily carved front door, following the girl. Carrying Thomas, she led them past several rooms, well furnished with lamps, chairs, divans, and many colorful wall hangings, and came to a large, heavy-hewn door. The girl stood back and Brice knocked.

"Come on in!" a deep, gruff voice called from within.

Entering, they met a large, graying man. Seams and creases lined his craggy face. Warmth emanated from his gray-hued eyes. He rose from his chair and held out a large paw. "Welcome to the Circle B, the Bidwell Ranch. We've been expecting you to visit us again for a while now, Brice. Good to lay eyes on you again. How's that surveying business?" His eyes took in Hannah's slight figure. "Now who's this young lady?"

"This is Hannah Carlson, Mr. Bidwell." Brice brought Hannah closer. "We hoped you might find a place here where she could earn her keep. She's on her own with a baby to boot," he added. "She's had trouble."

"Mighty nice to know you, ma'am. I'm Jesse." Jesse looked into Hannah's eyes as he enclosed her small hand in both of his great paws. "Well, now—" He hesitated a moment. "How might you be at nursin' an ailin' lady? My wife's been taken real poorly and don't seem to be gettin' any better." His eyes darkened in sorrow before he went on. "She's needin' a woman's help and there's only so much a man can do in this situation."

"Yes, sir, I'm glad to be here and I'd like to meet your wife." She indicated Thomas in the Mexican girl's arms. "If she wants me, there's my small son, about five months old. I couldn't stay anywhere without him." Hannah stood firm about her son. "I'm afraid I've lost track of the days to be sure of his exact age."

"No trouble a'tall, ma'am. The wife would likely take to a young'un prattling about. We had three sons ourselves. The fever took our youngest, Jimmy, and accidents took the other two, Lance and Hal." His speech halted as a hitch caught his voice. "We have no sons now, and it's been a hardship on my wife and me. Always hoped they'd be takin' over this spread in time. Reckon they won't be doing that now," he said, his voice lost in sorrow.

He moved stiffly from his office chair, beckoning them to follow. "She's in her room, stays there most of the time. We'll see what she says."

They followed the rangy old man as he led them toward the back of the house. Hannah saw rough walls covered with old pictures, hanging blankets, baskets, and *ristras* of drying chilies. All in all, the house had a comfortable, homey feel to it. Hannah, looking about for Thomas, saw the Mexican girl following along with them, cuddling the little boy.

"Lupita, you're a spoilin' that young'un already." Bidwell laughed as they met a closed door. He tapped gently. "Leatha, we've got visitors, all right to come on in?" His voice held a soft, gentle tone, belying his rough exterior.

They heard a weak voice from within and Bidwell nudged the door open. His wife lay propped up in bed. Her finely drawn face looked pale and pinched. Her hair bore tinged remnants of a corn-silk color. Her faded blue eyes took on a soft glow when she saw Jesse. She waited for her husband's question.

"Darlin', we have a visitor, and one I hope can take better care of you than I'm up to. Name's Hannah. She's got a small baby. I don't know a lot more, but she needs a place to stay. Maybe you'd like to have a chat with her so we can decide about keepin' her on. It'd be up to you," he said, introducing Hannah to his wife.

Her pale blue eyes fastened on Hannah. "Come here, child. It's been so long since I've even seen a young white woman. Jesse and I had sons but no daughters at all. Sit yourself down next to the bed." She waved the others away.

Hannah pulled a rawhide chair forward and sat down. Lupita had Thomas and Hannah had no worry about his well-being at the moment. "I'm pleased to meet you, ma'am. I came from Iowa about a year and a half ago, and I've had terrible trouble—but I'm well enough now, and if I can be of help, I'll certainly try very hard."

"My dear, I can see in your eyes you've known great sorrow. I won't ask about it. I know what my eyes see and that's enough to suit me. I'll be glad to have your company. We'll get along just fine. Now where is this baby?"

Hannah saw the eager look in her eyes. She rose to get her baby, her heart bursting with hope. Maybe she and Thomas would be able to rest here. How long, she had no idea, but this ranch looked to be a safe haven just now. She found Lupita, took the child from her, and brought him to Leatha's bedside.

Leatha's eyes took in the pink cheeked little cherub, with slightly wavy fair hair. "My stars, he's beautiful! You've been camping with a surveying crew? He looks no worse for it. How is he called?"

Hannah held her son out for inspection. "His name is Thomas. He's been a real good baby so far. I love him more than my life, ma'am."

The interview was finished. Leatha handled the baby and fussed with his hair, twirling her thin finger in it. "I'd like you to stay on here, my dear. I'd be glad of a woman's help. It's too much for Jesse." She laughed. "Men aren't much good at nursing a sick woman, you know."

Assured she was employed, Hannah said, "I'm sure he did his best. He seems to be a fine man. Thank you for having me." Nodding, she left the room.

Lupita waited out in the hall for her, took her to a room, and said in accented English, "This is for you, *senora*."

"Thank you, Lupita." Hannah closed the door, with Thomas in her arms, and saw a good sized bed spread with Indian blankets, walls thick and whitewashed, and the ceiling low. Brightly woven rugs graced the dark stone floor. The window had glass, and she looked out toward dark fringed mountains behind the ranch house. "It's really beautiful here, Thomas."

She wept at this safe haven. Brice had been her savior once again. Her few belongings were in the room, placed here along with the crib Brice had made. It would last a while longer, but with Thomas growing like a weed, he'd need something bigger at some point.

"Oh, Brice, I'll miss your strength when you leave me,

and for sure, I'll miss you," she whispered, feeling desolation and loss at the thought.

Later, with Thomas asleep, she walked outside in the cool evening air. The smells of a busy ranch came to her, along with the scent of wild things growing across this beautiful rangeland. Hearing steps crunch behind her, she tensed inside, and drew away.

"It's just me, Hannah. I needed to walk about some myself," Brice said, his voice low, for her ears only.

"I'm jumpy, can't seem to help it. I'll get better in time. You'll be leaving in the morning, won't you?" Her heart felt heavy at the thought of not seeing his big, spare body and dark blue eyes.

"I'll come sometimes if we're near enough. Seeing if you and your son are doing all right, that's what I'd like to know most of all."

Overwhelmed by his caring, Hannah couldn't stop her tears. "I'm sorry to cry. Sometimes I wonder if you think that's all I do, but how can you do so much for someone you don't even know?"

"I know you, Hannah. There's none better as far as I can see." He came close, took her into his arms, and pressed her close against his body. "I reckon you're the best thing that's ever happened to this old loner. Why? Who knows? I only know I need the sight of you, and I'll miss that like hell around the camp, and that little boy, too" He bent her back in his arms and reached down to her lips. Holding her in a grip of steel, he kissed her over and over. "I'm sorry, but I've wanted to do that for a long time."

She didn't struggle against him, but nestled closer into his warm, solid, body, enveloped in the overwhelming comfort of his arms. The touch of his firm lips set her blood to racing. "Oh, Brice, I don't know what I'll do without you. You've become so much a part of my life it's hard to think of any other time." The remembering Hank, she knew she had to tell Brice about her ugly encounter with this sinister man. "I need to tell you something."

"What is it, then?"

"That man, Watkins, came up to me down by the creek one day when I was getting water. He wanted to know if I had a husband and asked if I was thick with you. He became terribly angry when I refused to tell him about myself. He said he'd find out about me! On its own, it doesn't sound so terrible, but the meaning in his eyes..." She felt her own face tighten and saw Brice's draw into a jaw-clenching frown.

His brow crinkled. "Sure as hell, he was one of the men I sent into Flagstaff this morning. I'll keep an ear out. Try not to worry too much, talk should be dyin' down about your husband by now. He's not likely to know many folks—decent ones anyway." He held her close, taking in the smell of her hair and skin. "I'll miss you every day Hannah," he murmured softly. "You're all healed now and no one around here need ever know what we know."

Hannah's heart soared at his words, and certainly, his touch. "I'm glad I told you about Watkins. I didn't want to burden you with it, but I guess it's better that I did. If you keep an eye on him, he won't know you're doing it, will he?"

"No, honey, he'll not."

He called me honey! No man has ever done that! Her heart beat so rapidly she felt breathless, and all her worries fled. "I'll be fine here, Brice," she assured him. "They *are* good people, aren't they?"

She moved away from him. "I'd best go in now, Brice."

She hugged his strong, male body. With reluctance, she left him, not wanting prying eyes to make something untoward out of her meeting him like this. She sought her bed and lay there wondering why she felt slightly uncomfortable in Brice's arms. *Will I never be able to enjoy the embrace of a good man?*

Thomas was asleep. Someone had changed him again. Lupita had tended her child and Hannah felt a kindred feeling between herself and the diminutive Mexican girl. Unsure of things, she wondered if anyone had seen her meeting in the orchard with Brice. Fear reached her again. He'd been her friend. They all knew that.

ოჯეჯ

In the morning, she saw his wagon hitched up and ready. After a last few words with her and Thomas, Brice gave her a warm smile. "You'll do fine here, Hannah, and don't worry so much."

He mounted the wagon, clucked to the mules, and flashed a wide smile at her as he drove away.

She watched him disappear from sight, wondering when she'd see him again. She hefted her increasingly heavy son in her arms and turned to re-enter the house and her new life.

CHAPTER 10

Hanna soon realized she had many willing hands to help. Lupita took Thomas frequently, as well as the ladies in the kitchen. It freed her to spend more time with Leatha Bidwell. The lady required a great deal of help in her daily routine. Her condition weakened steadily, making Hannah wonder what lay at the cause of her illness. She went to the lady's room and gently tapped on the door.

"Come in." Her voice sounded very weak this morning.

Entering, Hannah saw Leatha lying in mussed linens with her hair awry. "What would you like me to do first, ma'am?" She touched the lady's hair. "Your hair needs fixing." She laughed. "You need a bath, to eat, and a change of clothes and bed linens, too."

"I'll not have you become a servant. I'd like your help with things more as a daughter, if that's not too forward of me to ask." Leatha sighed. "There is something about you, my dear. You remind me of a sister when we were young girls. She's gone now—long since—but you remind me so much of her."

Hannah agreed readily but, seeing the depth of Leatha's illness, wanted to know more. "I see how ill you are, and you're steadily declining, but how do you know what's wrong? Have you seen a doctor? Are there doctors in this area? It's seems so far from everything." Hannah wanted to deny the truth before her, but, without doubt, this fine lady had long since resigned herself to death.

"I have seen a doctor, yes, six months ago when we went to Flagstaff for supplies. For quite some time, I'd known something was very wrong." Leatha smiled and shrugged. "I saw the doctor while Jesse did business. He told me I have a large and deadly growth in my body. He said nothing could be done for me. I couldn't tell Jesse the truth about that visit—I couldn't find the words." A tear escaped and ran down her cheek. "The doctor gave me laudanum to ease the pain. I use it when I need it, but Jesse has never seen me take it. Since you'll do most of the caring of me, you need to know the truth of things." The long discourse left her panting for breath.

Hannah brought her a drink and helped her take a few sips. "Thank you for telling me. I want to help as much as I can." Tears stung in her eyes, but she held them.

"Go ahead, child, cry if you like. Let it out. It's not good to keep things built up inside. Sometimes I wonder if that's what happened to me. As we lost our sons one by one, I held the heartache inside and Jesse was left to grieve alone while trying to comfort me. He isn't well either and I know it. It's one more thing we hide from each other. I wish he'd tell me, I know he wants to, but he doesn't." Leatha looked at Hannah. "We've been secretive for too long."

Hearing that Jesse faced death, too, Hannah felt her world slipping from beneath her. She'd accepted the loss of Leatha, but not his—

Silent, in shock, she had no ready answer to Leatha's words. That Jesse was ailing brought a fresh chill over her. Regaining her strength, she put it aside.

She was there to help Leatha. She aided her to a chair, combed her hair, and brought warm water for a semi bath. Lupita brought fresh linens, and together they made up the bed.

"*Tomas sueneo*," Lupita said.

Hannah guessed he was at rest somewhere in the house. She smiled and nodded her thanks to the little dark-haired girl.

This became the general routine most days unless Leatha felt too sick and weak to move at all. A pity, Hannah thought. Such a lovely woman, and with a husband who dotes on her.

She read books, keeping Leatha company on those days

when it was difficult to leave her bed. During those times, the lady frequently asked to see Thomas. Hannah thought she enjoyed the sight of this new little person who reminded her of happier days when her sons were children.

Leatha had kept many of the clothes her sons had worn and freely offered them to Hannah, along with the use of a slightly battered crib her sons had used so many years ago. "My boys were a rough lot and used the crib pretty hard, but I believe it's still usable." She chuckled, remembering those days.

"Just in time for this growing child." Unable to refuse a genuinely sincere offer, Hannah accepted and planned to make good use of it. He'd grown out of the one Brice had made. With love, she placed that crib in a store room. Looking at it warmed her heart, remembering the strong hands that had crafted it during her darkest hours.

In the kitchen, two portly Mexican ladies worked at putting food together each day. They spoke little English and Hannah's offer of help fell on deaf ears. They made Mexican custards, *flan,* and light foods for Mrs. Bidwell, and served her in her room if Hannah wasn't nearby. Their caring of the ailing woman made Hannah realize the high regard they had for her.

The Mexican ladies introduced Thomas to mashed fruit and spotted pinto beans. She worried about it, but they shushed her, laughing. What they said made no sense to her, and Thomas tolerated the added foods just fine.

"*Muchacho mucho gordito,*" the women said.

By now Hannah knew it meant good in some way. Their names were Guadalupe and Conchita. Hannah slowly became familiar with Spanish names and some of the words, new to her mid-western tongue. *This is a whole new way of life for me.*

One day they brought a chunky baby boy for Thomas to play with. The babies lay kicking and wriggling together on a large blanket laid out carefully on the kitchen floor and talked to each other in the universal language of the very young.

"*Su nombre es Pedro,*" they said, telling her his name.

The dark-skinned baby and the fair, light headed baby

babbled happily as they reached out to touch each other. They examined faces, noses, pulled on clothes, touched hands, and made baby sounds with bubbly spittle drooling from their soft little mouths.

The loving care the Mexican ladies lavished on her baby delighted Hannah and brought her great peace of mind. Lurking in the back of her thoughts lay the haunting possibility of leaving a motherless child behind if they dragged her off to prison, or worse, to hang on the gallows for murder. She knew very well it could happen, and she'd never see or care for her son again. What would become of Thomas? Would some other woman care for him and love him?

The days passed slowly. Things, being quiet and peaceful, lulled Hannah into a sense of security. Her bond with Leatha had become near that of mother and daughter. Mr. Bidwell was out on his ranch much of the time, placing his wife's care almost solely in Hannah's capable hands. She felt strong, useful, and needed—a feeling of competence sorely missed. She welcomed it.

Brice seldom left her thoughts, and she looked for him every day. Gazing out over the trail where he would appear when he came again to the Bidwell Ranch, she whispered, "Oh Brice, where are you today?"

To her delight, a month after her coming to the ranch, she saw him ride into the yard on his big dapple gray, Romer, and ran out to greet him. He was dusty, with sweat-stained clothes. His angular face and dark blue eyes touched her deeply and set her heart racing. Contrary to her better judgment, wild flames flickered within her and sent her body in a spin.

He leaped off Romer and swept her into his arms. "Howdy, Hannah, I thought to see you and the boy. How're you faring these days?"

Caring and warmth shone from his eyes. Her heart swelled with joy because he'd come.

"Brice, I've missed you so! How was your ride? Are you far from here now?" She found herself babbling in excitement at his presence. But deep within, lay unspoken questions. What had he heard about Moore? She couldn't hide the worry in her eyes and wondered if his answers might be too painful or too fearful to mention. "It's a good place, Brice, like you thought it would be. Leatha is a lovely, fine woman. She treats me as a daughter, but she's sicker each day. She hardly gets out of bed anymore." She frowned. "If something should happen to her, she said I should stay on here. How could I do that?" She felt selfish mentioning it.

"I wouldn't worry just yet. You're happy here, then?"

"Oh, yes. It's peaceful and it feels safe. The Mexican women take care of Thomas so I can take care of Leatha. They bring little Pedro over to play with him." She laughed with joy. "Oh, Brice, you must see them together. No language problems with those two."

He handed the reins to Manuel, who took the tired, dusty horse to the stable. Brice walked beside Hannah to the ranch house. "How've *you* been then?"

His dark blue eyes looked into hers. A thrill spun its way down, coiling around her midsection like liquid flame as he touched her honey-colored hair. It looked good these days and she looked better, filled out, and the darkness beneath her eyes had gone.

His question meant her feelings, her safety, and her worries. "I love it here, but you know I worry, waiting to hear if you've learned anything new." Hannah knew happiness these days, though the long shadows of her crime hung silently and darkly over her. Fear of discovery seldom left her. Secure as she felt with the Bidwells, she'd never know the feeling of real safety.

With a sinking feeling, she saw a frown cross his brow. "I have news, but let's wait until later. I need to speak to Jesse just now."

His spurs jingled with small bell-like sounds as he walked down the long hall to the heavy wooden door. Hannah watched and admired the way his long frame moved easily down toward Jesse's office. He knocked and went in. What did he have to tell Bidwell? Was it about her troubles?

Brice remained closeted for a good long time with the rancher. They came out chatting amiably and she saw them shake hands. Supper forestalled further conversation. Waiting eagerly to meet with him alone, she held her questions, caring for Thomas and her patient.

Leatha never left her room, nor did she eat well. Hannah tried what she could to encourage her dietary intake, but with little success. Her patient declined daily. "Ma'am, you must try to eat a little better. You don't take enough food to sustain yourself. You're getting too thin." She tried to keep alarm from her voice.

"Go eat with the others, child. Mr. Fowler is here, and you'll want to see him. I have no wish to eat now, maybe a bit of tea and a nibble of tortilla later." She lay back against her pillows with a tired sigh and closed her eyes.

Hannah felt she continually failed Leatha, but had no answer to the dilemma. Fighting a desperate battle and slowly losing her patient, despite all her efforts, filled her with an increasing sense of hopelessness.

After the supper hour, she met Brice out under the trees in the orchard. "Come with me, my dear, we'll sit here and talk." He led her to a sturdy bench under a straggly apple tree. Some of the apples lay on the grassy ground, shining in the moonlight.

The slightly sweet odor of semi-ripe fruit filled the surrounding air and somewhere far off, she heard the soft hooting of Great Horned owls. Sometimes they silently swooped over the orchard in their quest for small game, rabbits, mice, and such. She often marveled at their quiet, deadly sweep through the night air.

Her anxiety wouldn't let her wait for him to begin. "Please, Brice, if you have anything to tell me, please let me hear it."

"Hannah, there was talk back in Flagstaff," he said. "There was some mention about a woman being out there at the Moore place, but no one ever caught sight of her while she lived there. What this comes to, I don't know. Watkins was way too curious about you. I had it out with him and fired him."

"I knew this place was too good to be true!"

She turned to him, her face shining white in the soft moonlight. He saw the look of despair on it. "I'll make the next trip to Flagstaff, myself, and see what I can learn," he said.

"It's that Watkins. He'll dog this to death to bring me down. I know he will, Brice. He reminded me of Moore in some ways. Do I see that in every man, or was it some evil gleam in his eyes?"

Brice took her in his arms. "Well, you don't see that evil streak in me, now, do you?" He held her out from him. "You'd better not." He laughed then became serious. "If you could leave here now, would you want to head out for California? It's far off, and no one there would know or care about Moore."

"It wouldn't be right to leave Leatha. I couldn't do that, Brice."

"If the worst happens, and they arrest you, I'll do my best to clear your name. After all, lady, you were trying to save yourself and your baby. How in hell could they not understand that?"

"It'd be best to have it out and cleared up, unless it went the wrong way and they hang me. What'll happen to my son with me gone?" She held her face down in her lap and hugged her arms across her chest. "And no, you've never made me think of Moore."

"Let's not spend too much time worryin' for now, but you needed to know what I have found out, little as it is. You're safe enough for now, bein' here. These folks set a great deal of store in you. He thinks of you as family these days, tells me you're doing a great job with his wife."

"They're very good to me, Brice. Gave me things their babies had used. Thomas has grown out of everything and eats food from the Mexican women too. He's strong, growing like a weed, and doing very well." She smiled up to him, forgetting her worries in the joy of her child.

"You look wonderful, Hannah. I've missed seeing you, holding you." He took her into his arms, held her close, and bent to kiss her upturned lips.

"I've missed you, Brice, I look for you around every corner, and wait for you every day." Her arms tightened around his lean, hard body. "Oh, God, what will I do when you're gone away? What will happen to me and my baby?"

"Maybe I won't be gone, girl. When things get sorted out, what would you think of marrying me?" He held her close in his arms, his face nuzzling her hair as he added. "I've been thinkin' on it for some time now, Hannah."

Dizzy with his scent and the intensity of his voice, Hannah gasped at his proposal. He turned her in his arms and held her out, looking deep into her eyes as light from the rising moon filtered through the trees creating a dappled pattern over them. He waited for her answer.

Her heart leaped with joy at his words, until she gave thought to what marriage to a man meant, the thought of enduring physical intimacy once again sent icy chills of hideous remembrance racing through her. "W—well, I'd have to think about it." She didn't want to hurt him, but shaking in his arms, she drew away from his warm embrace, hugged her arms around her body, and began heavy, deep, weeping.

Sorry he'd brought her to this point, he exclaimed quickly, "We'll talk about it later when things are squared up. I understand you might have bad feelin's about such a thing, but I'm not like Moore. Good God, woman, not every man is that way!"

He took her by the shoulders and held her out to look into her eyes while he declared his feelings. "Darlin', think about it leastways!" He shook her gently. "I wouldn't want to live the rest of my life without you. I've been a loner for a long time, but now I can't seem to get along alone. Funny the way things go in your life. Just out of the blue you come to my cabin in the night, like it was meant to happen. Something brought you my way that awful night."

Hannah sniffed and dried her eyes on the hem of her skirt. "I do care for you, Brice. If I can ever care for a man that way again, it'll be you. It'd only be you." Hannah shook her head at what he'd said.

He'd called her darling and her heart told her he was a

man, good and true, but a deep fear clawed at her insides, clouding all other feelings. The atrocities committed on her person by Moore invaded her mind. It made her sick with dread.

"Forget about these things now, Hannah. I see you can't think of it yet. You need a man to stand for you and a father for Thomas. I'd never thought much about marryin' but since runnin' into you and seein' how bad you've had it in your life, I can't think about much else. I love you, girl. I don't know what else there is to say, and I'm not even sure what love is. It's not that you've had a bad time either, it's the woman of you that calls to me, all soft and smellin' nice. Bein' beautiful ain't all that much, never was. It's who you are, that's what it is for me."

Hannah realized the heat of his emotions had sent his semi-cultured speech back into his Texas drawl. "I have deep feelings for you, Brice, but with all that hangs over me, it just can't be—not yet." With regret, she said it and felt relieved to distract him from his pursuit of her.

"Let's walk a little, darlin'. We've time to think about this. My work in this area will last several more weeks."

He placed a friendly arm about her and they walked together under the trees. The moon came up brighter, casting shadows and dappled spots of creamy light over the trees and mountains.

"Walking with you like this takes all my worries away, Brice. Just now, I'm at peace and can't think about what might lie ahead. I don't want to think of it. Life here is wonderful." She stopped and faced him. "My lady is a fine woman, but there is a sadness about her that's beyond me. She told me what's wrong and has no hope of recovery. But I wonder if it's that or is it having lost all her sons? Is it that all the dreams you had when you're young, and starting life, have come to a sad, defeated end?" Hannah sighed and leaned closer to him. "If we have a life together, will it end like that, too?"

"Things don't always come to naught. A person has to try. We might have a wonderful life, girl, but things happen and there's nothin' to be done to change it. It's the way life is and catchin' what happiness that comes your way seems all the more important. There'd be the two of us facin' life together, remember that, Hannah, darlin'."

"You give me hope and courage, Brice Fowler. Maybe we could have a life together. I will think about it. As you say, there's no hurry. I'm healing in mind as well as spirit. My bruises are gone, but there's more than that. He hurt me inside, real bad."

She looked up at him, her eyes shadowed from the moonlight. The warm light in his blue eyes gave hope for their future, but she wondered. *Is there any chance at all I can survive this and live a normal life?*

CHAPTER 11

B rice rode away the next morning, and Hannah sighed as she watched his lanky figure grow smaller. As he faded into the distance, the desolation she felt at the loss of him struck her deeply.

Later, as she gently combed Leatha's hair, the woman sensed her troubled heart. "My dear, are you well? You may confide in me if you will. Life out here is hard on women, believe me, I know. I'd be pleased to help."

She seemed especially pale this morning. Hannah worried over her rapid decline. She would soon lose this new friend. Confiding in her would be a great release, yet, could she tell her troubles to anyone but Brice? What would a gentle lady like Leatha think about what she had done?

"I'm all right, ma'am, just sad to see Brice leave, I guess."

Seeing Hannah's confusion, Leatha said, "I know my time is short, my dear. I want you to know you may stay in this house as long as you need to. It's a safe haven for you, I see that, too."

Her words made Hannah's face tighten with apprehension. *She's a friend, I know that. Could I possibly tell her what I've done?* She protested. "I don't know what to say."

Leatha had said Mr. Bidwell was not well, and Hannah worried what her future held when Leatha passed on, and Jesse, what then?

As if reading her mind, Leatha spoke softly. "Hannah

dear, Jesse agrees that you should stay on here when I'm gone. You'll be the daughter he never had. In so many ways, you already are."

"Ma'am, are you sure?" *Would he want a woman like me living here, if he knew everything?* "You've made me feel at home here, but if you plan on my staying, there is something you should know. It's very difficult to speak of but it's only right you know my story."

"Go ahead, my child, let it out. Keeping dark things inside is never good. As you know, I believe it's some of what ails both Jesse and me."

Hannah slowly began her story. After a silence of many months it was difficult to speak of the brutal treatment by her husband. But she told of her sad life with Moore. Seeing understanding in Leatha's eyes, she laid out the brutality, and how she'd finally struck back in fear for her life and fled into the night with her child.

"Oh, my God, dear girl. I knew you'd suffered, but that way, with such brutality? I see the truth of it in your eyes. Please, I'd like Jesse to know of this, if you'll allow me to tell him. He'll understand, my dear, he will." Her pale blue eyes relayed the depth of her concern.

Hannah's head rose up in fear. "Are you sure? Would he want a woman like me taking care of you?"

"He would if I say so. He'll take you and your son into this house to stay when I'm gone. Jesse will believe you. He's a man of great understanding."

Sensing she had no alternative, Hannah acquiesced. "Yes, you may tell him, and I'll be in the room with you if you like. He may want more details."

"We'll tell him together." Leatha beckoned Lupita and sent her for Bidwell. As they awaited him, Hannah knew an intense anxiety. Again, her life hung in the balance, and there was nothing for her to do but face up to it. She had Thomas to care for and saw no way out. With deep foreboding, she waited.

The man came into the room. Rugged and sometimes gruff, Bidwell became a gentle presence before his wife. The glow in Leatha's eyes, as she gazed into his rugged visage told of her love for him.

"My dear, we have a story to tell," Leatha said. "Hannah has told me the circumstances of her tragic life and why she is here with her tiny son." Her voice became weaker with the effort of talking. "If I can't finish, she will answer any questions you might have." She began the story, and when her voice became inaudible, Hannah continued on.

"I had to save myself and my child. The madness in his eyes told me he'd lost all reason. My fear now is that I'll be arrested and held for murder. What will become of my baby? Brice saved my life that night. He can tell you how I looked, what he saw. It took nearly a month to heal enough to meet his crew." Hannah held her head high as she completed her tale of horror.

"Honey, Brice and I have already discussed this matter. He bound me never to speak of it, but I'm glad you've had your say on it. Try not to worry too soon. If you're arrested, we'll watch over your baby. He'll be safe here." He rose to put a friendly arm about her and patted her shoulder.

He followed Hannah from the room, tears coursing down his leathery cheeks. He took hold of her arm. "Hold on, Hannah." His eyes held deep sorrow. "I know my wife is failing and failing fast. She thinks I don't know, but I've known for a while. We play this game of putting on a brave face, and have done it far too long. I wish I knew how to break this falseness away. I'd like her to be honest with me. My God, she's dying and we can't talk about it!"

"Mr. Bidwell, why don't you tell her how you feel? Have it out with her. You can cry with her, but you'll be together in it. Wouldn't you both feel better with nothing hidden? You're very gentle with her. I'm sure it'd be for the best. She's been real lucky to have a loving husband like you, for all your losses. Believe me, I know."

"You're right, Hannah, and call me Jesse from now on, if you will."

Hannah sought her room after the exhausting ordeal with Jesse and Leatha. Getting her past out in the open was a good thing. Now, if they could open up to each other, it would be a good thing for them as well.

Thomas was gone. She surmised the women had him in their care.

"Brice, they know it all now," she whispered to herself. "Thank you for standing up for me. How many times can I say it?"

She threw herself on the bed, relieved, worn out, and too tired to look for Thomas. Her milk flow had decreased and, since he was taking other foods, it was little loss for her child. With her nursing duties, it had become a blessing. She curled into her bed, trying to quell her spinning thoughts.

"I'm living in comfort and safety for now, but I'll never rest until everything is over and done. Maybe I could have a life with Brice, God bless that man! Sometimes I wish I'd never left home. At least I'd know where I was in life." She uttered a soft laugh. "Nowhere, an old maid that's what I'd be, and I wouldn't have Thomas. I wouldn't know these good people, or a man like Brice Fowler." She marveled at the way her life had gone.

Sleep was slow to come. A sense of foreboding came over her at times and, at this moment, it was intense.

☙❧❧

In the dingy barroom, drifting smoke, acrid and thick, served to limit visibility. Whiskey flowed freely, glasses clinked, and a tinkling piano played in the background.

Hank Watkins heard it in the far recesses of his mind and none of it bothered him as he sat in a quiet corner, playing poker with three other men.

The occasional titter of saloon women frequenting the place, looking for a night's pay, a bit of fun or both, barely reached his consciousness.

Hank was drunk, and slurring his words when he asked, "Shay, any talk around about a little yaller-haired woman with a kid?"

"Nope, ain't heerd of none like 'at around." Jack Coombs

sat across from Hank. "Why you askin? Woman of yours, walked out on you, did she?"

"Shut your ugly face, you nosey coyote. I'm jest sayin', a while back I saw a woman like her out at the place I was workin'. Closed mouthed as hell, she was. Yesiree, snooty little bitch, wouldn't give me any time a'tall." He lowered his voice. "I swore I'd fin' out about her is all." He scoffed. "Hell, she weren't no woman of mine."

Coombs laughed. "Hell, why would she have the likes of you? A drunken loser like you, musta knew a useless skunk when she seen 'im."

"Ante up, you bastard, an' finish the game here. I got to mill aroun' for a while." Hank dealt a round of nicked and battered cards, took a drag on his cigarette, and the game went on amid the soft din that rose above the fuggy atmosphere.

A quiet little man, neatly dressed, sat in on the game. "I just might have heard about that rancher called Moore."

"Naw, never heard about any rancher. So wha's about it?" Hank had no interest in the subject, but in the dimness of his mind felt it polite to ask.

"Seems they found him with his head bashed in by a skillet. The sheriff did some investigatin' but no one's heard anything more on it. Seems there was some traces of a woman livin' there. Baby clothes were found, so I hear."

"What happened to the rancher, daid is he?" Fuzzy from the liquor, Hank frowned as he worked to make out what was said. "They find his woman?"

"Naw sir, that's what's queer about the whole deal. They say he was dead all right, and in real bad shape by the time they found him, been a layin' there quite a while. Kept to hisself, so he wasn't missed for some days an' when he didn't show up to claim his stock at the round-up for three-four days, some boys went a lookin', that's the last I heard of it, though. Ain't been nuthin' since then said about it," the man finished.

Hank began to take interest, and his mind struggled to work through his alcoholic fog. "Shay, what's yer name? Live 'round here?"

"Name's Ordway. I own a small store down the street

called Clay's Mercantile. Live upstairs, me and my wife." He shifted in his chair, "Well, I got to get goin' afore she gets to worryin'. Night, you-all." He rose from his chair, picked up what money he had left, settled his hat on his head, and shuffled through the swinging doors.

Hank continued card playing and drinking until the small hours of the morning. Later, he weaved his way out into the night. He stayed at a small rooming house with rude little cots—all he could afford. He'd been lucky at cards, or even that would have been beyond him.

დოდი

The next morning, Hank nursed a grand headache as he swilled two cups of coffee and tried to eat some of the fare the landlady put forth. "I'm a little put off this mornin', ma'am." He reached for the pancakes and slathered honey over the few he'd put on his plate. "Looks good, this here does." He began to shovel in the food and his rioting gut settled down some.

"Hey, you damned hawg. Save some fer the rest sittin' here," It was a portly whiskey-swilling man, Al Partin, who'd been recently tossed out by his wife. "You smell like a whiskey keg set out to air."

Al grabbed the remaining food and placed his arms around his plate to protect his hefty breakfast.

"Hawg yourself, mister." Hank moderated his tone. He wanted information to fill out what he'd heard at the saloon. "Any of you yahoos heered about old Moore gittin' his head bashed in?" He was sure he'd heard the name right last night, even though he'd been drunk.

The landlady forestalled trouble by bringing in another platter of pancakes. "Now don't git in no trouble, I'm warnin' the lot of ya, or I'll be kickin' some of you useless yayhoos outta here!"

Hank watched her walk away, muttering, tugging at wispy graying brown hair, and tucking it under the ragged cap she wore while cooking.

She shook her head and moved her generous frame up to

the cast iron stove. "Ain't never seen sich as these, always hungry, they are."

Hank figured Ella Barnes had seen about every kind pass through her poor hostel. He'd started asking about the death of Moore and had been talking about it ever since he'd awakened this morning. He decided to find out if she'd heard anything. She might tell him it wasn't any business of his or did he have some other reason? Maybe he'd ask her about it later when she didn't look so mean. He knew it made her mad as hell to see him sitting around instead of hunting for a job.

When they had a moment of quiet, she said, "I heard you askin' 'round about that Moore fella. What's yer interest in it then?"

"Nuthin' much, jest heard he'd had a wife, wondered about it an' what ever became of 'er?" His head ached like hell, but he was glad to have the subject opened, and glad the dead man's name was right.

"Well, I heered talk about thet. Some say he got married here, more'n a year ago. Nobody's ever seen him since, though, to know about any woman. I guess that scrawny lookin' preacher might be the one to ask 'bout that. Why don't you ask around? Maybe you'd find a body who knows, seein' yer so almighty interested in Moore's woman."

"Jest might, jest might do that, ma'am. Thank ya."

Hank turned to climb the stairs to his bunk. His head hurt with all the talk and clanging of dishes and he had some thinking to do. Maybe the numerous cups of coffee he'd swilled would help.

Later, when his head cleared, he pulled on his scuffed old boots and went out on the street. "Got to nose around a bit. Oughta be lookin' fer work, but time enough fer that. I got me some checkin' to do. Might just be a reward fer what I know," he muttered to himself, thinking of spending the reward money as he shuffled down the splintery, sun-whitened boardwalk. "Damn it all, I got to knock off on the drinkin'."

The town was busy. People bustled about with wagons loaded with supplies, cattlemen on horseback, and women shopping in their faded sun-bonnets, most of them dragging a child or two along. Flagstaff bustled, and clouds hung over the Peaks, making ready to douse them with a shower like most days in mid-summer. A brisk wind picked up, causing him to shiver in the high thin air.

He saw the sheriff's office and crossed the dusty street. He approached the deputy—sitting back, hat over his face and feet on the desk.

"Say, there's been some talk around, heard any news about thet Moore feller?"

"Who's askin'?" Deputy Lin Johnson sluggishly roused to attention. He moved his thin, wiry frame, took his feet off the desk, and sat up His watery blue eyes squinted at Hank. "What's your interest in the case?"

"Well, I jest might have some information 'bout a woman thet came from here 'bouts, an' wonderin' if she might jest be connected to the killin' in some way?" He couched his voice in low confidential tones, even though the office was empty except for the deputy. He did hear sounds of talk from the back and guessed that was where the jail cells might be.

"What you got to say, and who are you to come in here with your talk?"

"Name's Hank Watkins. I was workin' way out on a surveyin' crew off toward the southwest of here, when the boss comes a draggin' in with this little woman and her young'un. Little bit of a mite he was. Jest couldn't figger what she'd be doin' out there like that." He shifted his weight, his heart took a leap, seeing a light of interest flicker in the deputy's eyes. "Heard any talk 'bout a woman might be hiding herself out?"

"Wait until tomorrow, when the sheriff gets back. Come on in with your story then. Where can we reach you if he wants to see you sooner?"

"I'll be at Ellie Barnes place or the Roarin' Duck where I play a few cards with the boys. Jest let me know when he comes in. He might be wantin' to hear what I got to say." His chest swelled with the importance of his information.

Hank left the sheriff's office and, feeling at loose ends, wandered the town, looking for nothing in particular. He knew a few men, but mostly those associated with his card games. If he loitered about the mercantile, maybe he'd overhear something or other. He sauntered over and went in.

The interior was warm and dark with odors of molasses, grains, harness leather, tack, and woolen goods. It brought up memories of his childhood, not a happy one, except for a few times he remembered going to town with his stepdaddy and spending time in a store like this. Sometimes he got a piece of candy to chew on and the man never hit him in front of people.

"Say, Sarah, did you hear that there was a woman out to the Moore place?"

Hank overheard a work-worn woman asking a friend. They were picking over yard goods, holding it out, and commenting on it.

"Now this here's a purty print, don't yu' think?" Sarah asked.

"It's right nice." the other woman, Martha, agreed. She kept on with the subject. "I heared there might a been a baby out there too. They found some baby clothes, weren't much fer a young'un, so I heard."

"Now where'd yu' hear tell of that, Martha?"

"I hear things. Sometimes it's real important, and this sounds like it." She wandered farther down to the bonnets on display. "Some drunk has been asking around town about it. I heared him over at the hostel. Makes a body wonder what happens a-way out on a place like 'at. Never heard much about the man, kept hisself away from people—queer sounding, I'd say."

Hank heard enough to quicken his heart rate and toughen his resolve. There was something about a woman. Maybe it was that snooty little bitch who'd scorned his advances. His excitement increased along with his burning desire to avenge himself on that standoffish female.

"Mebbe it's her, sure could be or I miss my guess, comin' outta nowhere like that and about the same time," he mumbled.

Sheriff La Force rode in later that day, dusty and trail-worn. He listened as Lin Johnson passed on the information from Hank. "Queer sort, a useless drunk to my notion. No idea why he'd be takin' an interest in old Moore's death, but he sure was awful nosey about it. He's been askin' around, like he's real curious about it." Lin frowned. "Wonder what interest a man like that'd have with a married woman, anyway."

The sheriff frowned. "Well, Moore's been dead a while. Trail's cold if there is a trail. I'll worry on it tomorrow. I've had a hard ride. Been out to the ranch, and I did see some evidence of a woman, and a few poor lookin' baby things. If there was a woman there, she sure had little enough to work with. There's some as think he was a mighty hard man." With that, La Force said goodnight and headed to his home, trail weary, dusty, and very thirsty.

He stopped for a few drinks at the Roaring Duck but, needing his rest, he headed out the door for his quarters then halted as a man stepped in front of him.

The man eyed the battered metal star on his sweat-stained vest. "Might you be the sheriff?"

"So, I am. What's on your mind?"

"I got somethin' to say about a woman I seen out on the trail, an' wonderin' if they's been a reward put out on anybody yet?' Hank weaved about, spittle oozed out the side of his mouth and down the front of his sweat-stained shirt. He reeked of sweat and alcohol.

"I'm too tired to bother with a damned snoot full," LaForce said. "Come in the office tomorrow and we'll talk. Good enough for you?" He left the useless drunk standing without a backward glance, having no time for a man like that.

The man stood in the doorway, sputtering. La Force heard him snarl. "Well, to hell with ya', I can find out without your help."

LaForce turned to see the man wander unevenly out the swinging doors and shrugged. "I'll see that useless bum again."

CHAPTER 12

The next morning, La Force, stopped at the mercantile and overheard Clay Ordway's wife Sarah talking with a female customer.

"Did that good-looking young feller ever come back?" Lorna asked.

Sarah frowned. "What good-looking young feller?"

"That one coming in here askin' for women's clothing and all the possibles to go along with what a woman might need, you know, under things an' all?"

"My stars," Sarah said, "You're right. That was powerful strange. Yes, I do remember that, now that you mention it. But why do you ask?"

"Well, there wasn't no sign of a wife. He just told you to pick out a few things about your size. He didn't look it over either, embarrassed over the stuff, was my guess at buyin' women's personals. He did say he thought a blue dress would be about right. He bought a load of sewing things as best as he could. Didn't know two hoots about that either." Lorna chuckled. "He sure was a nicely dressed young man."

"Laws, a body jest might see about anything, these days," Sarah countered. "Didn't know 'im at all, eh?"

"In those clothes, you could see he was no cowhand, had money on him, too." Lorna added.

Sarah nodded. "If they got money, we don't generally catch the name unless they come in a lot or ask for credit."

La Force found the conversation more than interesting. It

triggered an idea that had been fomenting in the back of his mind. He approached Mrs. Ordway. "Say, ma'am, sorry to be listenin' in on your talk, but I was wondering what more you might remember about this man buyin' woman's things?"

"Nothin' much, except he said her colorin' was near to mine and she was about my size. Nice young man. He was, not a cowboy or one of the usual rough-necks we get in here, seemed sort of genteel like, he did." She shrugged. "It was out of the ordinary, I thought, him buying women's clothes like that."

"Didn't give his name, did he?"

"Not as I remember. It never came up. We generally don't ask that unless they cain't pay up. Then we have to know who they are—business, you know. Sure seemed like real nice feller," she reiterated.

La Force thanked her, shouldered his supplies, and headed out the door.

Later on in the day, he was at his desk in the sheriff's office. Hank sauntered in. "Say, sheriff, there's somethin' you might be interested in knowin'."

La Force waved him to a chair. "What's on your mind? Sorry about last night, but when a man's tired, he's got no time for drunks."

His comment wasn't overly friendly, but the likes of this man didn't set well with him.

Hank, sober this morning, tried to appear sincere. "Well, its jest that when I was out along the trail to the west of here, our party chief, or boss, he comes into camp haulin'a woman and her young'un along with him in his wagon. Little mite, the baby was. The woman kept pretty much to herself. Right snooty to my way of thinkin', but I knew there was somethin' fishy about the deal. Wouldn't say a thing about herself, not a word did she let on, jest hung on the boss mostly. She wasn't his wife, I know that cuz he ain't got one. Wonderin' if you'd know somethin' about a woman like that."

"What would your interest be in this woman?" LaForce didn't like the look of Hank's ugly scowl and found himself reluctant to pay him any mind. But knowing information often came from unlikely sources, this tidbit was not something he could dismiss. It fit with what he'd seen at the Moore ranch.

"Jest wonderin' if you'd heard anything about a woman like that, a runnin' from somethin'd be my guess. She'd git a scared look about her if you surprised her when she wasn't payin' attention."

"Did you creep up on her? That'd be enough to scare a woman all to hell." La Force didn't mind razzing the drunk, though he appeared sober this morning. Hank wasn't much of a man, La Force saw that about him. "Well, I'll think this over and see if it brings anything to mind. And no, I haven't heard of any reward. What'd you say she looked like? It might help in case I do hear anything."

Hank shuffled his feet and rose from the chair. "Well, she was small and not especial purty, but nice enough, womanly, if you know what I mean. She had light-colored hair, sort of like honey, kept it in a big braid down her back. Had a little boy she called Baby Thomas, fed him the natural way, if you know what I mean. He was real young, not walking or anything. Never heard his age, though. Jest you keep in mind I was the one as told you. If anything comes to light, you remember now, I was in on it."

Hank finally left the office, leaving La Force with something to consider. Could she be the woman who'd lived at Moore's? She'd had a small baby. He decided to ask around and see if anyone ever saw him with a wife.

La Force made his way down the dusty street. The sky, dark and threatening, clouds hung heavily over the tall peaks outside the town. Nearly every day in the summer, those clouds moved over Flagstaff, bringing refreshing showers. During those times, the sun often shone through the rain, creating a magical sight.

A few heavy drops splattered over the dusty street throwing up small puffs of dust when he turned into the preacher's yard. "Reckon he'd know whether or not Moore had a wife, if he'd married 'em," La Force mumbled. He stepped onto the porch, and rapped on the door.

A spindly, middle aged man with thin, graying sideburns

came to the door and seeing the battered star on the man's chest, opened the door. "Come on in, sheriff. What can I do for you?" he asked, beckoning La Force in to his dark, musty sitting room.

"Howdy, Pastor Elkins, you busy just now?"

"Never too busy for the law, Sheriff. Set yourself down. My wife'll bring somethin' to drink. Looks like we got us a short downpour out there again today." He indicated the falling sheets of rain, hammering on the tin-roofed house and turning the street into a muddy mess. "So how can I help you, then?"

"Well, I've a few questions to ask of you, wonderin' if maybe you'd remember a rancher named Moore. He was found with his skull bashed in about three-four months ago. I'm sure you've heard around town about it. A bit of information has come to light and you might be some help with it."

"Have a cool drink, Sheriff."

The pastor's wife, Martha, handed him a drink. She matched her husband in her frail, dried up appearance. The drink was ginger water, with tiny flecks of the spice floating around. He remembered how precious spices were in this country.

"Thanks, ma'am, this looks real fine." La Force raised the glass and took a long pull. "So now, do you remember ever seeing Moore, or if he had a wife with him?"

Pastor Elkins shook his head. "No, I cain't rightly remember a man like that. He wasn't a member of our congregation, or I'd know who he was."

"Dear, could it be the couple we married here, you remember, over a year or so ago? Never saw them before or since. I can look it up in the register. We keep a record of marriages, births, deaths and baptisms, too." The wife stood with her hands on her hips, her arms akimbo. "Sir, do you know what they looked like, might jog our memory a bit."

"He was big, a surly man, a loner, they say. I never saw a wife myself, but he had a woman living out there, signs of a young'un too," La Force added. "There was evidence of both when we investigated the killin'. We found some ragged woman's things and a few baby things, looked like she kept her baby in an old feed trough." He shook his head at the idea.

Martha brought the ledger they kept of births, deaths, and marriages. "Let's see." She turned the pages back until she came to the area she sought and pouring over the pages, exclaimed. "Yep, here's the name of Moore. Look right here, Will. Don't you recollect marryin' them? It says he married one Hannah Carlson. If I remember her, I believe she was a small woman, with real nice light-colored hair. She'd just got off the train, as I recall, didn't even know the man. It always seemed a mite strange to me, marryin' a man she'd never even seen afore that day. But things like that happen purty often out here." She placed the book in her husband's hands. "See, Will? Look right there." She put a finger on the names.

La Force took a good long look at the register. It was there before him. Moore married a woman here in Flagstaff. Maybe she'd had a baby for him, and who knows what the hell happened after that? He puzzled over it, but at last the picture was clear enough. He knew he'd have to take action and had a bad feeling about it.

It had stopped raining when he stepped out onto the weathered porch. "I thank you, parson, for your help in this, and thank you, ma'am, for the cool drink."

He tipped his hat and took his leave. His boots picked up a thick layer of mud as he made his way back toward the office.

La Force knew he'd have to have a talk with Hank Watkins again and found it distasteful. He detested a drunken lout like that but it had to be done. Changing directions, he headed for Ella Barnes boarding house, leaving thick muddy tracks as he crossed the rain-soaked street. The air smelled fresh and clean, and a few clouds remained, clinging around the San Francisco Peaks.

Looking at the lofty Peaks, Jake recalled the old story. It was said, at night, you could see the lights of San Francisco from the lofty, upper reaches of those mountains. The western air being so dry and clear made something like that possible.

Ella answered the door. "Howdy, Sheriff, good seein' you. Needin' something', are you?"

Her hair was awry, and her cheeks reddened, from baking, he guessed, by the flour on her hands and arms and stains
on her apron.

"Hank Watkins around?"

"Naw, he ain't here right now, might look down to the
Roarin' Duck. That's where he spends his time, 'stead of
lookin' fer work." The look of curiosity spread over her face.
"What's he done, now?"

"Just want to talk to him, that's all, ma'am." La Force
turned and headed for the Roaring Duck. "Damn, I hope the
fool bastard hasn't gone and drunk himself into a sodden mess
like the other night."

La Force found Hank disgusting on a good day, and now,
because of his calling, he had to deal with the man again,
drunk or sober.

Adjusting his eyes to the dim interior, he spotted his man
smoking, having a snort or two, and shuffling the worn and
warped cards provided by the establishment. Occasional bursts
of raucous laughter erupted from the group.

He walked over. "Say, Hank, got a minute?"

"Well hell, if it ain't the sheriff! What you callin' on me
fer?" Hank rose out of his chair, more than eager to chat, and
yelled back at the table. "Hey you jokers, don't touch my
cards, ya hear me now?" His chest swelling with importance,
he walked with La Force to another table. They pulled out
worn, scratched chairs and sat down.

La Force ordered a drink for each, hoping Hank wasn't
too far gone already. It was early in the day for it. The drinks
arrived and the sheriff began, his voice low. "So tell me everything you know about this young woman and baby you told me
about."

Hank's reddened eyes held a sly look. "Found out somethin', did you?"

"Not so far, but I might want to follow this along for a
while. I'd appreciate what you can tell me, and no, there's no
reward, not at this time. We don't know enough to put out anything like that."

Hank detailed where he'd seen a woman named Hannah

and her baby, what they looked like, and anything he could remember about her. "Snooty bitch, she was. Don't fergit as how I told you everthin', Sheriff—remember—everthin' I know about the woman." He snorted his drink down and headed back to his poker game.

La Force left the Roaring Duck, deep in thought. He decided to ride out in the morning to check out Hank's story. There'd been traces of a woman and baby out at the ranch— going by the things they'd found. Maybe there was somethin' to it. He felt hesitant, a new thing for him. He shrugged and headed to his office.

Lin Johnson sat pushed back in the chair with his feet on the sheriff's desk. He straightened himself up and asked. "Learn anythin'?"

"Looks like I'll be out on the trail a while. You take care of things here. I don't know how long I'll be, but for sure, three-four days." LaForce was tired and, for some reason, felt a deep reluctance about what he had to do.

"What've you' heard, Jake?"

"There was a woman out to Moore's place, and a baby. I'll follow up on Hank's story. They had a record of her marriage to Moore at the preacher's. He married her right off the train almost a year ago. No one's ever seen her since that I can find, not even for her baby's coming—strange to my way of thinkin'."

La Force sat a while thinking about the things he'd learned. "I've got a feelin' about this and I don't like the way it's shaping up. I sure don't."

CHAPTER 13

At the Bidwell Ranch, Leatha's condition deteriorated to the point she laid gasping and sweating on her bed. Hannah carefully bathed her brow and limbs with cool water. Her heart ached at the pain of her friend and patient. Medicine kept her in some measure of comfort and Hannah gave it often.

"Do the cool cloths help at all?"

"Yes, my dear. It's very soothing, thank you." Leatha closed her eyes, grimacing as pain swept over her frail body. "I know my time is very short now." Her breath came in short gasps. "Nothing can change what's happening to me. I'm falling into a big soft cloud. It reaches out for me. Looks very peaceful and, sometimes, I see my boys." She panted as she struggled to communicate with Hannah. "Please don't be upset, my dear. It's for the best. Might I have a bit more medicine please? I'm so tired." She fell back on her pillow, her breathing labored with a rasping sound. "Oh, you're so beautiful," she murmured to someone she saw, though her eyes remained closed.

Hannah poured the laudanum in a spoon, placed her arm beneath Leatha's head, and put the mixture between her pale bluish lips "Shall I call your husband? He's asked me to call him Jesse, now."

"Not yet—he's not doing well with this. It hurts him so much. But we have talked. He knew all along." Leatha tried to smile and, after a long pause, continued. "Can't fool that man, never could. I have a few more days yet, Hannah dear, I think, before I go to lie beside my sons." Fatigue lined her pale face and kept her voice to a low whisper.

Hannah turned away from the bedside to hide her tears. She needed to check on Thomas and as soon as the medication sent her patient into a shallow sleep, she eased quietly out of the room.

In the passageway, she met Bidwell, his craggy face creased with worry, his body bent from the struggle of keeping death at bay and losing the fight day by day.

"How is she, Hannah? Don't try to mislead me I know how sick she is. She hides it from me even now after we've talked it out."

"She's asleep now, sir. I've given her more medication. She doesn't want to worry you. She told me she has a few days left. She's very tired and ready to go to her sons. Jesse, I'm so sorry." Hannah felt she disobeyed Leatha in telling him, but he wasn't blind to the situation. They needed each other now more than ever, in these last few precious days.

Hannah went with Jesse into Leatha's room. He sat at the bedside and took her thin, pale hand. Her eyes flickered open when Jesse spoke to her in low, loving, tones. "Leatha, you've been the best wife a man ever had. I know how it is with you. We can't play games anymore, my dear. Please talk to me. After all the heartache we've known, this is just one more stone across our path. We'll be together again, and it won't be so very long."

Roused further from her drugged sleep, Leatha smiled at him before lapsing back into her shadowy reverie. Jesse had finally connected with his wife and the thought of it comforted Hannah. She'd helped them face what lay ahead.

In the kitchen, she found Thomas, crawling on a blanket and playing with Pedro. He sat up very well these days and practiced it often when he got to the floor. Seeing his mother, he shrieked with joy and held up his arms. When she took him up, Pedro cried and Lupita swept him up in her arms. Both babies gurgled in delight.

"*Tomas es muy bueno, senora.*"

Thomas reached out to Lupita and Hannah knew he'd found a friend in the Mexican girl. She'd have to leave Thomas behind one day, if they came to arrest her. Bidwell would take him in. Thomas would be safe in this spacious ranch home, but she knew that wouldn't last, the man was seriously ill. Despair swept over her as she considered the facts.

"Mi hijo," Lupita murmured to Thomas, her voice cooing softly as she touched his soft baby cheek.

The girl called Thomas her boy and Hanna took a bit of comfort from it. Someone else loved him.

It would all come out as time unfolded. A heavy sense of foreboding told her that, and a safe place for her child lay heavily on her mind. Could Lupita take him when her own father, known for his brutality might interfere? Hannah prayed that Jesse Bidwell would be able to oversee his care as he'd promised—but for how long?

Leatha's time came in the early morning hours. The summer sun began spreading its faint rose and mauve hues over mountains and grasslands, creating an ethereal scene of nature's splendor. Hannah felt it was a fitting welcome for her mistress as she passed to the glory beyond. Hannah did her best to console Jesse.

The splendor of that wondrous sunrise was soon lost to her as she dealt with the heavy sorrow and desolation in the darkened ranch house. The sounds of weeping and mourning surrounded her.

කුළු

Two days later, Leatha's funeral was conducted in the early part of the day on a hillside in the rustic little cemetery. The grassy mounds where her sons lay were encompassed by a protecting grove of trees out a ways from the ranch house. One grave, very small with grass and wild flowers growing over it, belonged to Hal, their youngest. He must not have been much older than Thomas. That small plot of ground reminded her of the uncertainty of life.

The thought caught at her heart and she barely heard the

service, remembering what Brice had said. '*You have to live life the best you can, and can't change much the way of it.*' She wished him here on this sad, lonely day.

Leatha's coffin, made by Jesse's Mexican workers, had been done some time earlier at his request. Prepared for his beloved wife, padded and lined with a soft silky material, it bore clever artistic carvings on the heavy cover.

Leatha appeared at rest with a gentle look of peace on her thin, ravaged face. Dressed in a long sleeved pale blue dress that ruffled softly in the low winds of morning, her cold, pale hands held her bible and a sprig of wild-flowers. Her dreadful battle was over and the worn look on Jesse's face told of his deep pain and loss.

A tall young man conducted the service. A reverend McDonald, she thought someone said. Hannah, relieved to see this pastor was not the one from Flagstaff, felt she'd passed one more hurdle in her troubled life. She'd never seen this man before. *Thank God! He wasn't the one who married me to Moore.* She sat beside Jesse during the services. He'd asked her to, and she believed it helped him.

The mourners enjoyed a large layout of food provided by the two cooks. They'd roasted huge chunks of beef, venison, pork, and several chickens as well. There were vegetable dishes from the bountiful gardens as well as pies, sweetmeats, and fruits from the orchards. An unhappy occasion for a barbeque, but folks who came from such far distances required food. They expected to eat and spend some time at the ranch. Hasty arrangements were made for their comfort.

Hannah wouldn't have believed there were so many people within a day's ride, but the evidence was there before her eyes. She wondered if there'd been that many near Moore's ranch that she'd never known about.

Bidwell introduced her as a relative from back East. "This is my niece, Hannah Carlson from the Midwest. She came to help out with Leatha during her illness and I'm mighty glad to have her. She's a widow woman and that little feller there is her son." He indicated a chubby, gurgling, Thomas, held snugly in Lupita's arms. "I'm just hoping she'll stay on with me a while yet. I've grown attached to her and the young'un."

"How do you do," Hannah said in greeting and shook many outstretched hands.

She'd never remember each and every face and unconsciously searched among them for the tell-tale signs of trouble. At last she felt at ease and left off worrying.

The mourners from neighboring ranches knew of the many tragic Bidwell losses over the years and felt a deep empathy for Jesse. Death was no stranger to any of these hardy, ranch folks.

She met a woman named Bessie Morris, a big, strong, work-worn ranch wife, and a small, tidy little woman called Hettie Bell among the many others. Hannah felt especially comfortable with these women, and longed for further acquaintance with them. Numerous children ran about. Death sat lightly on the young when it wasn't close to them. It gave hope for the future, seeing the young finding play where they might, reminding everyone else, that life did go on.

Jesse had gone to the end of the patio to chat with his rancher friends. Alone, Hannah felt edgy, seeing a good number of rough appearing cowboys. They gave her more than a passing eye and it made her wonder. Was it because they were lonely men or was there one among them who'd be questioning or threatening like Hank Watkins? She murmured a polite response when it was required then hurried away to a secluded corner of the patio. Overhearing a few comments before she reached the quiet spot she sought, curiosity made her stop to overhear their words

"Wal, what's got her tail in a twist, now? Ain't overly sociable is she?" she heard a dark eyed, lanky rider, with leather chaps hanging loose, say.

"I reckon she probably got too close a look at your ugly mug, Harry." A man named Dink chuckled. "Thet's enough to scare off any woman."

A slight sandy haired cowboy laughed. "Right as hell, ya see how quick she took off runnin'?"

"Aw, go to hell, Dink, she didn't look at you thet I saw. Ain't so much with the wimmin folks yerself, now air you?"

Hannah caught sight of Harry edging him with an elbow.

Suffering a round of catcalls and disparaging remarks by the others standing around, Harry, Dink, and the rest of the men headed off to the loaded food table, took up thick crockery plates, and dug in.

A heavy set man with narrow pig-eyes commented. "She's a right nice little woman, ain't she now? Might do fer some lonely cowboy, lookin' fer a wife."

Something about this cowboy gave Hannah an unsettled feeling.

"Got herself a nice little boy there, too," a cowboy called Pardee said. "Don't go gitten any idees, Tug Parker, you big slob. She wouldn't have to do with the likes of you, anyway."

"Hell, you say!" Tug, tired of jibes about his size, didn't like the unfavorable comments. "We'll see about that, you damned ol' chuckwalla."

He slapped his dusty hat against the side of his leg and headed toward the heavily laden tables set out on the spacious patio.

The cowboys busied themselves piling generous portions of beef, beans, and all the fixings to go along with it on their plates. Coffee spilled and food dropped, splattering on the patio stones as the mourners partook of the generous outlay of solid ranch food.

Hannah moved across the patio, looking for Jesse. He sat at the far end, finding a quiet moment. She felt his sorrow, and his many losses over the years, but wasn't sure how best to comfort the man.

He shook his graying head, as though to drive away his sorrows. "Sometimes it's more'n a body can bear, losin' all of 'em like I did," he said softy. "I don't know why—I just don't."

She heard his whisper and laid her hand on his shoulder in a gesture of comfort. "I don't know what to say, Jesse, you've truly had more than most to bear. It doesn't seem fair somehow. That's the way Brice sees it, too. We talked about it. He said you have to try your best. It's about all you can do and there are no guarantees of anything, good or bad."

"You're a comfort, girl. I'm proud to have you here with me," he said as tears coursed down his leathery cheeks. "I wonder if Brice knows about Leatha's passing. He'd be here if he knew. He's a right good man, Hannah."

"I wish he was here too. I miss him very much and always wonder if he's heard anything more about my trouble. I worry every day about it, more for Thomas than myself." She regretted her selfishness in worrying over her own problems when Jesse's sorrow was so great.

"Don't borrow trouble," he said. "Wait and see. Maybe it'll come out right for you. If anything happens, we'll watch over your little fella until it's made right."

"Jesse, I'm grateful for this haven. When I struck out with Thomas that night, I had no idea where to go or what to do. I just knew I had to escape from the murder burning in his eyes!" She trembled at the memory. "Everyone I've met has been kind, except the one man at Brice's camp. He wanted to get close and know everything about me. I refused him and he became enraged; said he'd find out about me, and he meant it. He sent vicious looks at me after that, but hid them from Brice or the crew."

"Did you let Brice know about it?"

"I finally told him. He fired Watkins later after I came here." Hannah sighed. "I don't know what he has done or said since."

Jesse lowered his voice and smiled, forgetting his sorrows for the moment. "By the way, Hannah, remember meeting that little woman, Hettie Bell?"

"Yes?"

"Did you know she came out here as a mail order bride?"

"Like me?" Hannah's eyes filled with wonder. "If she was, her life went so differently. How lucky she was! She looks happy, Jesse. That was what I'd hoped for, so long ago." Hannah wanted to cry.

Jesse turned her attention to the faint outline of a horse and rider. "Say, I believe that's Brice showin' up now, coming over the rise there."

He pointed toward the horizon where she saw a cloud of

dust, that rose from the horses hooves, float away on the evening breeze.

Hannah, her heart pounding, felt a hot flush rising over her face and forgot everything—her worries and even her tiny son. Her eyes didn't leave the sight of Brice's spare figure nearing the ranch yard. Tears came, but she blinked them back. It wouldn't do to let anyone see them. "Yes, I believe it is, Jesse. I wonder if he's heard about Leatha." She hoped she sounded casual enough.

Jesse smiled down at her. "Well, we'll just ask him. He's almost here."

Brice rode in on a sweaty, done in, Romer. He swung off beside them and slapped some of the dust off his clothes. "Sorry, sir, I just heard late yesterday and came soon as I could. Damned shame about your Leatha. She was a fine woman, Jesse." He reached for Bidwell's hand and shook it firmly. "How you makin' out?"

"Passin' fair, Brice. It's hard to handle but as Hannah here says, you have to live life as it is. Don't make it no easier, though." Sorrow lined Jesse's weathered face.

Manuel came to take the tired horse and wipe him down.

Jesse sighed. "Come on in, son, there's food a plenty, and some of my neighbors are still around." He nodded toward the house and started off.

"How're you makin' out Hannah?" Brice's dark blue eyes took her in and, by his look, knew he sought the gentle female part of her being.

Though he'd greeted Jesse first, his full attention had been on Hannah and she took comfort from it. After the passing of her patient, she'd felt increasingly vulnerable. "I'm fine, Brice. Jesse said he'd like me to stay on even though Leatha's gone. It's safe here and the women love Thomas. He plays with Pedro most every day. Jesse says he'll watch over Thomas if they come for me. "What have you heard, Brice, anything?" She felt comfortable using his name, and it felt good crossing her lips. He'd sweep her up and crush her to his chest when he got the chance. That would happen later and she prayed for it.

"There's been some talk in Flagstaff that Moore had a wife. The preacher's wife remembered you. It could go bad for you, I'm afraid. Hank's been stirring trouble as much as he can between his drinkin' and cards." Brice walked beside her toward the house, wishing he had better news. "Let's walk out again tonight, Hannah, will you?"

"Yes, I will. There's no moon, though." Her heart leaped in her chest. A flush heated her cheeks. She tried to hide her emotions, but he'd seen her confusion.

He laughed. "I'll just eat a bait of supper, and see you later on. I have more to tell you." He left her and headed for the still generous trestle table.

Hannah watched his familiar figure walk away. The feeling of rightness and familiarity swept over her. She felt more connected to Brice than she'd ever believed possible. Heavily tinged with caution and fear, a soft glow swept throughout her body and she trembled, unable to make sense of her feelings.

"Am I so numb from the dreadful beatings from Moore that I can no longer feel normal things?" She went to her room, flushed of face, and excited. Asking for a pan of water, Hannah freshened herself then fed Thomas and put him down to sleep for the night.

CHAPTER 14

As the deep dark of night encroached on the ranch, Hannah walked out to the end of the patio. It was dark enough that she had to feel her way. It was idyllic in the walled patio and the night air was cool with the sweet odor of cut hay drifting on the soft breeze. She waited for Brice.

"Hannah!" His soft voice came out of the gloom.

"I'm here, Brice." Her voice wavered with excitement.

He stepped up and took her arm. "Let's walk out in the orchard again Hannah." He swept her into his arms, crushing her against his chest. He bent and kissed her deeply. "God, it's good to see you."

She didn't struggle and that made him go farther. His hands moved over her body, making her heart race and pound in her ears. But in her fear of intimacy, she stiffened in his arms. She'd fight against him if he went further.

"Do you know how long I've waited for this?"

"Oh, Brice, I'm happy to see you too." She pulled away. "So much has happened here, and most of it tragic with Leatha's passing. Jesse's lost without her and, after the loss of his sons, this only adds to it. He's a broken man anymore. It's like he has lost all hope."

Brice pulled her close again. "Darlin' we talked about this before. You do the best you can. What else is there? You take happiness where you find it, before it slips away. Have you given thought to what we talked about last time?"

"Of course, I have. It's all I think about. I feel safe with you, even with all that's hanging over me. It wouldn't be right for us until I know I'm clear of this thing." Nestling closer in his warm, safe arms, she buried her face in his chest. "Brice, right now, this feels so good, so right, I can forget everything." Then she remembered. "You said you had more to tell me. What is it? You know I worry they'll take me away."

"I've heard things. About three-four weeks ago, the sheriff came to the camp. I wasn't there, and the crew didn't know where I'd gone. Said he wanted to ask you a few questions. Campy told him I'd taken you to Seligman and put you on a train to the East. Where he came up with that, they haven't said." He chuckled. "Reckon they know more about this than they tell me. Thought a lot of you, I know that."

"What else?"

"Hank Watkins was blatherin' about the woman he saw out on the trail, and told the sheriff about it, described you to a tee, too. After askin' around town, the sheriff asked the parson and his wife. They remembered marryin' the two of you back then. 'Another mail order bride,' she said." Brice laughed softly. "It's a stroke of luck he thinks you're headed back East. The men said he seemed right glad to hear of it, maybe pleased to be shut of the whole thing."

"Still hanging over me—if Hank ever finds out I'm on this ranch—God help me, Brice! All because I wouldn't take notice of him." Tears flooded her eyes. "Eventually, someone will tell the sheriff about the woman out at the Bidwell Ranch."

She sank down on a handy bench, and Brice sat beside her. His arms around her were all she had to cling to, as thoughts of her own helplessness filled her with anger and desolation.

"Try not to worry so, dearest Hannah. It might be a better thing if it all comes out. Then you can get shut of it and we can go on with our lives. For now, he appears to be satisfied you've gone back East."

His words comforted her and she clung to him for security. With the onus of what hung over her, passion was lacking, but she knew she'd have him for a husband down the road when things cleared up. "Maybe you're right about having it all come out." Hannah sighed with frustration and a creeping sense of doom she couldn't dispel, even in the comforting warmth of Brice's arms.

"Tell me, have you ever heard of a woman killing her husband, even in fear of her life, and not going to jail or worse yet, the gallows?" She felt compelled to ask. "And there was the life of my son, as well,"

"No, but I've never heard of a case like this. Maybe some have. I'll discuss it with Bidwell. He might know." Brice pulled her closer into his arms. "We'll worry about it in the morning. Right now I need to hold you. You've got a hold on my heart, Hannah, my girl. What am I going to do about you?"

He kissed her deeply. Kissing came naturally to him. He was good at it, she was sure of that, and responded until it frightened her.

"Brice, I love you. I know you're a good man, I've seen it time and again. I wish with all my heart this was all over and we could go on with our lives." She pressed into him. "Where will we go? Where would we live? If we did go now, I'd be free of all this."

"I couldn't up and take leave now, Hannah. I've heavy obligations with my work and all." He nuzzled into her ear, making her giggle and squirm. "It'll come right for us, dearest, I know it."

༄༅༄

Tears in her eyes, holding Thomas in her arms, Hannah bid Brice goodbye once again. He and Bidwell had spent a long time together in the ranch office and, though she wondered about that, it was no business of hers.

"Hannah, dearest, I'll keep my eyes open and ears out for news. But please remember, I'll stand for you, no matter what takes place, you know that." He took one more kiss while Thomas tugged at his hat with his baby fingers. Chuckling, he said, "He's a mighty fine boy, Hannah. I'll be proud to be his daddy."

He mounted and turned Romer out the wide, swinging gate. He managed a few backward glances with raised eyebrows and a wide grin gleaming white against his tanned features. His antics brought giggles to Hannah's lips along with desolation so deep she could scarcely believe it as she watched him ride away.

☙❧☙

Hannah and Brice planned marriage one day. Jesse knew of their intimate walks in the garden. She'd never dishonor Jesse's house in any way, and hoped he realized it. Intimacy would wait for the wedding day and the mere thoughts of it made her shiver. *I wonder if I can be a proper wife..*

Their love for each other had deepened past the point of passion for Brice, but Hannah, fearful of intimacy, knew a desperate happiness clouded with doubt. *Would she face the end of her life, never knowing the love of a good man?* That thought crossed her mind all too often.

At loose ends with Leatha gone, Hannah, never a slothful person, looked for purposeful things to occupy her time. Jesse doted on Thomas, talked to him, or chucked him under the chin. He shrieked with joy as the old rancher carried him around on huge shoulders.

She believed the boy brought back happy days spent with his own sons. The state of his declining health had become a worrisome factor and dampened her joy in life on this peaceful ranch. Hannah loved Jesse as a father, as much as the loving man who'd raised her back in Iowa.

"Would you like to ride out with me, today?" Jesse asked. "We'll be checking the herd just south of here. There's been coyote activity on some of the calves. A few were pretty cut up—the ones that lived." He held a braided leather bridle in his rough, scarred hands. "The boys drove the varmints off—too late for some. We're lookin' them over for the cripples and we'll kill the ones that are too bad off. An injured calf won't make it out in the open. The coyotes keep sniffin' around. Always lookin' for a chance. If we have to butcher some, we can always use the meat. But of course, that's not my first choice. Too bad, but that's the way of ranchin'." The old man shook his head at one more loss.

"Why, yes, Jesse, I'd love to ride out with you. I'll ask Lupita about caring for Thomas. She probably has him in tow, anyway." Hannah left him to made hasty arrangements. Earlier, Jesse had offered her the use of his late wife's clothes, her dresses, outdoor things, and any other item she could make use of. She'd readily accepted them saying, "These will do fine, and I thank you for the use of them. Leatha wasn't very big either, about like me."

She worried the sight of her dressed in Leatha's clothes would trouble the lonely old rancher, but she needed them and he'd offered. The outmoded clothing fit her well and, dressed in Leatha's fetching riding clothes, Hannah stepped out for his appraisal.

His eyes filling, he grinned with approval. "Dear girl, they fit you just fine. Leatha used to ride with me and wore those same togs."

Tears glistened in his fading blue eyes and made her imagine he saw his young wife, her long, pale, golden hair, streaming in the wind, her cheeks red with excitement, while she rode at his side.

Moved by his sorrow, Hannah offered no condolences. Riding out was good medicine for the craggy old rancher and her own flagging spirits, too. "Which way is south, Jesse?"

He brightened with the activity and, indicating the direction, nudged his mount into a trot. He rode well, considering his increasing pain. Seeing him now, remembering Leatha's words, Hannah wanted to doubt his ill health.

His idea of "just south of here" differed from Hannah's. After many hot, sweaty hours under a broiling sun, they heard the bawling and saw the dust of milling cattle.

"There they are, Jesse!"

She'd never seen any of Moore's herds and this was new to her. The cowboys sorted the herd, looking for strays and injured animals, working through thick clouds of dust swirling up from a multitude of sharp hooves.

"We'll pull up under this tree right here and give the horses a blow. How're you doing? I'd have to say you ride pretty blamed good for a dude girl. Where'd you learn to ride like that?"

"We had horses where I grew up. They were the big draft sort, but we rode them once in a while. My home was in farming country. I had eight grades at school and two more years at the Normal School in Ames. I think they intended me to become a teacher, but I had other ideas."

Hannah laughed at her idealistic youth. She'd been so young then. "My father was completely against my coming West. I don't think he'll ever forgive me, and mother didn't say. I had a brother, but he was away. I never knew his thoughts," she added. "As far as riding goes, the neighbor kids had ponies too, and we rode those, mostly bareback. In fact, I'm still getting used to a saddle."

It was long ago to her now. Another life lived by someone else. Hannah felt she'd lived at least three lives so far, and wondered if she would even have another life if they arrested her. Maybe she didn't deserve to live. She thought that at times, until she remembered her baby.

She dismounted, removed the wide-brimmed hat, and enjoyed the cool breeze streaming softly through her hair. Her legs, stiff from the unaccustomed time in the saddle, had several worn, raw spots burned on them. "The shade of this tree feels good. I'll just sit here awhile." She took a long pull from the canteen strapped to her saddle. "That tasted wonderful!" It tasted of tin and was warm, but she drank her fill and wiped her lips with her neck piece.

"I know you aren't used to riding so long, but I have to say, you did me proud, girl. I'll come back when it's time for chuck. I'll have the wagon pulled up right here unless he's already got a fire going. If so, we'll eat down yonder when it's ready." He stood looking downward. "See the wagon sitting out near the stream? I'll just wave my hat and you ride on down and eat with the hands. I have to warn you, girl, a young, single, female is mighty rare around here; they'll be showin' a lot of interest."

He chuckled as he rode away. He'd come alive and forgotten his sorrows for a time. The old man cut a fine solid figure, sitting straight on his horse.

Hannah sat for a long time, thinking of Brice. She no
longer feared him, but for the sexual act—she shuddered, remembering the beastly things Moore had done to her. She did
her best to shut out those thoughts, to put them far from her
mind. Brice had always been gentle with her. His solid male
body and the warm strength of his arms held her in its own sort
of spell. It felt like coming home when he held her.

Brice loved her child, had already been a father to him. If
he turned out wrong, she'd wish for death. She squared her
shoulders, determined. *I'm no longer the same young girl who
trusted too much.*

Gazing down, she watched the cowboys move the calves
into groups. An occasional pistol shot ring out. Skinned carcasses hung from nearby trees, their pink flesh looked naked.
Hannah's attention drifted away from the rough and dirty scene of working cattle to see the rugged beauty of the place
while resting in the breezy shade. This ranch was beautiful.
She felt sorrow for Jesse's losses. What had his life come to?

The West fascinated her. Lost miles of wasteland faded
into purple hazes, and massive high craggy rock formations of
red sandstone or pale sand-colored stone monuments. Lofty
soft feathery trees grew in the high places and, at this level,
there were rolling hills thick with grass and brush. Her heart
sang for the wild splendor of the place. "No wonder Brice
loves it here."

A white hat waving back and forth caught her attention
and roused her from her pleasant daydreams. Hannah mounted
her horse and rode down to Jesse and his men. Meeting more
cowboys could easily be an unpleasant ordeal, but she steeled
herself. Any new person could be the one that guessed her
identity. She never stopped searching their eyes for signs of
curiosity, or undue interest. If she was recognized or tied to
Moore's death, her secure haven would disappear. Head held
high, she reached the dusty, milling scene.

Everything stopped. The cowboys reined in their mounts,

watched her ride in, and took in every move as she dismounted, throwing the reins onto the ground. The dread in her heart
lay hidden behind her smile and, halting before the cowboys,
she stood firm.

"Hannah, dear, these are the cowboys from this side of
the ranch. Some others are back in the higher mountains, got
wolves and coyotes both up there." He led her toward the suddenly quiet men who waited to meet her. They stood ready,
faces wind-burned to shades of dark bronze, features generally
clean cut, and eyes sharp and squinty from the relentless sun.
They wore clothes worn and soiled from their work.

"Boys, meet Hannah, my niece from the East. She came
to help me with my late wife, an' I'm hopin' she'll stay on
with us for a while." He laughed. "Now don't go scarin' her
off, you wild bunch of yahoos."

Hannah laughed as she met them one by one and shook
their hands. Some held on unnecessarily long, until she went
on to the next. "I'm pleased to know you," she said several
times over.

They seemed a friendly lot. Boyish in their manner,
though tough and hardened from the life they led.

She met Slim Pardee, Harry Elkins, Dink Hand, Len
Green, Tug Parker, and a few others. It would take time to
place names with each face and she realized she'd met some of
them at Leatha's funeral. That they were fascinated with her
was inescapable. She wondered at their names, believing some
of them couldn't possibly be real. How lonely their lives must
be living way out from cities or even small villages, to find a
woman, any woman, so interesting!

The gleaming pig-eyes of the heavy set cowboy, Tug Parker, set her to trembling inwardly. Though he said nothing, she
felt he was overly taken by her petite femininity. She could
almost see his mind taking in her soft body. He gave her an
uncertain, queasy feeling and gazed more than any man should
at her breasts. He exuded overt interest. Silent and brooding,
he finally turned away from the gathering and moved toward
the chuck wagon.

The cook rang a small triangular bell to call them to eat.

He had a nice bench set up for Hannah under a shady tree and handed her a plate of beans, beef, and biscuits. "These are so fluffy. You did a fine job with them." She indicated the high crusty bread and bit into one sopped with sauce from the beans. "Tastes good, too, Jack."

The cook, a wizened older man, whose rider days had ended from a horse-related incident, was called Jack. She heard rabbit mentioned in passing, accompanied with friendly ribbing. A good natured sort, he limped about keeping the cowboy's plates full and pouring strong black coffee.

They became quiet. Only sounds of clinking tin plates, forks, knives, and the occasional low murmur of deep voices broke the silence. Hannah knew her every move was furtively watched, but she stopped worrying over it, understanding they were hungry for the sight of womankind, be she plain or pretty.

Jesse sat with her, shoveling in his chuck. His presence gave her a measure of comfort. "Why do they wear those big leather things on their legs?" She hadn't seen chaps worn before. Moore never put them on that she knew about, though she'd seen them hanging on one of the walls.

"Those are chaps and the boys wear them to keep from getting their britches all tore up. Some of the brush out here has nasty thorns, and then there're the cattle, horns, hooves, not to mention ridin' all day in the saddle. They help with that and keep their legs warm in winter, too."

Hannah remembered the cat claw bushes that shredded her dress the night she'd fled from Moore. "I see how good they are but never gave it much thought." She looked up at Jesse. "Thanks for telling me. I guess I've a lot to learn about this way of life."

From then on, she tried to take in everything, but her breasts were full and beginning to tingle and throb. She looked at Jesse, and flushed pink. "I think we should start back, I need to feed little Thomas. I didn't realize how long we'd be away."

His face flushed. "Shore, honey, an' if I didn't go and forget all about that. Leatha used to take care of our boys that way and got uncomfortable sometimes. We'll get a move on."

He rode over to have a word with his foreman, Harry, for a few minutes before they turned to leave. "We'd best take it easy goin' back. Will you make out all right?"

If he felt remorse over his lack of consideration, Hannah forestalled any thought of it. "I'll be fine. I've had a wonderful day, Jesse, and fully enjoyed riding, even meeting the cowboys, and seeing some of your cattle. With Thomas taking other food now, it isn't so much to worry about." Surprised at being able to speak so freely about a feminine situation, she felt ever closer to the graying rancher. She could never have said these things to her father.

CHAPTER 15

The ride back, with full aching breasts, seemed endless, but at last they entered the ranch yard. Tired, happy, and bursting with her need for Thomas, Hannah hastened into the ranch house to find her baby. Lupita ran to meet her with the fretting baby in her arms. "Oh, *Tomas* need you, Senora, he *tiene mucho hambre!*" Lupita laughed and so did Hannah.

"And I thought my milk had eased off!"

Thanking the girl, she took Thomas to her room to care for his needs. After washing herself, Hannah put on fresh clothes and went to dinner, carrying Thomas in her arms.

At dinner, the weariness and defeat in Jesse's face told her the ride hadn't been easy for him. Hiding her concern, she thanked him again. "It was a wonderful day, Jesse. I believe this ranch is one of the most beautiful places on earth. Thank you for taking me."

"Just thought you'd like a look-see at the place, we always thought we had a kind of Eden in this ranch." He cleared his throat, before going on. "There'll be a dance later this month at Seligman, would you want to go?"

"Well...I don't know." Hesitant at being seen in public, she asked, "Would that be a good idea? Will you be going?" She saw Jesse Bidwell as a protector, and wouldn't consider it otherwise.

"Of course, I'll be goin' and everyone else that can get away. You'll be all right. It's far enough from Flagstaff." He smiled at her. "You're a young woman and need to get out a bit, not hidin' away here with the help."

"I'll think about it. Who'll go from here?"

"As many of the boys as can get away, and Lupita. She might like to get away from her old man. He's a mean devil, treats his family like dogs." He nodded, smiling. "You think on it, my dear," Jesse added. "People from all around will be there, camping out for three-four days."

The impending dance, a fourth of July celebration, excited Hannah. Thoughts of it thrilled her. Dancing, twirling about a slick dance floor with other young people had been forgotten. She wished with all her heart Brice would be there to hold her in his arms. Thoughts of it made her long for him all the more. "Brice, where are you now? How far away?"

Her wishes, uttered aloud, made her blush, hoping Jesse hadn't heard. But he only said, "Come along, Hannah. Lupita will be with us, and you'll have to bring Thomas. Do you both some good, how about it?"

"I will. It's been a lifetime since I've danced. Wonder if I'll remember how." Hannah laughed, remembering dances in the past, strutting along with the music. Lost in memories, she forgot everything until Jesse spoke again.

"It won't matter to the men there. You'll be lucky to sit down. A nice little lady like you won't go unnoticed. You can bet the ranch on it." His lined face wreathed in a wide smile, he patted her shoulder.

⁓⁓⁓

They set off in a large wagon, heading north-westerly toward Seligman. Bedding, food supplies, finery for herself and Lupita were packed. With the sun barely above the horizon spreading the glorious colors of dawn across the vast broken escarpment of mountains and grasslands, the sight of it caught at the heart. Looking at the wild beauty of the Circle B Ranch, Hannah cried, "Oh, Jesse, this is the most beautiful place on earth!" She'd said it many times.

He smiled his agreement, nodding his head. "Yes, Hannah, it sure is. In all the years we've lived here, it never changes, a little cold during the winter months, a little hot in summer, but all in all, right nice country."

Along the trail, a number of cowboys, dressed in the little finery they had, kept pace with them, hooting and yelling, unlike their usual laconic selves, instead exchanging insulting barbs to one another in good natured tones. Clearly in a celebratory mood, the boys were getting a head start on the occasion.

Hannah tried to remember if she'd met this bunch. One or two rode close to their wagon just to get a look at the young women. She thought some of them looked familiar and wondered if she'd met them momentarily. "How many men work for you, Jesse?" she asked.

"Don't rightly know, just now. They tend to come and go."

One of them she'd met out on the round-up with Jesse kept pace with their wagon. The heavy-set cowboy Tug, watched her more than the others. He'd decked himself out in a bright red shirt and because he observed her too often, his presence made her feel uneasy.

Hannah shook off unpleasant thoughts, preparing to attend a real community event for the first time. She planned to enjoy herself. There'd been no great gatherings other than Leatha's funeral, and those people were about as good and solid as any she'd known in Iowa. She felt comfortable with them.

They stopped to rest and eat along the way. She fed her son and Lupita had already changed him. She shook out her hair in the flowing breeze. "It's good to sit here in the shade a while," Hannah exclaimed to the Mexican girl.

"*Si Senora, es bueno aqui,*" she replied.

The soft wind ruffled their clothes while they downed burritos stuffed with chicken, cold *frijolies,* and fruit pies made by the two Mexican cooks. They washed it down with icy water and mugs of strong black coffee made over a hastily built campfire.

The cowboys fed themselves close by, but refrained from

close company. Hannah guessed they waited for the dance to invent chances to get close to the young women. She hadn't spoken to any of them in close conversation, which suited her just fine. She didn't want another run-in like the one with Hank Watkins. Thoughts of that always gave her the shivers.

She was tired of sitting and jostling on the hard boards of the wagon seat for more long hours, but relief came in sight when Jesse pointed out the small collection of windswept, gray, weathered buildings ahead. The raw little town of Seligman was set in open country studded with stunted greenery, and rocky buttes. It looked miniscule and lost in the vastness of the country around it.

Occasional dust devils swirled in high columns of rusty-tan-colored funnels. A wind-swept settlement at best, it lay before them, spread out haphazardly alongside the gleaming rails of train tracks. A rough wagon track accompanied the railroad line, heading westward.

"Well, ladies, there she is, pretty new for a town, came with the railroad, only a few more miles to go until we're there." Jesse boomed the words, waking them from the fatigue of their long drive.

"Thank God!" Hannah muttered, wondering if her legs still worked. Looking into the back of the wagon, she saw Thomas asleep on a pile of bedding and Lupita next to him, just awakening.

The girl's eyes seemed unusually bright and shinning. *Must be the dance,* Hannah decided.

"*Senora, eet weel be fiesta* soon!"

The dreamy glow across her face made Hannah wonder. Did the girl know someone here or have a special beau and was anxious to see him? Hannah wanted Lupita to have ample opportunity to attend the dance. Perhaps there would be someone among the rancher's wives she could ask to watch Thomas. She'd met several friendly women at Leatha's funeral gathering, weathered and strong ranch wives.

Certainly, most of them would attend this celebration with life so lonely and the people living out so far. A celebration like this provided the opportunity to renew friendships, catch up on news and gossip, and enjoy a bright spot away from the rigors of their daily lives.

Pulling in to the camping area, they found a clear space and set up the tent. Jesse tamped in the tent pegs after removing offending rocks from beneath the tent. They settled in with their supplies. He left, saying, "I'll be back soon, ladies, got business to attend to." He took his team and rig.

They laid down on pallets to rest from their arduous journey. Hannah took Thomas onto her chest, played with him, fed him, and held him close to rest. Maybe it was a fool's paradise, but she felt happy, a feeling that had eluded her for so long. She couldn't stop the smile spreading across her lips as the excitement of the celebration captured her completely.

"Lupita, you awake?" Her words meant little to the girl, but the friendly tones were clear enough.

"*Si, Senora*, I wait for *la fiesta*."

"*Esta amigo aqui?*" Hannah essayed her limited Spanish and heard a giggle from the dark-eyed girl. "Ah ha, Lupita, *amor, no?*"

"*Si, senora, no es hombre Espaniol*, he Frenchman, I teenk." The woebegone look betrayed her secret.

"What is wrong with that, Lupita?"

"*Mi madre y padre* say *es muy mal, es necessito mi esposo Espaniol*."

"I see." Prejudice came in many forms. Not knowing what to say, Hannah offered, "Maybe one of the women here would watch Thomas and we can both go to the dance."

"Oh, senora, I wish *que mucho* go!" Lupita flushed pink. "To see heem would be *muy bueno*." Her little hands fluttered to her throat and Hannah knew Lupita was more involved with a man in Seligman than she thought.

Later as the sun sank below the horizon, the two young women left for the dance wearing the best they had. Hannah wore a frilly blue dress of Leatha's, nicely nipped in at the waist with a flowing skirt, laced with ribbons and scalloping around the bottom. Lupita wore a low necked, gathered blouse, a colorful skirt, with a bright paper flower fixed in her long black hair.

Hannah left Thomas in the care of a weathered rancher's wife, Bessie Morris, who had several young'uns of her own running about with companions among the assembled ranch folk. She had said. "Now don't go a worryin' over this child. I've had a passel of 'em and he won't be no problem fer me."

Hannah remembered her from Leatha's funeral. Bessie, a good natured woman, had helped her husband start his ranch some years ago. Her work worn hands looked capable when she took Thomas and cradled him against her ample breasts. He would be safe with this woman.

They entered the hall to the strains of rustic dance music. Hannah saw two men with fiddles, one with a guitar, and another thumped a piano hard enough to make the deep beat of a waltz pulsate through the wooden walls. It filled the air and added to the festive feeling. The hall appeared crowded with folks of all ages, dressed in the best they had. Inside, the long rectangle building looked to be a school room. There were no desks but some of the items she noticed hanging on the walls—maps, childish drawings, a few scattered, worn books and low-level coat hooks—gave away the purpose.

Jesse, lounging against the far wall, spotted them and came over. "Sorry, ladies. I got to jawin' here, and forgot to escort the two best lookin' women in the place. Well now, aren't you both a sight!" he exclaimed as he came close. "So where'd you leave off your young'un, Hannah?"

"Bessie Morris. She didn't care much for the goin's on and would keep Thomas." Lupita was to care for the baby, but Hannah quickly added, "Jesse, Lupita is young and needs a bit of social life, don't you think? Besides, I think she has a beau here and wants to attend this dance."

"Shore, I reckon so. Bessie's a right good woman." He laughed before he left them to rejoin some of older men. "Now, you ladies have a good time dancin'."

Hannah wondered if he thought of his Leatha, seeing Hannah wearing the good lady's ruffled frock. It must have brought back nostalgic thoughts of his late wife. She saw an escaping tear course down his cheek when he left them to rejoin his old ranching friends. Her heart ached for the man in his loneliness. Before she had time to look around or even find a seat, a young man sauntered up to her. "Howdy, ma'am, care to have this here dance?" a lanky, blond-headed cowboy in a green checkered shirt asked.

He looked familiar, but she wasn't sure of his name. "Certainly." She rose to join the slender-built man.

His arm snaked around her and felt like corded steel as they began a waltz. His first steps were strained and awkward, but the natural grace of the rider quickly came to his rescue. To Hannah, he seemed skillful and she enjoyed the feel of swirling across the floor. A warm night, all the windows and doors were open wide and a cooling breeze swept through the swirling dancers.

"Name's Harry, Miss Hannah, I work for Bidwell, foreman on the southern section. Met you out on the range the other day an' sure was hopin' you'd consider dancin' with me. I'll be havin' the laugh on the rest of the bunch, bein' first."

He flushed as he related this information. Sweat had formed on his brow with the effort of dancing, an unusual activity for this cowboy.

"I remember you. I live at the ranch for now, but you boys know that." She smiled up at him as they whirled about. Out of the corner of her eye, she saw Lupita in the arms of a slim, dark-eyed man. He sported a thin mustache and dressed too well to be a cowhand. Was this the man Lupita had told her about? The girl was deep in earnest conversation with him, looking deeply into his eyes, and Hannah knew that Lupita saw no other man at this dance. Her rapt attention to the dark-eyed stranger was fully returned. His lips moved as he held her close. The girl's eyes shone, her lips moved, and her cheeks flushed with joy in response.

Across the floor, Hettie Bell swirled in her husband Ezra's strong arms. Looking at the tall slender rancher Hettie had married, Hannah's heart ached, knowing how different it might have been for her. But she'd met and married the wrong man.

The music stopped and Harry returned her to a seat along the edge of the floor. "Thanks, ma'am. Maybe we could dance again later?" He flashed a friendly smile with his question.

"Yes, I will, Harry." She no sooner said farewell to him and sat down when the fiddlers started a reel.

Tug Parker stepped up in his bright red, sweat-stained shirt. "Howdy, ma'am, care to have a dance?" His face, moist and ruddy, the smell of spirits heavily on his breath, made Hannah involuntarily draw away. Taking in his bulk and small, red-rimmed eyes, she decided he was not the best looking of the men. Not wanting to cause hard feelings, she nodded. "Yes, I'd like to dance." She rose to move out with the portly cowboy.

"Name's Tug, seen you around the ranch a lot, mighty nice little boy you got there, too." He pulled her close against his sweaty body when they moved out onto the cornmeal pol-ished floor. Jesse had mentioned how the folks around the area used it for slickness as the dancing feet ground it into a fine, slippery powder.

The alcoholic fumes of his breath and his sweaty clothes made her feel nauseous. She pulled away. "Please, I don't care to dance so close, if you don't mind."

"Girl, you feel real good in my arms. A man could easy get used to a nice little woman like you." He pulled her even closer against his protruding belly and soggy shirt.

With disgust, she felt the moisture. Rising alarm in the situation made her push away. "Please, don't hold me like this. I don't care for it and don't call me girl. I have a name."

Having said that, she immediately knew she didn't want this man to know that much about her and prayed the dance would end. She thought she might faint in her disgust of him.

"Aw loosen up, deary, I don't bite, name's Hannah, I hear tell." He ignored her request and, pulling her close again, weaved widely as they turned until she feared they would fall.

"Please take me back to my seat, if you would, please!"

"Problem here?" It was Jesse. His deep familiar voice made Hannah want to cry with relief at his solid presence. She felt Tug loosen his hold. The breeze cooled her damp clothing. "Mind if I cut in, Tug?" His firmness made Tug back off.

"Naw, no problem, sir, just havin' a little dance with this purty young woman here." Tug's sheepish face and bloated presence told Jesse all he needed to know. Anger flushed red up his neck and into his craggy face.

"Okay with me, sir. Here she is." Tug handed Hannah over with a scowl across his reddened face. He stood glaring while Jesse steered Hannah away.

"Oh thank you, Jesse, he was getting too close, and he's been drinking. I was frightened of him. Maybe I shouldn't have been, but I couldn't help it. There's something very ugly about that man." Thoughts of a kind and gentle Brice rose in her mind. Though definitely masculine, he'd never threatened her. How different men were. *Oh why can't Brice be here?*

"Well, we won't have any more of that, Hannah, don't you worry about Tug. He's a good cowboy, but maybe not so good at socializin'."

He whirled her across the dance floor, and Hannah realized he was a wonderful dancer. "You're a fine dancer, Jesse. I was thinking how much Leatha must have enjoyed these dances. Did you go very often?" She smiled up at him.

"Shore did, honey, we went to *all* of 'em."

Hannah realized, though he'd hoisted a few drinks himself, he was a pleasure on the dance floor. Safe and comfortable in Jesse's solid embrace, she thought of her father, though she'd never danced with him.

Later, while Hannah was having a moment's rest, Lupita joined her, her face aglow with excitement. "Oh, senora, he es so wonderful, he want to kees me." She indicated the slim, dark-eyed man approaching. Lupita did her best to introduce him to Hannah as she clasped the man's arm.

"*Enchante, madame,* nice to meet you." He introduced himself with a slight bow. "I am Pierre Solnier, come from France to see your wonderful western lands. Lupita's Spanish, close to my language, we converse quite well together." He raised his eyebrows and smiled down at Lupita.

"Nice to meet you, Mr. Solnier, I hope you'll enjoy this part of America. It's quite new to me as well, but I love it all the same." Hannah worried over Lupita mixing with a foreigner. Yet he seemed a gentleman. He certainly dressed well, but she knew from hard experience how deceiving looks could be.

Several more cowboys danced with her, their names whirled in her mind. She wanted Brice and he was not here. Her constant desire to be near him with murder hanging over her was unrealistic, yet she wished for him all the more. "Someday," she whispered.

Lupita danced only with Solnier, refusing other offers. Hannah, watching her, wondered if she was in over her head with the man. He looked like a good man, and he certainly cut a dashing figure in his finely cut clothes.

It was late when they sought their beds. Hannah had visited Thomas, fed him, and changed him earlier. She took him from the rancher's wife, placed him close beside her, and fell asleep with thoughts of Brice's dark blue eyes looking into hers under the trees in the moonlit orchard.

CHAPTER 16

The stay in Seligman lasted several days. The next evening, cowboys and ranchers attended a barbeque held for visiting ranch folk. Hannah met people she knew from Leatha's funeral and took the renewed opportunity to further acquaint herself with her neighbors.

Tug Parker furtively kept an eye out for her and his overtly leering eye contact sent icy chills racing down her spine. "That man makes me feel uneasy." she murmured, fearing she'd made another enemy like Watkins. Not wanting a repeat of an unwelcome incident, she decided to try a friendly approach.

Walking over to him, she said, "Good evening, Tug. How are you?" With those few words, a heated gleam rose in his small, pig-like eyes. Seeing it, she shrank away, regretting her attempt at civility.

"Why, Miss Hannah, I'm just fine. Sorry I had too much hooch last night. It got away from me. I can see that a fine lady like you wouldn't like drinkin' much. Don't care for it much myself. A reg'lar teetotaler, that's me."

The stale odor of alcohol and tobacco smoke reeked on his breath, but Hannah was determined not to let it bother her and treaded a fine line between friendliness and interest. "I thought it was a very nice dance, didn't you?"

"It sure was, but it could'a been a hell of a lot better if you know what I mean, girl." He waggled his eyebrows in a suggestive way.

Sickened by the nasty innuendo, she knew her friendly approach was wasted on a man with his animal-like tendencies. She turned to leave. "I'm sorry, I must see to my son."

Tug grasped her arm, his filthy nails biting into her tender flesh. "Wait a minute, my girl, you can't go a flirtin' wi' me that-a-way and just walk off. You've had a baby an' you're feedin' 'im too. You know what I'm talkin' about."

His leering gesture and meaning were unmistakable. She fought the rising gorge in her throat giving her the urge to vomit.

"Leave go of me. I'll scream if you don't. You're insulting me. Mr. Bidwell won't take kindly to that. I don't want to cause trouble, but you'd best leave me alone!"

She feared Tug saw her trembling in disgust and fear as a sign of weakness. But she finally understood—gentleness was the very behavior that fueled aggressive behavior in certain men, and unfortunately, she'd attracted her full share of them.

Realization changed her. Determined never to allow such behavior again in her life, she firmed her jaw and ignored Tug. He released her, cussing under his breath. "Go on, then. Git outta here, you bitch!"

She made her way, stumbling over rocks and tent ropes, to the safety of their tent. The sickening confrontation with Tug's foul and lecherous comments, angered and nauseated her. She sought privacy to massage away the bruised areas where he'd dug into her arm with his filthy nails.

Lupita wasn't there. She'd been gone for quite some time. Had she met Pierre somewhere alone? How safe was she with that handsomely dressed man? Upset at her conflict with Tug, Hannah couldn't worry over it. She lay down on her pallet, shaking in anger. Thomas was with Bessie again. "Oh, God, what will happen next?"

༄

ᎾᏩᎾ

After buying such supplies as Seligman afforded, Jesse hitched the horses to a wagon piled high with needed goods and seemed in fine spirits as they headed back to the ranch.

Hannah sat in silence, worrying about her run-in with Tug. Lupita was in such a dreamy state she barely interacted with anyone. That had Hannah worried. *What has the little Mexican girl gotten into with that very handsome stranger?*

Her thoughts held her attention to the point she had difficulty remembering the enjoyable events at the gathering. Most dance partners had been gentlemanly and fun, but her ugly encounters with Tug had dampened everything. She wanted to ask Lupita about the Frenchman, but not in the company of Jesse. He didn't need added problems.

Unable to shake the feeling of being hunted by Tug, Hannah wondered about herself. *Something about me attracts men like Tug, yet other women are soft and gentle and have no trouble. Brice and Jesse are the best men I've ever known.* Hannah sighed. *I need to be tougher.* Straightening her shoulders, she held her head higher.

Wishing for the sight of Brice and wondering how far away he'd gotten with his surveying work, she reflected about California. Jesse's failing health meant they couldn't leave this country immediately. That fact ended those thoughts—he was ill and she'd never leave him.

The journey proved long and the wagon jolted constantly over the rugged track. Neither young woman had much to say, each of them deep in their own thoughts. The passing scenery went unnoticed. Thomas, with his baby ways, broke the monotony for them both.

"*Oh mijo, es muy dulce*," Lupita giggled as she took him from Hannah, her dark eyes pensive and near to tears.

"Lupita, what has happened?" Hannah kept her voice low, excluding Jesse from this very private conversation.

Lupita whispered, "Senora, he make love with me, I no could stop heem. I afraid now—mi padre beat me, he know."

"Oh, my dear, does this man wish to marry you?"

"*Si*, he say so many time before thees, but mi padre say no." Tears flowed as she recounted her lover's soft words. "*Mi amore te amo mucho.* What I do, senora?"

"The Frenchman must speak to your father. He can make this right."

"He say he weel, but I so afraid." Fear of her father shone in her eyes. "Sometime he beat me, senora, I so afraid heem."

Another sadistic man who beats those smaller than himself. Maybe it's their culture. I don't know, but she fears her father more than she loves him, I see that readily enough. Hannah felt sorrow for the young girl. Life for the small and weak proved dangerous without a protector.

Again they lapsed into silence, each thinking their own thoughts. Hannah forgot her own worries, contemplating the fate of Lupita.

In early dusk, they pulled into the ranch yard. Jesse, stiff from driving all day, appeared gray and sweating. Hannah knew it was his failing health. Undoubtedly, in considerable pain, he had difficulty getting down from the wagon. His youth and vigor had gone, leaving a tired, pain-filled old man.

Manuel came for the team and wagon. Other men appeared to carry supplies into the house or barns. Hannah wondered if one of them was Lupita's father. Carrying Thomas on her hip, she entered the welcoming confines of the ranch house. He needed a bath and she wanted one too.

So like coming home. She inhaled the odors of cooking food and polished wood. The familiar dark interior of the sprawling ranch house gave her a sense of security. Thoughts of California frequented her mind, but she never wanted to leave this place. It had become much more than a haven.

Lupita knocked on her door. "Senora, I help you?"

"Thomas needs a bath," Hannah said. "Could you do that while I freshen up?" The girl was tired, but had something to say. "What is it, Lupita?" Hannah asked.

"I speak with you, weel come later, senora," the girl said and took Thomas out of the room.

Dinner was quiet. Jesse, looking refreshed and pain free, asked, "Well, little lady, did you enjoy getting out a bit?"

He wore a big grin across his weathered face. Hannah had the idle thought that Brice's face might look that way someday.

"Oh, yes, I sure did, and I think Lupita may have too." Toying with the idea of confiding in him regarding the fate of the Mexican girl, she asked, "May I see you after dinner, sir?"

"Why shore, honey, anytime, just come to my office." He wore a mildly puzzled look as he answered.

He'd brightened and regained his usual robust self. *Was it medication?* She knew it was.

They didn't see Lupita again, but heard the cooks chatting and giggling in the kitchen as they played with the babies.

Jesse welcomed her to his office. "What's on your mind, my dear. You look so serious. Is it Tug Parker that's got under your skin?"

"Well, no, he hasn't bothered me since the dance, but there is another matter I think you should know about." Hannah had decided not to mention how Tug had accosted her the next day in Seligman. She didn't want to antagonize him by getting him fired and make him more of an enemy than he was.

She related what she knew about Lupita and the Frenchman. "She is afraid her father will beat her if he finds out, and there is the possibility she could have gotten in the family way."

"I wondered about that after I saw them dancing, often and with no one else. He kept her all to himself. I'll try to find out if the man is on the level. He could be. She's a nice girl, if not too smart in the ways of men."

"I'm glad I told you, Jesse. I want to help her if I can, but I don't know what I can do."

"We'll see what happens. Maybe he'll show up here and have it out with Papa." He grinned. "That's what I'd do if I had eyes for a pretty young girl."

Relieved and glad for the action she'd taken, Hannah felt closer to Jesse than ever. "Thank you, sir, I feel better about this." She leaned over and kissed him lightly on his head, an act she'd never taken with her own father.

In her bedroom, Hannah found Lupita there with Thomas. The frightened look on the girl's face spoke volumes. Tears lay near the surface in her troubled eyes.

"What is it Lupita! Tell me." Hannah saw bruises on the girl's arm, her reddened face swollen from crying, but from heavy blows as well. "What happened to you? Who did this?"

"*Mi padre, senora,* he beat me. He say, he keel me, I see Frenchman again." She buried her head and sobbed into her skirt. "*Mi amor*, he say he come for me—*por Dios!*"

"If he comes to see your father, Lupita, let them have it out. You can go with your man as a married woman then, but it's better to have your father's blessing. *Su padre y su amore hablar, is bueno, no?*" Hannah did her best with her halting Spanish, but the girl seemed to catch her meaning.

"*Si*, es *possible, bueno*." She brightened a bit with those words and, taking a last look at Thomas, she moved slowly out of Hannah's room, her pretty face a picture of pain, fear, and indecision.

The beaten appearance of the little maid filled Hannah with anger. She could not interfere, but would inform Jesse in the morning. Taking a last look at the sleeping Thomas, she sought her bed. Sleep was slow in coming as she pondered the cruel things in life for some. It didn't help to know she was not the only woman to suffer brutality at the hands of a man.

The next morning in his office, she asked Jesse about Lupita's father. He nodded. "Pasqual is a mean bastard. Always been cruel to his children—wife, too. I've done my best to give them employment, him especially, if only to keep them out of his way. It's not my place to reprimand the man. He'd only move on and settle someplace else, but the cruelty wouldn't stop." He shook his craggy head. "I don't understand a man like that."

Hannah shuddered, remembering. "I don't either, Jesse, but I know first-hand how they are."

CHAPTER 17

Life drifted peacefully for several weeks. Thomas grew daily. He played most days with little Pedro and searched about for him if he was not there. The babies found new ways to move about. No blanket held them now, and the cooks were ever more careful.

Hannah blessed Lupita's help in caring for her child. The closeness between them grew into a loving bond, which was a comfort for Hannah. Lupita would be one more safety net for Thomas if she was arrested.

Three weeks later, while preparing for bed, Hannah heard a timid knock on her door. She opened it to find Lupita standing there, alarm in her eyes.

"*Senora, is muy necissito hablar!*" Her features were pale, and she'd been crying.

"Lupita, what's wrong?" Hannah led the girl into her room.

The distraught girl threw herself onto the bed, sobbing and twisting in agony. "*Senora, is possible, I encinta—bebe, senora!*" Lupita indicated her abdomen with trembling hands.

"Oh, Lupita, you sure?"

"I seek in morning each day, I dizzy, *mi madre* she say, *si encinta*. Senor Pierre, he no come!" Her distraught face was drawn, and whitened with fear. "*Mi padre, he keel me!*"

"We will speak with Senor Bidwell. He will know what to do."

Hurriedly, she threw on her clothes and, they went to him.

Hannah knocked on his office door, sorry to lay this new burden on his broad shoulders.

"Come on in." The gruff voice held a measure of comfort for Hannah as she ushered the tearful girl in.

"Jesse, we have a problem. Perhaps you can help Lupita?"

The girl renewed her sobbing.

He surveyed the weeping girl, trembling before him. "Come on, out with it. It can't be all that bad."

"Sir, Lupita is in the family way with that Frenchman in Seligman." Hannah laid it out for him, hoping he had an answer for the situation. "Her father wants to kill her. He'll beat her and she's afraid."

"Well, he won't be doing that. I'll take care of him, but what about the Frenchman? What are his intentions toward this girl? She's very young and the dirty bastard took advantage of her innocence." Jesse's ire rose up his neck, his face flushed ruddy, and he pounded his fist on the desk.

"Oh, no, senor, he say he love me, he kees me, he love me. He want marry me. He say he *hablar mi padre*."

"Then where the hell is the man? He ought to be here taking care of this mess he's gotten you into!" Settling a bit, he gave thought as to what must be done. "If he don't show real soon, I'll go get the bastard myself."

"Maybe he come soon. He say *dos meses* he come." Lupita brightened at the thought of her handsome lover riding up to face her father.

"We'll see then, we'll wait a while. Meanwhile, keep her here in the house. Her father won't come here with his threats. We've had a few run-ins before. He's a mean one."

"*Oh gracias, senor, gracias!*" Lupita kissed his work-roughened hand.

"*De nada, senorita.*" Jesse's voice comforted her as he turned to Hannah. "Take care of her, keep her with you. She's good with Thomas and busy as he is these days, she'll be kept mighty busy runnin' after the little tyke." He frowned. "We'll see if this man shows. She seems to believe he will, let's hope to hell he does. It'd be a better life for her away from here."

Putting her arm about the distraught girl, Hannah drew

her away from the office and into her own room.

Nothing was said until Lupita gushed, "Oh, senora, he weel come, he weel, I know thees."

She sank into a chair and stared blankly at the wall, her hands spread wide in hopelessness. She had no tears left, only the lingering hope her beloved would come for her, and soon.

∽∾∽

Weeks dragged on for the little senorita. Hannah watched hope fade from her eyes, until the girl finally believed she'd been a fool for the dashing Frenchman. Afraid to return to her father's house, she kept close to Hannah and Jesse, availing herself of their protection. After storming the ranch house in a towering rage, her father left, in fear of losing his work at the ranch.

Out by the corrals, looking at a mount Jesse had offered her, a gentle chestnut mare called Fancy, Hannah looked up to see dust roiling on the horizon. Shading her eyes, her heart raced at the thought of Brice riding in on his dust-covered roan, Romer.

As the figure neared the ranch, she saw it wasn't her dearest friend and love, but a stranger driving a team of beautifully matched blacks, their sweating bodies dressed in silver trimmed harness. They pulled an elegant black coach with gleaming silver appointments. Sorely disappointed, and not wanting to be seen, Hannah returned to the house. She'd never lost her edge of fear when strangers approached.

Jesse stepped out on his wide porch as the team and chaise pulled to a halt. "Howdy, stranger, step down and welcome to you."

Surprised, yet glad to recognize the errant Frenchman, he stepped off to make the man welcome.

Hannah, standing just inside the door, heard him mutter. "About time you showed up, you cowardly bastard." He did not voice those thoughts to the visitor, only smiled and held out the hand of friendship to a travel-weary man.

"*Monsieur* Bidwell, I bid you good day. I am Pierre

Solnier." He bowed slightly as he took the old rancher's hand. "I come seeking a young girl, Lupita. I am told she lives here. She has promised to be my wife."

Hannah saw his black eyes flash as he faced the rancher, all the while, searching about as if hoping to catch sight of his Lupita. His rig and horses were splendid, and the fine cut of his clothing, though travel-worn and dusty, spoke of a man of some means. Hannah found comfort in that for Lupita.

Jesse's smile broadened across his face. "Well, good to meet you, sir. Come on in. She's here, and if I don't miss my guess, she'll be mighty happy to see you." The men crossed the porch to enter the sprawling ranch home.

Hannah, sighing with relief, ran to find Lupita. Finding her in the kitchen minding Thomas as well as little Pedro, Hannah whispered. "Lupita, make yourself pretty, you have a visitor."

Lupita's face went white, as she tried to grasp Hannah's words. "*Quien? Senora, Señor Pierre—es heem*? Tears formed in her wide eyes as magical rays of hope brightened her face and took over her soul.

"*Si*, it is him, dear girl, now maybe he can speak to your papa and make things right," Hannah replied.

"*Mi papa keel heem!*"

"No, Lupita, he will not—not this fellow! Come now and greet this man you love." Hannah gave the girl a little shove and they went to Jesse's office. Lupita approached the heavy door with trembling hands and timidly knocked.

"Come on in." The rancher's voice was tinged with excitement.

They entered, and Lupita, seeing the dark clad man before her, nearly fainted. "Oh, *senor, es* you!" Her little hands fluttered in helpless wonder at the sight of her lover. Hearing relief in the girl's voice, Hannah knew it was a renewal of lost hope. Scarcely believing it was him, the girl asked him, "You come for me?" She could barely speak.

"*Oui, mademoiselle*, I come for you."

He started for her, but Jesse intervened. "Sorry, sir. I must know what you intend here." He studied the man before him.

"This girl has suffered too much already."

"She promise to marry me, sir. I would speak with her father *nous devons parler de masculin* as soon as I might." Pierre flashed a smile at the trembling girl.

Smiling joyously, she waited to throw herself into his arms.

"I'll send word and we'll get this out on the table." Jesse bellowed for Manuel and sent the boy tearing for the Mexican village.

Lupita ran into the Frenchman's arms and nestled there, her eyes shining with happiness, wild to see him, expressing relief, and beyond rapture that he'd come for her. Hannah noticed she didn't question his tardiness, only reveled in the fact that he'd come.

Dinner was called and they gathered at the table. Guadalupe and Conchetta served a fine meal of grilled beef, corn chowder, greens, tamales, breads, fruit dishes from the orchards, and later, custard of *flan,* served with strong black coffee. Hannah observed the Frenchman's polished table manners and the way he handled his cutlery, using both hands.

Lupita sat at the table tonight as a family member, rather than her usual position of helping about the house and caring for Thomas. When they heard the loud pounding of footsteps on the wide front porch, her eyes widened in fear at the forthcoming confrontation with her father. Hannah smiled to see Lupita shrink close to her Frenchman for protection.

Pierre put a steady hand on her shoulder. "*Non, mademoiselle*, have no fear, my sweet."

Rising from the dinner table, they met the flushed and angry father. Jesse allowed no noisy outbursts from the father and took him, Pierre, and Lupita, down the hall to his office. Hannah, relieved to miss the ugliness, should there be any, gladly stayed behind. Lupita, had her man to speak for her now.

Sounds of angry voices, tearful sobbing, and Jesse's commanding tones escaped through the door. An hour later, they emerged smiling, shaking hands, and uttering a laugh or two. Hannah waited for Lupita in her room.

The girl came, seeking her friend. "*Senora*, we weel have wedding. Pierre, he speak my father, he brave man." She blushed with happiness. "Now I go with heem, I love heem too much, *senora*." Lupita, flustered with all she had to do, left the room in haste and Hannah, happy for her, wondered if this day would ever come for her and Brice.

Within a few days, an impromptu wedding was held. A visiting padre performed the service, and Lupita became a bride. Her darkly handsome groom, sided by Jesse himself, beamed with pride. Lupita stood resplendent in the white wedding dress of her mother's with flowers in her hair. Hannah, Maria, a sister of the bride, and two others stood with her. Her father, holding in his fury, gave her away. Whether by choice or not, he complied. The affair proved quite elaborate under the circumstances.

The fiesta began soon after with music and wild dancing, continuing long into the night. Lupita had the first dance with her husband and the next with her father. Hannah saw no signs of animosity in the man, and wondering if a few dollars had crossed the man's palm, decided they had.

The bride and groom spent this night apart. Delighted, Hannah learned he wished them to begin their life together in the new house he'd just completed for her. Lupita told her. "'*Mi marido*,' he say, '*Cherie*, I take too long to build our home, *mi amour*, but I want to give you fine home. Is ready and waits for us.'"

Lupita's joy was complete, and Hannah, happy for the girl, helped her while she rushed about preparing to leave with her husband. She could barely collect her things in her excitement, though pitifully few they were. They both believed her new husband would correct that deficiency in short order.

℃℃℃

The newly married couple left the ranch with her scant belongings in the early morning. Hannah's sense of loss was tempered with well wishes for her friend, Lupita. Not only marrying out of her culture, but into a foreign one at that. Hannah prayed for her happiness. "Please God, make sure that she'll be happy!"

Remembering her own wedding day, she hoped the new couple would find happiness. Reflecting on her own eagerness to become a wife and the hideous outcome, a chill passed through her. Could any bride truly know her future?

∽∾∼∾

That same day, Brice rode over the ridge, through the wide gate, and into the ranch yard at dusk. Manuel ran quickly to take his sweating, dust-caked horse. Romer looked about done in. Hannah figured he'd had a long hard ride.

Brice clapped him on the shoulder. "*Gracias, mi hijo*, walk him a bit, *por favor*."

Hannah knew his legs were stiff and tight by the way he walked to the ranch house, slapping dust from his worn clothing. Heading straight for her standing on the porch, he ran his hand through his dark curling hair.

Hannah cried out as she ran into his arms. "Brice, it's been so long! I've missed you terribly. A lot has happened, some of it very nice, too. Lupita is married now, can you believe it?"

"You don't say! Married, is she? I'll have to hear about that! Sorry in takin' so long getting' here, but we're far away now. Took an all-day ride to come see you and poor Romer's the worse for it." He grinned into her eyes. "I just had to come and set eyes on you. Been so long. You all right?"

His roughened hands and lean, hard body caressed her as he pressed her against him.

"Yes, I'm fine, Brice, just waiting for you."

"I'm dirty as hell, shouldn't be hangin' on so tight, but I just can't help it. I love you, girl, God help me, I do."

She flushed at his words. "It's been quiet around here, Brice—after Lupita's wedding, that is. Her father wanted to kill her for a while."

She laughed into his wind-burned eyes. The whites were reddened some but they were the same dark blue she remembered, even through the dust and sweat of his long ride. She couldn't let him go. The male smell of him and the touch of his hands on her body set her heart soaring beyond anything she'd ever known.

"Let's meet in the orchard again. I need to make love to you." He chuckled. "Well, as much as you'll allow, anyway." His eyes twinkled mischievously, setting her aglow all over again. "I've missed you so much, girl." He put her away from him. "I've got to see Jesse if he's here."

Her eyes took in the sight of him and his wide smile and she loved what she saw. "In the office, I think. He was here for dinner," Hannah replied, smiling back into his eyes.

She let him go and went to her room.

Lupita's younger sister, Maria, watched Thomas for her these days. She rose to her feet, "*Senora, que pasa?*" she murmured, seeing her mistress so flustered and glowing.

"*Es bueno, mi amore, senorita,*" Hannah reassured her and gave her leave to go. She fed Thomas and put him to bed. He needed little from her these days, taking so much more by spoon. He was growing—crawling, and jabbering most of his waking hours—developing into a happy, healthy baby. A beautiful blond-haired boy, her son had crept silently into her heart, never to leave. "Brice loves him, too. Thank God for that."

Concerned that Brice had information, she wondered what news. Things were so peaceful at the ranch these days. Would his evil tidings chase her security away?

In the darkness, with outstretched arms, she felt her way toward the orchard and gasped in surprise when he swept her against his work-hardened body.

"How does it go for you these days? My God, girl, I've missed holding your little frame!"

"You frightened me!" She couldn't suppress a happy giggle. All her worries were absent when she was with this man. He'd taken her into his life, became her protector, and, at last—her dearest love.

"Come, darlin', let's walk a bit." He wrapped his arm around her and they moved farther into the orchard. "There isn't much that's new to tell. Hank Watkins is still mouthin' around town about the woman and baby, says they must have been Moore's woman and child," he added. "He's still put out as how you escaped on that train to the East." Brice chuckled at that. "He was after the reward, something to sooth his ruffled feathers, I'd say."

"How good of Campy to tell the sheriff I went home, a great stroke of luck for me." She buried her face in Brice's shoulder. "There's always the chance I'll be found out, but I've been safe and happy here and Jesse treats me as a daughter." She told him about Lupita's wedding. "Jesse came to her rescue until the bridegroom came. He took so long in coming, she'd about lost hope, poor girl. I hope it will be a happy union, but who knows about things like that?" she told him. "Brice, that man had Lupita in the family way, one of the reasons her father was so angry."

"I'm glad Jesse stood up for the girl, and damned glad that Frenchman finally came for her. It's like Jesse to take care of the poor girl. And I'm mighty glad he's taken to you that way, Hannah. He's lonely with his wife gone, isn't he? And not so well either. I found that out by accident—saw him takin' medicine, and not the alcoholic kind."

"Brice, I know about it, Leatha told me but I wasn't sure how much medication he used. He's already suffered too much." She sighed and pressed closer. "But as you say, life is the way it is. It fairly breaks my heart." She clung tight in his arms. "I want to be your wife. I know that for sure. When your work is done, could we leave this country and never think of all the things that happened here ever again?"

"Only a few months now, but you'll want to see Jesse through to the end. He's taken real sick and needs you."

"No, I'd never leave him, Brice, I couldn't. I want to get so far away, I'd never have to worry, but after the gracious way he and Leatha took me into their home and lives, I'll stay and see him through this, whatever comes." Heart hammering, Hannah felt the trap closing around her. Getting away was no longer a possibility, only a fanciful dream, and her mind flew into a mad whirl at this new realization.

She clung to Brice, hiding her fears.

"I'll be startin' on back in the mornin', darlin'. We're going into the mountains northwest of Prescott, and, with the rough goin', the men need me more than usual. I send the stuff off from Prescott these days. Doesn't amount to much as a town, but growin' enough to have a telegraph. I won't be gettin' news from Flagstaff anymore."

"You're leaving so soon?" Tears formed in her eyes. "I'm lonely without you, even with these wonderful people here, but it's not the same. How did this happen, Brice? I never thought I'd marry again, or fall in love. I was too afraid to think, just to survive, and now here you are!"

"We'll never know why, but something brought a poor tormented soul to my cabin in the middle of the night. Like I say, life is worth the living, and I'll be the best man for you I can be, but I'm not perfect, by a long shot." He added. "Hannah, it takes all I've got to stay away from you anymore." He drew her closer, kissing her over and over.

"I warn you, I'll never be beaten again, Brice, you know that. I'm much stronger, no longer an ignorant girl." She laughed at her own words.

He was nothing like Moore. But in her heart she knew a strength of purpose she'd never felt before. No, it'd never happen to her again!

They spent long, happy hours together in privacy beneath trees now hanging heavy with ripening fruit. The aroma clung in the air, creating a magical aura that enhanced the sense of wonder the two lovers felt in their growing union. If clouds formed on her horizon, they dispelled in his arms.

CHAPTER 18

Brice left on Romer the next morning and, again, Hannah fought her sense of desolation at his leaving. His last kisses lingered softly on her lips, and his strong hands had left their heated traces on her body. She wiped away a few tears, shrugged and watched for long moments as he rode out. Then she returned to the ranch house and sought Jesse.

His pallor, sweating, and lagging steps dwelt heavily on her mind. The craggy old man was very ill. Leatha had said it and now Brice. Unable to avoid thoughts of where she'd go if he died, she scolded herself. "It's very selfish of me, but what will become of my son and me?"

She found him sitting in his office. He invited her in and gestured for her to a seat. "What's on your mind, little lady? Now that Brice's gone, you're looking for somethin' to work at, eh?"

He laughed, and Hannah thought he looked well enough.

She left off worrying and didn't say what worked on her mind. "Maria is watching Thomas. I thought to take Fancy out for a ride if I'll be safe alone."

"Hell, yes, oughta be! Haven't seen any outlaws in quite a spell." He laughed. "I'd go with you, but got some figgerin' to do. Always hated paperwork. Damned stuff ties me up."

"Maybe another time, I'll ride out by the big pond," Hannah said. "It looks nice and green from here and I've never been there. If I get lost, I'll give Fancy her head. She'll bring me home." She took her leave and dressed for riding in Leatha's old riding habit, faded blue with a small ruffle on each side of the row of buttons, and a flounce around the back in the way of a small bustle. She made a fetching figure wearing it.

Fancy hadn't been ridden for a spell. Nervous and fretful, the mare settled down into a gentle walk-trot after a short run, a gait that made for excellent riding. Hannah handled her well enough and the fast-flowing air during the run was exciting. The sun hung hot and high overhead. Heat waves danced on the dry ground before her and made the distant mountains float like a mirage.

The sight looked magical to Hannah. She mopped her brow and took a good drink from the canteen. "Hot one today, Fancy. We won't stay out long unless it's cool enough by the pond."

Arriving at the watering hole, she found shade trees, brushy growth, and a few patches of tall, waving grass—a cool, inviting place fed by a constant spring. She dismounted and tethered Fancy near a handy bunch of grass. The glossy little mare fed, eagerly snipping the succulent grasses and munching. Hannah watched the movement of the mare's busy jaws under the smooth velvety skin that covered them. A huge dimple just over her eyes moved in and out as she chewed. Everything was mesmerizing today.

Sitting on the pond bank, she let the cool breeze fan her flushed face and hair while she drowsed languidly, daydreaming of her life with Brice. Wondering how Lupita fared in her new marriage, Hannah let her mind enjoy a restful hour. She took off her boots and stockings and dipped her feet in the water. It looked clean and felt refreshingly cold.

"Oh what a paradise this ranch is! Wouldn't it be wonderful to live here forever with Brice?" she murmured and lay back to watch the lazy movement of a few scudding clouds.

A soft breeze kept the trees swaying above her and the occasional bird wheeled about, scolding—no doubt waiting for her departure so it could visit the edges of the little pond.

Her reverie was interrupted by hearing Fancy's snort. She

tossed her head and, with ears pointed forward, whinnied in welcome. Hannah turned, pulled her dress down over her bare legs, and felt her veins fill with icy dread.

Tug Parker rode into the shady area near Fancy. "Nice day fer swimin', now ain't it? I seen you ridin up here. Me an' some of the boys are workin' cows just over the rise there. Whew! It's sure a hot one, good day fer a swim." He ground hitched his mount near Fancy and, casting his beady, fat-rimmed eyes on her, moved closer. "What d'ya say, sweet heart? Want to take a dip, er cain't you swim?" He pulled his shirt open, ripping off some of the buttons in his haste.

Hannah froze at the sight of this man, utterly disgusting in speech and appearance. Her heart hammered in fear and anger. A big man, and strong, he had the potential to do her great harm. Not wanting to antagonize him, she said in her lowest tones, "Hello Mr. Parker. No, I don't swim, and I was just leaving. I need to get back to my baby."

Her breasts had the ache of fullness, and though her milk had lessened, she needed to take care of her child. "You might want to cool yourself off as soon as I leave. It looks clean and it's really nice." She pulled her feet out of the water and reached for her boots to pull them on.

The dampness made the stockings stick. Wiping her feet on her riding dress helped. Nervously fumbling in her efforts to pull them on, but unable, she decided to ride without them. She rose from the ground to catch up her mare, attempting to avoid Tug. He was too quick. He lunged for her, grabbed her arms cruelly, and pushed her back to the ground.

He knelt at her side, his sweat-fouled scent assaulted her nostrils. "Here, now, little lady, lemme help you wi' them boots."

Feeling befouled, she jerked her feet away.

He grabbed her riding skirt and pulled it up, tearing the fragile cloth. "Here now, let me hep you! Say, you got nice little feet there!" He reached for Hannah's leg and caught hold. As he bent nearer to her, his grasp on her leg tightened. His hand pushed her skirts higher and his greedy eyes followed.

The odor of his foul breath and the overwhelming smell

of his body made her nauseous. "Please, I can put them on without help!"

She tried to pull away, but her evasive action made him move his bulky, malodorous body even closer. He grasped her arm. His nails bit into her flesh.

"Let me have 'em, missy, I ain't a gonna hurt you none. You don't need to be skeered o' me. I ain't so bad. Lots of ladies have told me thet, if you get my meanin'." His fetid breath hit her full in her face and she fought a rising need to vomit.

"I said, leave me alone! You have no right to talk to me like this. Mr. Bidwell will have something to say about your behavior! Go on now and I'll not mention this to him."

Hannah understood fully the lascivious intent of this huge, powerful man. It loomed threateningly in his little, yellowed pig-eyes, as he leaned closer and grabbed her dress front.

"Aw, ya never said anythin' to him in Seligman. There's a reason behind that, now ain't there? What is it—hidin' from somethin' or afraid of gittin' yourself in a fix?" He reached for her breasts.

Hannah screamed. "Leave me alone, you monster! Why are you doing this? Why torture me? I've never bothered you. Let me *go!*" She struggled against his powerful grip.

"That's why. You won't give a man the time of day, except maybe that skinny surveyor feller. Got somethin' goin' there, have you', daddy of yer youngun' is he?"

He fixed his glowering leer into her eyes and saw her fear. It only made him bolder.

"He's a friend. A longtime friend if it's any of your mix." Hannah, angry as well as afraid, struggled to escape him. Her boots lay far away on the grass as she twisted away from his grasp. Getting to her feet, she ran toward Fancy with blood dripping down her leg from his filthy fingernails.

"Naw you don't, little missy. I got you now an' there's nobody aroun' to cry to." Leaping to his feet, he grabbed her around the waist and pulled her against his sweat-stained shirt.

She felt his course, work-hardened hands grasp her breast and squeeze. She cried out in pain and fought her faintness from his assault on her body. She kicked at his lower torso and clawed his face, leaving long bloody trails of torn flesh. His bleeding face quickly became a wild mask of insanity, as he clutched her tighter.

If he felt the clawing of his flesh, he gave no sign. She realized he was intent on something else.

"Now jest let me have some of the same as thet baby gits. You got a'plenty thar. I can see that much!"

He yanked her dress open, making the fine little buttons fly into the grass, and bent his protruding lips to her full aching breasts. Her mad struggling only made him more inflamed.

In horror, Hannah screamed, "Please don't! Oh please don't do this!"

Unable to escape his heavy grip on her body, she raked his face again with her nails. His strength easily overpowered her and Hannah felt the darkness overtake her as his foul lips closed over her breast.

With his evil mouth, pulling and draining, blackness nearly overcame her. Bloody trails snaked down his purple, bloated features. In his passionate frenzy, he never seemed to feel any of that, as he availed himself of her soft female flesh—until a voice rang out.

"Hold on there, Tug, you Goddammed bastard! I thought I saw you headin' over this way. Leave go of her, or I'll gut shoot you and leave your carcass for the coyotes to finish." Jesse's voice—angry, low, and menacing—confronted the sweating, inflamed cowboy, his gun barrel gleaming blue-black in the sunlight.

Tug dropped Hannah onto the grass. She lay limp and pale, her riding habit torn away. Drops of thin, bluish milk oozed from her bruised breast.

"She asked me fer it. She sure as hell wanted me, she did. I ain't a-lyin' about it neither!" His florid cheeks dripped sweat and blood, but he'd gone pale.

"You filthy bastard, get your gear and be gone before I get back with her. If I see you again, I'll kill you, you God-damned rotten son-of-a-bitch!"

Jesse's face, white-hot with anger, drove Tug back. Jesse

took another step forward, his six-gun aimed at Tug's swelling gut. His finger itched like burning hell to pull the trigger. Hannah lay on the grassy bank, awake enough to see her rescuer and moan in pain.

"Yessir, I'm a goin' now. No need a gitten' so riled." Legs shaking with passion and fear, Tug caught up his horse. Mounting, he jerked the bit painfully in the animal's mouth, and spurred him cruelly. Drops of blood dripped down his horse's flanks as he took off at a mad gallop.

Jesse knelt next to her. "Hannah, wake up. You're all right now. Tug's gone and we'll never see hide nor hair of him again." He snorted. "Not if he wants to see another sunrise." He pulled her torn habit together, trying to cover her naked breasts. "Come on now, you'll be all right, honey. I got here in time."

"I'll never be all right!" Hannah sobbed as she crawled to the water's edge and splashed water over her face and breasts, desperately attempting to wash away the foulness of Tug Parker. She moaned, then vomited into the weeds. "Oh Jesse!"

Remembering again the horror at the filthy hands of Tug Parker, she began long, deep, broken, sobbing, shuddering as she came fully awake and vomited again onto the grassy banks of the pond.

Jesse pulled her clothes together, patted her, held her close, and wiped her face with his scarf.

"Oh, God, why do these things happen to me, Jesse? What do I do that makes men want to do me harm? What will Brice say when he finds out about this?" She gasped for breath. "He'll want to kill that man and he deserves it, but I'd hate for Brice to get in trouble over it. He's gone too far helping me as it is."

Jesse stroked her hair. "Honey, no man could go too far helpin' you and don't worry about Brice. He knows some men aren't right in the head that way. You're a very gentle girl. Maybe that attracts the wrong kind. I can't figure men sometimes, honey, but I'd better never lay eyes on Tug Parker again. I know it and he sure as hell knows it, too." He dried her eyes and helped her to her feet.

"I need to get these boots on before I can ride." She sat down and pulled on her socks, and the boots. Her feet were dry, and she had no need to hurry now. She looked up at him, grateful tears filling her eyes. "Oh, Jesse, there's not enough ways to thank you for saving me from that horrid, ugly monster."

"Now, honey, don't take on so. Had I known what kind he was, he'd never worked a day on my ranch."

He helped her to her feet and brought her mare Fancy close. Helping her mount, he patted her, soothing her frayed nerves at this latest onslaught against her person. She wondered if she'd ever dare trust a man again. Her rising nausea made her shudder violently, and she slumped in the saddle, crying her heart out as they rode slowly toward the ranch.

She prayed Tug would be gone, not wanting another killing because of her, and Jesse would certainly kill him, if he wasn't gone when they got back. Her left breast felt bruised and flowing milk had wet the other side of her torn, soiled habit. Head hanging low, tears falling, she fought her revulsion at what had happened. Understanding evil men—like Tug, Moore, and Hank Watkins, too, for that matter—was beyond her.

Hannah crept to her room, hoping she wouldn't be seen in her disheveled state. How could she answer questioning looks? What could she say?

When she asked Maria to bring her water to bathe away the grimy feel of Tug's evil touch, the girl made no comment, but the look of sorrow on her face, and her silence, spoke of curiosity as well as concern.

A river of water would never be enough to wash her horrors away. If Jesse hadn't come when he did, what then? Feeling cleaner after bathing, she took Thomas to her breast, avoiding the bruised and painful side.

"Oh, baby boy, we have another enemy now. I couldn't stop it from happening, unless I'd never left this house. It shouldn't be this way!" Angered and feeling lower than a snake's belly, she sobbed and rocked her baby gently as he fed.

Later, Hannah joined Jesse in his office. Sickened and shocked, she sought his comforting presence.

Still visibly upset, he exclaimed, "Goddammit, Hannah! Brice left you in my care. He won't take kindly to what's happened, but he's got to know." His face had taken on a sweaty pallor and, seeing how quickly he reached for his medicine bottle, she knew for certain he used laudanum the same as Leatha had, and more frequently these days.

"I hope all this will be over soon so I can go to rest beside my Leatha. Your Brice's a good man, he'll work it out." He laid his graying head down on his desk, murmuring, until the waves of pain passed. "Brice, you'd better show up here pretty damned soon. Your woman needs you now."

Hannah quietly left him to his reverie. The medication had taken him to a comfortable state. Sickened over the day's events, she regretted adding to Jesse's problems.

CHAPTER 19

Tug spurred his horse and rode hard for Flagstaff. He needed a drink and needed it bad. "Damned that little snip of a whore, won't give a man the time of day. She's got a young'un. She knows what's goin' on, damned stingy of her to my notion. Keepin' herself fer thet skinny surveyor feller, that's what's goin' on. An' I know'd it." Seeing no blame in his actions, he only remembered the taste of Hannah's female flesh and wanted more. "Selfish little bitch!"

He snarled his rage. He never felt the flaming scratch marks that reddened his grizzled face, nor did he see the blood stains down the front of his shirt.

Nearing midnight, he rode into Flagstaff on his exhausted, trembling mount. Handing him over to the stable hand, he headed for the nearest bar. "Goddamn, I hope to hell there's a woman available. I'm needin' one—real bad."

He heard the tinkling of a piano and a sudden roar of laughter as he passed Lillie's Place. "Some lucky somabitch's scored at cards." He pushed the swinging doors open and sauntered in.

His mood foul, he attempted nonchalance. "If I'm nice, maybe one of them girls might take me on fer the night. Barkeep, pour me a whisky, an' one fer thet little lady sitting over thar an' see if she'd join me in a drink or two." He gestured toward a blowzy woman sitting at a table, casting her eyes slyly about for a night's action.

"What in hell happened to you? Tangle with a bear, did ya?"

"Never you mind my business, now, just tend ta yorn."

The barkeep spoke to the woman then motioned Tug to come to her table. Tug sauntered over, tipped his hat, and sat down. "Howdy, ma'm, would you like 'nother drink er two?" He motioned for the barkeep to replenish their glasses.

"Why thank ya, sir, that's real nice of ya, name's Mollie."

Tug saw how cunningly she sized the possibilities of a sweaty, tired rider. Ignoring the bloody marks on his face, she waited to see what he might be willing to spend on her.

Conniving' bitch, this one, now ain't she? His eyes squinted as the bartender poured another round. "No time like the present fer a little fun," he said to the woman. "I always say. Anyplace a feller could clean up? I been a ridin' most of the day. Near wore my horse down to nuthin' just tryin' to git here."

He smelled of acrid body odor, dirt, and sweat. His clothes were dirty and worn, and the blood down the front of his shirt had dried into black stains.

"I kin see a need or two a man might have." She smiled. "We got a right nice place upstairs here, might do fer ya."

A cunning gleam crossed her eyes, and Tug saw it. Her smile, marred by broken, yellowed teeth, disgusted him, but he wanted a woman, and any of 'em would do, including the slatternly cow who sat before him.

He needed to get the hurt of his dismissal and the fine, petite body of Hannah off his mind. He hated her deep in his gut. He'd hate the little bitch till the end of his days. "Teach her some manners one day, I will." His low words were only half heard by his companion.

"What's at ya say, dearie?"

"Nuthin', honey, let's go upstairs and have us a nice bath, what'd ya say?" He sniggered beneath his breath and threw an arm around her, pulling her thin print dress awry as they headed for the stairs.

Later, above the sounds of carousing, card playing and the thumping piano, the occasional scream could be heard.

Tug gave her a hefty swat, saying, "Just shut ta hell up, woman. A body's needin'a bit of fun, no cryin' now, happens all the time with my women."

She screamed again and, in a rage, Tug slapped the whore repeatedly across the face as he slammed into her soft body time and again. In his mind, he extracted hate and revenge on Hannah, violently using the bar-girl cruelly in her stead.

Much later, Tug staggered out into the night. "Damned bitch wouldn' even lemme stay the night." The front of his clothes were stained with fresh streaks of blood drying into the fabric. He weaved from his alcoholic intake and headed for the stables. "Dunno what's wrong with females anymore."

He found the stable, warm from the heat of the animals, and settled into a pile of straw. Before drifting into a heavy snoring slumber, he felt rivulets of alcohol-laced saliva run from the corners of his mouth down into the straw bedding.

 exex

The sun stood high. Tug came awake when a young stable hand kicked at his inert form. "Ouch, Godamm," he yowled when the light of day struck his bloodshot eyes.

"Hey, mister, this ain't no boardin' house. If you're lookin' fer a place to sleep, try Ella Barnes's place. Beds ain't that much, but the cookin's good, so I hear tell." The kid stood with a pitch fork in his hand. His stance gave Tug the feeling this young man had enough authority to enforce his words.

Tug shook the straw off and stood up. "Thanks, sonny— bad night. I'll take a look-see at this Ella's place—new in town." He heaved his bulk out the stable door and worked his way into the center of town.

The boy had frowned, looking at him. Tug wondered if he'd seen the tell-tale blood stains on his crusty, travel-stained clothes. The kid'd likely keep his mouth shut, he figured. Things happened. Maybe the kid didn't want any mix in it, even if his curiosity was aroused. But Tug figured, what the hell, and gave it no further thought.

He lumbered down the boardwalk until he found Ella

Barnes's rooming house. Hoping his disheveled state, alcohol fumes, and befouled clothing wouldn't give the woman second thoughts, he took a cot in a room with several others. A dollar was a dollar, and he guessed she'd seen some bad ones come through her place but minded her own business. After eating a good breakfast, he sought the lumpy bed and slept most of the day away.

◌◌◌

Near sunset Tug thumped down the stairs wearing fresh clothes. Seeing Ella cleaning the table, he asked, "What's fer play in this here town." He looked about for other roomers. "Any food around?"

"Supper's at six, if you're around. I don't trot out no food 'cept at meal times. Ain't no house slave to you lot of saddle tramps. You kin find yer own fun." The woman sniffed as she turned to her kitchen. He heard her mumbling to herself. "Sorriest lot of men yet, never did see the like."

Tug lumbered out into the fading sunlight. Blinking his eyes against the evening light, he headed down the street. "I wonder how my sweetie is after the good time I give 'er last night?" He passed the bar called Lillie's place, sure this was the place where he'd had a hot time with a woman called Mollie. He shook his head at his confusion. "Must have had a snoot full last night, can't remember nuthin'."

Entering the dimness of the tavern, he thought he saw the woman. Approaching her, he asked. "Say, ain't you my woman from last night?"

"Hell no, you dirty bastard. After what you done to poor Mollie, you'd better high tail it on out o' here 'afore Glen Parks comes in. He's the owner. He's gunnin' fer ya' after the way you ruined that poor girl. She'll likely never get over what you done to 'er last night."

The anger in her eyes told Tug he'd gone too far again. "It's that snooty lil' bitch what set me off, an' lost me my job in the bargain," he mumbled. Deciding he'd better not hang around to face the saloon owner, he hurriedly turned away.

He returned to the boarding house as the sun went down, hoping the promised supper would be ready. Some of the boarders were gathering at the large oval dining table. Tug essayed a smile as he took in the scene. "Howdy, fellers, I jest got in town here. Any excitement around this place?"

Al Partin was already at the table, waiting for the forthcoming meal.

Tug saw a bigger man than himself. "Guess I ain't the only big feller around town." He introduced himself.

The greeting was acknowledged with a grunt, "Names Al, been here awhile, lookin' fer work."

Tug sat across from him, watching as the men gathered around. A motley bunch, mostly down on their luck, he thought. *That'll be me now the bitch got me fired.* His lips thinned and his face tightened just thinking about it.

The conversation was muffled by the noisy sounds of eating. Supper was good tonight—roast beef, potatoes, corn bread, a sweet pudding, and juicy fruit pies for dessert. *That boy was right about the cookin',* he thought. *Better than that damned cook at Bidwells, that's fer damned sure.*

"Say, ma'am, this here's a mighty fine meal you put on." The man next to him smiled into Ella's flushed face. "Yeseree, mighty fine."

Tug thought this man was someone he'd like to know.

"Wal it won't be so fine if'n you don't pay up, an' right soon, Hank Watkins," Ella asserted as she piled on more biscuits. "I don't keep nobody as cain't pay, you all know that." She stalked off toward her kitchen.

"Ella don't give a body no break a' tall." Hank frowned. "Women will be the end of me yet. Goddamned the ornery, mule-headed bitches."

"Amen to that brother," Tug responded. "Had a few run ins with 'em myself. So what's yer gripe? One of 'em git to ya?" He laughed in Hank's face.

"You can shut ta hell up, mister, non o' yer mix, no how."

Embarrassed, and increasingly angry about the reference to his finances, Hank's face flushed red with embedded resentment. The latest turn his fate had taken, all due to a female, had him mad as hell. Tug saw in him a kindred spirit, one who'd run afoul of unwilling women all his whole damned life.

"No offense meant, pard, just observin' that's all." Tug wanted to make a friend or two, and insulting a man wasn't the way. He worked at smiling.

"It's all right, I guess," Hank muttered. "I've had a few hard knocks an' mostly it's them females, always actin' so damned snooty, gitten' a man fired."

"Well, we'll have to have a talk. I'm in the same boat," Tug offered.

"You like cards? We go down to the Roarin' Duck of a night. Might hit it good now and then so's a man can keep on eatin'" Hank showed a rise of excitement as he mentioned playing poker. He had the gambling habit, and mostly it paid off for him, kept him in a cot and food.

Tug felt a beginning comradeship with this troubled soul. "Sure, I'll join up with you' if it's no bother."

"We'll just mosey on down thar right now, then. Sun's gone and things are likely stirring up down to the place."

The two left together, and Tug felt a kinship he'd been lacking. Most of his working cowboy friends tended to be leery of him.

The night wore on with little luck for either man. "I jest can't win a hand. Some damned luck I've had. Fired, out of a job, turned down by some stuck-up bitch of a female, and now I'm losing what money I had left." Tug was fast approaching a raging fury. None of it was any fault of his. Luck was running bad again. That was what it was.

"Hang on, Tug, it's bound to change," Hank encouraged him, and it felt good.

Dark-eyed Jack Coombs was playing and doing well. "Hey, keep on playing. You're not doing so bad. Didn't you win a hand a few deals ago?"

"Hell, you say." Tug wanted to accuse the man of double dealing, but couldn't bring himself to accost Coombs. The man's glittering black eyes told of a hidden deadliness, and Tug didn't have the guts to accuse him. It could cost him his life and he knew it. He'd met men like Coombs before. Tug snickered knowingly. "Deal 'em then. I ain't got all night, got me a little woman huntin' later on."

The slapping of a new round of cards and heavy tobacco smoke, filled the air. "Here you are, boys. Take a look and ante up." Clay Ordway laughed. "Say, Hank, did you ever find that woman you was a huntin'?"

"Naw, the sheriff said she went home to the East somewheres." Hank's disappointment showed on his face and, again, Tug saw a fellow soul that wanted revenge on a woman. Hank continued. "Sure would have liked to see that little bitch hang fer what she done, killin' her husband with an iron skillet. Bashed his head in with it an' ran off in the night with her little kid. They never caught the bitch either. Hell of a thing, lettin' a killer like that get away."

"What'd this woman look like, anyway?" The twinge of familiarity in Hank's words set Tug thinking, maybe—could it be the same one?

"Aw, nuthin' special, had nice colored hair, though, all yella' it was, little bit of a thing, an' snooty as hell, wouldn't give a man any time a'tall. She jest had eyes fer that skinny surveyor feller."

"What? Surveyor feller!" Tug got excited. "What about her hair, an' that baby of her'n. Tell me all about thet woman. Maybe she ain't gone like you think. I seen one like 'at, had hair the color of honey, purtiest thing about her. She was always a holding that kid, a boy, I think it was. Fed 'im herself the natural way, she did, if you know what I mean." He sniggered at mention of a nursing mother. He could see the picture in his mind, the baby going at her, and felt himself engorging to the point of pain. He needed a woman again, and bad.

"Goddamn it! Thet yella' haired bitch threw the sheriff way off. It's got to be the same woman, ain't thet many around here like 'at."

Hank's comments set Tug on fire. He got restless and lost interest in playing cards.

"I'll be seein' the sheriff in the morning about this," Hank said. "Where 'bouts did you see this woman?"

"Why you askin'? Know this woman, do you?" Tug queried, wanting in on this in a big way. He'd get his revenge.

"Hell, yes," Hank snarled. "I know 'er! It's on her account I lost my job, wouldn't give a feller any interest, what with her hangin' on thet surveyor feller.

Tug wanted to hear more. "By God, I knew she was a hidin' somethin'. Kept to 'erself, mostly. I danced with 'er, tried to be sociable. She wouldn't have nothin' to do with me a' tall. She didn't squeal on me neither. I knew she was afraid to tell Bidwell, an' she never did. I see why now. She's a hidin' out, didn't want no notice takin' of 'er."

"I can see why she didn't go fer you, Tug. She likes 'em skinny, not a damned tub a lard like you."

Hank laughed. Tug knew he'd had a few too many and was becoming quarrelsome.

"I'll have 'er yet, never you' mind, you sorry bastard. I know where to find 'er an' you don't."

"At the Bidwell Ranch, that's it, aint it?" Hank, elated at this new information, grew reckless.

Tug rose in his chair and directed a powerful punch into Hank's face. "Teach you, ya bastard. You cain't horn in on me, pull my leg like 'at an' git away with it!"

Hank slid to the floor, his chair overturned, and blood ran down his face into his mouth. He moaned, but stayed put. Tug figured the man had enough of his big fists and bull-like size.

Maybe thet Mollie'll be a waitin' fer me. Tug's thoughts went back over last night, what he could remember of it. "I'm cashin' in, had enough card playin' fer the night." He rose to leave, sweeping up what little he had left. More important things burned on his mind now.

He wandered down the street until he came to Lillie's, pushed the swinging doors open, and sauntered in. "I'm lookin' fer the little lady I met up with last night. Anybody seen 'er? I fergit 'er name."

"Ya mean Miss Mollie?" the barkeep replied.

"Yep, I guess that's the one. A hot one, she is." Tug leered at the barkeep, winked, his little pig-eyes bloodshot from drink.

"Just a minute, I'll see."

Tug felt a nudge. "Are you the fat party that manhandled Mollie last night?"

Tug looked into the glittering, fiery eyes of tavern owner, Glen Parks. "Cain't say as I manhandled the little lady. She wanted everythin' she got—an' cried an' screamed fer more." He faced a large, graying man with a face tougher than shoe leather, and an expression of anger to match. "I never pay no mind to such talk. Ain't she here?"

Glen's rigid face, grew dark and flushed. His jaw set firm, he faced Tug. "I said if you had the guts to show yourself in here again, I'd kill you. Didn't you hear that today?"

Finally, Tug understood Glen's snarling words.

"I'll give you one chance, and that's all you'll get," Glen backed away. "Now, draw, you filthy bastard, so's I don't have to commit murder. You laid that girl up for at least a month. She's still crying and moaning from what you done to her."

Tug stared into the face of death.

"I said draw, you filthy, rotten animal!" Glen backed farther, giving him room.

"Aw, now, no need to git so all fired worked up. I was jest a funnin' with 'er." Tug's face tightened. Instantly sober, he knew what he faced. "Give a feller 'nother chance," he begged, slobbering the words as stains of urine ran yellow down the front of his pants.

"Draw on count of three, you son of a bitch." Glen began his count. "One...two...three..."

Tug tried to pull his gun, but Glen, in his fury, was much faster. Within seconds, Tug lay dead on the floor, gun in his hand—unfired.

"There, you ugly pig, try funnin' with the ladies now!" Glen blew the smoke from the barrel of his gun and holstered it. "Somebody get this rotten carcass out of here, and call the sheriff while you're at it."

Jake La Force entered the barroom. He heard no sound of tinkling music, or laughter at the moment, but he had heard the gunshot. The patrons, sobered at what had occurred, scurried to obey Glen's orders. La Force liked the man. Glen wasn't one to mess with, and La Force respected him for it. He watched some of the men grab Tug's legs and haul his bloated body across the barroom floor and out the swinging doors, leaving a smear of blood in his wake.

"Want to tell me what happened here?" La Force, always terse and to the point, questioned the owner. "Hell, I heard the shot away down the street."

"You might want to speak with Mollie," Glen said. "She's upstairs."

The men mounted the stairs and entered one of the rooms to find a sobbing, tear-stained woman lying on the bed. Seeing them, she burst into tears again with eyes already red. "I tried to sleep, but I couldn't." She tried to sit up at the edge of the bed. Clutching her breasts and lower abdomen, she went pale and fainted back onto the bed.

One of the girls attending Mollie, a petite blonde woman, Clara, said. "He hurt her real bad, Sheriff."

"He won't be a botherin' Mollie again. He was a bad 'un, real bad." Another girl named Alice went on to relate the story told by the bleeding and sobbing Mollie about last night's vicious attack.

Word spread around the small town, as it does anywhere when violence rears its vicious head. La Force investigated and found no fault. An unfired gun was found in Tug's hand. After interviewing a sobbing Mollie as to how Tug had savaged her, he concluded that Glen had rightly defended his working girl and saved the community further trouble from a hell-bound cowboy in the bargain. Relieved of the incident, he dismissed the entire thing.

CHAPTER 20

The next morning, La Force sat in his office, musing about the events relating to Tug's demise. The man wasn't known about town that he knew of. A no-account drifter, he guessed. For some reason, this incident reminded him of the Moore case. That had been resolved rightly, if not legally, resulting in Moore's death, and La force felt satisfied with the outcome.

Boots sounded on the doorstep and Hanks Watkins sauntered in, his chest puffed out and a sneaking smile across his face. He doffed his hat. "Pardon, Sheriff, if you ain't too busy, I got somethin' to say."

The cocky leer on the man's face made La Force want to punch it in, but holding his disgust in check, he said, "Spit it out, I ain't got all day." He had no time for the likes of Hank.

Hank couldn't stop the self-satisfied grin spreading over his face. "You know the fat guy, got hisself shot last night? Well, he told me somethin' you're needin' to hear." \

La Force waited, his jaw tight. "Get on with it."

"Wal, thet feller got hisself fired from the Bidwell Ranch. Rode in here night 'fore last. Said he got fired because of a yaller-haired gal that lives out there. She had a little baby, too, he told me. He said she had a visitor sometimes, a surveyor. Now, don't that beat all?" He waited expectantly for the sheriff's reaction.

"Might be somethin' to it, Hank."

La Force got up and put his hat on, he meant this as a

dismissal, but Hank hastened to add, "Anybody could see Tug was a damned pig. Got what was comin' so I hear. But what he told me bothered me an' I had to come see you."

La Force felt regret stirring in his gut. "Sounds like something I'll need to check out. Anything else, he said?"

Hank leaned forward in his chair, chest swelling out, knowing his news was important and had to be looked into. "Nothin' more 'cept he bothered her some and she wouldn't tell on him. Figgered she was hidin' somethin'. Didn't say why he got fired, though, but from what I hear he done at Lillie's place, I can guess he must'a got too close to the gal and Bidwell fired his sorry ass."

"If that's all you know, you can go, but I may need you to be a witness later on, so don't go nowhere." La Force bit off the words.

He had to pay heed to Hank's story, but the man dragged his feet in leaving and halted on his way out. "Say, Sheriff, I was wondering about a reward. I figured you'd be square if there was one. I was pretty sure about that."

Greedy bastard, La Force thought. "Hank, I'll let you know on a reward, but there's no talk of it, fer now."

La Force sat down again and tilted his chair back. "Wonder if that crippled up runt of a camp cook was lyin' to throw me off the trail. Maybe he didn't know where the woman went, but I'm figuring he did. Tomorrow, I'll head out to the Bidwell Ranch and take a look around." He shook his head. "Damn, I thought I was done with that damned case. Moore was a mean bastard, and probably got what was comin' to him. Now it falls to me to arrest the woman if she's there, an' I'm sure as hell hopin' she won't be."

ↄↄ

Life settled into a pleasant routine at the Bidwell Ranch and Hannah slipped into an uneasy security. No one had come to arrest her after so long a time. Dared she hope the investigation into Moore's death had died and was forgotten?

Though she did her best to cheer Jesse, he continually

missed his Leatha and mourned her passing. Now he was morbidly ill, and she believed the man looked forward to lying in the ground beside his wife and sons.

"It isn't right." She shook her head in sorrow. "Dying belongs to the future and rarely thought about."

Though, in truth, her own imprisonment and death loomed before her if she gave it thought.

Brice came again, and the excitement of seeing him ride over the ridge, through the wide gateway, sent thrills of heat through her body, making her forget her worries. He slapped his hat to rid it of dust and grinned at her. "Come here, darlin'. It's been too long." He crushed her in a bear hug and asked, "How is everything?"

Fearful of what Brice would say about Tug's mauling of her, she decided against telling him. "I'm fine, Brice, just missing you."

Keeping things from him caused feelings of guilt, but if she told him, he'd leave his work to square things with Tug. He'd likely kill the ugly devil and he wasn't worth a bullet. Why God allowed men like that to live, she didn't know. She kept her secret and hoped Jesse hadn't told him. She hugged him closer.

Later, when they walked out under the trees in the orchard, she declared softly, "I love you Brice, I know it deep in my heart now. You're everything to me. I miss you dreadfully when you're not here." She sighed. "My heart aches with it."

Being close against him helped ease the memories of Tug's lecherous attack. That monster's evil touch aroused revulsion and nausea. She'd never feel safe again until she was Brice's wife, not until then.

"Darlin', it won't be much longer. There's two more months left to this job, and then we'll be married. I'll be Thomas's daddy and give him my name if you'd allow it. Thomas Fowler, how's that sound?" He chuckled, and Hannah responded with joy.

"Oh, yes, Brice! You've been his father in every way and the only one he's ever known. It's a wonder how good you are with him, and me too." She giggled in her happiness. "Brice, where will we go then? Where will we live? I can't leave Jesse when he's so sick and this wonderful ranch too. I've come to love it here."

"If things work out like I've planned, you won't need to worry about that or anything else. Don't worry over it now. Things will work out, I feel it in my bones." He kissed her deeply. "I'll be leavin' again in the morning, darlin', an' it gets harder every time I do." He held her close for long hours in the starry night. His hands strayed over her body, as far as he dared. "Oh God, you're nice, just right in my arms," he murmured soft and low into her hair, sending shivers of delight through her.

Hannah stirred against him. "Brice, being your wife still frightens the daylights out of me...you know what I mean?" She flushed but the darkness hid her confusion.

"Hey, girl, we can handle anything together—that, too." He kissed her soundly and nuzzled in the softness of her hair.

∽∾∽

In early morning, Brice mounted up to ride away. He'd kissed her and her son as long as he could, and again she watched her love and protector ride away. Her heart ached as he rode over the ridge beyond the wide ranch gate, and longing for him set in again.

She wondered about what he'd said. *Everything will work out, he was working on it.* What had he in mind? Euphoric though her thoughts were of her life with Brice, the cold chill of worry niggled in the back of her mind.

Days later, setting out with Jesse for a ride to the western reaches of the ranch, upward toward the hazy mountain slopes, Hannah started in delight. "Oh, Jesse, could that be Brice coming in again so soon?" She thrilled at the sight of the man on horseback off in the hazy distances.

"Don't know, child. We'll soon see when he gets here, doesn't appear to be Brice's horse. That's no dapple gray. It's either a black or dark bay the man's ridin'." He shielded his eyes with a hand held across his forehead.

Any stranger riding up to the ranch brought concern to Hannah, and she watched with apprehension as the tall rider, wearing a battered leather vest, rode into the ranch yard. When she saw the dull gleam of a five-pointed star on the rider's vest, she felt ice replacing the warm blood in her veins.

In silent horror, she watched the man dismount from his sweating horse, hand it over to Manuel, and stride toward Bidwell, hand outstretched. "Howdy, sir, you're Jesse Bidwell, I take it?"

Her breathing stopped and her face grew cold. The man indeed wore a metal star on his vest. "Oh God, it's happened! He's come for me," Hannah whispered to herself. Her heart pounded. She stood firm as the two men greeted each other and waited for her happy world to crash around her.

Manuel took the tired mount to the barn. Murmuring "*Gracias*," to the boy, the sheriff introduced himself. "I'm Jake La Force, sheriff out of Flagstaff. Seems we got hold of some new information on an old case, an' maybe you folks here could be of some help." She felt his sharp, pale blue eyes sweeping over her. "I'd like to ask a few questions of you, Mr. Bidwell, and the young lady, here, too."

Hannah fought the shock taking over her body. Her baby would soon be motherless and she faced the certainty of it. The fearful dreams she'd had so many, many times had just become stark reality. Yet, in another way, relief flooded over her. It was out in the open. Tight with apprehension, she lifted her chin, ready for the sheriff's questions.

Jesse appeared calm. "Well, come on into the office. We'll make you comfortable while we have this out. You must be worn a little after that long ride. I've done it myself many a time."

Hannah wondered what his thoughts were.

They entered the coolness of the ranch house. Jesse led Hannah and the sheriff down the long hall. The usual hustle and bustle of the house was eerily silent, adding to the dreadful suspense building in Hannah's soul.

Certainly, the sheriff had come to the ranch to question her about Moore's death. As they moved through the house, she felt La Force's keen eyes on her. Was he making sure she didn't run? He wasn't one to fool with. It was in his mien, straight stance, and definitely in his quiet voice. Ice crept into her bones and across her scalp. She'd have to leave her son. *Oh God, my poor baby!*

Jesse bade him to a wide leather chair and poured the man a drink. "Well, Sheriff La Force, what brings you out here?"

Hannah sat to one side, waiting for calamity to fall.

"There was a killin' out at the Moore Ranch about six-eight months ago," the man began. We never found out just what happened exactly. The man's head was bashed in, but what the story was, we never really learned. No one knew the man personally and we found no answers. Women's things were found, and a few baby clothes. A drifter around Flagstaff kept on about this woman out at a camp, nagged on it day after day. Figured there was something unusual about her being out there with a tiny baby, and no man. A surveyor feller brought her there and kept watch over her."

He continued on and Hannah's mind whirled in panic. "Now, we do know that Moore married a woman off the train, a mail order bride, they said. The preacher's wife kept the marriage record in a book. Nobody saw the woman after that. None of Moore's neighbors knew he'd married, never said anything that way." He cleared his dusty throat, sipped his drink, and went on with his story.

Hannah quietly listened to words that doomed her life on the Bidwell Ranch.

"The preacher's wife remembered the marriage and described the woman," the sheriff continued. "I checked on that information with the informant and found enough similarity to investigate the matter. Seems he'd found out from another drifter that the lady in question was stayin' right here."

La Force bent a glance toward Hannah. "When I went out the first time, a man out there, a cook, I believe, said the head surveyor had taken her to Seligman and put her on the train to the East. Didn't say much about her, nor mention a baby."

He frowned. "Seems like he was coverin' for the woman, an' maybe his boss, too. Shore threw me off the trail."

A knowing smile crept over his tight-lipped face.

Hannah sat pale and shaking. She nearly fainted when he directed his next words to her.

"Ma'am, you fit the bill from the descriptions I've had of this woman, an' if you are the mother of a small child. I'd like to know if you'd know anything about this. Will you speak now? I have identifyin' witnesses in Flagstaff, so don't try keepin' anything back. I'd like to hear the full story."

Hannah felt the man disliked what he had to do. Unbelievably, she saw in this sheriff, a friend. "He'd have killed us both, sheriff," she began, her voice weak and shaky. Her strength returned as she spoke of her husband's cruelty and the beatings she'd endured. "I knew he would, right then, I knew it!" She gasped in pain. "He'd become increasingly violent as time wore on, and in all those months, never looked at his baby son or held him. Murder was in his eyes, and I knew he'd kill us both." She held back the tears as best she could. Relieved to have it out in the open, her fears were for Thomas, not herself.

"Just go on with it, ma'am. It's a hell of a tale you have to tell. I'd heard he was a hard man, but nothing of that sort."

She took encouragement from his words. "When he stopped beating me and fell into a drunken sleep, I took a heavy iron skillet and hit him over the head as hard as I could. There was a little blood, but I didn't stay there after that. When he woke up again, he'd be so bad, sheriff." Hannah fought tears. "I couldn't let him hurt my baby. We wouldn't have lived another day. I saddled Concho, packed what I could, and we left in the middle of the night. I could barely sit the horse, I hurt so terribly. For some reason, he'd beaten me extra hard that night." Her voice choked on the words, and tears filled her eyes. Hannah took a deep breath. "After a long time riding in the dark, I found a cabin and went in. A man was there, and I fainted dead away. He took care of my baby and me too." Her voice wavered into a whisper. "He saw the way I looked. He can tell you about that. His name is Brice Fowler. He works for the Land Banks, he said, surveying land for new settlers."

Hannah held her head high as she finished her story. She'd had no choice but to do the desperate things she'd done.

What happened now was out of her hands. Her life lay at the mercy of others. Her baby would be safe with Jesse, but if he died, what then? She raised tear-filled eyes to the steely-eyed sheriff. "What will become of my baby now, if I'm arrested?"

Bidwell stepped in. "Never you mind about Thomas. He has a home here as long as he needs one."

"It looks like I'll have to take you in to jail until we get this worked out. There'll be a trial, and you can tell your story to the judge and jury." La Force looked at Bidwell. "I'd like to spend the night here so we can get an early start in the mornin' if you're of a mind to offer as much."

"Certainly, Hannah has a good horse to ride, a nice gentle mare I've given her. She's a fine young woman, Sheriff. We feared this day might come. I hope you'll watch out for her in Flagstaff." Jesse turned to Hannah. "I'll come to Flagstaff as soon as I can, but I want to get word to Brice. Try to hold on. It'll come out all right. Who could expect a woman to put up with what you did out at that ranch? Nobody of a right mind could find a good woman like you guilty. They just couldn't Hannah!"

She saw the tears lying thick in Jesse's eyes and turned to La Force. "Sheriff, don't think I'll try to run away with my baby tonight. There's nowhere I could go. I'm afraid, but glad, too, to have this out in the open. I'll trust the law. I only hope they'll see my side of what happened. There was nothing else I could think to do. If they hang me, at least my child will live. I'll never regret saving him."

La Force smiled at her, which gave her a moment of comfort, but he had his job to do. She wondered what trials he'd seen. It could easily go hard for her. Taking her in, putting her in a cold jail cell was his duty and his job. She saw in his flint-blue eyes that being sheriff had tragic moments and this was one.

Hannah took her baby into her bed and held him in her arms as long as she could stay awake. Sleep was hard to come by, with swirling thoughts of a trial, leaving her child, and wondering when Brice would come in her desperate hour of need. Her eyes hurt from crying. Would Maria be as loving as

Lupita had been? "Oh God, if you can hear me, take care of my baby boy!"

CHAPTER 21

Early next morning, she sought Maria. The girl knew what Hannah faced, the tears in her eyes attested to that. Hannah tried to instruct her about Thomas's needs, but the girl knew him as much or more than she, so she could care for him. He wouldn't have mother's milk from now on, but he already handled solid foods and was able to drink from a cup. She had Jesse's promise he'd provide for Thomas and that became her comfort.

❧❧❧

Prepared for her trip into Flagstaff, La Force told her it was a long hard horseback ride and allowed her hands to be free for the trail. The ride would take most of the day. She wore one of Leatha's riding dresses and packed other things she now thought of as her own. With frantic last-minute instructions to Maria, and a tearful leave taking of Jesse and Thomas, she mounted Fancy and followed the tall spare figure of Jake La Force out of the wide gate.

Leaving Thomas behind nearly broke her heart, but jail was no place for him. Eyes swollen and reddened from crying, she urged her horse along behind the sheriff, barely keeping to the trail. She didn't know the terrain and didn't care one way or the other.

"You'll do fine, ma'am. Looks like you know ridin'. I'm glad for that, makes for an easier trip."

His look, one of kindness, gave her a measure of comfort. Others would not regard her with approval. Her life lay in the hands of strangers now.

"Sheriff La Force, who was it who talked about me around Flagstaff?" Sure it had been Hank, she needed to hear it.

"It was some saddle bum who drinks too much and won't get himself any kind of work. Name's Hank Watkins, ever hear of the fellar?"

"Yes, I know him. He tried to get familiar with me while I stayed at the surveyor's camp and was furious when I refused him. Brice Fowler, the head party chief, fired him. That's what they called the boss around there." She grew grim, her teeth clenched, remembering the ugly words Hank had thrown her way. "Looks like his threats to find me out have come true."

"He ain't much to brag about, ma'am, but he'll be a witness against you in the court, at least the little bit he knows. Then again, all he really knows is that you appeared in the camp with a tiny baby and no husband. Most men would find that unusual," he continued. "Funny thing is, at your surveyor's camp, the cook there told me the boss-man had put you on a train to the East so we quit lookin' for you. It was another of your admirers that pulled the plug. A man called Tug Parker. Seems he came ridin' into Flagstaff burnin' with hate against all women. He roughed up one of the girls at Lillie's place and got himself killed for it."

"He's dead then?" Her heart ached at the thought of another man dead because of her. "He was an ugly beast, that man." She shuddered. "I can't say how he attacked me. It sickens me to think of it."

"No need, Bidwell told me all about it. Son-of-a bi— sorry, ma'am, fer cussin'."

La Force had about seen it all, Hannah guessed, but taking it as usual wasn't in his make-up. A man like La Force wouldn't understand a man like Tug, either. No decent man would.

Remembering how Tug had hurt her, she thought of Thomas and made her filling breasts hurt and tingle. She'd heard that if you bound them tightly, the discomfort would last for a few days and then be over. Her time with Thomas was over for now—maybe forever. Fighting tears, she didn't reply to La Force. What was there to say?

The ride to Flagstaff proved long and arduous, but the sheriff stopped several times to rest the horses and prepare food. Hannah appreciated his consideration, even his doing the few camp chores. Her fear and sorrow were tempered with hope that Brice would somehow rescue her.

The terrain grew steep, rocky, and pine-filled. The cooler air refreshed the tired horses and riders as they entered the heights around Flagstaff. The familiar scent of the rust-barked ponderosas filled the dry air. No anticipation of happiness awaited her at the end of this ride, and the coolness of the dry pine scented air and shady glades beneath the giant trees gave no comfort, only memories of the small cabin where she'd first met Brice.

Her tired, aching body longed for the end of this miserable journey for whatever awaited. With spirits low, and desperate hope, she clung to the saddle. They rode on. In another two hours, with the sun sinking below the heights of the San Francisco Peaks, she saw the beginnings of the small town of Flagstaff.

A few dim lights shone from store windows, but Hannah, worn from the long ride, found it difficult to care. Thoughts of dismounting and finding a quiet place to lie down were uppermost in her mind. "Are we almost there, Sheriff? I can't ride much farther."

"Just about, ma'am. We'll find you a quiet cell and bring you some supper. That might help a bit." His face told her he hated to use the word cell, but that was her reality now, and nothing could soften the fact of it, other than a few kind words offered here and there.

Hannah noticed several observers on the street watching the sheriff bring a woman in with him. She wore no handcuffs or ropes, and they showed only mild curiosity, until La Force stopped in front of the jail.

Interest quickly flamed into wild speculation. "Hey, Sheriff, whatcha got in tow there?" a male voice called out.

Another voice rang out as the crowd thickened. "He's gone and brung in some woman. What's she done, Sheriff?" the man kept on. "What'd she do, Sheriff, kill somebody?"

Hannah flinched, hearing that.

Several men and a few women crowded around. An item of curiosity, Hannah kept her head up. Despite fatigue and despair, she stared forward, ignoring the people who crowded around.

"Get on back. Go on about your business." La Force dismounted and turned to help Hannah to the ground. Her legs were stiff and she nearly fell before he grabbed her waist to steady her. To the crowd, he yelled, "This is none of your mix. Get on out of here or I'll arrest the lot of you, now get!"

"She's a little thing, ain't she?" Hannah heard a man call out. "What's she done, Sheriff, kill somebody?" The man snickered.

Shuddering at the ugly words, she was grateful when La Force ushered her into the jail. "Is this what I'm to face, Sheriff? They're curious. They care nothing about me, just the excitement of a woman being arrested. Will they all hate me and be against me?" She noticed the look of surprise on the man sitting behind the desk.

"It might be pretty bad for a while," La Force told her. "Most of the folks around here know about Moore's killin', but it'd sort of died down. Now, I suppose it'll be big news again. We don't ever get a case like this one. I'll find you a lawyer if you'd like, maybe he can help you." He ushered Hannah down between iron-barred cells. The smells of rank male sweat, stale body odor, cigarette smoke, and left-over food assaulted her senses. Her snugly bound breasts ached painfully, adding to her abject misery.

For Hannah, her hell had just begun. Bringing Thomas here would have been terribly wrong. She was consoled that he was in safe, loving hands with Jesse. Stared at by the other inmates, she held her head high as she passed by the many cells before reaching the one allocated to her. Looking at them would only encourage unwanted comments and she wanted to be left alone. Unbelievably, they were silent watching a woman prisoner being led to a cell, a relief to her battered senses.

The last cell was cordoned off enough for a bit of privacy. "What is this cell, screened away from the others? Were you expecting a woman prisoner?"

"No, ma'am, we keep this one for those goin' to the gallows. That way they can have some privacy, if they want." Seeing that this was shocking information to her, he quickly added, "Well, we use it for others, depending on the need, so it's not just for the hangin' ones," he said, trying to soften the fact of her situation, and regretted using the word hanging, even though it could certainly become a reality for her.

Lin Johnson shuffled in with blankets, a pillow stuffed with some crunchy material, corn husks? Or some other dried material, she didn't know. Hannah felt he was a kind man, in spite of his intense scrutiny.

She believed he was curious to get a look at the woman Hank Watkins had gone on about for so long, a woman who'd done murder. "I guess I'll be an object of curiosity from now on." She shrugged, looking for a place to rest.

Hannah felt pure exhaustion from the long ride and didn't care what the deputy thought or the rest of the town. The narrow bunk and crunchy pillow, rustic but inviting, waited for her. An old chair leaned against the wall. Dispirited and worn, she cried softly. "Oh, Brice, where are you, tonight?" She dropped onto the unyielding surface of the bunk and fell into a dreamless sleep.

She was rudely awakened by the rattling of her iron-barred door.

A voice called to her. "Supper's here, ma'am." It was Lin, attending to her needs. He passed the tray of food through a slot onto a narrow shelf. "Here you go, ma'am. It's from Ella Barnes's place. She's generally a mighty fine cook."

Hannah took the tray and sat on the bed to eat. They were tasty victuals and she was famished along with her fatigue. Her breasts ached terribly, but she left them bound. She'd have to endure a few more days of it. Thinking of Thomas caused more pain and thoughts of him caused her milk to flow which increased the aching of her breasts. Thinking of his baby face and chubby little hands reaching out to her, she prayed he was happy and well.

The night held strange sounds for Hannah. Men snoring, belching, and farting during the night were noises she'd rarely heard. It worked to remind her of where she'd come to be. In surprising contrast to the cruder sounds she'd heard, the soft strains of one lonely male whose low voice echoed softly as he sang a tune, subtle with his words, not offensive, only sorrowful. Even in here, most men were gentlemen in their rustic ways. Without knowing their particular infractions of the law, she appreciated their consideration. She crawled into her cot and drifted off.

Morning brought a fresh wave of noises, men growling, cursing, and scratching themselves. "Now I've truly died and gone to hell," she groaned. "I wonder what this day will bring. What hellish thing awaits me?" Hannah sighed. "Brice, oh Brice, you'll not want me now, will you?"

ତ୍ରେତ୍ର

Jesse sent a man to find Brice. He had to be told of Hannah's arrest. What he could do about it, Jesse didn't know, but he could hire legal advice. If not, Jesse would take care of that himself. Little Thomas had cried much of the night, which increased Jesse's fatigue, as well as the nearly constant pain he suffered these days. He helped himself to a good sized dose of laudanum and called Maria to come to the office.

The girl entered shortly. "*Si, señor?*"

"*El niño*—the child—he's not feeling well, no?"

"*Si, Señor, es* sad, he *madre* gone. *El niño* cry *en la noche.*"

Jesse sighed and shook his head. "Very bad, *no madre, señorita,* very bad."

He motioned for her to go. She and the cooks would care for Thomas in their own way. Most all Mexican babies, he'd noticed, seemed fat and happy. Hannah would approve of the care her son received, he was sure of it.

Jesse imagined what Hannah endured in that Flagstaff jail. His heart ached for her while he awaited Brice's arrival. Hannah was part of his family, and her arrest for murder, though there'd always been the prospect of it, was unbearable to him.

ଏଓଏଓ

Within three days Brice arrived, tired and sweaty in his trail-worn clothes and worry lining his angular face. "Tell me about it, Jesse."

They sat in the roomy office. Jesse related the arrival of La Force, Hannah's arrest, her concern over her baby, and how she looked as she rode away with the sheriff. "The whole damned thing cropped up again because I had to fire one of my cowboys. That bastard attacked your Hannah!"

"What the hell! I'll kill that son-of-a-bitch!"

"Settle down, son. Sheriff La force told me Glen Parks already took care of that lousy low-life."

"I've got to get to Flagstaff, Jesse, and soon. Thomas'll be all right here?"

"Shore, man, the Mexican women love Hannah. Her baby's in good hands. He cried for his mother the first few nights, but Maria sleeps near him now, and he's some better."

Brice heaved a sigh of relief. "Jesse, I've got to ride to Flagstaff soon's I can set a horse. Mine's plum wore out. I'd sure as hell appreciate the loan of one of yours." He staggered to his feet. "Hell's bells, Jesse, I can't think what Hannah's goin' through."

"I know you'd want to set out now, but killin' yourself won't help her," Jesse said. "Wait for sun-up. I'll go along with you if I won't slow you too much."

"Why not take the buggy then? Might go easier for you."

"Good idea, you know I'm sick as hell, and I'm glad you do, but I'd like your confidence on it." He felt himself filling with pain, sweating as he spoke. "I don't want it spread around for now. Later won't matter much," he continued. "I'd hate to worry Hannah with all she's got to face."

"Jesse, she knows. She told me about it. That little lady doesn't miss much, especially with people she cares about." Brice sighed. "She was happy here. You and your wife were folks to her, like her own. She didn't say so, but I saw it plain."

"There's something else you need to know about." Jesse related a bit further about Hannah's run-in with Tug. He told it all as he'd seen it. "It took her days to stop crying and having nightmares over it. She was doin' pretty good until the sheriff showed up. Now it's all out on the table, and we've got to help her, Brice."

"God damn that filthy bastard! I'd a killed the bastard myself if I'd a got hold of him. In Flagstaff, you say? And he's the one that fingered Hannah?" Fury gripped Brice's features, setting his jaw tight and hands into clenched fists.

"Too late for killin' anyway, son, as I said before, got himself shot to hell in a brawl over what he did to one of the girls at Lillie's place, roughed her up real bad, he did. That son of a bitch was a danger to any woman he met. I say good riddance."

"So, how'd it come about regarding Hannah?"

"Thing is, Tug got next to Watkins. The man you fired. They got talking about women doing 'em dirt I guess and Hank put two and two together about Hannah."

Jesse understood Brice's temper, but angry though he was at the injustice that seemed to follow his woman, the thing with Tug was settled.

"I know you're anxious to get to Flagstaff, Brice. We'll get a good start at sun-up. I want to see Hannah, too, and see what I can do. You're worn out and so is your horse."

"Your right, Jesse," Brice replied. "We've got a long ride tomorrow, and you've got too damn much pain." He frowned. "I'd ride through the night, myself, but this is for the best."

Jesse nodded agreement. And another night's rest would help the old man.

∽∾∽

"You got a good horse for me? Mine looks like he needs a few more days' rest."

"Shore do, son." Jesse loaned Brice Monty, a dark bay that looked like a sturdy mountain horse. Morning's pale light saw the men on their way. Fortified with medication, the old man rode in the small buggy, pulled easily over the rocky trail. He drove with grim determination, gritting his teeth as each irregularity on the trail caused him a new and vicious onset of pain.

He'd steadily worsened over the past few weeks, and Brice selfishly hoped he'd hold out long enough to help Hannah. He felt no reproach for those feelings and cursed as he rode. "I worry over Hannah—woman like her shouldn't be put into this position. Bastardly turn of luck!"

Stopping for rest and medication, Brice asked Jesse, "Ever know of other trials along these lines?" He looked for signs of hope in the old man's answer.

"A few through the years," Jesse replied. "It seldom went well for a female guilty of killing. A jury would have little sympathy for a woman who'd killed her husband." He shrugged. "If women were on juries, might make a difference. I guess there's little comfort for Hannah in that, Brice."

CHAPTER 22

A gentle rattling on the bars of her cell, awakened Hannah.

Lin shoved a tray into the slot and waited for her to take it. "Here's yer breakfast, ma'am."

She saw curiosity in his eyes, but kindness lay there too, an innate kindness, even friendship.

"Doin' all right, are ya?" He couldn't miss her disheveled state.

She didn't have a lot of privacy for bathing and getting herself together. *What is he thinking? How a small woman like me was strong enough to bash a man's skull in for him?*

She took the tray and thanked him. The smell of coffee aroused her senses somewhat, but she had little appetite. Her breasts were painful in the extreme this morning—something more she must endure. Sighing, she picked at her tray. The bread looked good, but the thick, rancid, spread made her nauseous. Thinking of the cheerful breakfasts enjoyed at the ranch made her sick with longing. She wondered which cook created this unfortunate meal.

She did her best with the breakfast. She needed to bathe and wondered how that could be accomplished. When he came for the tray, she asked, "Lin, could I have enough water to bathe?"

"Why sure, ma'am, I'll bring a bucket of warm water."

She offered a weak smile of appreciation. "Thank you, Lin, maybe it'll help me feel better."

Walking away, he muttered, "Shore is a clean little thing."

The men took her request upon themselves. "Hey, Lin darling, would you bring me one, too?"

"Me too, I'm just so darn awful sweaty this here mornin'."

The male prisoners omitted the use of profanity and Hannah gratefully welcomed their consideration. She planned to ask for her needs in lower tones the next time, but found humor in the exchanges. The other inmates seemed friendly and accepting of her, for the most part, but she wondered how they thought of her. *Do they believe I'm like them? Am I?*

Lin appeared, carrying a battered bucket with warm water and some rudely woven fabric to use. She bathed as furtively as possible, considering the open bars of her cell with her blanket across the chair to provide privacy.

What would happen today? Could Brice help her survive this ordeal? Would he marry her now? Maybe he wouldn't want her after this. Feeling discouraged, but cleaner, she dropped on the bunk to wait.

Later in the morning, La Force came. In low tones, with serious mien, he said, "We're holdin' you for the murder of Jacob Moore, your husband."

"That's the charge against me?"

"Yes, ma'am." His reluctance in the announcement was evident. "We have a lawyer coming to help you. There's another one in town, so when your friend comes, he may want some changes. That'd be all right with us. The judge'll be out of town for another week or two. He's got a few cases before your hearin' yet and they usually give enough time for your defense, so there won't be a trial for quite a while yet."

Now it was official. She was being held for murder. "Thank you, Sheriff La Force. I'm waiting for my friend, Brice, to come. He's been wonderful. He saved my life that night, my baby's, too."

"I believe he did just that. Take it easy for now. Rest yourself and wait for him." La Force smiled at her. "I told these ornery gazebos in here to hold it down some. They can

get pretty rowdy, an' havin' a woman prisoner is a bit of excitement they ain't used to. Don't take much around here to get
them yahoos in a twist." He left Hannah to mull over his
statements.

Hugging her tender breasts, she lay down to rest until a
tap on her cell aroused her from a half sleep.

"Yes?" she said.

"Howdy, ma'am, name's Herbert Larkin. If you'd want,
I'm your legal representative, or close enough. I've had
schoolin' that away an' I'm here to help you, if you agree to
it."

Hannah saw a young man at the bars of her cell, tall and
nearly thin as a razor blade. Clothes hung loosely on his narrow frame, his hair, scanty and sand-colored, along with his
watery blue eyes, presented a rather poor picture.

However, to Hannah, he was a small ray of hope and she
asked Lin, "Let him in, if you can, please."

In some odd way, she felt sorry for this unfortunate appearing gentleman. Lin turned the iron key and slid the bars
open, allowing the lawyer in, locked it again, and turned away
to allow them privacy.

"It's good to meet you, Mr. Larkin. I'd be glad to have legal help. I have no idea what I should do." She motioned him
to the end of her bunk. "Have a seat. I'll use the chair."

"Nice to meet you, Mrs. Carlson, or it'd be Moore, I suppose, isn't it?" he began. He held out a hand in friendship.

Hannah took it momentarily and replied softly, "Yes, I
suppose it is. I haven't gone by that name for quite a while
now. Call me Hannah if you will, that'll be just fine with me.
Will you be able to help me?"

His face was serious. "Why not begin at the beginning?
Tell me everything from then until now. Maybe there's something in your story we can use in your defense. Tell me exactly
what happened in the death of Jacob Moore."

She felt his eyes taking her in. She wondered at Herbert
Larkin's appraising gaze. *What does he see? A small, slight,
young woman, not big enough to do what I did?*

Hannah pondered these questions and how to pay his fee

as well. "Mr. Larkin, I have very little money for your services, you should know that."

"That's no problem for me. My fees are low and I make out well enough. Don't you worry about it now, just begin your story, ma'am." He didn't miss the way her hands twisted together in her lap.

His pale blue eyes looked friendly. "You must think I'm an evil murderess. Would anyone believe that, looking at me? You haven't heard my story yet. In telling it, I must relive it all again."

He made no reply and waited. Hannah began detailing the painful events, and kept at it, reliving the horrors of her marriage to Moore. Noting the look of pain over the lawyer's face, she murmured, "There you have it. I don't know what else there is to say. I had to escape that man to save my son. He was only three months old at the time." Hannah shrugged and looked at Larkin. Could this thin little scarecrow of a man save her from the gallows?

"You certainly had reason enough for what you did, or I should say, were forced to do, but it's hard to say what a jury of these hardened men around here might say. They often go hard on a woman who shows too much independence, some of them, anyway."

Hannah felt little reassurance from that.

Larkin rose to take his leave. "I'll have more questions later on, and keep you advised, ma'am, on what's happening." He called for Lin to let him out and Hannah thanked him for his help.

After the attorney left, she dropped onto her bunk again. Exhausted from her interview with him, she lay there, wondering about her baby. Thinking of his soft little body and pink, baby mouth, painful tingling stung her breasts as her milk tried to flow.

"Maybe Brice is tired of me and my problems. He's had more than enough of them since he met me."

Dreaming of open rangelands and high, mountain peaks, she fell into a deep, dreamless sleep.

എൻ

The time dragged slowly with no activity other than the daily food service, the deputy walking by, and the sounds of the other prisoners who lately had taken to entertaining her by comments, singing, and the occasional mild expletive toward one another. Books to read would have filled her empty hours, but she had none, and Brice had yet to come to see her. Would he?

Lying on her cot, wondering if her child cried for her, she heard footsteps approaching and heard Lin's voice. "Mrs. Moore, you've got a visitor."

Her heart leaped with joy when she looked up to see Brice standing just outside her cell. For a moment she could only stare at him.

Grabbing onto the bars, he cried, "Hannah, I'm sorry to see you this way. Are you all right?"

The intensity of his worried tone struck her, and soothed her feelings of abandonment. He'd come!

She rose to touch him through the bars. "Oh, Brice, I thought I'd never see you again. It's been so long!" Tears started in her eyes, but they were from joy at the sight of him. "I worried you wouldn't want to see me in here."

"I started as soon as I got word, darlin' We're a long ways from the ranch now, closer to Prescott, these days." He smiled into her eyes, sending the familiar thrills coursing wildly through her. "Jesse's here, too, lookin' to see what kind of legal representation they've got around here. He had a hard ride comin' in—he's pretty sick, Hannah."

"I know he is. He tries to hide it, but I've seen him doubled over with the pain. I'm afraid for him, Brice," she told him. "A man was here, a lawyer of sorts, Herbert Larkin. I told him everything. He hasn't been back since." She shrugged. "He's not a real lawyer, but about the closest thing they've got around here. He said he'd studied law. I don't know what to think about it." She reached through the bars to touch his craggy, square-jawed face. "It's so good to see you. I've been going crazy, sitting here day after day." She clutched at his hands. "Thomas, have you seen him? Is he well without me?"

"He was fine when we left the ranch. Maria is doing her

best with him. She said he cried for several days, but has taken to her pretty well. He looks for you, but doesn't cry any more, she told me. How're you makin' out in here? Do they treat you well enough?"

"Yes, they've been good to me, but nothing seems real, being in here. It's like a bad dream. I wish they'd let you in here, I need you close. I'm so glad to see you," she babbled and couldn't stop. "The judge is out of town now, so there won't be a trial until he comes back. Sheriff La Force says he had several cases ahead of me. Maybe more time will help."

He stood close to the bars for a long time, soothing her, reaching through to touch her, letting her talk on, pouring out her desperation and longing for her baby. His heart ached for her and he determined to find a way to free her.

At last she squared her shoulders. "I only know this. I'm sorry Moore died, but I did what I had to do. I'm ready to face whatever they do to me."

A new determination had formed in her eyes. The toughness that had enabled her to fight for her baby's life lay glowing in her face and his pride in her soared.

"I wish they'd let you out for a walk, Hannah, but walkin' isn't the real reason. I want to hold on to you and never let go."

His dark eyes crinkled at the corners. Her eyes took his measure and couldn't get enough.

She laughed. "You can't imagine how much I want that, too. I dream of it." She touched his stubbly cheek. "I wonder if we'll ever be together again, sitting under the trees in that wonderful orchard."

"We will darlin', we will, I know we'll do that and so much more." He kissed her through the bars. "So much more, Hannah, just you wait!"

She blushed happily. "I love you so."

They heard footsteps coming and a booming voice. "Hold on there. Let me see this little lady."

Jesse's words warmed her heart. He wore a wide encouraging smile as he moved closer. No signs of pain or illness marked his features at present.

"Thank God, you've come, you and Brice. I've been so

worried about you. Was the ride to Flagstaff hard on you?"

"No, honey, I rode in the buggy just like a city slicker." He shrugged and laughed.

She wasn't fooled. His pin-point pupils betrayed the laudanum that fortified him, body and spirit.

"Have you found a better lawyer for me?"

"No, but I've had good reports on the Larkin man."

He sounded serious, and she worried. What talk had he heard? This small town likely wasn't in her favor. She wondered at their general tone and had already formed the idea that her trial would be a wild event when it got started.

"I'm happy you're here, both of you. Now, please, tell me all about Thomas, tell me everything!"

"He's doing fine, plays with Pedro most days, but he's lookin' for you all the while he's playing and eating. I see that little head turn too often not to think it."

She fought bitter tears at that picture. A lonely little boy, looking for his mother.

"I wish Lupita could be with him. They had a special feeling together. I'd like to let her know what's happened. Do you think I should?"

"It's fine with me, and maybe we'll find out if she's happy," Jesse replied. "If not, I don't think it'd be a good place for Thomas, if she needed to take him."

Hannah would never want her child exposed to abuse of any kind but, in her situation, she was powerless. The thought of it gave her chills. These days everything seemed dreadfully final.

"Don't you worry a minute over that boy. We'll take good care of him," Jesse said.

He was very tired from his rigorous trip to Flagstaff, and pain was setting in again. The lines around his mouth deepened, though he tried to hide the increasing pain of his illness.

"Brice, Jesse looks tired after that long ride. You're staying in flagstaff for a while, aren't you?" She looked at him, concern for the older man etched on her face.

At her suggestion, Brice faced Jesse. "Let's go on over to the hotel. We'll come back later on," he added. "I've got some lookin' around to do, and I want a confab with La Force."

It gladdened her heart he'd come and worked to gain her freedom.

The men took their leave. Hannah rested better now they were here, while wondering how they could possibly help her. She'd already confessed everything to the sheriff. She was guilty. Should she have tried to deny her role in Moore's death? Shivering, she lay down again, knowing she'd been right to come clean with La Force.

઼

Brice headed down the boardwalk toward the center of town while Jesse rested at the hotel. Passing the Roaring Duck, Brice stopped to listen. Loud, raucous men's talk might reveal some of the town's feeling toward Hannah. His hat pulled down, he walked in. "Whiskey," he told the barkeep.

"New in town?" the man asked.

"Been here before, just coolin' off." Brice took a chair between the bar and a noisy table of card players and adjusted his ears to the busy hum of activity. After sundown, the place slowly filled with people looking for a night's relaxation. An outburst from the card players caught his attention.

"Hell, you' say? Sure as hell, you're off your game tonight, Hank. Now button it up and play if you don't mind. What the hell's got in to you anyhow?" Al Partin had the deal and slapped a round of cards. "You playin' er not?"

"I'm in, I'm in. No need gittin' riled up. A feller can celebrate if he's got a right to, cain't he?" Crowing, Hank held his cards close.

Brice recognized the voice of Hank Watkins.

"What in hell's got you actin' so all fired loony tonight, Hank?" slim, dark, Jack Coombs asked in low, subdued tones.

"Just like I been a sayin' all along, there was a woman out to the Moore place and she's the one bashed the man's head in. Talk's around that the sheriff brung 'er in to jail three-four days ago, from the Bidwell Ranch. Been a hidin' out there, that's what. I been tellin' the sheriff 'bout it fer weeks now."

Hank wore a self-satisfied look on his reddened face that even heavy slugs of booze couldn't erase. Brice's blood ran hot, hearing his words.

"Getting' a reward, are you, Hank?" Clay Ordway asked. "The way you're playin', you'll be needin' some dollars real soon like."

"Ain't been no notice of any. I asked about it. Ain't heard no different. Worse luck, if it hadn't a been fer me, she'd still be a hidin' out there gittin' away with her killin'."

Brice wanted to smash a fist in Hank's face after hearing the drunken bum's bragging, boastful discourse.

"Quit the palaverin' and get on with it. Feller might's well be home in bed for all the damned card playin' gittin done here," Al grumbled. "Ain't any promise of nuthin' in my future, and I'm sick as hell of yer bragging and blowing about a windfall of reward money."

"Tried to git back with yer woman, eh? Bet she wouldn't let a fat-ass loser like you in the door."

Hank's nasty comeback tickled Brice.

"Ante-up, you bastards," Al grumbled. "You'll be damned lucky as hell if I don't paste thet ugly face of yours to the floor, Hank."

Brice quietly sipped his whiskey and mused. *So Hank's been stirring up trouble for Hannah. Should've fired his sorry ass long ago, wish I had.* He sat there for a while, waiting to hear more comment on the female prisoner.

Hearing no more on Hannah, Brice quietly rose and left the saloon. It was getting late, too late to visit her again. At the hotel, he sat with Jesse. "There's a lot of talk, most of what I heard was from, Hank Watkins, the man I fired. Getting back at Hannah is all he thinks about, damned jackass!"

"Think it'll go bad for her, Brice?"

"Hard to tell. I haven't heard enough talk, yet. Reckon I'll go see the parson in the morning. See what he's got to say. Seems he was the primary one to identify Hannah as Moore's wife."

"Brice, she told everything right out to La Force. So there's no going back on any of it." Jesse shrugged. The lines of pain had creased down the sides of his grayish features.

"It's best that way, out in the open. One way or another, she'll be done with it." Brice shuddered inwardly at the thought she could be convicted. Wracking his mind for ideas to help Hannah occupied all of his time. "It could go bad for her. Is there anyone who saw her life with Moore, at all?"

"She said they never saw any neighbors," Jesse said. "He had no mix with anyone 'cept at roundup, and those gents never went to the house."

"The only person she ever mentioned to me was an Indian woman called Neebah," Brice said. "Moore brought her in to help when Thomas was born. What she'd know, I couldn't guess. If I knew how to find her, I'd ask her about it. It's an idea, might turn out to be the best one. It could be Hannah's only chance if the trial goes against her."

"People won't listen to anything an Indian woman'd have to say, even if you found her and got her to come in and testify. I know how they feel about Indians around here. You're barkin' up the wrong tree there, Brice."

"Let's turn in and work it out tomorrow. Maybe the lawyer would know where we could find this woman." Brice couldn't give up his idea.

The old rancher lay on his bed in obvious pain and Brice helped him take another dose of laudanum.

"Hell, Jesse, you're hurtin' real bad. Tomorrow, we'll see the doctor about it. Might as well, we'll be here a while, anyway. Maybe he'll know something new to help you."

"I'm feelin' some better now, Brice, thanks for spoon feedin' me. I won't be around too much longer. It don't bother me a'tall, but I hope to hell we can help Hannah before I go."

His face took on a dreamy look and he drifted off into a peaceful sleep, leaving Brice awake and thinking.

Troubled, he sought his own bed but, tired though he was, he lay awake for long hours before sleep came to him. Hannah lay heavily on his mind and he wracked his brain, thinking of ways to help her. With no credible witnesses to Hannah's life with Moore, would a jury of twelve hardened men think abuse from a husband reason enough for killing him? He was her best witness, but his interest in her would make his testimony doubtful.

Brice was troubled by Jesse's increasing illness and knew nothing could be done to save him. The man had little will to live without his Leatha. A visit to the doctor might help, but he knew instinctively it would not. A good friend, newly found, Jesse's death would be a great loss.

CHAPTER 23

The next morning, Brice sought out the parson. Asking directions, he made his way down the dusty street to the weathered little home. It wasn't Sunday, and he found the man at home. The weather was cool and a good breeze kept the silver dollar-like aspen leaves fluttering and turning their silvery sides out. A pleasant day, Brice would have enjoyed it if his mind wasn't preoccupied with Hannah's trouble.

Knocking on the door brought a hurried response from within. The wizened little parson met him at the door. "Welcome, stranger, step right on in."

"Thank you, Parson Elkins." Brice entered. "Wonder if you'd have the time to tell me about the woman you married to Jacob Moore?"

This request aroused the parson's curiosity. "How's it you'd want to know about that?" Looking about for his wife, he called, "Martha, we've got a visitor, will you step in here, please?"

The woman presented herself. "Yes, Will?" Her questioning eyes examined Brice, head to toe.

"Martha, here's another man askin' about that young mail order bride who married Jacob Moore." He turned to Brice. "Can you say what your interest in this woman's all about? I hear she's locked up in the jail for what she done to her husband. A body can't help being curious about your interest in the matter."

"I know a lot about what went on that night and wondered

if you'd seen anything about him one way or another in the way he might treat his woman?" Clearing his throat, Brice went on. "She and her baby son happened into my cabin and the poor woman collapsed on the floor, nearly dead from her husband's beatings. I helped her out and found her a safe place to stay."

"My stars, Will, I never heard tell of anything that way about him, but we only saw the man on the day they were married." Martha looked at her husband in distress. "When you marry folks, you don't know what they'll turn into after they're married a spell. Poor little soul, was she all right then?"

"Yes, she is now, but they're holding her for his murder." Brice twirled his hat in his hands. He wasn't getting anything from these two.

"She married him right off the train from the East,' Martha volunteered. "Never stopped in town that I heard of, just went on out to their ranch. Never seen hide nor hair of 'em since. They never come in to church, not even once."

"My wife is right. That's all we saw of 'em." He shook his head in dismay at Brice's story. "Martha, best we pay a call on the poor lady. She might have a need fer some prayin' over, seein' the fix she's in."

The wife nodded. "Good idea, Will. She'll surely be needin' some good Christian prayin' over." Her gleaming eyes told Brice she relished the idea.

He thanked the two and took his leave. He'd talk to the sheriff next and turned to the part of town that boasted the sheriff's office and jail.

He walked among the scattered, busy people on the street, not expecting to meet anyone he knew. In no hurry to face that sleazy character, Watkins, Brice would have a few choice words for the man when he did. For now, he didn't want to stir up another incident to endanger Hannah.

Entering the sheriff's office, he approached the desk and introduced himself. "Howdy, Sheriff, I'm Brice Fowler. You've heard of me, I reckon. I'm the skinny surveyor they talk about." He grinned as he leaned over the desk to shake the proffered hand.

"Right glad to know you, Fowler. Jesse Bidwell speaks real high of you and your service to Mrs. Moore." La Force frowned. "Nasty business, lockin' her up, but there's no help for it, with her confessin' the way she did." He shoved some papers aside. "Likely would have brought her in anyway, but tellin' it all makes it easier for us to prosecute the case." Regret lay in his eyes, voice, and the slump of his shoulders. La Force offered Brice a chair and joined him. "She told me how he'd savaged her, and how she feared for her child. Likely the bastard needed killin', but hell, it's agin' the law."

"I'd be glad to testify as to what I saw that night." Remembering that night, Brice felt his anger rise. "Ran for her life, and barely made it to my cabin. Anyone's got the right to fight for their life, and her baby, too. I can't figure a man wanting to kill his own young'un, just can't."

"She filled me in on how you did for her. I'd of done the same, Brice, and I agree she had the right to defend herself and her child. That'll be what the defense has to prove." La Force rose from his chair. "Had breakfast yet?"

"Well, no, I guess I haven't, but I'd like to visit the prisoner before I do. Another thing, Bidwell's at the hotel, might ask him too."

"He's down with the little lady. We'll see if he's hungry." La Force led Brice down the corridor between the cells.

Cat calls were thick and heavy. "Hey, Sheriff, goin' ta visit down yonder, are you?"

Course laughter rang out.

La Force stepped to the bars and threatened, his voice low. "You bastards'd better cool it off or I'll settle the hash of the lot of you, an' if you don't think so, ask old Homer over there, sulkin' in the corner. He'll tell you. The lady's got trouble enough without any truck from no-goods like you-all."

Brice appreciated the sheriff's protective attitude toward Hannah.

Jesse sat on the bunk in Hannah's small, crowded cell. She jumped up at the sight of Brice and stepped to the bars. "Brice, you're here! Maybe the sheriff will let you in to see me. Could you, Sheriff? Jesse was allowed in."

Brice had never wanted to hold her more than right now.

"Maybe later on," La Force said. "Right now we need to have us a confab. We'll be going over to the hotel for breakfast." Turning to Jesse, he asked, "Care to join us in a bite of vittles, Jesse?"

"Why shore I will, Sheriff." Jesse turned to her. "Girl, excuse me whilst I commune with these two for a while. We'll be back soon's we can."

Brice felt her eyes on him.

"I'll be waiting." Her words, though casual, were heavy with love for him.

He didn't want to make too much of their relationship, but hiding his feelings would be difficult indeed.

The men crossed the street to the hotel. The dining room was quiet at this time of morning and their conversation more likely to be confidential.

They ordered and took coffee. "What is there that we haven't discussed?" La Force began. "We need to help this woman, and as sheriff, I'm over steppin' the bounds in askin' it."

"My testimony as to her condition the night I found her in my cabin should be important," Brice replied. " they wouldn't believe that, what the hell would they believe?"

"She's well healed now, so it's just your word and hers against a dead man with his head bashed in." La Force shook his head. "Sometimes these people take it in their heads to go hard on some poor soul. No way to figure that ahead of time that I know of."

Brice frowned at this news.

The food came and they bent to the meal of hotcakes, thick slabs of bacon, eggs, and hot strong coffee.

"You don't make us feel too good, Sheriff, with your talk," Jesse said. "That girl nursed my wife like a faithful daughter, and she don't belong in jail fightin' to save herself from hangin'."

Brice quietly listened, seeking any small sign of encouragement from the sheriff. The man shoveled in his food and had little more to say concerning the case. Brice wondered about Hannah's breakfast. "Sheriff, what's the best way to defend her in this? Is that lawyer fella worth his salt?"

"If we had a witness to her beatings at Moore's hand, that would help out, maybe quite a bit." La Force ate another forkful of eggs. "We don't know anyone who'd ever seen the inside of that house. Why don't you nose around and see if you can find out if there is anyone else who might have seen her in that condition?"

Brice nodded his agreement.

Jesse spoke up. "Good idea, son. We'll mosey around this pile of shacks and see if we hear anything. I'll go all the way to help that young woman. She's the daughter I never had."

Jesse looked grim, and ate sparingly, and Brice wondered if pain was taking his strength again.

Returning to see Hannah, Brice asked her, "In all the time you lived at the ranch, did anyone ever see you all cut and beaten like I did, on the night you came to my cabin?"

"No one at all, Brice. He never brought people around and we never visited any neighbors either. I thought it strange, since most country people neighbor with each other like at Jesse's ranch. I guess he didn't want anyone to see what he'd done to me."

"You had an Indian woman to help with the birth of Thomas. Did she see you that way?" La Force asked.

I don't know where she is, and she'd never speak before a jury of white men." Hannah looked at the floor. "They'd never listen to her anyway, would they?"

"I'd like to talk to her if I can. If she saw you that way, she'd be a real witness, the kind we need." Brice nodded his head, imagining a shy, reluctant witness on the stand. "Maybe La Force can give me some idea how to find the woman."

"She pretended not to notice my cuts and bruises. I could see she feared Jacob and I couldn't blame her for that. Where she came from, I have no idea, and I never saw the woman afterward. Her English was very limited, Brice," Hannah offered.

Her voice bore the tones of hopelessness, and Brice feared she was losing her determination. Saving her baby's life was the price for what she faced now—and she'd do it again to save him.

"Hannah, I'll be checkin' on a few things. Anything I can bring you?"

"Yes, get inside here and hold me. That's what you can bring me." She trembled. "I need the touch of you, Brice."

"One day I'll remind you of that. You may live to regret wanting that much of me, darlin'." He laughed softly and kissed her through the bars.

Brice left the jail and walked the town, hoping to find someone who'd seen Hannah's beaten condition, knowing all the while there was no such person, except an Indian woman, lost to them, somewhere out on the Navajo Reservation. Discouraged, he returned to the sheriff's office. To La Force, he said, "I'll be tryin' to find that Indian woman who helped Hannah with the baby when her time came. That's all we've got. Indian or not, she saw her battered condition, even in the family way. Didn't say a word about it, though. Afraid of Moore. I reckon I can figure that."

"People around here aren't likely to pay any attention to some Indian woman off the reservation. Too many around here think them no better than dogs. There's still a lot of fear where Indians are concerned." La Force shrugged. "Too bad. They've never been overly troublesome in this area, considerin' how the white folks have moved in and took over a lot of their land."

"Hell's bells, that's all I hear. They won't listen to what an Indian woman has to say?" Brice swore. "Dammit all to hell!"

Jesse entered the jail. "Howdy, Sheriff, anything new?"

"Not a lot, Jesse. Brice, you might see that lawyer fella and see what he's come up with."

La Force shuffled a few papers and Brice left him to his work.

They stopped by to see Hannah and found her deep in slumber. They looked at each other.

"Poor little soul, let her sleep. She won't be worryin' for a while," Jesse said, as tears formed. He wiped his eyes and they left the jail. The old man hurt for Hannah as much as he did for himself.

CHAPTER 24

"Any chance of me seein' thet woman you got locked up in here, Sheriff?"

Hank stood in front of the worn, wooden desk, hat in hand, reeking of yesterday's booze. The smirk pasted on his unshaven face set La force off.

"What's your business with the lady? Ain't you done enough hound-doggin' her?"

His very presence here insulted Hannah. La Force wondered what Hank had in mind. Obviously, the man hated her, and, from what La Force had seen of him, Hank's twisted, worthless personality lay at the bottom of it.

"You won't be seein' her until the trial." La Force scoffed at the man. "She wouldn't see you, Hank, knowin' how you've talked all over Flagstaff, tryin' to bring her down. What'd she ever do to you, Hank, run you off? If so, that shows a hell of a lot of sense on her part. Now get your worthless carcass out of here before I arrest you for loitering."

"Go to hell, you son-of-a-bitch," Hank mumbled under his breath.

"How's that, Hank?"

"Nuthin', Sheriff, nuthin."

La Force laughed. Hank didn't want any truck with him or any man who'd put up a fight. Hat in hand, the man shuffled out the door.

Hank saw Brice on the street. In a foul mood after his visit with the sheriff, he called out, "Well, if it ain't thet skinny surveyor feller, a lookin' after his woman. That's what they call you hearabouts." He scowled. "Wonder what the hell she sees in you. Ain't so much to look at no how, nowhere near as good lookin' as me." He spat the words toward Brice as he spoke. "I'll be a sittin' in that court room, you damned bet. Wait'll she sees me lookin' her in the eye, the snooty bitch!"

"You'd better hightail it away from me, you trouble makin' bastard. I've a mind to bash your head in. Might do you some good."

Hank, satisfied he'd made the surveyor mad as hell, grinned, and Brice's anger flushed up his neck.

His scornful look made Hank lash out. Brice figured a good fight would satisfy something in the man, maybe make up for his off-center idea of what the woman had done to him.

"Aw, go to hell, Fowler," Hank snarled. "You ain't my boss no more. She's out'n yer reach now. I seen to that, too!" A smug look crossed his sneering face. "I'll be seeing the yellow-haired bitch get what's coming to her."

A coward, he wasn't up for a fight and, seeing Brice's bunched fists, hurried away.

Hank had riled Brice in the extreme. Not wanting a fight drawing attention to his attachment to Hannah, he withheld his desire to assault the man. She didn't need a brawl carried out in her honor. He'd deal with Hank in due time. The trouble-making scum had it coming. The fact that Hank had accosted her during her days with his crew still burned. Brice could see that hate-filled man sitting in that courtroom, crowing. Getting even with Hannah consumed Hank.

Continuing down the weathered board walkway, Brice felt confused. There had to be some way to contact the Navajo woman, Neebah. He often felt eyes watching him. It gave him an eerie feeling, one he'd had as soon as he'd come to Flagstaff. Not knowing the reason for it, he decided to bide his time. It was a mystery he had no answer to. In a quandary about how to find answers for Hannah, it occupied his mind to the point of frustration.

A visit to the lawyer might be a good idea, maybe clear up problems she faced that he might not know about.

Brice consciously kept an eye out for a likely Navajo. Maybe a man who spoke some English. Someone like that could help him. He meandered slowly along the street, deep in thought. Clouds formed rapidly over the peaks again and he looked for shelter before the daily downpour. The winds gusted and aspen leaves trembled and shook in the breeze, turning inside out as they lashed about. He ducked into the general store, just as the rain came pelting down.

The welcoming warmth inside filled with the familiar odors of supplies—piece goods, harnesses, saddles, and items needed by surrounding ranchers, farmers, and townspeople— gave the store a comfortable feeling.

"Needin' somethin' I can help you with?" Clay Ordway stood nearby to direct Brice toward needed items. "Stranger in town, are you?" he asked.

"I've been in your store before, a while back, just thought I might have a look around." The rain poured in sheets outside. "Might be needin' a few things."

"Oh, my, you're the young man who came in here some months ago to buy ladies' possibles." The quiet, feminine voice belonged to Ordway's wife. She moved quietly to join them.

Brice wondered if she made the connection between him and Hannah. "Yes, ma'am, so I did. Thanks again for your help. Everything was just right."

"Wasn't that about the time old Moore was killed? Aren't you the man who helped that poor little woman out? I hear tell she had a tiny young'un too. We wondered at the things you bought, sure weren't what a lone man would be needin'."

"Why do you ask?" Brice replied, taken aback at the boldness of her questioning.

"We know about the woman prisoner there in the jail house, and how you and that other man go to see her. Just wondering is all. None of my business, I guess. A body can't help what she's thinkin', mister."

Brice saw she couldn't help her curiosity and answered her. "Yes, I did help her. She came draggin' into my cabin in the middle of the night so savagely beaten she could barely stand up, with that baby strapped to her chest, hurtin' so bad she couldn't even hold on to him. She had nothin' but the clothes on her back and a few things for the child. I saw the fix she was in and helped her out. I reckon anyone would have done the same, ma'am," Brice said. Maybe explaining Hannah's plight would help someone to see her side of what happened that fateful night. "Once she got over her cuts and bruises, she took a job at the Bidwell Ranch, takin' care of his ailin' wife. She did well there. They set quite a lot of store by the lady. Never had a daughter, an' took to her right away, baby, too."

"Oh, the poor dear. How terrible the man drove the poor girl out in the middle of the night. But she did kill him, didn't she?" The woman shrugged, holding her hands in a gesture of indecision. "That's not a good idea in this country. Men don't take kindly to somethin' like that around here."

"She didn't know he was dead, just afraid he'd find her and kill them both." With a sense of futility, Brice kept on. "All I know is she fought for her own life and her baby's. You'd have done the same way, ma'am, and your man would have done the same as I did."

"Yes, I reckon so," Clay agreed. "How's a body to know when a stranger comes to your door, what they might have done. As you say, maybe she had the right to do what she did. Little mite of a woman to do in a big man like that."

Brice couldn't determine the man's state of mind regarding Hannah's deed, but did want to catch the feelings of the townspeople toward Hannah's murder charge. In another vane, he asked, "Ever see any Navajos in here to talk to?"

"On occasion, we do. They generally don't want much to do with the *white eyes*, as they call us. The government has pushed their reservation farther out this way. Had to get it done right away so's the Mormon farmers didn't claim it all," Clay told him. "They settled most every place where things will grow. Some of the Indians around here work at odd jobs or ranch work. Mighty fine riders, I'm told."

Hoping for some assistance in locating Neebah, Brice put the question to Clay. "Would you know of one I could talk to?

I'm looking for a woman who might be able to help Hannah. I'd at least like to have a talk with her."

"If I run into one that speaks a little English, where're you stayin'?" Clay replied. "Of course, you couldn't get one of 'em to go in a hotel. It'd have to be around outside somewhere— shy around white folks the way they are."

"If you'd send word to the hotel, I'll talk anywhere. Just send a kid around to let me know, if you would." Brice selected a shirt of soft cotton material and, seeing the rain let up, paid up and left the store. His emotions were strained tight with worry.

As he stepped onto the walkway, the briskly flowing air swept a cooling freshness through the streets. It generally happened after a summer squall, but he paid no mind, as he headed toward the hotel.

He'd see how Jesse held out while waiting to hear from Clay Ordway. Brice had had dealings with Indians in the Texas area. These Arizona natives might just be the same, expecting to be thought of as wild savages, not men like everyone else. *You can't blame them for stayin' shy of us.*

Jesse was gone from the hotel. Seeing Hannah, Brice guessed. When Brice entered the jail, La Force called to him. "Say, you know that Watkins fella? He's been tryin' to get in here to see Hannah. I sent him packin' but he'll keep tryin', maybe even get hisself in trouble to get in here. He's sure a man with vengeance on his mind. No wonder she wouldn't have anything to do with the no-good bum."

"I met up with him," Brice said. "Reckon we'll have a run-in yet, the trouble makin' bastard. I've tried to keep things peaceable for Hannah's sake. She don't need more trouble on her account." He frowned, not understanding how a man could hate that way. "He worked for me. When Hannah came to the camp, he accosted her, and I had to fire his sorry ass. Now he's a mean trouble makin' no-account, livin' off his gamblin' if I heard right. It's the drink, I reckon, that's got to him."

"It may get ugly at her trial. Hope she's stronger than she looks," La Force commented. He rose to lead Brice down to Hannah's cell. "Jesse's there."

Her delight at the sight of him gladdened his heart and toughened his resolve to find someone who could testify on her behalf. "Darlin'! You're a delight to these sore eyes." To Jesse, he said, "Seein' our gal, are you?"

"Find out anything we can use, Brice?" Concern furrowed Jesse's wind-burned brow.

"I'm workin' on a couple things, Jesse. I'll be leavin' town for a while if I find the right guide." Brice reached for Hannah through the bars. "I have an idea how to help you. I'm going to find this Neebah if I can." He kissed her lightly. "So far I have no one who knows who she is or how to find her. I'll keep lookin', darling."

Jesse nodded. "Good idea, Brice, but you know damned well these men around here will never pay any attention to an Indian woman. They just won't, man." His sorrow lined his face and he rose to leave. "I'm done in, Brice. I'll be needin' to visit my hotel room." His craggy face had paled and sweat dripped from his brow. In deep pain, he needed his medicine.

Jesse left, and the deputy allowed Brice to enter the cell.

"Come on over here, my darlin'." He reached for Hannah and they spent an hour holding each other.

Though they were quiet, the other prisoners knew about it and set up a cacophony of cat calls, thankfully, never vicious, just friendly banter from her brother cell-mates. Brice felt relief knowing it.

She had trouble enough and didn't need any from the other inmates.

Lin came and sent him on his way. "We can't have this ruckus in here, Brice. You'll have to head on out now."

Chuckling, Brice left Hannah.

Out in the office, Lin said. "We have a hangin' in a day or two and the boys are riled up over it." Speaking low, he said, "We've tried to keep it from Hannah, bein' she might be headin' that way herself."

"Fine way to talk, Lin. Don't let her hear you sayin' a thing like that. She might panic, hearing that bit of news."

It wouldn't be a secret for long, and Brice wondered if she didn't already know about the hanging. People in these situations weren't usually too kind. If she knew, she'd given no sign.

Seeing the sheriff, he asked. "Say, Jake, where's the lawyer that came to see Hannah? Reckon I'll have a chat with him and see how he plans to defend her or if we can help."

La Force gave him directions. Sick at heart, and worn-out from disappointing opinions, Brice left to rejoin Jesse at the hotel and found him pale, sweating, and doubled over in pain.

"My God, Jesse! Needin' some of the medicine?" Brice had never seen him this bad. "I'm sending for the doc. Maybe he can do something."

"It'll pass soon, Brice. Just hand me the stuff. This is the worst I've had it so far. I hope to hell I can make it through Hannah's trouble. I'd like to live long enough for that. Don't tell her how bad off I am. It'd only worry her, and she's got enough on her plate."

"Well, dammit, Jesse, take more medicine then, or is it runnin' out? The doc'll fix you some more." Brice helped him to the laudanum then left to bring the doctor, despite Jesse's protests.

It had deepened into night as he made his way along the street to find the doctor and, as he passed an area between intersecting streets, a figure sidled toward him.

"White man, you look for In'dan talk English?"

"Yes, I am." Brice looked at the tall Indian. "Man, will you wait for me? I must find the doctor, my friend is very sick. I wish very much to speak with you." He took in the man, his black eyes and hair, skin mahogany from the sun, a beaded buckskin shirt and deer-skin leggings made his outfit. He wore high-legged moccasins with a nice beaded design on his splayed feet. Brice repeated his question. "Will you wait here for me?"

"I wait," the man grunted softly.

"Thank you." Brice shook the man's hand. "Be back very soon. What are you called?"

"Me, Katchee Tsinijinni, long time work tradin' post. Speak purty good English. You come quick, eh? I wait."

"Yes, very soon." With that Brice hurried to see the doctor and found the man at home when he rapped on his door. It opened and he asked, "Doc Haskins?"

"Yes sir, how can I help you?"

Brice introduced himself. "Could you see Jesse Bidwell at the hotel? He has severe pain and his medicine no longer helps him. He's real sick, Doc."

"Of course, I'll go see Jesse. I know him well, and I knew his wife. Damned shame what's happened to those good people." He picked his bag, heaved a sigh, and made to follow Brice. "Lead the way."

"Sorry, Doc, I have to have a chat with someone. Bidwell is in room four on the second floor. I'll come soon's I can."

They parted and, as the doctor hurried away, Brice walked to the intersection where he'd met the Indian. He approached slowly, waiting for contact, unsure of anything with the man. Did he fear white men? He'd have good reason, Brice knew.

"White man, I here." The darkly clad Indian appeared out of the dim moonless night. Scents of campfire smoke, and sweat, emanated from him.

"Thank you, Mr. Tsinijinni." Brice, stumbling over the difficult name, smiled in the darkness. *Maybe at last, I'll find the only witness for Hannah that knows what she suffered, besides me. Oh God, I sure as hell hope so.* Brice felt taut with hope. "Maybe you can help me to find someone, a woman named Neebah."

The man before him stood cloaked in darkness amid the shadows. The earthy smell of outdoor life clung about his person. "Why you look for dis woman?" The dark glitter of Tsinijinni's eyes shone in the cast-off light from Lillie's place.

"I wish to speak with the woman called Neebah. She can help a friend of mine, the lady in jail. My friend said this woman helped her with birthin' her baby out on the Moore ranch. It happened about eight, nine months ago." Brice's voice took on the tone of urgency, though he tried to be patient and adopt a casual mien. He wanted this man's cooperation if it could be coaxed from him. *Does he even have knowledge of such a woman? If so, why would he want to help a white man?*

"Her not here now, go far away—Navajo Nation."

"I wish to find this woman. Can you take me to her?"

"Her go away from bad one. Her man work for white man, Moore, and now Neebah say him spirit walk earth."

"He's dead now. He can't hurt anyone." Glad to impart this news, Brice thought it would help his case. That this man knew of Neebah and could find her filled him with hope.

"Him spirit walk now, no rest for bad one."

With a sinking spirit, Brice saw his one chance slipping away. "Is there no way I can see her, talk to her?"

"Mebbe I talk her, tell about dis woman. Mebbe I find her. I will talk you later. I find dis Neebah. She know many thing." Tsiniginni drew his blanket closer and turned away. "White man, I find you."

"I thank you for helping me," Brice said. "I must speak to this Neebah. She can help my friend. Please, she may be the only one who can help."

"She no speak white man house, be 'fraid," the Indian said this in parting before melting into the darkness, leaving Brice alone in his desolation.

"I'd go out there and find her myself if I could." He spoke into the darkness where the blanketed form had faded from view. *If he can't find her, by God, I will go out there, myself.* His discouragement was tempered by hope and his strong will to free his beloved.

Returning to the hotel he found the doctor with Jesse. "How is he, Doc?"

"I've given him a good supply of laudanum, but as far as his condition goes, nothing has changed. His time is limited at best." Doctor Haskins shook his head at the futility of his ministrations to the ailing rancher. "Damned shame, that's what it is." Turning to Jesse, he said, "Old son, take as much as you're needin' to keep you comfortable. I know you're wanting to help the young woman in jail. I hope this medication will see you through that."

"Thanks, Doc, appreciate your help. I know how it is with me, and barrin' the little lady, I don't mind it so much. I got a lot waitin' for me over on the other side." Jesse shook the doctor's hand. His gray, sweating face bore out his rapidly declining state of health.

Brice saw the doctor to the door then turned to his friend. "Well, Jesse, I found an Indian man who may be able to help us find the midwife. Says she's afraid of Moore's spirit, said it walks the earth. I get the idea that this man knows a lot more than we do about this whole situation. I don't know why."

"Hell, Brice, Moore's spirit probably does wander the earth, bastard that he was. No way to know how or what that Indian fella knows. Just hope to hell he'll take you where you need to go." Jesse managed a laugh. "May's well turn in, can't do more tonight. I'm so full of medicine, sleepin's all I can do."

"See you in the morning, then." Brice turned out the lamp and sought his bed as the wick burned down. "Damn, Jesse, I'm seeing that so-called lawyer in the morning to get his fix on Hannah's case. Hope he's got an idea or two."

Jesse didn't reply and it was long into the night before slumber found Brice's troubled soul.

CHAPTER 25

Daybreak saw Brice up and ready. Jesse was lost again in heavy slumber, and Brice knew he'd used his medicine during the night, and often. The once-burly frame of the old rancher appeared to shrink a bit more each day. Shaking his head in futility, Brice slid quietly out of the room.

He breakfasted in the dining room, and La Force joined him.

"Sheriff, I talked to a Navajo man last night. He'll help me find Neebah, the woman who helped with the birthin' of Hannah's baby."

"Might be a good idea to hear what she's got to say. They don't have much truck with whites, and she may hang back. Most of the men on a jury would scarcely pay mind to any female, let alone an Indian woman," La Force commented while shoveling in thick chunks of bacon and bread sopped with grease and eggs. "Damn shame nobody else saw the fix she was in, kept her away from people, and no wonder. I hear tell he was a hard man. Bastard had it comin' to my way of thinkin'."

Brice nodded in agreement. Breakfast over, he took leave of the sheriff and walked to the office of Herbert Larkin. He found it small, crammed with books and papers, and giving off a musty smell.

Larkin had just walked in, his clothes hastily thrown on, and hair awry from sleep. He looked at Brice, a question on his lips. "May I be of assistance to you, sir?"

Brice, hat in his hands, asked, "I've come to find out how you intend to help a friend of mine, Mrs. Hannah Moore. I'm the skinny surveyor you've heard about." Brice took the only seat available. "I know the lady is innocent. She tried to save herself and her son. Didn't even know she'd killed the man."

"Yes, I had a talk with her. She told me how you helped her that night. To be honest with you, I fully believe in her innocence and that she acted in self-defense. She had to, really." A worried look crossed his face. "Thing is, there's no one to back her story but you, and if your interest in her is what I think it is, a lot could be said to cloud her story, as well as your testimony. They'll say you and she hatched up this deal so you could get her away from her husband. If they do, and sound convincing about it, it could go bad for her, real bad."

"God Almighty!" Brice wanted to pound the man's desk. "All I hear around here is what *might* happen, what people *will* believe, with no one standing up for the poor woman. Larkin, the man was bent on murder! What's so damned hard to swallow about what she did?"

"Well, I believe it right enough. I see she's a fine young woman, and I believe her. But by my experience, I know how these things can go. It's hard to fight a killing under any circumstances, and worse yet, the woman confessed the whole thing to Sheriff La Force. There's plenty of folks that don't hold with raising a hand to your husband, no matter what the reason."

"Anyone would understand a woman protectin' her child, Larkin. My God, why in hell wouldn't they? What if I find a witness to her battered condition? There is such a person. I just haven't found her yet." Brice's heart sank, but he continued. "It's the Navajo woman who helped her when her baby was born. She saw how Hannah looked, all battered and cut up."

"A Navajo woman! My God, they won't pay attention to anybody like that. We'd be laughed right out of the courthouse, Brice."

"Hell, man, if the woman knows what happened, and what Hannah's condition was at that time, why can't she testify about it?" Brice slumped back into the chair. "I'm going to find the woman anyway, Larkin. I reckon that's about all there is. And the fact that anybody can see what a fine woman Hannah is."

"I'll do all I can, Mr. Fowler. I believe in her innocence. The judge is a tough one, too. He doesn't make things any easier. He's square though, certainly, he's that."

"What's his name, maybe I've heard of him."

"Name's Judge Rufus B. Jant, been here for two, three years now. I've tried quite a few cases before him. Don't put up with any nonsense, but he's been fair to my way of thinking." The lawyer went to the door with Brice and shook his hand. "Any witness is better than no witness, good luck to you."

Entering the jail, Brice asked to see Hannah. "How's she doin', Lin?"

Lin escorted Brice down the corridor between the cells. "Pretty low some days, misses her baby real bad."

It was deathly quiet today, too close to a man's hanging, Brice guessed.

"Hangin's set fer tomorrow. Man's a hoss thief. Wonder they didn't string him up out on the trail," Lin added.

Hannah rose from her bunk to meet him. "Brice, oh Brice, how are things? How's Jesse? He's worse every day, isn't he?" She looked at Lin. "May he not come in with me? It would mean everything—just a little while?" Her entreating eyes held the deputy's.

"Why shore, ma'am, I reckon he can." Lin opened the cell, let Brice in, and walked away as Hannah rushed into her man's arms, seeking the warm comfort they held for her. "How I've needed this!" She rested her head on his chest. "Oh God, Brice!"

"Are they treatin' you all right?" Worried, he hugged her back and looked into her eyes with his question.

"Yes, they're nice enough, considering what I'm charged with. Lin makes sure I have what I need. I hear a lot of comments, though, and not all about me. Did you know they'll hang a man tomorrow?" She shivered at the mention of it. "They're trying to keep it from me and I appreciate it, but word leaks out. Oh, I wish we could ride out in the sunshine again—just once!"

"We will, darlin', we will." He held her close, needing it as much for himself as for her.

He heard the false ring in his own voice when he spoke. Did she hear it? Was Hannah losing hope? Was he?

"That parson and his wife came to see me this morning." She smiled, in spite of herself. "They're sure I'm guilty. It's in their every word. I've heard all there is to know about repentance. They didn't get around to Hell's fire but came close. I wouldn't feel bad if they didn't come again." She shrugged. "I hope that parson won't be on my jury." She switched thoughts before going on.

"Brice, I'd like to see Thomas. I have to see him! It's harder every day without sight of him. Who knows? It could be for the last time. Maybe they'd let him stay in here with me just for a little while, maybe overnight?"

The pain in her voice shook Brice. "I don't know, darlin'. I'll send a telegram and ask Lupita if she isn't too far along havin' her baby. You did say she was in the family way, I believe. She could bring Thomas to you. We may have to ask Maria. She'll do it if her father don't raise a ruckus." Brice saw the desperate tears lying close. "Try not to lose hope, Hannah, I'm workin' on something, and I need to leave town to do it. It may be the best chance for you."

"You mean the woman, Neebah. I hope you find her Brice, but whether it'll help, I don't know." Hannah sighed. "She was kind to me and I even had the feeling she pitied me. I've heard that Indian men beat their women sometimes too, but hopefully not the vicious way, like Moore."

"I've made contact with a man who'll guide me. How long that will take, I couldn't guess, and then I'll be away from you, maybe during your trial. Thank God, Jesse's here to be with you. The Indian said this Neebah's afraid of Moore's spirit walkin' the earth. Maybe it does—seems like he'd have gone right down below, but maybe the devil didn't want him either." Brice chuckled at that idea.

"Brice, right now, I'm in heaven just sitting here with

you. I think about being your wife. It'd be right between us. I had to think about it a lot, but I'm ready to marry you." Though she smiled shyly with her words, he knew she was unsure of intimacy, as well as the probable futility of planning any future.

"Hannah, I need to leave you. I'm going out to nose around. Maybe that Indian man will show up again. Is that parson coming back?"

"I hope not, unless they convict me. I might want to see him then." She grinned. "My church at home never went in for fire and brimstone."

"Jesse had a tough night, Hannah I'm worried about him. He wants to see you through this and then he's ready to join his wife, he told me that. It sounds like the man has given up, but in his place I reckon I'd feel that way. If I lost you, I'd feel that way."

When Jesse entered the jail, Brice took his leave. Hearing Hannah's soft voice mingling with Jesse's, was a comfort to him. She had his solid support and had come to love the rugged old rancher.

Brice wandered about the streets of Flagstaff, not sure what action to take. He went into the telegraph office and wrote out a message to Lupita, telling her of Hannah's need to see her baby, and asked her to bring Thomas to his mother. Solnier had the means to bring it about. Brice would have to wait and hope they'd get it done, since he couldn't leave Flagstaff when he awaited a visit from the Navajo.

Drifting about, going into the mercantile, the barbershop, and even to the stables to check on their horses, Brice heard nothing of interest. Returning to the barbershop, he settled into a chair for the "works." His face was covered with a steaming towel, which rendered him anonymous. Quietly listening for comments from townspeople, he hoped to get the tone of feelings regarding Hannah's trial.

"Say, Jack, there's a hangin' tomorrow and people are crowdin' in town already. You goin'?" The voice sounded deep and gruff.

Brice couldn't see who asked and waited for the reply.

"Hell yes, wouldn't miss out on it, Bill. Won't be missin' out when they string up the woman they got locked up, neither. Right bashed her man's head in, she did. Little bit of a thing too, so I hear." He coughed up a wad of spittle and aimed for the spittoon. Brice wondered if he'd hit it. "Ain't had no trial yet," the man continued, "but the judge is due back here any day now. Course, he's got a few in front of 'er, so I reckon it'll be a while yet."

"Hell, Jack, ain't you the ornery one wantin' to see some-thin' like that."

"You fixin' ta go, Bill?" It was asked with a knowing snigger. No one in the town missed these events and they both knew it.

"Might's well if it comes to that. Wife's real upset over it. She thinks the woman did right fightin' for herself and her ba-by. Just might be something' there, too if that's the right of it," he said to the barber. "Hey, leave me somethin' up there, Cal, I don't want my wife to think I been to a scalpin.'"

"Haven't heard what any other folks are thinkin' about it, Bill. There's some around here don't believe in what she done, though. Lot of talk about it, too. Sort of takes the mind off the one fer tomorrow, Don't it?"

Brice heard Jack's reply with renewed interest and took it as a good sign for Hannah that someone believed in her. The barber turned his attention to Brice and he relaxed as he re-ceived a shave and haircut. It took his mind off things for a while and he welcomed it.

He left the barbershop believing no one there knew him. He hadn't been asked, not even in casual conversation. A tremor of apprehension flickered through him, and that made him uncomfortable. Maybe they knew who he was and didn't say anything, believing him mixed up in Hannah's case, the hidden lover and conspirator?

Shaking off his negative thoughts, Brice returned to the hotel and found Jesse laying on his bed, writhing in pain.

"Hell's bell's, Jesse, what's goin' on?"

"Aw, Brice, this is the worst attack I've had yet, and I didn't want to worry Hannah over it, so I left the jail before it hit me too bad," he groaned. "Brice, hand me the medicine bottle, will you? It took hold on me so bad I couldn't get to it."

Brice helped Jesse to a generous swig of laudanum and waited until it took effect. When he saw Jesse relax, he commenced what he had to say. "Jesse, I've been listenin' around town. Some at the barbershop can't wait for the hangin' and some believe she did the right thing. They acted like they didn't know who I was, but I had the feelin' some of them did." He shifted in the chair and hurried to finish. Jesse had become glassy-eyed and was nodding off. "Jesse, I've sent for Hannah's baby, and I'm going out on the reservation with a guide to find the midwife." That was the end of it. His friend was unconscious from the medicine.

He sat for a while. He needed Jesse to stand by Hannah while he was gone with the Indian guide. Would he find Neebah and how long before he'd get back? Brice felt time closing in on him. He'd have to be two men to be where he was needed if Jesse was laid up. He couldn't help what he had to do and prayed it'd it be in time to help Hannah.

CHAPTER 26

A long about high noon the next day, the sheriff led the horse thief out before a loud, partially drunken crowd of townspeople, ranchers, and ranch hands. Brice heard cat calls, snickering, and obscene remarks fill the air, along with the sounds of a woman sobbing her heart out. Even a horse thief like Hack Jones had someone who loved him and would mourn his demise.

When the rope settled around his neck, the crowd quieted with anticipation. They waited to hear any last words he might say. Did he fear death? That titillating thought sent shivers down the spines of many in the bunch as they watched. Brice was sickened by the crowd's participation in the gruesome affair, but a hanging was one of the highlights enjoyed by frontier people. He drew his body up tight. This business held no luster for a man worried that his woman might be next.

The rail-thin parson stood close by and, with solemn voice, intoned a final prayer while the white-faced Jones stood ram-rod straight and tight lipped, ignoring the minister.

Looking down from the lofty height of the gallows, he yelled his defiance at the howling, bloodthirsty mob spread out below—many drunks, some even enjoying a picnic lunch. "You all kin go straight to hell!"

Hannah heard the roar of approval from the boisterous crowd as Jones stepped boldly over the trap door and waited. She stood on her bunk to peek out her only window to see the defiant look on his face. His bravado told them he wasn't afraid, though the pallor on his face said something else.

Hannah turned away and sat quietly, thinking of Brice and little Thomas, two men who needed her.

Brice, in disgust at the raw animal instinct displayed by his fellow man, turned away, but a shock went down his spine when he heard the heavy wooden sound of the trap-door spring. Then, after a short bit of shocked silence, came the quieter comments of the on-lookers, enjoying the spectacle of a man strangling and kicking as he died. Of course, the man was a horse thief and a man's life depended on his horse. It could not be tolerated, and it wasn't.

Were it not for Hannah's situation, the hanging ran true to the normal way of things and wouldn't have bothered Brice. He couldn't help seeing Hannah's slight figure swinging slowly to and fro from that scaffolding, and it chilled his mortal bones. Seeking reprieve from the circus-like atmosphere of the hanging of a horse thief, he headed for the jail to see Hannah.

Jesse had elected to stay with her during the execution. She was aware of everything, and the noisy circus atmosphere of the onlookers upset her. Brice worried she'd be distraught.

Elbowing his way past the rapt watchers of a man's demise, he returned to the jail to check on her and found her frozen to her bunk. "Hannah dear, it's all over now. Try not to think about it."

"Will you say that when it's me swinging out there?" White-faced, she could barely raise her head or look into his eyes.

"Oh God, Hannah, you can't say that!" He reached through the bars. The deputy was at the hanging and Brice couldn't get to her.

"Brice, I just want to hold my baby once more. Could you arrange that for me, please?" She didn't care about anything else. He saw it in her eyes and heard the defeat in her voice. She tried to hold back the tears. "I'll always love you, Brice, and other than that, I don't know what to do anymore. All I know is that my baby will have a chance to live."

"Hannah, that man out there was a horse thief. He stole another man's way of makin' a livin' and that's death in this country. You must know that. You're not the same—you're no killer. They've got to see that!"

Jesse sat quietly on Hannah's bunk, listening to their exchanges. "It'll come out all right, Hannah, dear. I have a feelin' and I'm usually right." He shot her a smile to give her hope. "As soon as Lin gets back, I'll get out and leave you two alone, that is, if Lin lets you in for a visit, Brice." He managed a chuckle. "They sure do go on over hangin' a hoss thief, and this little lady stood on her bunk and saw the whole thing."

Jesse's attitude lightened the mood.

Brice looked in surprise at Hannah. "You didn't?"

She held her head high and returned his look, her lips firm and her jaw tight. "I'm no coward anymore, Brice."

He saw Jesse had improved over his sad condition of last night in the hotel. The pain must come and go, Brice mused, keeping his eye on Hannah.

Time dragged on for Brice. He had no word from Tsiniginni. Her trial was on hold for several cases before hers, thank God. It gave them more time, but for what good? The lawyer had nothing new to offer.

While Hannah waited, some prisoners left the jail to freedom, some left for the state penitentiary in Yuma, a hellish mud-walled hole with cells dug out of solid rock and steel bars set across the front of each. To be sent there was nearly a death sentence. Hannah told him they had a women's section. Which would be worse—the rough prison or the hangman's noose? Brice shook his head at the comparison.

༝༝༝

It was moon-dark when he left Hannah's cell, and as he walked the boardwalk, he heard the familiar summons: "White man, I talk you."

Brice's heart leaped with hope. "I'm here waitin' on you."

"You come along me, go fin' Neebah, she much afraid evil man spirit walk." His blanketed figure emerged from the darkness. "Go early, bring food, need strong horse."

"I'll be ready and damned glad to go with you. I must

speak with this woman. Only she can help my friend, Katchee." He stepped forward and shook the Indian's hand. "I thank you, and will find a way to pay you for this service."

"Sun come up, you be ready, come outside town, north. I wait you." The man turned and disappeared like a wisp of smoke on the soft night breeze.

"Thank you, God. At last there is something I can do for Hannah." Brice cried and headed for the hotel to find Jesse. This could be the chance he needed to save her. They both thought that.

He found the man lying in bed. "Jesse, how are you to-night?"

Jesse had the trace of a smile across his lips. "I guess I'm about the same, Brice. This thing comes and goes on me."

"I've heard from the Indian tonight. He's takin' me to find Neebah in the mornin'." Brice said. "Hannah will be in your hands, Jesse, while I'm gone. I don't know what I'll run into or how long I'll be gone, but it's the best we've got going, the only thing I know of."

"Well, it's sure as hell a chance, Brice. You've got to go. I'll look after the little lady as much as they'll let me." Jesse heaved a labored breath. "I haven't heard from Lupita yet about the baby. I'll be busy here and don't you worry none about Hannah. She knows you're doing your best to help her."

"Thanks, old boy, I guess they wouldn't let me in to see her, this late. You'll have to tell her for me."

Jesse grinned. "I shore as hell will, Brice, first thing in the mornin'."

ℰⱮℰⱮ

The first tinges of pale pink in the eastern sky saw Brice ready with his bedroll and supplies secured behind his saddle. The horse, frisky with the coolness of morning, as well as a good rest, gave Brice a few moments of battle. But good Texas horseman that he was, he got the horse in hand and headed north.

He climbed areas of cinder and shrub, then into tall pon-

derosa-forested areas with thick pine needles carpeting his
way. Of the Indian he saw no trace, but took this as a sign of
the man's natural caution. He'd learned to trust his feelings
about Katchee.

After several hours, he heard a soft whistle and the Navajo came up next to him, riding a white man's saddle on his
paint horse. Brice, happy to see him, called, "Good morning to
you".

"You come dis way, white man." He grunted the soft
Navajo accented words, indicating a northerly direction.

"Call me Brice, I'd like that."

"Unh, I call you Brice. You call me, Katchee, okay you?"

"Sure as hell, Katchee, okay me."

Nothing more was said. They climbed for another hour,
and at first, Brice caught glimpses of vast expanses of purple,
orange, ocher, and many shades thereof as they skirted through
huge trees. In a bit, the trees thinned into scrub oaks and cedars
as they started down a long steady slope into the vast, wide
reaches of open country.

Lonely stretches of seemingly empty, scattered mesas
reached into a hazy horizon as Brice and Katchee entered this
different landscape, one Brice had never seen. The mystery of
its vast reaches seeped gently into his mind as he followed the
Indian across the wild, tangled vistas into his homeland. Brice
thought little could grow there and wondered how the people
managed to eke out a living when it appeared so barren and
waterless. A beauty, such as he'd never seen, held him in a
state of enthralled awe. He couldn't help wondering if it had
been surveyed.

They descended slowly onto flat, open, and desolate
plains, with gullies and canyons that held green trees and occasional spots of water. It grew much warmer in the lower altitudes, and Brice divested himself of his coat and gloves. He
grew thirsty and drank from his canteen. Katchee didn't seem
to need water and, as time passed, Brice wondered if he did
without food as well.

After many hours, they stopped under the scattered shade
of twisted and dwarfed cedar trees to let the horses rest.

"Brice, want eat?" Katchee asked.

"Reckon I wouldn't turn it down. I have a few things in my pack if you'd care to join me." Brice offered thick meat sandwiches he'd gotten from the hotel kitchen. The worse for wear, they wouldn't last much longer in the heat.

The Indian took a sandwich. "Um, dis good meat." He ate without further comment. Thirsty, he knelt near a small pool and drank at length, putting his face deep into the water.

Brice followed suit, knowing he had much to learn if he was to survive this ride into the unknown lands of the Navajo. He found the water cooler when he held his face lower in the pool. He filled his canteen and watered his horse before they began again on the long ride to find Neebah.

He thought constantly of Hannah, wondering if they'd survive this trouble. Would they have a life together? He didn't know, but he'd do the best he could. She was the first woman to make him feel that way. He continually imagined living his life with this soft, feminine woman. Thoughts of it filled his mind with endless possibilities, and a smile spread across his lips.

They rode into sparsely settled red sands, interspersed with clumps of twisted cedar and cone shaped, pale-colored mounds that looked to be piled there by the workings of men, though he knew they couldn't have been. It added to the wonder of the land. Occasionally, they passed mound-shaped dwellings that Katchee called a *hogan.* Brice learned it meant a house. Sometimes small children played about and scampered away at the sight of strangers.

At dusk, Katchee pulled to a halt under a twisted grove of cedars. He threw the reins of his sweating horse over the branch of a tree.

Brice decided the winds and dryness made the cedars stunted. Survivors of a harsh land, they struggled for water and fertile soil, finding little of either. He noticed the leaves were deep green and emitted a pleasant odor. Worn from the long ride and worry, Brice rested in their shade.

"We sleep here, Brice." Katchee said. Later he added, "You want eat?" His face was expressionless, but his eyes held a gleam of satisfaction. This was his country and he knew very well how to make out in it.

"Yes, I reckon I could do with a bite of grub. I have a few crumbs left in my pack." Brice offered what he had left of lunch.

"I make food," the Indian said and slid away on silent feet, saying, "Make fire, Brice."

Gathering dry cedar faggots, Brice made a conical pile and lit small bits of bark and twigs beneath it. The smell of cedar smoke met his nostrils most pleasantly. It was peaceful, waiting and watching the smoke drift about on a wayward breeze which followed his every move. He lay back on his saddle, waiting for Katchee.

The Indian returned, holding two fat rabbits in his outstretched hands. He smiled at his catch. "Now we eat."

He quickly skinned them and gutted the carcasses. Putting a slender branch through them, he propped them over the glowing coals.

Brice stepped up to turn them at intervals. "Looks great, my friend."

With gusto, they ate the roasted rabbits, ignoring occasional bits of hair and grains of sand. They drank their fill of a nearby trickle of water and hobbled the horses in a patch of tough stringy grass that grew where it could. Brice felt deep satisfaction with his guide thus far. The man was smart, resourceful, and was certainly his pass into the lives of the people he'd meet out here in this wonderful land of lonely ridges and dunes.

"Brice, you want dis little woman for squaw?"

"Reckon I do. She is a good woman, very gentle, and has a fine boy child as well."

"Mebbe we find Neebah. Mebbe, she help. She much afraid of devil man."

Katchee's bronzed face was expressionless in the firelight and Brice felt a growing respect and friendship for this man of worth.

Nothing more was said, and they sought their beds. Brice lay awake on his hard bed, watching the stars gleam overhead.

His thoughts were ever of Hannah and her tiny son. They were his as far as he was concerned. The breeze blew a few ashes about. This place was very peaceful, and he would have enjoyed it immensely, were it not for his desperate mission.

The morning saw them off again. Brice already felt dried out and lean as a piece of beef jerky. The country changed, growing increasingly desolate and dry. Vultures circled about overhead, waiting, watching, for the scraps of a kill made by another creature, or some unfortunate traveler who'd lost his way. Brice shivered at the sight of the circling scavengers and appreciated the skills of Katchee all the more.

Later in the day, they neared a *hogan*. Several small children scampered behind the building to peek out at them with great round eyes. A man came out to meet them, *"Yah-ta ay,"* he said, his hand raised in greeting.

"Yah-ta-ay," Katchee returned, greeting the elderly man. After suitable verbal exchanges in Navajo, Katchee indicated Brice.

"Welcome." The old man waved his hand and nodded in greeting. He motioned Brice to dismount and enter the home.

Brice did as beckoned. The round house was floored with rugs of many colors and designs. The walls held tools, pots, and skins, among other items strange to the eyes of a white man. He nodded. "Hello, and thank you," to the squat, black-eyed woman sitting near the back of the dwelling. He heard quiet giggling from her as well as the curious children who peeked in at the door, giggled, and skittered away when Brice took notice of them.

Katchee explained the reason for their travels to them and nodded to Brice the affirmation of his actions. "He like you, Brice." He indicated the old man.

"Does he know of Neebah?" Brice hoped he wasn't in too great a hurry, pushing for information.

"He know, he say she go to land of big stone mountains. He say she have people there—husband."

With this knowledge, Brice felt futility edge into his thoughts.

"We go," Katchee added. "We find dis Neebah, Brice."

Brice voiced his gratitude. "Thank you, Katchee."

They pushed on after partaking of cold mutton, a flat sort of bread, and a dish of acorns or pine nuts offered by the old man's wife. It was good, he decided, if strange to him. The nuts were not bitter as he'd expected. He expressed his thanks to the man and woman and winked at the children as they took their leave. Brice heard them chattering when they rode away.

Turning eastward, they rode steadily until dusk.

"We stop here for sleep," the Indian said. He foraged once again and brought in three small hen-like birds.

Partridges, Brice thought, and damned welcome, too. They roasted them to a wonderful juicy brown before he tore into his share. He thought he saw a trace of humor cross Katchee's face. "It's damned good, you know that. Thanks again to your hunting. A mighty hunter, you are, Katchee."

"Go sleep, white man."

Brice wanted to laugh, but kept silent. "Good night, Katchee," he said and slept heavily. His aching body, so desperate for rest, accepted the harsh desert earth. It seemed softer than before.

CHAPTER 27

Starting early, they passed through increasingly difficult terrain. Their mounts slipped and plodded over the rocks until Brice's horse threw a shoe and they drew to a halt. He had no way to replace it and no choice but to go on, knowing his horse would be lame in short order. The hard and rocky ground cut rapidly into his hooves. Having always been shod, his hooves were not hardened against the rocky shelves and rock-strewn mountainsides.

When it became obvious his horse could go no farther, Katchee said. "Need horse, Brice. I find." He left over a rise.

Brice sat down under a ragged pinon to let the moving air cool his sweat-stained head. His eyes burned from the sun, and parts of his skin exposed to the fierceness of the rays had burned, peeled, and turned to an even darker bronze. "I've always been an outdoor man, but I'm turning into a strip of jerky on this ride. Hannah won't even know me when we get back."

He thought of her, wondering what was happening, and if he would get back in time with Neebah.

After several hours, Katchee returned with a bony Indian horse. "He strong, not much look good." He handed Brice the rope holding a dun colored gelding that looked like he'd seen better days.

Brice removed the tack from his mount and placed it on the scrawny horse. "What about this horse?" He indicated Jesse's stock horse. "Turn him out to find what he can?" He already knew he had to do just that, knowing Jesse would understand the loss of his horse. Brice had left Roamer at the Bidwell ranch and couldn't help feeling glad about it. He'd hate to part forever with that faithful horse.

They set off again, and Brice found his new mount close to torture with his short jouncing walk, but the bony nag was sure footed, managing the rocky terrain with desert-hardened hooves. Brice appreciated him for that.

Climbing high into a pine forest, they enjoyed the coolness of a ride beneath towering aspens interspersed with strong, straight, black-trunked firs. He wondered if the Navajo had gotten off the track, but kept his council. At length, they came out on a high precipice, and Brice gasped as he looked over the purple depths of a vast valley, stretching miles upon miles to the horizon.

Placed whimsically by the hands of the gods were uncountable masses of rock, weathered and shaped by eons of winds, rains, and sand storms. Unbelievable beauty lay before him overlooking the valley of stone mountains as mentioned by the old Navajo they'd met.

"Unbelievable!" Brice said as he gazed out over the vastness. "These are monuments, each one a marvel of nature!"

They stayed the night on the cool heights under the tall pines that graced this high mountain precipice. The gobbling of wild turkeys as they settled in the trees out of harm's way drew Brice's interest. "What the hell is that?"

Katchee laughed. "Big bird, he good eat."

"Hell, you say. Let's get us one if they're good eatin'."

"They wild, not easy catch him, Brice, you want try?"

"You bet, let's go huntin'! I could do with a big meal before we go down into that wonderful valley full of sand, rocks, and who knows what else." Unspoken were his desperate thoughts of finding Neebah.

They set off on foot, padding softly on a thick mat of pine needles, careful to avoid twigs that snapped or any other noise to warn the wily birds of their coming. Brice's blood ran high at the adventure of it.

At length, drawn by the putt-putting sounds of roosting birds as they settled for the night, they spotted several rows of turkeys roosting above them on some of the lower branches, safely out of reach of a stalking predator.

Katchee putting his finger to his lips in warning to Brice, brought out a loop of cord, and fashioned a sort of lasso. Creeping closer, he made ready to rope one of the big birds. With a soft whistle of moving cord, he settled the noose over a sizable tom and jerked him to the ground in a fury of thrashing wings, talons, and beak. The resulting furor caused a wild fluttering of wings and gobbles of hysteria among the remaining birds. They flew off the tree limbs into the darkness, crashing onto the ground or into brush and trees, making them easy prey to other animals for the remainder of the night.

"Good, Katchee! You've got him!" Brice quickly slashed its throat with his knife and the big bird hung limp in their hands. They returned to camp with a good catch of meat, enough for a day or two. Brice thought they might take a few more, but to destroy a life when the food would spoil before being eaten went against the common sense of both men.

After plucking and cleaning the carcass, they built a green wood frame over the remaining coals and set the bird to roast. It would hold better cooked and they spent long hours tending it. After roasting sufficiently, they each ate a good bit of turkey meat. Tough though it was, Brice found it delicious to his semi-starved palate. They covered the rest of the carcass in leaves, a bit of canvas and hung it in a tree to keep it safe from hungry night hunters.

Katchee laughed. "Maybe big bear come, he eat meat."

He settled himself to sleep, and bade Brice the same.

Disturbed by the yowling of huge mountain cats, called puma, and the hooting of owls, Brice's worry over a stalking bear never materialized and, with thoughts of Hannah, he finally rested.

∽∾∽

Morning came, and sizzling pieces of turkey made their breakfast. A full belly gave him needed strength to begin the descent into the wondrous valley of monuments where Neebah would be found. They wound their way about the huge trees, heading downward, ever downward, and the trail became narrow and torturous with sliding rocks and rolling boulders. They dodged and slid, as they worked their way down for hours. The temperature climbed at lower altitudes, creating further discomfort.

They finally reached a wide area of sand dunes and gullies full of green growth and occasional short streams of water that meandered for a distance before disappearing beneath the sand.

To Brice, this extremely rough and rugged place created a magic of its own. Nearing one of the great weathered stone monoliths, he saw how the wind-carved contours lay in sun and shadow, creating a magnificent work of nature.

He wondered if these monuments were held as objects of worship by the native people, and by observing the worshipful attitude of Katchee toward them, concluded they were. If these magnificent wind-carved monoliths held religious importance for the Navajo, he reasoned, why not? This place could only be a creation of God. These ancient people easily recognized it and worshiped the Gods that lived there.

Without warning, the strong winds created a boiling turbulence. Looking northeast, Brice saw a massive wall of orange tinged dust slowly covering the blue of the sky and enveloping every living thing with swirling clouds of smothering, choking, rust colored dust.

It whistled and roared as it rapidly overwhelmed them. They took cover in one of the washes and hunkered down beneath thick brush to wait it out. Katchee covered his face with his blanket, wetted down with water, and Brice followed suit. After an hour, a stinging, lashing rain washed everything clean, and soaked them to their skins.

The sun came out again, bathing everything in brightness. Mounting their horses, they continued on.

"Hell's fire!" Brice commented. "That was one damned blow!"

Katchee grinned. "We go, white man."

This was the place he'd find Neebah. Was she here in this

strange and lonely place? Could he prevail upon her to come to Hannah's aid?"

ల౩లు

With Brice gone, Hannah's days dragged on endlessly, and she drifted between optimism and hopelessness. Keeping track of days became difficult.

The lawyer came to see her regularly, but never with positive news, or ideas. "You must tell me about Moore, your routine at the ranch, and the abuse you suffered. I need to understand Neebah's service to you and the events leading to the assault on your husband, including the flight into the night with your child. I'd be able to present a clearer picture to the jury of that desperate night." The man worked hard to find a way to help her, but she thanked him with little hope.

Her saving grace was the constant care and concern Jesse offered. He visited often and brought necessities, new clothes, and a few books. Lin let him in to see her. The ailing rancher became increasingly ill, but neither of them mentioned it. She realized it was the same way Leatha had been with her husband, and he with her. Bad news was hard to speak of. Hannah understood that easily enough.

She needed him more than ever with Brice gone, and thoughts of his demise frightened her. Jesse Bidwell was all she had. Brice had gone searching for a witness into a vast and terrible wasteland. Would he ever come back or did he lay dead somewhere? Would she ever know?

Jesse appeared one day with a beaming smile across his weathered face. Hannah sat up and cried in joy as Lupita appeared, carrying Thomas.

"Oh, my God! It's my Thomas! Lupita, thank you!" she cried in her happiness at the sight of her baby son. "He's grown so big," she babbled with joy.

Lin let them into her cell and watched her take the boy into her arms. She cried into his clothes for a moment and held him too tight. He squirmed, and she held him out for inspection. Thomas wasn't too sure about her at first, but soon knew her and babbled as he reached for her face and hair. She delighted at his attempts to stand and walk alongside her cot on his chubby legs.

Lupita beamed in joy at what she'd been able to bring about. Her husband and Jesse waited outside the cell. "Hannah, *mon cherie,* how does it go for you?" She giggled at her ability to speak a bit of French.

"I'm well enough, but let's see you!" Lupita's slightly protruding abdomen took Hannah's attention for a moment. "You are happy, then?"

"Si, senora, I very happy. Pierre, he good man." She turned rosy. "He make *casa muy hermosa* for me." Amid Lupita's happy chatter, Hannah saw a dark shadow cross her eyes, a slight coldness crept over her, but it was soon lost in the joy of seeing and holding her child.

"I'm happy for you, Lupita." She looked at Solnier, who'd come to stand outside her cell. Handsome and dapper as ever, Solnier beamed at Lupita while she sat with her friend in the dark jail cell.

"Senora, we go back soon, I weesh to take *Tomas* with me." Her eyes turned to the little boy and told of her love for him. Hannah in her desperate hour of need seized upon this offer of help with gratitude.

"Oh, yes, Lupita, he may go with you. I thank you for that. I don't know if I'll ever be free, or even live. Lupita, if they hang me, this will be the last time I'll ever see my boy!" Tears flowing down Hannah's cheeks bespoke her thanks more than words.

"Oh, senora, do not say a thing so sad!" Lupita sobbed for her friend's pain. Meanwhile, Thomas gurgled to Lupita in his baby way and reached out to touch her hair with chubby hands.

"He loves you, Lupita, he always did, right from the first day you met each other." Hannah wasn't sure how much of what she said got through to Lupita, but there was never a question that she would love Thomas as her own.

"*Senora, Maria es aqui.* She help with *Tomas,* and me, when my time come." She proudly indicated her enlarging belly and grinned sheepishly.

This came as a welcome surprise to Hannah, since she worried Lupita would be overburdened with both babies. At least now Thomas would have two mothers in her absence. "That's wonderful, Lupita." She looked to Jesse, seeking his approval of the plan.

"Sounds good, Hannah. Thomas will be safe with them." He left unspoken his relief that the baby would have loving care. In his declining health, he'd not be up to it. They saw him heave a sigh of relief. He'd been standing outside the cell with Solnier, his face pale with fatigue and pain.

Lin came and sent them out then turned to Hannah, who'd kept her child for the night. "I have something to tell you—the date has been set for your trial." His look of concern said more than Hannah wanted to know.

With dread, she waited for him to enlarge upon his message.

"Your trial will begin Monday next. I know you've been a wantin' to get it done with, ma'am. I shore hope it goes the right way for you." He turned to leave. "That's a mighty nice little feller you've got there."

He left and Jesse returned alone. "I heard about the trial date, Hannah."

He sounded lost when he said it, maybe knowing how it might go, but smiled his best.

Hannah held her child and prayed for Brice to return. "As long as Thomas is cared for and has a chance at life, I believe I can handle anything they might say against me at the trial. No matter what happens to me, I know what I did was right. I had to do it. I hope Brice gets back for the trial. Oh God, I need him so."

The distraught expression on her face must have hurt the old rancher deeply and she regretted it.

"Brice is doing the best he can to find Neebah. He didn't know how long he'd be gone. His biggest concern was he wouldn't get back here before your trial. Now, looks like he won't."

Jesse's worry made Hannah say, "He wanted to be here, but he's doing the only thing he knows to help me, Jesse."

"I know he is, girl." Jesse took his leave of Hannah, saying, "If you have everything you need for Thomas, I'll come back in the morning. Lupita's outfit is leaving then. She has to travel slowly these days." Hannah knew he returned to his hotel to take a good dose of the laudanum. It would help him—for a while.

Exhausted with worry, Hannah sought her bunk. Her greatest joy was seeing her child and knowing he was safe. In her heart and mind, she inhaled the warm baby smell of him, his tiny face, and his chubby body. It felt so good to hold him in her arms and hear his babbling as he examined her face, hair, and looked into her eyes. In her prayers, she blessed Lupita, her new and beginning family, and prayed for Brice's success.

That done, she squared away in her mind to face what was to come. Her baby was safe in her loving arms tonight. Sleep found her as she curled around her baby, breathing in his scent, and they both slept well.

CHAPTER 28

Brice and Katchee moved rapidly over the soft sandy floor of a long, shallow depression. The horse's unshod hooves found relief from the punishing, rocky shelves and areas of broken ground. The going was better, but the high sand banks cut off much of the winds and turned the heat and burning sands into a suffocating furnace. Brice emptied his canteen and silently hoped they'd find water soon. What had looked so ethereally wonderful from afar now burned and dried Brice's very soul.

To Brice's thinking, it bothered Katchee none at all. Either that, or he put up a tough facade. In silence, they rode on until they came out onto a high, long slope leading close to one of the huge stone monoliths. "My God!" escaped from Brice's cracked and burning lips. "These damned things are a hell of a lot bigger than they looked from up there. They're mountains!" He whistled as best he could from his parched lips.

Coming to another shallow depression, they entered a pleasant area of grass, trees, and water. That Katchee had known of it was a given. Brice, wondered how well Katchee knew the area and decided he knew it well.

"We rest here, Brice."

They dismounted, led the dusty horses to drink, and did the same for themselves. "This is a welcome bit of a green, Katchee, but this valley of monuments is not for the weak or faint of heart for all its beauty."

Brice threw himself on the grass, took off his hat, and let

the breeze cool his sweating head and body. They shared some of the turkey, with a few grains of sand included, and added a few pinon nuts to the mix. The water in the draw was cool and slightly alkaline in taste. The men and horses drank their fill.

"Why does this woman believe Moore's spirit wanders the earth?" Brice asked. He felt he intruded on native beliefs in some way, but hoped for an answer.

"She say he long in house and bad when men come. Her man work 'round ranch. He see dis. Man need be covered soon and hogan burn up to clean. She say his spirit much angry, like bad man."

Brice felt Katchee's discomfort discussing Navajo beliefs on death. "No wonder she believes that way," he replied, "being evil like he was. I said the same thing. Even the devil didn't want the bastard."

Knowing how the woman felt about things might help when he met her. He nodded his thanks to Katchee. Looking out over the huge valley, he wondered where they would search for her, but knowing this man, maybe he already knew.

✦✦✦

The next morning, Hannah said her goodbyes to Thomas, Lupita, Maria, and Pierre. They came to her cell for a few moments to collect Thomas. She'd feasted her hungry eyes on his baby face for as long as she could and held his little body in her arms while he slept, knowing it could be for the last time. She couldn't stop her tears, but smiled bravely. "Thanks for your care of my son, Lupita. May God bless you and your child to be."

Lin opened the cell door and slid the iron bars back. She whispered her last words to Thomas and reached out to pass him into another woman's arms. As Lupita reached out to take him, her sleeve fell back and Hannah saw a large, dark bruise, slanting down the outer aspect of her arm. Hannah's blood ran cold at the sight! Lupita started at her reaction, said nothing, but her face had gone white. Wordlessly, she passed out of Hannah's sight, carrying Thomas in her arms. Sick with apprehension, Hannah watched Pierre guiding her along by her elbow as any dutiful husband would.

Her scalp turned to ice and she wanted to scream her questions to Lupita! Was that handsome, dapper husband of hers in reality an evil brute? Could there be some other explanation for the dark bruise on her arm?

In jail and unable to care for Thomas, Hannah sank to her knees to pray for the safety of her child. His safety, even his life, lay in Lupita's care now, and they'd left on the long, arduous journey to Seligman. Had she placed her helpless child in danger?

Jesse came soon after in good cheer, thus well medicated, and frantically, she told him. "I saw a big, dark bruise on Lupita's arm. Could her husband be abusive?" She gasped in pain and worry. "They have my Thomas—have I sent him into a dangerous situation?"

"Hell's bells! I hope there's another reason for something like that, Hannah. Surely he's a better man than that. Please, God, this will be over soon. We'll get your baby and go home." She heard the longing for his home and the peace he waited for. But in his voice, she also heard the deeper meaning—to rest beside Leatha.

"I hope so, Jesse, oh how I pray for the end of it all, too." Hannah struggled for answers. She hated that he'd become so heavily involved in her troubles. He loved her, but the strain of her murder trial and the surrounding heartache, further wore on the rugged old man.

"Don't worry over Thomas. Lupita loves that child as her own. If anything is going on, she'll protect him, you can be sure of that." He sighed. "I hope all this is wrong. It's all based on one bruise, isn't it?"

"I cling to that, Jesse, and hope you're right."

"Are you prepared for the trial, Hannah? Parts of it could get ugly. Hank will be testifyin', you can be sure of that. That mean-son-of-a-gun wouldn't miss out on gettin' in a few licks at you."

"He tried to get in here to see me, Jesse. He wants to have the laugh on me. It'll be hard to face that kind of hate." Hannah shrugged. "Whatever happens, I'm ready for it. It's been hanging over my head for so long, I'll be glad to have it done with. Maybe I'll be found innocent, maybe not, but I couldn't do anything other than what I did."

"Be strong, Hannah, like you've been all along. It takes a brave woman to fight like you did. Maybe that'll swing 'em in your favor." His face had gone ashen, and pain filled his eyes. "I'll have to go back to the hotel and rest, honey."

"I see that, Jesse. Try not to worry over me. You've been so good taking me in. I won't let you down, no matter what happens."

Later Herbert Larkin came to see her. "Well, we're set for it, ma'am. Are you ready for this trial?" He wore a quizzical expression. "I haven't seen young Fowler around lately—any word?"

"Nothing, Herbert, he's looking for the midwife, that's all I know. Mr. Bidwell is here and will come for the trial. He's my only friend, anymore."

Hannah worked to put a cheerful face on the forthcoming events and found it exceedingly difficult. She worried about Lupita and Thomas. That she was helplessness to do anything in that regard angered her and brought desperate tears. "I'll be glad to get on with it. I know you'll do your best for me."

"I certainly will, ma'am." The lawyer sat with her for long hours, going over every detail. It brought all the horrors back again, and the trial would add to that substantially. "See you tomorrow, Hannah. Wear your best dress. Look like the lady you are." With that, he left her.

Hannah felt exhausted from her long hours with the so-called lawyer, found her narrow bunk, and pulled up her blanket. "If they find me guilty…"

ℰᏏℰᏏ

After two days of wandering the valley of stone monoliths, meeting and talking with people in hogans they found scattered along ledges, gullies, and long grassy depressions, Katchee and Brice rode into another long valley with grass and trees. A steady little stream kept everything green. Rows of corn, planted in clumps with beans, grew thick, dark green, and lush. A few goats grazed among the plantings.

Brice wondered why they were in a garden area. "Wouldn't those goats be destructive to the garden?" he asked, observing the fertile growing area.

"Goat eat weed, good in there," Katchee offered.

Going farther, they saw the home where they'd been informed, Neebah lived with her husband. The rounded house faced the east to catch the first rays of the rising sun and was set near a sheltering wall of black-and-orange-streaked sandstone amid two or three shade trees. Several chickens clucked softly while scratching in the red-tinged earth for tidbits.

"This is a right nice place here," Brice commented. *Could this finally be the home of this illusive woman I seek?* He held his breath in fervent hope.

"Come, we see."

Katchee dismounted and indicated for him to do the same and together they approached the dwelling. There were no locks on the homes of Navajo people and anyone who passed by was welcome to enter and make use of whatever he found or needed. For Brice that was no different from any western home. Strangers were always welcome. It often meant their survival.

They bent down and entered, only to find it empty. "Mebbe with sheep, belong her, all sheep for woman." He shrugged. "We wait." He settled himself on a tussock of thick green grass after freeing his mount. Brice followed suit. The clear water in the amber tinged stream was cool and sweet to his dried lips and parched throat.

Anxious though he was, Brice relaxed and dozed off while they passed the afternoon waiting. If Katchee did the same, he had no idea about it.

Late afternoon sun still warmed the air when they heard the tinkle of bells. Anxious, with pounding heart, Brice waited to meet Neebah.

They sat in the shade, watching for the herder. Tinkling bells, scraping of tiny hooves, and confused baa-ing of ewes, who hunted for lost lambs, gave evidence of an approaching flock.

The band came in view with a squatty older woman herding them. She edged them into a large corral near the stream. She wore a gathered purple velveteen skirt, topped with a bright green tunic studded with silver coins sewn in various places. She wore buckskin boots, calf high with beaded designs on them as well as fringes of buckskin trim. Nearing the Hogan, she saw the two men who waited for her. Brice saw her face blanch pale when she saw him.

They rose to greet her just as a man approached from the wooded area behind the home. Meeting together, Katchee spoke to them.

Brice heard a long exchange of greetings, which he took as offers of hospitality. With an invitation to the home, the two men entered and took seats in the proffered area.

"Dis Neebah Gray Wolf and her man, Manny Alchesay," Katchee said. "They welcome you."

Brice nodded his acknowledgement of them. He looked at Katchee. "Can you ask her what I wish to know?"

"Soon, white man, eat first."

And Brice had to wait. Neebah glanced at him but averted her eyes if he looked her way. She went about her business, preparing food. Over her cooking fire, she placed a pot of cooking grease. When it was very hot, she mixed the dough into round balls, then flattened it into a circle and made a hole in the center before throwing it into the smoking grease. He saw it puff and brown slightly as she turned it side to side with a forked stick. She made a stack of these and set them aside to cool. Then she put a pot of cold mutton stew over the coals and, in time, they enjoyed the stew and bread. She had a crockery pot of golden honey to top the leftover bread. Brice drank only water, though some sort of brew was offered.

The meal over, they sat together in the hogan. Katchee spoke to both the man and woman at length. Brice saw Neebah's eyes widen in alarm.

She spoke then to Katchee, and Brice knew it was for him. He waited patiently.

"She know more than what he did to your woman," Katchee said. "I ask her come Flagstaff and talk white judge. She say white man's hogan must burn to free him spirit. Him spirit can sleep, not walk here."

"Fine, we'll do that. No one would live there after what happened. You say there is more that she knows? Has she told you?"

"She want tell you."

Brice directed his attention toward the woman. "Neebah, what is it you have to tell me?"

Trembling and with shaking hands, she moved close to Brice. Softly in his ear, she began her say. She kept her voice very low as if to say it aloud would bring dreaded calamity upon them all.

He felt his face grow cold while he listened in disbelief to her words. "My God, Hannah *did* know what he intended for her. Somehow down deep, that poor, defenseless little woman knew his evil soul!" He asked her very gently if she would tell what she knew to the white judge, his voice nearly pleading with her. This woman could help Hannah if he could get her to speak before the magistrate in Flagstaff.

"When evil one's house burn, I talk white man." She looked into Brice's eyes. "You good man."

Later, trying to sleep, Brice mulled over the horrific things this woman had told him. The judge had to hear her story, Indian woman or not. He'd see to that. Please God! Let it be in time for Hannah!

CHAPTER 29

Hannah determined to wear her bravest face for the trial. She dressed carefully in one of the new dresses Brice had brought in, one with a high neck and long sleeves, and a blue print that complemented her eyes. She brushed her hair to a high buttery sheen and, though her hands trembled with anxiety, plaited it into a thick braid that hung down her back. Jesse came to wait with her. He'd brought his medication with him, and he'd taken one dose already.

"Hannah dear, don't be afraid. It just might come out right for you. I can't see how they could go hard on you. All they have to do is look at you to know you're a good, decent woman."

She appreciated his reassurance but he cared for her and wanted a positive outcome. "Thanks, Jesse, I'm glad you're here with me. I hope Brice finds help for me. I know he's trying. Having you two on my side means the world to me. It gives me strength. I'm as ready as anyone facing the hangman's noose could possibly be." She uttered a half laugh.

"Hush, child, don't talk that way."

Footsteps sounded in the passageway and they looked up to see Herbert Larkin. "It's time, Hannah. The sheriff's coming for you. I'll walk in with you and Jesse and it'll be up front in the courtroom."

La Force appeared, unlocked the cell, slid the bars open, and stepped in. He held handcuffs before him. "Sorry, ma'am, I'll be puttin' these on for now. Maybe I can take 'em off later." He snapped them over her slender wrists, being careful they weren't too tight. "Let's go then."

He took her elbow and assisted her to her feet. Even now, La Force was her friend, and it comforted her.

In solemn procession, the four left for the courthouse. The other inmates quietly offered their support.

"Good luck out there, ma'am."

"We're hopin' fer the best, ma'am."

"Sheriff, you watch out fer the little lady now, ya hear?"

"Hey, lawyer, do better fer her then ya done fer old Hack Jones!"

"Shut ta hell up, you dumb bastard!"

She heard a scuffle.

"Beggin' yur pardon, ma'am, fer the cussin'."

Hannah couldn't help but smile as she heard the encouraging comments from her fellow inmates. To a man, they favored her side in the case. Though she hadn't met any of them, she felt accepted and even the worst among them had kept his language along decent lines.

The building used as a courthouse lay across the street. She walked beside the sheriff toward it and whatever awaited her, but, she couldn't cross the street without loud murmurs from the onlookers. They'd all waited to get a look at the female defendant, or murderer, depending on their point of view.

"Ain't very big, is she? Wonder where she got the muscle to do what she done, takes a mite o' strength to smash a head in, don't it?"

Loud guffaws accompanied that comment.

"Looks all prim and proper, the little lady does. Hard to believe what they say about her, ain't it? Coulda fooled me."

Tired of the many comments, and leery of crowd mentality, La Force shot a menacing look at the throng. "All right, move on out of here. This ain't no damned circus. Move away or you'll be in the hooscow yourselves."

He made a tentative move in a man's direction, and she saw the man shrink away. To Hannah, it was obvious La Force had control of the situation.

The crowd quieted some, but Hannah heard mention of

"lady killer," "hammerin' Hannah." Raucous laughter accompanied the comments as well as shushing from some quarter.

Having run the gauntlet of townspeople, she finally reached her place in the front of the courtroom. La Force sat her in the chair and turned her over to Lin who took a seat next to her. "Jake has got to accuse you in this case, him bein' the one who took down the evidence, did the investigatin', and brung you in to jail."

Lin's information and sympathy warmed Hannah. She gave him a look of appreciation. He'd been a good friend to her, as much as he could, in seeing to her needs and comfort. "Thanks, Lin," she managed.

She didn't see the judge. Herbert Larkin sat on her other side and Jesse as close as he could. He'd be a witness as to her character and had good standing in the community. If only Brice sat on the other side! In her fear and apprehension, she wondered. *Why is it when I need him so terribly, he's always gone somewhere? I understand why, I do, but I wish he could be with me during this horrible trial!*

She sat with her back to the crowd of onlookers and was grateful for that fact. Hank Watkins had to be among them, and she'd eventually have to look into his hateful face, knowing how hard he'd worked to put her here. Even so, facing Tug Parker would have been infinitely worse. She sometimes saw his little piggish eyes glaring with lasciviousness and hatred in her nightmares, but he'd met his maker and deservedly so. With Hank, she could look him straight in the eyes with pride. She had done what any mother would have done, and if they never believed her, so be it. She took a deep breath and readied herself for the trial ahead.

The judge walked in and a hush settled over the little wooden courthouse. He came from the back, and turning, Hannah caught a look at the man who held her future in his hands. It depended on the jury to decide her fate, but this man had power even over them.

He stood tall and gaunt, middle-aged, with course, unruly gray rimming the bottom parts of his thinning black hair. Thick bushy eyebrows hung heavily over his piercing black eyes. His clothes were dark, of homespun fabric, and he wore them with dignity. His no-nonsense persona stood out to the unruly crowd before him and, by the hushed quiet in the courtroom, she sensed they greatly respected this man.

He took his seat. "Harrumph!" He cleared his throat. "Now, Sheriff, what's this crime we're here to decide?" He directed his attention toward La Force. "Have you selected the jury, Jake?"

"Not yet sir, we waited for you. We'll get 'er done right now, Judge."

Hannah turned to Herbert Larkin. "Please don't let them pick Hank Watkins or Parson Elkins. Hank hates me and the parson and his wife believe I'm guilty. I realized that when they came to visit me in jail. Maybe it's because we didn't come to his church."

"I'll attend to it, ma'am. Thanks for telling me. I wasn't aware of that."

In questioning the crowded room as to service on the jury, a forest of male hands were raised. Jake and Herbert Larkin questioned each in turn.

"I'd be real willin' to be on thet jury, Sheriff," Hank declared as he stepped forward, clearly eager to sit in judgment against Hannah.

"Don't think we can use you, Hank," La Force objected. "You got too much a'gin the lady. What's your say, Larkin?"

"I agree, Sheriff."

Hank muttered his disappointment and slunk back into the crowd. Hannah sighed with relief. He wouldn't be sitting in judgment on her, but he'd have his say later in the trial and his chance to spit his venom toward her.

The only other objection was toward the parson when his turn came to volunteer. The rise in voices and tone of the crowd expressed their wonder about the refusal of the parson. Larkin gave no reason, and his request was granted. Hannah wondered if a woman or two on the jury would help her case.

With the twelve men seated in their chairs, Judge Jant turned to La Force and asked. "Well, sir, what's this trial all about? Let's get on with it."

"Well, your honor, a man, one Jacob Moore, was found dead with his head bashed in about eight-ten months ago. When he failed to claim his stock at roundup, some of the boys went lookin' for him and found the man alone in his home. He'd been layin' there for some days, Judge. In lookin' the place over, we found a few female things scattered about, some baby clothes. Wasn't much of either, I can tell you. It looked like an old wood box was fixed up for a baby to sleep in. Nobody'd heard he'd had a woman out there, or ever caught sight of one, never neighbored outside of round-up, far as anybody ever heard." La Force looked over toward Hannah. "The body was in real bad shape, Judge, couldn't hardly tell what happened by the time we got there. Put 'em under right quick, I can tell you."

The murmur of the crowd bordered on humor at the mention of a rotting corpse. The judge banged his gavel for order, along with the narrowing of his eyes beneath his bushy brows.

"Get on with it, Sheriff. Where's all this heading?" His forehead furrowed, and his lips thinned.

"We couldn't figger out just what happened for a long while. Then we got a report of a young woman and her baby travlin' without a husband an' in company of a surveyor feller when she was seen." La Force paused then continued, if reluctantly. "I got to wonderin' if the man, Jacob Moore, and a woman were married here and visited the parson." He indicated Parson Elkins, "Turns out they had a record of the marriage and the parson's wife described the lady to my satisfaction, so I went to the surveyor's camp. The boss was gone an' the cook said he'd taken the woman and baby into Seligman and put them on the train to the East, back where she came from. I thought that was the end of it, but it wasn't."

La Force took a long drink and went on: "A big cowboy that got hisself shot here recently told of seeing a young woman and baby out to the Bidwell place, described her to a tee. I went out there for a look-see, and found this young woman working there taking care of Jesse Bidwell's ailin' wife." He indicated Hannah. "The poor lady was deceased by then, but she and her baby stayed on."

"This young woman we see here in the courtroom?"

"Yes, sir, she was Moore's wife. She told me everything that happened, and I have to say, I believed what she said."

"Where is this surveyor? He might have something to say in this matter."

"I don't reckon I know, Judge, maybe the little woman can have her say. She'd know, if anyone, his whereabouts. They spent a lot of time with each other." Hannah saw it hurt La Force in what he'd had to say, but the truth was the truth, and he was one to tell it.

The judge bent his look on Hannah. "Little lady, will you step up here?"

"Yes, sir."

She kept her voice as strong as she was able. She knew when she faced the crowded courtroom, she'd be looking into Hank's smug face. She held her head high and stood before the judge.

"Just have a seat right there, ma'am." He indicated a huge wooden chair set to face the crowd.

Hannah took the seat, faced the crowd, and was sworn in. Hank's gloating, grinning face stood out in bold detail, before any other, the same sneering man she'd known from the surveyor's camp. He was scum and she coolly returned his look, showing him her low regard.

"Now, ma'am, say your name, and where you're from."

Hannah did as requested, hating again to say the name, Moore. His bestial cruelty had brought her to this. "I came from Ames, Iowa, to marry the man. They call someone like me a 'mail-order bride.' I had only known him about an hour before we were married."

"Let's hear what happened out there at the Moore place. Now you just take your time. We are not in a hurry here today."

"Well, sir, everything was fine for the first three months, but then he began having rages of temper about everything and began hitting and kicking me, throwing me against the wall. He knew we were going to be parents, but he never stopped his cruelty to me. That last night, I knew for certain he would kill me and our baby son as well. It was in his eyes, Judge." Hannah's own eyes filled with tears, remembering. "I had to get away from him or see us both dead. I waited until he was asleep from drinking. I grabbed the only thing at hand and swung it hard against his head so we could get away." Hannah breathed deeply, trying to keep herself together. She took comfort from Jesse's steady gaze of encouragement and solid, comforting presence.

"I put the baby's things in a saddle bag, saddled a horse, and rode away. I hurt so much it was hard to stay on the horse, but I rode as far as I could. That's when I found a cabin and met the man you call the surveyor. His name is Brice Fowler, and he works for the Land Banks. He saved my life that night, sir."

"Where is this surveyor fellow?" Judge Jant asked.

"I don't know. There was a Navajo woman who acted as midwife. She saw my battered condition and he's gone to find her. I don't know if he's all right or even alive." Hannah choked back a sob.

"Why does he look for this woman?"

"He thinks because we plan to be married one day, and no one except him saw my injuries, you wouldn't believe him." She ignored the warning look from Larkin.

Too late. She'd said too much, but couldn't take back her testimony. She frowned with worry. *Now, for sure, they'd never believe Brice.*

"Who is this woman he searches for, Hannah?"

"She is a Navajo woman named Neebah. She helped me when my son was born. She was the only one I had. My husband didn't stay around to see me through the birth of his son and had no interest in seeing or even holding him. He didn't care about the baby or me. The woman, Neebah, saw how beaten and bruised I was, and she's the only one, sir."

Aghast at the effrontery of the idea, the judge exclaimed. "My God, woman, a Navajo squaw! You don't know her whereabouts, and if your man finds her, testimony from a native woman wouldn't be counted in a court like this. She'd never come in here to begin with or be allowed to testify."

Judge Jant's words caused raucous laughter from the crowd and Hannah's hope faded.

He quelled the outburst from the crowd then, addressed her. "Anything else you got to say, ma'am?"

"Nothing more that I can think of, except my son lives because of what I did, and I'll never feel regret for that, your honor—never!"

"Anyone else have something to say?" the Judge asked.

Hank stepped forward. "You bet I do. I got a lot to say, yer honor."

The judge dismissed Hannah and had him take the chair. "Go ahead, young fellow, speak your piece."

"Well, sir, she came out to that surveyin' camp, totin' her young'un. She was thick as thieves with our party chief, right close, she was, wouldn't take any body's offer of help er nothin'. They had something goin' on between 'em, I saw it plain as daylight. Mebbe she killed her husband to be with that skinny surveyor. That's what it looked like to me."

"Did you see any signs of the woman in question having been beaten or otherwise physically mistreated?" Judge Jant asked Hank.

Hank preened, his chest puffed out at the importance of his testimony. "Naw, sir, Judge, I never saw any sign of nuthin' like that. She looked all dressed nice, an' her baby too. Just hung around the boss, she did."

"All right, Hank, you may step down."

Hank stepped back into the crowd with his chest out and a smug self-satisfied look on his face. He'd done his duty and his snide look at Hannah as he returned to his seat told her his hatred ran deep.

"The hell with what that jackass says!" Jesse roared. "This little woman came to my ranch ready to work for her keep, and she did just that. Nobody could have taken better care of my poor Leatha than this fine girl. She hardly knew Brice Fowler when he brought her to my ranch."

"Yeah, that's why she came there, Jesse. She was a hidin' out so she could get away with killin' 'er husband. That's it, an' you know it," Hank shouted, red-faced.

Hannah saw Jesse's face grow livid, as the old man turned to have a go at Hank. "You're a Goddamned liar, you rotten bastard!"

The judge banged his gavel several times. "We'll have order in here or you'll both be thrown out."

Hannah was worried that he was becoming over wrought and would take ill again. "Please, Jesse, that's enough. Thank you for your defense of me. I'll never forget it." She got up from her chair and reached to help him settle back in his chair.

Judge Jant listened quietly. The truth came out best when anger reared its ugly head, but he held up a hand. "All right, Hank, shut your face, you've said enough, and I'll hear no more from you." He banged the gavel again to confirm his words. To Jesse, he said, "Tell me about Mrs. Moore's coming to your ranch."

The rancher took the witness chair. "Well, your honor, Brice Fowler had been by the ranch a time or two and the last time he was there, he mentioned a woman with a child who needed a place to earn her keep. I needed a woman to help me care for my late wife and said, bring her to the ranch and we'd see." He smiled at Hannah. "She's been a blessing to our home, Judge, and we've never seen any sign of a mean streak, just a loving mother alone in the world with a baby boy to raise and no man to help her."

Hannah felt tears rise at his loving words.

"Did she tell you the trouble she was in?" Judge Jant appeared to see the pain and weariness in Jesse's eyes, and his voice became conciliatory.

Jesse wiped sweat from his pale face. "Not for a long time. She told us just before the wife died. But Brice, the surveyor, laid it all out for me in the beginning. He wanted me to know everything about her."

"That'll be all for today. We'll have court again in the morning. Jury, you boys are dismissed and keep your ideas to yourselves, if you please."

Jant banged the gavel to finalize his decision to adjourn. He rose from his chair and left the room.

Hannah sat in a daze, believing things had gone against

her.

Lin came to Hannah's side, bade her accompany him back to her cell, and she was more than glad to go. "Maybe Brice will make it back before I go to the courthouse again," she said. He was always on her mind.

Jesse rose to walk beside her. "Jesse, please go and rest," Hannah said. "You look tired and it scares me to see you so pale."

Herbert Larkin had taken his leave as well. He hadn't said a word to her, either of encouragement, or of defeat. She hadn't even noticed his departure.

Jesse sighed. "I believe I'll just do that, honey. I thought it went pretty well today, didn't you?"

"I don't know Jesse, I just don't know. Hank didn't help, except to show everybody what a nasty, vindictive person he really is."

Hannah's voice had gone flat, and she kept her face expressionless. She needed Brice, and Thomas. She needed her life back. Jesse turned to go his way.

There were other comments as they left the courtroom, but Hannah scarcely heard them for the roaring inside her head. Exhausted, she stared straight ahead as they crossed the dusty street. Thomas worried her. Seeing the long, dark bruise on Lupita's arm made her wonder about the young woman's situation. Hannah wondered if she'd ever ride out in the sunshine again with Brice—a hopeless dream, a long way off.

In the quiet of her cell, Hannah flopped on the bunk and lay there, staring at the ceiling of rough, thick planks. It was an old jail. After hearing they were building a newer one, she whispered, "It won't be in time for me. Where are you, Brice?" She saw a baby face floating above her. "Thomas, my little boy, are you safe and well? Is Lupita happy, or does he beat her, and she lives her days in fear? My son, I pray I'll be able to come to you, and we'll have a good life with Brice."

Wondering if God would grant her freedom and bring these things to pass, she fell into a fitful sleep.

Jesse entered the jail just as Lin was taking supper to her. She awakened at the sound of his voice.

"Can I see Hannah? Poor woman had a tough day at court."

"Shore, I got to take her this chuck. She'll be glad to see you, Jesse."

Hannah waited while Lin let him in. He sat on the end of her bunk while she picked at her food. "Jesse, have you heard anything from Brice? He's been gone so long, I fear something has happened to him."

"He said it could take a while. Neebah is afraid of Moore's ghost or something. If he finds her, will she come with him?" She saw the worry in his eyes as he added. "Honey, I'll have to testify tomorrow, and I'll do the best I can to help you."

"I know you will, Jesse. I couldn't ask for better than how you've been to me." She smiled lovingly. "I'll take what comes and be glad to be done with it. Hanging's better than being sent to Yuma, so I might have some choices." She laughed bitterly at her own dark humor.

"Aw, honey, don't go sayin' stuff like that!" Shaking his head, he grinned at her.

The moment of lightness helped her, and she thanked him for the visit.

Herbert Larkin came. Still trying to find other witnesses that might help. "Maybe I'm not a good enough lawyer for you. I've always thought I was pretty good, but I see trouble ahead. They've more witnesses against you than we have for you. Even Jesse has to testify. He knows you and Brice are committed to marriage and that won't be in your favor, I'm afraid."

It was deepening dusk outside her tiny window. As Larkin left, she felt the darkness closing in around her. She lay down to rest. Her mind whirled with the events of the day and, try as she might, nothing cast a glimmer of hope her way. "Brice, where are you tonight?" she cried, muffling her sobs in her blanket.

CHAPTER 30

The next morning, she returned to the courthouse with La Force and Lin at her side. After yesterday, she had a better idea of what she faced and had mentally prepared herself. Hank had done his talking, and as long as he didn't yell out in the courtroom, she wouldn't have to listen to him unless he took the stand again. Then she'd have to look at his malevolent glare of hatred.

Jesse came in behind her and took his seat. "Mornin', Hannah." His smile gave her additional courage. She realized he must be well medicated. He looked very comfortable, a little giddy and glassy-eyed as well.

Without fanfare, Judge Jant entered, sat down at his bench, and banged his gavel for attention. "Harrump!" He cleared his throat. "Now where did we leave off this case, yesterday?" He nodded at Jake La Force.

La Force stepped up. "There's the merchant's wife, the parson and his wife, Jesse Bidwell, and the surveyor if he's here. There might be a few more as would like to have their say. How's that with you, Larkin?"

"About right, Sheriff."

"We don't know where Mr. Fowler is at this time, Judge. He's still out looking for the Indian woman."

"Haw, haw, ain't no Injun squaw can talk in this here courtroom, Judge, how'd somethin' like that look?" Hank yelled out, obviously hoping to wound Hannah more than he'd done already.

"I'll be the judge of who speaks before me, Hank. If you don't keep your yap shut in my court, you'll be thrown out." Jant banged his gavel on the wooden desk. "Let's hear from Jesse Bidwell."

Jesse stepped up and sat beside the judge. "Your honor, I met this little lady when the surveyor feller brought her to my ranch. Said she needed a place to stay and would work for her keep. Well, my wife was ailin' with only some of the Mexican women to tend her when I couldn't. I needed someone nice and gentle like. My wife took to her right away and her baby son as well. Right nice baby she has, takes real good care of him, too."

Jesse looked fondly at Hannah as he spoke. "She stayed on after my wife died. I didn't want to put her out in the world to fend for herself with her child. I'd have to say, I've become very fond of them both."

"Did you see any signs of her having been beaten, Jesse, any cuts or bruises?"

"No, Judge, she'd healed up right nice by the time she came to us. The surveyor, Fowler, told me how she looked when she stumbled into his cabin in the middle of the night, said she nearly died that night." Jesse shrugged. The way the wind was blowing, he feared the court would hold out for proof of her injuries. "I've been ranchin' around here for years, Judge Jant, and anyone will tell you I'm an honorable man, and don't go fabricatin' things."

"Thanks, Jesse, we might need to hear more from you later."

He called Clay Ordway's wife, Sarah, to the stand. He talked in a soft tone, and Hannah was glad the judge treated her gently. Though the lady was acquainted with most of the town folks, she appeared tense and nervous sitting in front of them in a situation that could decide a woman's life.

"Now, ma'am, I understand that soon after Moore's murder, the surveyor, Fowler, came in your store for women's fixin's and what not. Care to tell us what you can about that?"

"Yes, sir," Sarah began in a tremulous voice, her hands clenched together in her lap, "A nice young feller in all, dressed all nice and neat-like, different from the usual cow-boys we see around, you could easy see that. He asked if I would make up a pack of possibles for a woman, you know the more private clothes and needs for a female about my size and colorin'. He asked me to put in a few sewing things, some material for baby things, a hat, and blue dress, too."

She looked down at Hannah and shook her head. Regret lay in her voice. "He seemed right flustered to be askin' for such, I might add."

"Anything else you'd remember? Did he pick out any of the personal stuff?"

"No, sir, he was shy about things like that for a woman. Had me do it all and wrap it up for him to take. Kind of a shy sort, he was." Hannah saw her face light up as she suddenly remembered. "But he did pick out the dress, your honor, said the color would look good on her."

"Thank you, ma'am, you may step down." The judge dismissed her and called the preacher. "Parson Elkins, your turn, if you'll so oblige the court."

"Yes, sir." Elkins took the seat eagerly and waited for the questions. His thin, pale face wore the animated look of antici-pation.

Hannah knew he thought her guilty of a terrible sin and in sore need of God's judgment.

"Tell the court what you know of the Moore family."

"Well, what I and my wife remember is that they showed up out of nowhere and got themselves married. Right off the train, she was, never seen 'em before or since, your honor. They both seemed nice enough fer people that don't go to church regular. Far's we know, never went a'tall, neither of 'em."

"That's all you got to say, is it?" Jant looked to the wife sitting quietly waiting for her turn to speak. He beckoned her to come forward.

She exchanged seats with her husband. "Yes, sir, your honor."

"Any other information you have to tell in the matter, ma'am?"

"Well, sir, he seemed to be a gentleman to the woman. He took her arm to help her when she walked in and when she got into his buggy. He seemed like a real good man to me, Judge." She smiled a self-satisfied look at Hannah. "We never saw hide nor hair of either of 'em after that day. They never came to services or meetings, not even once, sir."

Hannah heard a snicker, but didn't see the gloating look cross Hank's face as he sat in the quiet courtroom. She'd forgotten his existence.

There couldn't be much more to say about the case. It must be almost over. Hannah held her breath. Was there anyone else that might wish to speak?

A weathered man wearing cowboy garb, stood up. His hair was red, tinged with gray. "I might have a bit to say, Judge."

Judge Jant leaned over his bench to get a closer look. "Well, sir, name yourself and speak your piece."

"My name is Ash Hardy, an' I own the Slash Five. It's just west of the Moore place. I never was asked to come to his house, Judge, sir. He was a neighbor and a loner. Never did a sociable thing as I know of. Worked hard at roundup, and that's all any of us saw of the man. We went to his house when he failed to show up fer his share of the roundup, cuttin' his calves and notchin' the ears. We found him, and it weren't a purty sight, Judge, head all caved in on the one side where blood had been a'runnin' out the ear and nose. The flies had been at him, we could see that much. We're the ones called Sheriff La Force here. If he was beatin' on his woman, I couldn't say, but somebody sure beat him all to hell. Not a pretty sight that tore up, bloody place. It looked to me like a big fight went on in there, too."

He bent a long look down toward Hannah, and it made her wonder what else the man knew of Moore.

Judge Jant dismissed the rancher. "Thanks, Ash, you can step down if you got no more to say."

Hannah felt the icy sensation of defeat stealing into her belly. There was no sympathy in Ash Hardy's testimony, none in fact, other than the mercantile owner's wife, and little comfort could be taken from her words. Hank kept his steady gaze directed toward her, almost constantly, and she could almost feel his gloating eyes burning into her back.

How could any man hate that much? It gave her a sick feeling in the pit of her stomach seeing the animosity flowing at her. *I did nothing to him! Every woman has the right to decide what man she wants to be with, doesn't she?*

Jesse stood before the court. "Judge, I'd have a few more words to say in this woman's behalf, if I might."

Hannah knew his medication was wearing off. Beads of sweat had formed on his brow.

"Why shore, Jesse, Have your say."

"It's beginnin' to look like this here fine young woman is being railroaded by the testimony given so far. Why is it so hard to believe her husband beat the livin' daylights out of her, month after month, even while she was in the family way? She was healed up on the outside when she came to us, but inside she was scared to death of any man she'd see."

Hannah worried Jesse was overdoing on her behalf, as he went on. "I've never seen a better mother than she's been to her baby, and a fine nurse to my poor wife. She's a very gentle woman, and I'm here to say I believe her story, and Moore, the rotten bastard, got what he deserved!"

"Thanks, Jesse, but while you're standing there, why don't you tell the court about Hannah and this Brice Fowler. Are they thick with each other? It's my understanding they're planning marriage. Isn't that so, Jesse?"

"That's right, Judge, they plan to be married whenever she gets shut of this killin' charge. She was afraid of him or any man for a long time, but eventually he got around her fear—of him, leastways. Brice wants to take care of her, maybe make up for what she suffered at that devil's hands. He's a fine man, Judge, make her a good husband and father to her boy."

Hannah feared Jesse had said too much, making it look even more like she and Brice could have plotted Moore's death.

"All right, Jesse, thank you, that'll do."

Gray of face and sweating, Jesse returned to his seat. Hannah saw him take a small bottle out and drink from it. It must be his medicine, and she was glad he'd brought it along. She needed his support, and while he sat there, she knew at least one or two people were on her side.

"Well, if there's nothing else anybody's got to say, let's close this case and let the jury decide what happens to this woman. Larkin, you're actin' as this woman's attorney. You got anything to say for this woman? You haven't done anything so far to help the case."

"Yes, Judge, I have a few things to say. First, I believe my client is innocent. We don't have reliable proof as to her condition on the night of the killin', but in knowing the woman and meeting the young man who aided her in her hour of need, I believe them both, and their story."

Hannah knew the man presented her case the best he could, having little to work with.

"Jesse Bidwell is a man in good standing in this community, and he believes her story too. I'd like to ask the court for the right to have Brice Fowler and any witness he brings in to have their say. It's only right, Judge Jant, and being an Indian woman shouldn't matter."

The judge had to quell the uproar from the courtroom. "Hold it down, you lot. Continue on, young man."

"She's got eyes same as you and me, and we need to know what that woman saw when she helped Hannah with the birth of her child. If she saw my client all beaten and bruised, that would make a difference in whether anyone here will believe her story." Larkin turned to the crowded courtroom. "It'd be the only right thing to do, Judge Jant." Wiping the sweat from his face, Larkin looked to the judge for approval of his request.

Hannah realized the lawyer knew his business when he requested the judge to hear any evidence Brice might bring in.

"Well, Larkin, I can't hold up the deliberation, but if we hear from the surveyor, we'll have a listen. That's the best we can do." To the crowd and the jury, he said. "If we've heard all the testimony, and there's nothing more to be said either way, we'll hand it off to this jury." His words brought Hannah's heart to a standstill. He turned to the jury of plain, honest men, some from the town, and some from surrounding ranches and farms, waiting for their chance to do the deciding. "You fellows have heard what's been said, and now it's up to you to decide the fate of this young woman. Did she defend herself and her child that night, or was she planning to run off with the surveyor and killed her husband to get free of him?" He took a breath. "That's what this case boils down to, and now it's up to you." He banged the gavel on his bench "Court's adjourned for today unless you get right to it."

The men of the jury huddled into a tight circle, and their voices mingled together. No one moved out of the courtroom. They waited for the decision. Frequent outbursts were heard. Hannah sat in a daze with Jesse, her hands clenched tight in his.

"Aw, the hell you say!" a man on the jury shouted.

"I don't know about that, what about—God, what a mess!"

Their comments, kept in lower tones, and hard to catch, offered little comfort to her.

Hannah grew tired and sick inside as she sat between Jesse and Herbert Larkin, waiting for those twelve men to decide her fate. She whispered to him, "Thank you, Herbert, for the nice things you said. I know you did your best. You didn't have much to go on."

Jesse looked better after taking the last slug of medicine. She was glad for his comforting presence but it was more than she could bear waiting for those men to decide life or death for her.

The twelve men deliberated for close to an hour, then stopped and turned to the judge. "We've got it decided, your honor."

"What is your decision, then?" Jant asked.

"Your honor, we find this woman guilty of killin' her husband while he lay asleep and helpless. She may have had good reason, we don't know fer sure about it, not bein' there, but it ain't right sneakin' up and bashin' a man's head in while he's asleep. If she's got another man, it wasn't proved to us, either. She's guilty of killin', we know that. She confessed it herself."

Hannah nearly fainted at the verdict. Jesse supported her with one arm and Herbert with the other. She gasped. "Oh God, my poor baby, he'll have no mother now!"

She was too shocked to cry. Her spine tingled, her face felt tight and dry, and her tongue was so thick it nearly filled her mouth.

"Serves ya' good an' right, ya snooty bitch!" Hank's vindictive mocking voice rang out in the courtroom. "Killed 'um, didn't you?" He laughed. "I knew there was sumptin' wrong about you all along. By God, I knew it!" Like a crowing rooster, he spat his vicious words at Hannah.

"Hank, shut your ugly mouth or I'll slap you in jail for disturbin' the court." La Force stood over the jubilant malcontent. "Git on out of here!"

Hank never moved, but he did shut his mouth. "I'll be quiet, Sheriff, jest want to hear what they'll be doin to 'er. I got the right. I'm a citizen, ain't I?"

La Force sneered into Hank's mocking face. "So you are, you damned maggot!"

Hannah, sickened by the hate directed toward her, clamped her jaw, held up her head, and awaited her sentence. Her heart hammered so hard, she thought it might burst. Would she die or go to Yuma Prison? She didn't know which fate would be worse. Would she see Brice's face once more?

Jesse put his arm around her for comfort.

Judge Rufus B. Jant banged his gavel. "Order, folks, order in this court!" He cleared his throat and began. "It grieves me to pass sentence on this young woman because there might be more evidence on its way, but the case is over and the verdict is in. Young woman, stand up and face the court, please."

Hannah complied and the judge passed sentence. "In accordance with the laws of Arizona in this year 1894, I hereby sentence you to be hanged by the neck until you are dead. This sentence to be carried out in twenty days." He banged his gavel. "Case dismissed and court adjourned." He stood up and walked slowly out of the courtroom, his shoulders slumped.

Hannah saw him shake his head at what he'd had to do.

She stood there, frozen, and her heart nearly stopped as reality sunk deep. She was to hang! "Jesse!" She couldn't say more, no tears, no weeping, only stunned silence. She sat down, felt no comforting touches and heard no kind words, as her boy's face drifted before her. "My baby!"

Jesse and Larkin sat with her until La Force came to them. He put the handcuffs on her slim wrists and helped her to her feet. "Got to take her back now."

As they walked toward the door, she saw the gloating look on Hank's face when she passed by. La force commented. "Sorry, ma'am, they sure didn't show you any mercy, did they?"

Hannah got hold of herself. "I knew it could happen, Sheriff. Maybe Brice will get back before it's too late. He's been gone so long, I fear something's happened to him. It's a big, barren place out there, isn't it? A man could get lost and never find his way?"

"Ma'am, he's got an Indian guide. He might get hurt, but he won't get lost."

She walked steadily beside La Force. His masculine scent comforted her somehow, but the trial was over, and her fate settled. If Brice was lost out in that wild place he'd gone, except for Thomas, she didn't care anymore.

Jesse followed. "Hannah, I believe I'll go to Seligman and see to Thomas. If he's doing all right, at least that'll ease your mind."

"Oh, God, Jesse, can you do that? At least, I'll die at ease if he's in good hands." She turned to embrace him, but the manacles on her slim wrists prevented it. Tears filled her eyes. "Jesse, I know how sick you are. It'll be very hard on you. I don't know what to say."

"It won't hurt me any more than sittin' around here doing nothing. Maybe I can help you that way. Seems I wasn't able to do you any good in court. I'll go easy and take my medicine along. I'll take a boy from here to do the drivin', just like a big city feller."

"You have my undying thanks. Undying, strange word to use, isn't it?" She uttered a tinny, hopeless little laugh.

"Hold out hope that Brice will make it back in time. If he's found this Neebah, and the judge'll hear what she's got to say, things might go different, then," Jesse said. "It could happen, girl."

Returning to her cell, she felt and heard the stunned silence of her fellow prisoners. Saying nothing, she accepted their silent regret at her sentence. Some of them faced the same fate, she knew, and had no feelings about it. She fell onto her bunk and lay there, quietly staring at nothing.

She refused her dinner when it came and turned her face to the roughened brick wall. "Oh, Brice, do you live? Will I ever see you again?" She cried softly to herself, thinking of all she'd lost in life, and sobbed silently and deeply into her rustic pillow. She didn't want sympathy from anyone and mentally prepared herself for whatever lay ahead.

CHAPTER 31

A week later, Lin came to tell her she had visitors. She prayed it would be Brice. Jesse had gone to Seligman with a young man from the stables, to drive for him. With anticipation she'd waited daily for Brice or Jesse.

Utter disappointment filled her senses as Lin ushered the preacher and his plain little wife to her cell. "Here's your visitors, ma'am"

Will Elkins greeted her. "Howdy, ma'am, we thought to come and bring you some Christian comfort and councilin'. We're sorry to hear about your sentence an' all, and want to help you prepare for the hangin' they've set up for you."

"Dear, if there is anything we could do for you in your hour of need, we'd be happy to help you," Martha, his wife offered, an expression of sadness and compassion on her long thin face.

Hannah felt the edge of her hypocrisy and the message in her pale, glinting blue eyes. She knew instinctively the woman's real thoughts. *You sinned and got what you deserved, you back slidin' hussy!*

In an even and controlled voice, Hannah replied, "Thank you both, but haven't you helped me enough already? Your sympathies are with my brute of a husband, not me. You wouldn't believe the truth from me or anyone who backed me. I feel glad now we never attended your services, but then again, if we had you'd have seen my cuts and bruises. Your sainted Jacob Moore would never have let that happen. We never once had a visit from you, nor did he ever bring anyone to the house. He kept me prisoner out there, with no one to turn to in my trouble. If you'd paid us a pastoral visit, it might have saved me from the hangman's noose! No thanks for help at your hands. It's too late for me or my son, who'll soon be, motherless." With that Hannah turned away from them and said. "You folks may leave me now—I wish to be alone."

"We'll be prayin' for you and for your soul, Mrs. Moore."

Hannah never looked at their departing backs, but did say loud enough for them to hear, "I need prayers, but not from folks like you, and I do not wish to be addressed as Mrs. Moore. I haven't been that for a long time."

She hoped she wouldn't have another visit from the parson and his skinny wife. If they came again, she'd refuse to see them. But the next morning, she had another visitor.

She greeted Hannah. "I'm Mrs. Ordway, name's Sarah. I wanted to see you to let you know we believed your story. My husband is a dear kind man and what happened to you is strange to me, but I hear tell of men like that. I met your friend Brice when he came in to buy things for you. He was mighty shy about it, too, a right nice young man, very gentlemanly in his ways." She sighed. "How are you makin' out, my dear, settin' in here day in and day out? Would you like some sewin' to do? Maybe make a few things for your young'un?"

Her kindness brightened Hannah. "Why thank you, Sarah. Brice told me how you made that pack of woman's things. I needed something to wear. My clothes were nothing but rags. In all the time I was married, my husband never let me go to town to get anything and my clothes were worn out. I cried when I saw that blue dress. I'll never forget it."

"My stars, you poor child!" Tears formed in her eyes, reflecting her sympathy. "Somethin' else, too—my husband and I have talked it over and, if the worst happens, we'd be real proud to take your baby boy to raise. We've never seemed able to have any young'uns of our own."

Hannah, struck deeply by the sadness in her voice, nearly cried at the woman's words.

"We'd be real good to him."

Overwhelmed by the good woman's offer, though horrified at the necessity of it, Hannah stammered, "W—well, I—I
don't know. Guess I'll think about it. I have a few more days
left. I keep hoping Brice will come in time with a witness who
can help me. She's a Navajo woman, and they might not want
to hear what she has to say, but she saw the way I looked,
beaten and marked up, when she helped me with the birth of
Thomas. Moore never stopped the beatings, even with me in
the family way. I think he enjoyed making me scream."

"He must have been a terrible man, Hannah. It's real bad
what he done to you, but you have your boy. Name's Thomas,
is it? That's a nice name he has. I don't want to pressure you
about it, but please do some considerin' on it." She looked
flustered for a moment. "Please don't be thinkin' that's the
only reason I come here. I don't believe you done what they
say, not the way they mean. A woman's got the right to fight
for her life. I believe that, Hannah." She turned to leave. "I'll
be bringin' you some sewin' and baby patterns."

Lying on her bunk and going over everything made Hannah more confused. *If Lupita is being abused, I might need to
make other arrangements for Thomas. Jesse, please hurry
back, I need to know my baby's all right!*

ↈↈↈ

The days dragged slowly and, with the sewing, her hands
were busy. Eventually Hannah heard the sounds of men
pounding on lumber and the occasional cursing as they hit a
finger. Nothing could drown the sound from her ears. It was
the scaffold for her execution they were building, and it made
her blood run cold. When that day came, she'd see Hank's evil
sneering face waiting for the trap door to snap open beneath
her.

Three days left of her short life and no sign of Brice and
nothing from Jesse. Knowing Thomas was in safe hands would
ease the way for her. Brice must be dead or lost out on the
vastness of the Navajo lands. Some nights, in her dreams, she
saw him wandering in the hot sun, dying of snake bite or thirst.

She heard Lin coming. He usually brought her food, and it was near noon time. "Ma'am, you've got a visitor."

Hannah looked up to see Jesse coming behind Lin. "Jesse! I thought I'd never see you again! What of Thomas, did you find him well?" She inundated him with questions in her desperate need to know.

"Yes, honey, he was fine, just fine. But I'm sad to say, Lupita was not so well off. That French bastard has been beating her, maybe not as bad as your husband, but the happy girl we sent off to Seligman was no longer the same." Jesse looked gray and extremely tired.

"What happened, Jesse? Where is Lupita now and what about her condition? Oh my God, Jesse, I'll never understand men like that!" It was like a ghost revisiting her own nightmares, hearing about Lupita.

"Don't you fret none on that, Hannah. I took care of it. I hired a big wagon full of straw, and sent her, Maria, and Thomas, to the Circle B. She's closer to her time, only two-three months to go, she said. I think she'll make it. I hired a couple men to drive them with orders to go slow. They should be there by now. It took me a while to make it back here, but I knew you'd want to be sure about your baby bein' safe and all."

"Thank you, Jesse, I feel better, but sad for Lupita. What about Solnier, he must have put up a fight to keep her."

"He's lucky I didn't shoot him, the mean son-of a bi—" He hesitated. "Sorry, honey, my tongue runs off on me when I get riled up."

"He'll not follow or try to get her back?"

"It's my idea the man is on his way back to where he came from. Hear tell he wasn't overly popular in Seligman, either."

Hannah remembered Lupita's father and mentioned him.

"I gave orders for Lupita to run the house until I get back, so that ought to settle his hash for the time being." He laughed. "She's a married woman and out of his control."

"This relieves my mind more than you'll ever know. I haven't heard from Brice either, and with my worry over Thomas, it had me near out of my mind. I only have three more days to live, Jesse—only three more."

Hannah began to sob, part of it, relief over Thomas, and part because her young life was nearing a horrible end. She'd spent many unwilling hours wondering what it would feel like when that rope bit into her neck. It might be quick. She'd heard that, but quick enough? She felt the ice circling her scalp again.

"Don't give up hope, honey, he's doing his best, you know that."

"Yes, but it might not help me even if he does find the woman. Maybe she won't remember me, or she'll be afraid to come here." She sighed. "Jesse, a woman in town here came to see me." She wanted him to know about Sarah's offer, that there was a safe place for Thomas. "Jesse, if I die here and Brice *is* lost out on that reservation, will you speak to the people who own the mercantile, for me? They asked to raise my son as their own. They're good folks, Jesse. With you being so ill, it could come to that and I wanted you to know about their offer."

"I promise, Hannah," Jesse said with tears coursing down his cheeks.

CHAPTER 32

In the far reaches of Monument Valley, Brice finally succeeded in convincing Neebah she must come to Flagstaff and tell her story to the judge. She refused to go without her husband, and Brice waited with agonizing impatience while they made arrangements for their garden and livestock. It took many days before they set out, their obvious reluctance evident in their laggard pace.

Brice felt a desperate hurry, not knowing what was happening with Hannah. "Please God, don't let me be too late." His dreams of a life with her seemed very far off these days. He nudged his boney nag to move a little faster, but he only got far ahead of the Navajos.

"White man big hurry," Katchee commented.

"Yes," Brice answered. "Yes."

He was worried about being in time for Hannah and understood the fear and reluctance of Neebah. She feared speaking to the white judge, and Brice appreciated that as well.

Brice would burn the ranch house to satisfy Neebah's fear of the haunting spirit of Moore. They were headed there, Brice believed, though he had no idea where it was. It only added to his desperation.

After three days, they came to the desolate ranch. He saw the place where Hannah had suffered the cruelest of treatment at the hands of her husband and it sickened him.

"I'll just be a moment," he told them.

He walked into the foul smelling place. Taking a lantern,

he splashed what liquid was left in it, struck a match, and walked out. He took nothing. She'd want nothing from that house.

The building raged with fire and was engulfed completely when they turned their horses toward Flagstaff. It could be reached by dusk if the Navajos would only move faster. They looked back to see the hotly blazing pile of refuse that had once been a place where hell on earth had lived.

"Good riddance," Brice said.

It was dark and late when they finally saw the lights of Flagstaff ahead. Nearing the town, the Indians made a rude camp. "You go Brice," Katchee said. "See judge. He talk Neebah, dis place."

"I will. Please wait for me. I will come soon." Brice went on alone, first to the jail seeking Hannah. Shocked, he saw the newly erected scaffolding! They must have sentenced her to hang! *Please, God, don't let me be too late.* In haste, he knocked on the door. It was answered by a man he didn't know.

"What you want so late, mister?" He shuffled his feet. "We're closed up fer the night, gittin' some shut-eye before the hangin' tomorrow."

Tomorrow! He still had time! "Is it possible for me to see Hannah?" Hat in hand, Brice waited for the answer.

"Naw, sir, she's sleepin'. Why'd you want to see the prisoner?"

"I'm engaged to marry her, and I'd like to see her."

"Where 'n hell you been, mister? Don't you know what's happened? She's up fer hangin' tomorrow mornin', ten o'clock sharp." He opened the door wide. "I reckon she'd want to see you. She's a nice little thing. Hard to believe she done what they said. Don't seem strong enough."

Quietly they walked down the corridor to her cell. Brice called softly. "Hannah, it's me, Brice!" He wondered why she slept at all, considering what lay ahead of her in the morning.

Hannah opened her eyes and looked at him. Brice saw the light of comprehension slowly come over her face. She flew off the bunk to the bars.

"Brice, I thought you were dead or lost!"

"No darlin', almost, but we're here now. I'll see Judge Jant tonight if I can, or in the morning, and get this thing halted. He'll hear what Neebah has to say. I'll see to that."

"You found her then?" Hannah nearly sank to the floor in relief, but she clung onto the bars. "Will the judge hear her? Will he believe an Indian woman?" She reached out to hold on to him, and Brice wished he was in the cell with her.

"I'll go wake the judge now, Hannah. We've no time to waste." He disentangled her arms. "Hope the old cuss won't be too hard on me for disturbin' his rest, but it can't wait any longer. I'll be handlin' things, try not to worry, girl."

He left her standing in awe. He hadn't time to ask her about Jesse, but God willing she'd have all the time in the world to tell him these things. If the judge would hear Neebah's words, it'd make a difference, and they'd know she hadn't lied about the abuse. He had to hear her!

౮౩౮౩౮౩

Brice found his way to the home of Rufus Jant and, seeing a dim light inside, knocked on the door.

An old woman answered. "What can I do for you, young man?"

"Please, ma'am, I must talk to the judge. It's extremely urgent."

"Well, I'll go ask him. He's still awake, I believe. Had a busy week again, and he's tired, ain't getting any younger."

She reappeared at the door. "Come on in, he'll see you," she said and ushered Brice into a book-lined room he took to be a library.

He waited, hat in hand.

Judge Jant entered wearing a robe and slippers. "Now what's got you so all fired up, young man, life or death is it?"

Brice introduced himself and saw the judge's eyebrows rise upon hearing his name. He'd heard it many times during the trial.

"So you're the surveyor we've heard so much about.

Were you successful in your mission, young man?" Jant har-rumphed. "The young woman hoped you'd get here in time to help her out. So then, let's hear what you have to say."

Brice lowered his voice and sat close and told the older man the information he'd gotten from the Navajo woman.

"My God, man! I'll put the execution on hold till we check out the woman's claim. It certainly would prove Mrs. Moore's story." Jant rose from his chair. "Son, I'll take care of putting a stop to that hanging in the morning. Then we'll go see the woman and hear her out. I respect her fear of coming into our courtroom, and I don't blame her. If her word proves out, she won't need to. I thank you, son. Hannah seems like a right nice woman, and it was hard to pronounce that harsh sentence on her, but I follow the law."

"Thanks, Judge, sorry to disturb you at this late hour, but this couldn't wait." Brice rose to leave. "Good night, sir, and thank you."

"We'll be seeing you early son, about eight, right after I have a word with the sheriff." He shook Brice's hand. "Good to meet you, Brice Fowler. We need people like you in this country. Hope you plan on staying."

Brice rode out to the Indian's camp. He found Katchee sitting near a small fire smoking a white man's cigarette. "Hey, where'd you get that, my friend?"

Katchee laughed softly. "I know where find, white man."

"Katchee, tomorrow, the judge will come here to talk with Neebah. He knows she fears the white man's court, but he wants to hear her words and see what she has to show him. He's a good man, Katchee, but she'll have to prove what she says."

"Neebah will talk judge. She say Hannah good woman."

Brice rode to the stable and told the sleepy stable hand to give his skinny nag feed, water, and a good rub down. He chuckled, knowing it would be the first time for that scrawny but extremely tough little horse. From there, he went to see Jesse at the hotel and found him groaning with pain. "What's wrong, old son?"

Jesse gritted his teeth with the pain. "My God, you're

back! Brice, I've never been so glad in my life to see a man. Did you find your woman?"

"Yes and the judge will hear what she has to say. You won't believe what she told me. I couldn't believe it myself. Moore was a hellish kind of devil, marryin' an unsuspecting young girl like he did." He took in Jesse's situation, and his pale, sweating face. "Getting' worse, is it?"

"Hell, yes, Brice, I'm near my end and I know it. I had to go to Seligman while you were roamin' the reservation." Jesse told Brice the situation with Thomas, Lupita, and the Frenchman.

"Well, I'll be damned. Who'd have thought he'd turn out that way? Too close to home for Hannah, wasn't it?"

"Yes, it sure as hell was. She saw a bruise on Lupita's arm and couldn't stop her worryin'. I had to go over there and see to young Thomas." Jesse doubled over with a spasm across his mid-section and Brice hurriedly gave him a good slug of laudanum. Minutes later, Jesse lapsed into sleep or unconsciousness. Brice wasn't sure which and didn't care. His friend was comfortable.

∽∾∽

Morning saw Brice at the jail. He wanted to be there when Hannah got the word her execution was being held. Waiting for Judge Jant to appear, he relaxed sitting in a chair with Lin. The deputy looked puzzled, and La Force stood waiting. His face bore little expression, but Brice saw a twinkle in his eye.

The judge swept in, the same as in his courtroom. "Sheriff, put a stay on the hanging. We have new evidence. If it bears out, there'll be a few changes in the sentencing."

La Force laughed. "Yes, sir, I'll be damned happy to do just that. Wait'll we tell that bloodthirsty crowd out there. They're gatherin' right now, elbowing everybody out of the way to get a good spot to see the hangin'. They ' won't take the disappointment real easy, Judge."

"Tell them there'll be no hanging today, or for at least

three days, depending what we find. Sheriff, I'd like to ask you to accompany Brice and myself. We've got some questioning to do."

"You bet, sir. Be right along, soon's I get my horse. Lin, you keep things quiet around here. If trouble starts, use your scatter gun. They won't argue with that." With that, Sheriff La Force shoved his stained, ragged hat on, and they headed for the door.

"Hold on," Brice said. "Hannah has to know about this."

"Sure, son, but don't waste time lolly-gaggin' back there. We got a lot of riding ahead of us," Jant laughed and headed out the door.

Brice went swiftly back to see Hannah. "Darlin', there won't be a hangin' today, or ever." He took in her look of shock, and happily, saw the first ray of hope cross her face. "I got to go darlin'. We got some ridin' to do."

And he left her standing there, mouth agape and speechless, trying to take in what he'd said. Brice wanted to tell her everything, but he left before she could utter a word.

꘎꘎꘎

The men approached the Navajo camp. A lazy spiral of smoke rose from their breakfast fire.

Katchee stood waiting, a hand upheld in greeting. "*Yah ta hay*, white man."

They dismounted and Katchee led them to Neebah. "Dis Neebah Gray Wolf." He indicated the husband. "Dis her man, Manny Alchesay."

They said their greetings and, after a reasonably polite time, the judge began to question her.

Judge Jant asked her, his tone gentle. "Ma'am, what can you tell us about the Moore ranch, what you saw there, how Mrs. Moore looked when she gave birth to her baby? Tell us the best you can, please, ma'am."

"Hannah good woman, she beat plenty, I help bring baby son." She hesitated, fear in her eyes. "Moore, he evil one, he devil man, have evil eye on him. I show you what he do—I know, I see." She pointed in a southeasterly direction. "We go, you see." She refused to say more.

They mounted their horses and, with dreadful expectation, followed the woman and her husband.

Brice Looked at La Force. "I know what we'll be seein', if she told it right. Prepare yourself."

It took most of the day to reach the Moore ranch. Brice rode Hannah's fine horse from The Circle B, and enjoyed the fine mount that she was. Approaching the Moore Ranch, they saw the smoldering ruins of the house. The barns and corrals were intact, and the place looked desolate. Nothing alive moved. No poultry and no livestock milled around. Ignoring the smoldering ruins, Neebah rode on and they followed.

"Come dis way, you see." She came to a shallow depression about a mile from the ranch buildings and stopped. "Dey here, white man." She pointed. "Down dere, they sleep—long sleep."

"What the hell?" La Force whistled. "Is she pointing to a grave?"

Katchee had a small shovel. "Use dis one, Brice." He didn't want to get near the shallow place. The Indians sat on their horses in respectful silence.

Brice began to dig and carefully unearthed the depression. Shortly, he came to a woman's shoe, attached by the laces to a skeletal foot. "God almighty, what the hell's in this place?" He dug carefully, at last uncovering a woman's desiccated, dried corpse, dressed in tattered bits of calico, and beside it, the tiny bones of an infant. It's skull gave shattered testimony to Moore's violence.

Jant and La Force stood quietly at the edge of the grave in shocked silence at the pitiful sight.

"This is what Neebah said we'd find, Judge," Brice offered.

"We'll send some men out to bring these poor souls in for a decent burial. I see broken bones on the mother, and oh, God, that baby's head!" Judge Jant exclaimed in horror, shaking his head at the tragic scene.

Brice knew it could have been Hannah lying there with

Thomas, if she hadn't fought for her child that fateful night. "No one would have ever known Hannah's fate or her baby's, and no one will likely ever know who this woman and child were, either," he muttered, horrified.

"It looks like your lady was telling the truth all right," Jant said. "Saw the imminent danger she and her son were in and did what she had to do. I wonder how many other women he married before this poor, unfortunate soul? Sheriff, do we know when the man came to this area?" he asked. "This happened after he came here and undoubtedly the same fate may have befallen some other woman in another place. Could be the reason he moved to a new area."

"I'll try to find out, Judge," La Force said. "But the man kept so quiet about his affairs, we may not ever know where he came from or who this unfortunate woman was."

His face was white with shock at this ugly, tragic sight, and Brice figured the man had seen a lot in his days as sheriff.

Brice went to Neebah. "Ma'am, if there is ever anything I can do to help you, please, you come and let me know. I thank you."

"No, white man, I happy for dis—he devil man. Now people know."

Pleased at the white men's gratitude, Neebah had reserve and dignity enough not to display it. Moore's spirit no longer walked the earth. Brice had taken care of that, too.

They camped the night in the ranch yard. There was water and feed for the stock. The house, now charred wreckage, went unmentioned, though they occasionally glanced that way. If any of them wondered why it had been burned, they didn't speak of it, nor did Brice mention it. He had no regrets about setting it on fire. That scene of great evil had to be destroyed and all evidence of it wiped from the face of the earth.

"It's been one helluva day, boys. I'm turning in, not used to much riding these days." Judge Jant rolled up in a thick blanket, his head pillowed on his saddle. "Good night, boys."

Brice and La Force sat around the waning campfire. He feared to see Hannah's face when she heard the news of their grisly find. Ugly though it was, it would square her with the law, but it could have happened to her. "Jake, what has to be done now to free Hannah?"

"I suppose the judge will recall that jury and give them the facts. We'll bring the remains in for them to see what Moore really was and, of course, a proper burial. That'll make it all legal like. Sure disappoint those folks come to watch the hangin'."

"You'll send a party out for these bodies then?"

"First thing, Brice, 'fore the coyotes get at 'em." La Force shrugged. "Hope we covered the grave deep enough."

Brice wrapped a blanket around his shoulders and settled on his saddle. "Neebah told me what we'd find, but tellin's not the same as seein' those poor souls laying there and no mark on their grave."

La Force watched the last of the coals cool and whiten into ash before he finally followed suit.

CHAPTER 33

Morning's soft, pearly glow saw them awake and ready to pull out for Flagstaff. They had nothing for breakfast, and a long, hungry day lay ahead, but the three men were elated at the thought of freeing an innocent woman and eating wasn't heavily on their minds.

La Force rode to the Indian camp and returned to say, "Well, our Navajo friends have ridden away. Went on home, I suppose. They did what we asked and it was more than enough. Brice, thank God, you followed your hunch about finding that woman."

Brice laughed. "Everyone said nobody would listen to an Indian, especially a woman, but they were wrong on that. Judge, you sure are one hell of a good man for the job. Fair and square, no matter *who's* talkin', thank God."

"I hope never to change that, Brice. I guess not too many judges would ride out this way either, but I wouldn't have missed being a part of freeing that little lady. She's the sort we need out here."

Brice felt Judge Jant was embarrassed by the comments, but pleased as well, enjoying praise for a job well done.

☙☙☙

Hannah sat in her cell, restless, wondering exactly what Neebah had told the judge. It must have been important enough to stay her hanging. When Lin brought her breakfast, she found it more than elaborate and realized, "Dear God, this was to be my last meal!"

Nervous, she paced about in her cell and ate little of the lavish breakfast. She tried, but her thoughts kept her on edge.

Is this delay a false respite for me, and they'll hang me before Brice gets back?

Lin came back, saying. "You have visitors."

"Who is it?"

"It's the parson and his wife, wantin' to offer you religious councilin'." He added, "They look real eager, ma'am."

"Please send them away. If Jesse comes in, bring him back. His is the only comfort I need, please, Lin."

Shortly, Lin brought Jesse back to her cell and let him in. "Jesse, what's going on?" she asked him. "They've held off on the hanging. What do you know?"

"Not much, but Brice seemed pretty chipper last night before I fell asleep, didn't see him this morning." The rancher enfolded Hannah in his arms. "Honey, it'll be all right, I'm sure it will. Brice is a fine young man, no quitter, that's for sure." He stroked her hair. "My wife's hair was most like the color of yours, Hannah, maybe a bit lighter." He chuckled with happiness for her reprieve and, in memory, thought of happier times with his Leatha.

Hannah heard the longing in his voice and it sent a chill through her. He talked about his wife as though he expected to see her any moment. He was terribly ill. *Brice, hurry back, for me—Jesse, too.*

The time approached for her scheduled hanging. She heard the noisy gathering of on-lookers milling about out in the jail yard. Standing on her cot, looking through the bars, she saw children running and playing, shrieking in their exuberance as their elders gathered beneath the scaffolding, waiting.

Someone called out. "Where is she? Bring 'er out, we're waitin'."

The roar of the restless crowd reached through the jail, dogs barking, men laughing and joking, and the clink of a bottle or two.

"They *want* me to hang!" She clung to the bars, though

Jesse tried to settle her. "What's wrong with people?"

"Now, Hannah, don't take on so."

"Hurry, Brice," she continued as if he hadn't spoken, "they hate me, and want to see me die, strangling to death at the end of a rope! How can they be so heartless?"

Hannah knew nothing of mob mentality. In her innocence, she couldn't help but think the best of people, though her recent past had taught her differently. How well she'd learned the evil intent of some people. From all walks, they existed to create hell for others. She thought of Lupita, whose experience so paralleled her own. Tug, Hank, even the parson and his wife, had a lack of human compassion, not so evil as Moore, but vindictive and hateful, nonetheless.

Lin came back to her cell. "Don't let 'em get to you, ma'am, Jake told me how to handle 'em." He shrugged. "They can get all fired up over a hangin' an' don't like to be shorted out of it. Jesse, you sit right here and try to settle her. Don't you worry none, ma'am. I got my orders."

Jesse tried to encourage her. "He'll get here, honey, said it might take a day or two. Lin can keep that crazy bunch in line. Sure wish I knew what Brice was goin' on about, but after I took my medicine, I fell asleep."

Hannah saw his fatigue and pain-lined face. "Jesse, I'm trying to believe what Brice said. The judge put a hold on the hanging. Something must be happening that we don't know about. It has to be his talk with Neebah."

Outside, the restlessness of the milling crowd increased. Hannah worried if their anger was so great, Lin couldn't hold them off. Her rising panic made her pace about her cell.

"Jesse, I'm frightened. That crowd is ugly. If they don't get to see a hanging today, what then?"

The other prisoners were restless as well. They were for the most part on Hannah's side, and often called out encouragement. "Hold on, ma'am, maybe it'll turn out all right fer you, at least you got another chance, seems like."

Someone else spoke up. "Ain't often anybody gits out of the noose, but if the judge is in on it, you just might. Hope ta hell ya do, 'scuse me, ma'am, fer cussin'."

Hannah smiled at the friendly commentary. "They've been nice to me in here, almost like brothers."

Hannah heard Lin step out to address the milling crowd. "Folks, there's been some new evidence come to light. The sheriff and Judge Jant are out takin' a look at it now, should make it back real soon. Put your millin' on hold for now. I got my orders from Sheriff La Force. Go on about your business, if there's a hangin', you'll get to see it, but there won't be one 'till he gets back. I'm here to see to it!"

"Tryin' to git herself out of it, is she? She's a sneaky one, believe me, I know her if any man does. She's tryin to get away with her killin'."

Deep icy chills of fear crept through Hannah's body, hearing the harsh, vindictive voice of Hank Watkins.

"Doesn't that man ever stop hating? In no way was I cruel to him, just didn't want to discuss my personal business. He dug his hands into my arm, trying to make me tell."

"What a bastard! Some are like that, ma'am. Hank hates to be a loser at anything would be my guess. Loses at cards, so I hear, maybe that's got him all fired up." Jesse said, trying to calm her with his words. "Hannah, I won't be leavin' you while this business is goin' on. No telling what that snake might get started. Lin might just might be needin' another gun hand. If so, I'm right here!"

"Thanks, Jesse. I wonder how this will end when everything seems so tangled and mixed up." She curled up on the bunk. "Brice, I'm waiting for you once again."

They heard a large crash and the fracturing glass of the office window. Jesse went to see. "What the hell's this all about, Lin?"

A large rock and shattered glass lay scattered on the floor.

"It's Hank, tryin' to work up a lynch mob. I've told them the hangin's been put on hold by Judge Jant. That ought to shut 'em up. The whole town respects him and Hank maybe don't know that, yet," Lin went on. "He'd best watch himself, or he'll be in here fer disturbin' the peace. Jake don't hold with riotin' and told me to use this scatter gun if I need to." He held the weapon in his hands. "Watch this, Jesse."

He put the barrel out the broken window and pulled the trigger. They heard a yelp of terror from Hank.

Jesse grinned from ear to ear. "What'd you aim at, son?"

"Just the top of his old hat, I aimed high an' no one was standin' behind him. I might have creased him a mite across the head and peppered him some, sure hope so." Lin laughed. "Maybe that'll quiet the useless son of a bitch."

With a roar of laughter, Jesse and Lin looked out to see Hank clutching his head and wrapping his filthy neck scarf around it to stop the blood. Lin called out. "You folks better scatter now. Judge Jant ordered a hold on this hangin', and I aim to see it carried out! Go on, now, git on out a here!"

Jesse felt a flood of relief seeing the crowd thin out. "You won't change Hank's thinking, Lin, but being a coward he won't come back for more. Sure as hell he won't."

Hannah couldn't rest with so much ruckus goin' on.

Jesse sat in the office with Lin, his face gray and lined with pain. "Excuse me, Lin, while I take a swallow of my medicine." He took a healthy dose and waited until it took effect. "I sure hope Brice gets back here soon, Lin, I'm near the end of my rope, gitten worse every damned day."

"God, Jesse, I hate to see it. You jest sit yourself right there and wait for it to settle you down." Lin wasn't much good around the sick, and seeing Jesse pale and sweating made him nervous.

Through the rest of the day and all night, they waited. The only person coming through the door was Ella with her food. "That Hank, he's madder'n a hornet, he is," she warned. "Been a plannin' some way to git himself even with you, deputy. I heered him talkin' it up with some of the no-goods around town as wants thet hangin'. He's sure got a big hate agin' thet little lady you got in 'ere. Wonder what she done to 'im?"

"Let the bastard give it a try, Ella, and if you see him, tell him to come on ahead. We'll be a waitin'."

Jesse, relieved by the deputy's firm control of the situation, stayed in the office and took liberal doses of medicine to ease his pain.

⌯⌯⌯

Brice, the sheriff, and Judge Jant rode in to Flagstaff in the early afternoon to find many of the remaining crowd still hoping for the excitement of seeing a woman hang. Some did their business while waiting, but others stayed close, hoping to see Hannah hang, and for no other reason.

Crowding about for answers, some flung out queries to the judge.

"What'd you find Judge?"

"Ain't they gonna be a hangin'?"

Brice found their animal excitement sickening.

"We found plenty. Now we need to get the jury together. Sheriff La Force, I'll leave that to you, and the sooner the better."

Brice watched while Jant handed those matters over to La Force.

A pall of silence came over the crowd.

"Well, what'd you find out, then?" The questioner stood with his hands on his hips, staring at the judge.

"You'll know everything after the jury does. Now go on about your business and quit your blood-thirsty slinking about waiting to see somebody hanging from the end of a rope." Jant rode away, leaving them in the street.

Loud muttering and scuffling of feet met the judge's words. The man was greatly respected and the disappointment of not seeing a hanging abated. The crowd dispersed.

Standing back, under the shade of a tree, his scarf wrapped around the bloody pits and marks in his head from the scatter gun, Hank stood fuming in disappointment. Brice watched in disgust. Clearly a slow burning hatred had consumed the man at the loss of his goal.

"I'll see the bitch get her due," Hank yelled. "Yer lettin' it slip away, by God. I'll see to it, myself. I'll find a way to take care of her, and you too, Fowler, you skinny surveyin' bastard!"

He slunk away, Brice guessed, to the Roaring Duck to salve his wounds.

Brice left the crowd and went inside the jail to see Hannah. Lin took him back

"Hey, darlin', you all right? This has been a terrible or-deal for you, but it's most over now."

Lin let him into her cell. Brice reached for her small body and held her like he'd never let go. He told her what they'd found. "Even that tiny baby'd been beaten to death. It was a God-awful pitiful sight, Hannah. Judge Jant believes he may have done this where he came from as well." He paused in thought. "We wondered about his behavior before comin' here. Did he ever mention where he'd come from before buyin' his ranch out here?"

Hannah vomited into her waste bucket and weaved against him, her face white from what he'd told her. "I knew he'd kill us both. I knew it that night! He was worse than I'd ever seen him. We had to get away from him. They'll believe me now, won't they?" She paused, remembering his question. "No, Brice, he never talked about much of anything, certainly not his past."

"Well, honey, the judge is recallin' the jury now. The bodies should be here sometime tomorrow. The sheriff sent some men out to bring them back and went with them to make sure they find the grave." He held her close. "I love you Han-nah. You still want to marry me?"

"Yes, I do, Brice. Nothing sounds better to me than hav-ing you and Thomas, and no more trouble." She kissed him over and over, wishing he could stay longer with her. "Where's Jesse? He needs to know what's happened."

"He's sleepin' out there in his chair, must have taken an-other dose of his medicine, a big one this time. Hannah, he's dyin' and wants to get back to his place. Maybe we can go soon. Thomas is at the ranch now, too. You can hold him as long as you want then, darlin'."

"He might not know me. We've been apart so long except for his short visit." She frowned." You asked about Jacob, where he moved from? No, in all that time, he never said any-thing about where he grew up, I thought that was strange, too. We'll never know who that poor woman was. It could have been me, Brice," she finished sadly.

Jesse came down the passage. "What's goin' on, you two?"

Brice repeated all he knew to Jesse. "Shouldn't be much longer, Jesse, they'll be back with those poor souls Moore did away with. That should set Hannah free." He grinned and gave Hannah a huge bear hug. "This lady here said she'd marry me. How about that?"

"Aw, that's no news to me. I saw that comin' away back when you first showed up at the circle B. You already had a closeness between you, more than either of you knew."

Brice laughed and Hannah blushed from head to toe. "Jesse, you need to get to the hotel and rest yourself. Thanks for standin' by my woman here."

Lin let them out. He took Jesse's arm and ushered him away.

"I'll come back real soon, darlin'," Brice said.

Hannah, with real hope for her future, fell onto her knees. "Thank you, God, for bringing this about, and bless Neebah wherever she is. What horrors she must have witnessed with no one to tell. Brice, I'll bless her and you too until the end of my days. You've saved my life all over again!"

CHAPTER 34

It had grown dark and, outside, a furtive figure slunk about, using the dense bushes growing about the back side of the jail to conceal his presence. Hank searched for the window of Hannah's cell. Listening carefully for the sound of her voice to direct him, he waited.

He heard Brice talking with Hannah. Laughing together, their voices carried through a small high-placed window, actually more of a narrow slit in the jail's strong walls, to let in the fresh, cool outside air of a mountain evening.

In the encroaching darkness, Hank waited, watched, and cursed the small opening. "A hell of a place, window's too damned small!" He had a plan, but the inadequate opening frustrated him, and he slunk away in defeat. His anger and hatred had grown into madness. "I'll find a way." He threw away the kerosene and unlit torch of rags he held and headed for the Roaring Duck.

Playing at poker, anger clouded his mind, and he lost steadily, muttering to himself. "If this keeps up, I'll get myself kicked out of Ella's place. God damned that stingy yeller-haired bitch. Look what she's brung me to." He hoisted a few more drinks, staggered over to an empty table, and sat down to sulk, his hatred unabated.

"What's got into ol' Hank tonight? Talkin to himself. Actin' mighty funny ain't he?" Al Partin commented.

"Maybe gittin' cheated outta seeing that woman hang. Ain't that the one he's been goin' on about?" another man put in. A newcomer to the gambling crowd, he called himself Bill Hite—never said where from.

"I dunno. I got a funny feelin' about Hank. He ain't right no more. This hangin's got to him. I'm a worryin' what he might take in his head to come up with," Al said. He shook his head, afraid Hank'd overhear their talk and their comments. Nothing they'd said would help the ugly look on his face.

"Doin' anything about it?" Clay Ordway said, wondering if he should warn the sheriff.

"Ain't my business, but I'm happy as hell it ain't me he's got it in fer," Al rejoined. "Glad as hell. Hank's a mean bastard, he is." He kept his voice low.

"Deal, or shut up, this ain't gittin us no place," Bill said.

Nothing more was said. Drinks were poured and the slapping of cards filled the air, along with a thick pall of cigarette smoke.

Hank heard most of the talk. In his rage, he dismissed any reference to himself. He didn't see his fault in any of it.

໒ๅຉ

Late afternoon with the sun beginning its downward drift, the sheriff and two men drove into Flagstaff with the canvas wrapped remains lying in the back of the wagon. The crowd remaining about in hopes of seeing a woman hang knew this evidence was the reason the hanging had been halted.

The judge was summoned, and as many of the jurors as could be found gathered around the wagon. "We were taken to the grave site of these poor souls," Judge Jant said. "The Indian woman, Neebah, who helped Mrs. Moore at the birth of her son, directed us to the site of their burial. She said Moore murdered them in a fit of rage and buried them nearly a year before he took Hannah to wife." He directed La Force to unwrap the remains.

The gasp of surprise came from many gathered around the wagon. "God almighty! Looks like Moore done in a baby too!" a voice from the group exclaimed, looking at the tiny crushed skull and fractured bones of an infant.

"That's right, Albert. That's what we all said. Now you jurors take a good look at what the man did to the last wife and child before he married Hannah, and decide if Mrs. Moore told the truth about the night she killed her husband. Somehow, the woman knew he'd beat her and the baby to death just like she said. Now do your looking, and let's go back to court and do some deciding. La Force will you bring the accused to the courtroom?"

"Yes, sir, she'll be there." La Force headed to the jail, a smile of satisfaction spread across his usually taciturn features. He came to Hannah's cell. Brice and Jesse waited with Hannah. La Force unlocked it. "Let's go to court, ma'am."

La Force offered Hannah his arm, but Brice intervened. "Excuse me Jake, but I'll take this woman over. Come, Hannah. Let's see what they decide, now they know all the facts of the case."

Jesse followed, his pale and sweating face betraying the fact his pain was on the rampage again.

Happier with hope, but with an edge of fear, she took his arm. "Yes, I'll go, but I still can't believe what they'll say. Will it really be over, Brice?" She raised her face to him, uncertainness in her voice.

"We'll have to see what they say, darlin', but it looks good to me. No one could find you guilty after what they've seen. Moore must have been insane."

She shivered. "Yes, Brice, I believe he was."

They entered the courtroom once again. Hannah realized La Force hadn't put handcuffs on her this time.

"We're here, Judge," La Force said.

"Well now, gentlemen of the jury, have you considered the new evidence regarding the acts committed by the accused?" Rufus B. Jant asked the men.

There were only nine present, the others having returned to their ranches, farms, or what pursuits they followed.

"Yes, sir, we have."

"What are your findings, then?"

Hannah held her breath and clutched Brice's arm. Jesse sat pale and sweating in his dreadful pain.

"We believe the lady acted in self-defense, defending herself and her child, and find her innocent."

"So decided!" Jant banged his wooden gavel on the block. "Hannah Moore, you are free of the charge of willful murder," the judge declared. "You're free to go your way, ma'am."

Hannah rushed to the judge. "Thank you, sir, not just for setting me free, but for going so far out of your way to find the proof, and believing an Indian woman." She looked up to him, tears in her eyes. "I'll never forget you, sir."

Brice stepped up, a wondering smile across his face. "Judge, it's true, isn't it, that you can marry folks?"

"Why yes, son, it is."

Brice turned to Hannah. "Marry me, girl, today, if you will? We can go back to the Circle B as man and wife." He looked into her eyes, waiting uncertainly for her answer.

"Uh...er...yes, Yes, I will Brice. I will marry you now if you like."

Brice understood her indecision and fear of intimacy. Overcome, her desire never to be separated from him again made the marriage right in her eyes. Her face flushed rose with excitement and happiness.

They turned to Judge Jant. "Well, sir?"

"I'd be more than happy to unite you two, I sure would. Are you ready now?"

"Just a minute, please," Hannah said. She turned to Jesse. "Jesse, will you walk me down the isle and give me away?"

"Yes, ma'am! Just wait till I take another dollop of this medicine." He took the small bottle out of his pocket and took a healthy drag.

They waited several minutes while it took effect, seeing the gray, lined, face become ruddy again.

In some degree of comfort, the ailing rancher rose from his chair and took Hannah's arm. "Nothin' in this world could make me happier, dear girl." He walked her to the back. "You ready, Mr. Fowler, to take yourself a wife? We're comin' down!"

The judge stood with Brice waiting as Hannah and Jesse walked down to stand before them.

La Force stood beside Brice. He chuckled. "Well, hell's bells, never thought I'd be a best man today."

Hannah looked at him and smiled her gratitude for the way he'd been with her. "Sheriff, you're absolutely the best man, any day of the week."

They were wed in the company of the jurors, and a few onlookers standing in the door who'd gathered to see what the judge and jury would do about Hannah and happened on a wedding.

෴

"Well I'll be horn swaggled if that don't beat all. She's done got off from hangin' an' married thet surveyor feller to boot!" one of the men standing in the doorway commented.

Outside, Hank overheard what was said. His fury rose to heights. "She ain't gittin' away with that! That bitch is a killer, an' now she's got off. Worse yet, she's up an married thet scrawny damned, surveyor!" He slunk back, away from the door, and walked across the street, shaking and fuming in his fury. "They've got to come out of the courthouse where I can get at 'em." His blood-tinged eyes burned with madness, as he fingered his pistol.

The jury filed out, along with the rest of the onlookers. Judge Jant stayed to make out the marriage papers and the bride and groom waited there to sign them.

The legal formalities completed, Brice and Hannah stepped out into the waning light of the day as man and wife. Those of the remaining crowd sent up a roar of approval and congratulations. Gone was the howling mob who sought her death, and Hannah wondered at their quickly changing minds. How deadly the unthinking mob had been at her nearly fatal end, how titillating the prospect of her hanging to these same people.

Bidding farewell to the judge, they turned to make their way to the hotel. Hannah didn't want to set foot inside the jail again and asked La Force, "Would you please tell the other prisoners that I thank them for the way they treated me? I never thought they wanted to see me hang, not once." She shivered and Brice feared she'd feel ill when she gave more thought to her narrow escape.

"Why shore, ma'am, I'll do that and bring your possibles over to the hotel later on." Laughing, he headed toward the jail. "This is one prisoner I'm mighty glad to see escape the noose, if you'll pardon me sayin' so."

Hannah gasped as a shot rang out, and a bullet thudded into the post beside her head.

"I'll git you yet, ya' damned hussy!"

She heard Hank's raging voice, his hate-filled words echoing loudly from somewhere across the street.

Acting on instinct alone, Brice backed Hannah into a nearby doorway and placed himself in front of her. "Stay right here, honey, keep back! Will that fool never give up?"

La Force crouched, gun drawn. "Come on out, Hank, I don't want to have to gun ya' down." He waited. "Come on ahead you sniveling coward, get on out here where I can see you!"

Judge Jant came out and handed the wedding papers to Brice as another shot rang out, striking him in the left arm. La Force followed the flash of gunfire and let loose with his six-gun. They heard a scream of pain from the shrubbery beside the building across the dusty street, where Hank crouched, waiting to get a shot at Hannah.

Hank came weaving into the road, blood dripping down his arm. "You winged me, you bastard, protectin' thet murderin' whore," he wheezed as he staggered forward. "You cain't be a shootin' me anymore now. I'm givin up! Lookie, my hands are up best as I can!" Only one arm had been raised. Terrified and incoherent, he stood there shaking with pain from his wound.

His whining words brought Brice out into the street, ready to kill, but the sheriff pulled him back. "We'll take care of this sick bastard. You leave him to us. You'd best take a look at the judge here. He's been hit." La Force handcuffed Hank Watkins to a nearby watering trough then turned to check on the others. "Everybody all right here, anybody else get hit?"

"He got the judge right enough, Jake." Brice, shaking with anger, had taken hold of Judge Jant's wounded arm and began wrapping his neck scarf tightly around it to stop the bleeding. "Don't look too deep, Judge, but it's bleeding too much. Have a seat here and Hannah'll stay with you while I send someone for the doc Didn't get far at goin' home, eh, Judge?" he added.

Jesse hurried over, weaving in the street from pain and fatigue. "If you got things under control here, Brice I'm going to go lie down, I'm sick as hell."

"You go on, Jesse. We'll take care of things here." Brice hated to see the man's suffering and hoped he'd make it back to his ranch. Now that Hannah was free, getting Jesse home alive was Brice's main concern.

Hannah put her arm around Jesse's waist, supported his weight. "I'll take him, Brice. Judge Jant, you'll be all right now. Just hold real tight on the bandage here." She indicated his wrapped arm. "I need to help Jesse. He's awfully sick."

"You go on, ma'am, and take care of Jesse. I'll be right enough with Brice here." Jant gave Hannah a smile of confidence and waved her on.

She led the ashen-faced rancher away.

Brice watched his bride walk away and felt pride in his new wife. She had a lot of heart. He lost track of everything, watching her.

La Force stifled a smile. "Hey, bridegroom, anyone go for doc?"

"I sent a kid right away."

Brice heard the judge laugh.

"Can't keep those two apart for long, can we, Jake? I think I'll be fine, soon as the doc comes. Put that miserable miscreant behind bars. He'll come before me in a court of law soon enough." Jant's tone foretold a tough trial for Hank Watkins.

Jant sat on the boardwalk, holding his bleeding arm. Brice's wrap had helped staunch the scarlet flow, but he needed the doc in a hurry

"What about me? I'm bleedin' myself. Ain't I gittin' no

doc to fix my arm?" Hank whined. His anger and hate had dissolved into self-pity and fear.

"Aw shut up, Hank. You ain't dying, an' who in hell'd care if you was?" La Force told him. He checked to see if his cuffs fit the man's wrists snugly enough. "Outta' hold you for a while."

Brice watched the doctor tend to Jant and asked with worried expression, "Doin' all right, are you?"

"Yes, I'm doing well enough, but I'll be glad to have this arm fixed up. It's been a hell of a few days, Brice. We don't get that much excitement around here most days. I'm happy the way it came out, damned narrow escape for the little lady, though."

La Force nodded. "Too narrow, Judge. I never wanted to find her, or arrest her in the first place. You're a damned good man, Brice. She was lucky to stumble into your cabin that night. She can make a good life with you."

"We plan on that, Jake," Brice agreed.

"Trouble seems to follow Hannah. I hope you can turn that around for her, Brice," Jant said, his expression troubled.

"Reckon I'll sure try."

"He'll do that for her if any man can," La Force put in as he watched the doctor expertly clean and dress the wound on the judge's arm. "I like a happy ending and haven't seen many in my line of work."

"There, that will hold you for a while, but come into my office in the morning and we'll take another look. A gunshot wound can be trouble, though this one ran shallow, and I cleaned it real good. It's getting along toward dark, and maybe I could have missed something." The doc shrugged. He'd done his best for "on the street" medicine. "If it gets to hurting too much, send someone by and I'll fix you up with something."

La Force hauled Hank to the jail and, as he was led down the passageway to his cell, he endured dozens of foul comments. The woman was gone and they had no need to hold their language down. Especially after Lin didn't stint in letting them know what Hank had done.

"Hey, Lin, put the nice man in here with me. I'll make

him real comfy," a deep voice called. Raucous laughter rang out.

"Come on in 'ere sweetheart. I'll whop yer godammned head off."

These comments, and a few more, made chills of fear course through the cowardly Hank. "Now, Lin, I got rights, don't I?" he whined "You can't put me in where I'll git beat up. Ain't I suffered enough?"

"You'll never suffer enough for what you tried to do, shootin' at that nice little woman," Lin said, wanting to put Hank in the worst hole they had, but figured Yuma Prison would make him suffer far worse than anything Flagstaff had to offer. That hell hole was just right for a man like Hank.

CHAPTER 35

Hannah helped Jesse get into his bed after he'd taken another good dose of laudanum.

"Hannah dear, I want to make it home before I die," he groaned. He looked into her eyes. "I want to go to my Leatha, I'm plum wore out."

"We'll do our best to get you there, Jesse, count on that. You stuck by me and took care of Thomas. You kept him safe, Lupita too. I'll never stop thinking of all you've done." Tears filled her eyes when she looked down on the gray, emaciated rancher. He soon slept, and she stroked his brow. "Poor Jesse, God bless you and keep you."

She waited for Brice. He was her husband, now. It'd taken place so suddenly she'd had no time to give it thought, other than knowing she wanted to be his wife, in spite of her fears. Her impending death had driven all thoughts of a future from her mind and now, suddenly, it lay before her without shadows.

Leaving Thomas motherless had haunted her most of all. Brice, in his search for Neebah, had left her in desolation, and she'd felt deserted, even knowing such feelings were unreasonable. Neebah had been her only hope. Now, she was free and married! Maybe they'd never be apart again. It was a lot to take in. In shock over all that had happened to her this day, she compared this marriage with her previous one. How different it was. Brice was good, solid, had earned her trust, and she was no ignorant young girl anymore. She knew wonderfully well the man she'd married today. But she wasn't ready for the intimacy of the marriage bed and tried her best to subdue that fear. Her thoughts drove her to heights of anxiety she could barely conceal.

The past month had tortured her in every imaginable way. In disbelief at how close she'd come to death at the hands of Moore, she felt chills course through her, imagining in her mind the fractured remains Neebah had shown the judge. Hannah paced the floor, wringing her hands. *Oh God! Will I ever be normal again?* Would Brice want her this night? He had the right, and she would not refuse him. But she needed more time to heal from the hell she'd suffered in her young life. Waiting with trembling and anticipation, she wondered and prayed. *Would he know her needs?*

Brice knocked softly on the door and entered. "How's Jesse?"

"He's asleep, Brice. He wants to make it home. I believe he means to die. He's so sick!"

He saw the imploring look in her eyes, but it wasn't about Jesse, and he knew it.

"We'll set out first thing in the morning, Hannah." He took her into his arms. "I understand your feelings about things, darling. I took another room for you. We'll have our wedding night, but after all you've been through, it wouldn't be right, this night." He kissed her deeply and led her to a room just across the hall. "Try to sleep, dearest. I'll be right across here if you need me."

"Brice—I don't know how to—" She tried to voice her relief, but could speak no further.

Brice embraced her and opened the door to her room. With feelings so torn and utter fatigue draining her, she accepted his gift and entered.

Inside, she saw her things from the jail. Seeing the garments she'd been working on for Thomas, she smiled. He wouldn't be going to anyone else.

"My life has changed so drastically, I hardly know what to think anymore, but I like it. I'm going to have happiness at last. I believe I am!"

ʚ๏ɞ

Morning saw them breakfasted and Jesse situated in a comfortable wagon loaded with loose, sweet-smelling hay. He lay on a thick quilt provided by the hotel.

"Aw, I don't need this babyin'!"

But he had a wide smile on his face as he protested, unable to hide his happiness at heading home to his beloved Circle B Ranch.

"Just you rest there, Jesse," Brice told him. "The hay'll cushion some of the bouncin' you'll have."

Jesse's smile was more of anticipation than of their kindness. He wanted to see the Circle B once more before he went to be with his wife and sons. Brice found that easy to understand. He loved the place, too.

They hadn't taken time to buy supplies with the urgency of returning Jesse home. There'd be time later for those things and with Hannah's trim little mare tied behind, Brice clucked to the team he'd bought, and they set off. Jesse's buggy was left at the stable along with his driving horse and the scrawny Indian pony. The doc had come around with a good amount of Jesse's medicine and bid them God speed. The sheriff, Lin, and a good number of townspeople stood there to see them off.

Driving out of town, they passed the parson's weathered shack. The couple stood in front of their home and looked silently on as Brice's party passed. They offered no smiles or waves of congratulation.

"I don't mind seeing the last of those people, Brice. I believe they think I'm guilty, in any case, and I've gotten away with it." Hannah chuckled. "They must believe a man has the right to treat his wife in any manner he wants, and she has nothing to say about it." She shivered at the thought.

"It's possible, Hannah." He nudged her arm and looked into her eyes. "I'm glad the judge was handy to do the marryin'. It's better, all the way round."

Hannah blushed. He knew she was thinking, sorting her feelings. "Brice, now we have the time, I've wondered. What about your surveying work? Did you complete it?"

"No, it wasn't done, had another month or so left to finish. I left Jim Emory to clean it up. He's capable enough. I did make out my letter of resignation and left it for Jim to mail in." He gave a self-satisfied chuckle. "It wasn't the best thing I could have done, Hannah, but I couldn't leave you in that jail with no one to help you. They were bent on hangin' you, girl, and I couldn't let that happen if I had to turn the whole damned reservation upside down to find that midwife."

"You know how I feel about that, Brice. I owe you my life twice and more. I promise to be the best of wives to you." She laughed uncertainly and blushed to the roots of her hair. "I guess I haven't been, so far."

"Don't you worry about a thing, darlin'. I'll keep you busy raisin' a family, and I hope we have a whole bunch of little ones." His eyes twinkled, seeing her rosy-hued face and fluttering hands. "Thomas will make a right good big brother."

"I want that too, Brice. I'm very happy. I don't believe I've ever had such a wonderful feeling. I pinch myself to make sure I'm not dreaming. I can't believe it's all behind me, after all the months of worrying."

"Say up there, I'm pretty damned happy too," Jesse boomed out. He was comfortable for the moment.

The ride, though a happy one, was hard on the older man. They stopped to eat the generous lunch provided by the hotel and rested the horses several times. Brice got Jesse out of the wagon to walk around at those times to relieve the cramping of his legs and stomach. He'd been eating nearly nothing and had gotten steadily thinner over the past weeks. It hurt them both, but nothing could change what was happening.

Jesse laughed in the face of his demise. "Let's move on, you two, I want to see my place again. At the rate we're goin', I'll die before we get there!"

In the beginning dusk, they drove through the wide gates of the Circle B. Jesse sat on the seat with Brice while Hannah took the wagon bed. Brice watched Jesse's hungry eyes take in every detail as they made the last few miles. Jesse was gray with pain again, the large doses of Laudanum easing it only a little with the uneven motion of the wagon.

"It's a beautiful place, Brice. I've had many happy years here with Leatha and my boys, before we lost them." Sadness lay in his voice, tempered with an anticipation that made Brice wonder.

"Yes, Jesse, any man'd be damned lucky indeed to live here for a lifetime," Brice answered, knowing the man's deep satisfaction in reaching his home once again.

Pride and sorrow filled Jesse's throat. "Hannah, we're home! Look, there's Manuel come to take the team."

Their homecoming was nothing less than riotous with the happy news of their arrival. Hannah ran into the house, frantically searching for Thomas.

Maria quickly brought him to her. "He big, stand up now, he walk, too," she exclaimed and handed Hannah her son.

"Oh, Maria, he's so beautiful!" She held him out before her, to look into his dark blue eyes, thankful that they were the eyes of her father and not Moore. Actually, they looked enough like Brice's dark blue eyes that he could have been the father. All memory of Moore would be eradicated from her mind if she could possibly do so, and in time, she would.

Lupita and the rest of the household stood laughing and congratulating them with joy at their return. "Brice and I were married in Flagstaff yesterday," Hannah told them, flushing as she revealed the news.

"Oh, senora, I so happy for you!" Lupita exclaimed and hugged her closely. "Now you married woman."

Hannah held her out for inspection. "How are you, my dear? Are you well?" She didn't mention the girl's swelling belly. It wasn't done.

"Si, senora, gracias, your help for me."

She choked up as emotion overcame her. She could not speak, but her tear-filled eyes told what she'd suffered. Lupita's dream of happiness with Solnier lay shattered from his cruelty. How well Hannah knew those sorrows.

"Lupita, we must talk, but later." Hannah wanted to see and touch everything. She couldn't put Thomas down long enough to do anything but walk around and look at all the familiar things she'd missed for so long.

Everyone's joy of the homecoming was dampened by seeing Jesse's poor state. The wedding fiesta plans had been started immediately, as soon as they'd heard the news of the marriage. It was planned for three days, hence. That would give them time to prepare and notify distant neighbors.

Hannah, taking pity on the suffering man, asked Brice to escort Jesse to his bed. Jesse took a hefty dose of his medication and fell into a drugged sleep.

In a flutter with all the excitement, not knowing what to attend to first, she didn't put Thomas down until he began squirming.

One of the cooks came for him. *"Pedro aqui, senora,"* she said as she took him in her arms.

Hannah heard him shriek with joy when they reached the kitchen. A burst of laughing and rapid-fire Spanish flowed through the door and Hannah knew her baby was in gentle hands and playing with his friend.

"Looks like my son has other interests now." She frowned as she wondered if she'd been gone too long. "Brice, do you think he knew me?"

"Of course, he did, but he's grown close to the people here in your absence, and luckily so for his sake. Don't worry your head about that for a minute. He looked wonderfully well. He's had the best of care."

"Yes, he has, but Lupita has suffered, Brice. I know what she's been through. I can help her." Hannah shivered involuntarily at thoughts she never wanted to have again. "Let's look in on Jesse. He wasn't looking too well. He worries me. He won't last much longer, Brice. I'll be sorry to see that wonderful man go."

They found him where Brice had taken him without overt thought, sleeping in Leatha's bed, his breathing ragged, and his face pale, almost waxy.

"Oh, Brice," Hannah whispered quietly. "I don't know what to do for him anymore. I'm glad we made it here. I'll try to get him to the supper table, and they'll be callin' it soon."

"Jesse, can you make it to the supper table?" Brice nudged the man gently to wake him. "Sorry, man, to disturb

you, but you might want to sit at your table again. I'll help you
if I can."

Jesse came awake slowly. "We're home, aren't we,
Brice?" He smiled. "Hell, yes, I'll make it to the table. I can
handle myself. You and Hannah go on, I'll be right along."

They heard him groaning as he roused from the comfort
of the bed.

Supper was a quiet affair and Lupita joined them. She'd
become a family member, and they thought of her as such.

"*Senora,* you free?" she asked.

"Yes, Lupita, I am. Thanks to Brice." Hannah leaned
against him and felt him respond almost electrically. It gave
her a wild, pulsating thrill—one she'd never felt before. She
flushed heatedly, from her neck to her hair.

Lupita giggled. "*Ah, senora, es amor, no?*"

Hannah couldn't speak, but her rosy features spoke for
her.

"Those two have been through a lot, Lupita," Jesse said.
"Time will heal them."

Hannah didn't think Lupita understood him, but Brice
did.

Jesse turned to his food, though he ate poorly. After ex-
cusing himself, they watched him move slowly down the hall
to his bed.

"*Senor es muy malo, eh?*" Lupita shook her head in sorrow and left the table, dabbing her eyes as she moved away.

CHAPTER 36

Later, Brice and Hannah walked in the orchard. Most of the fruit had been harvested, but a fruity odor lingered, sweet in their senses. They said nothing for some time. She knew Brice wanted her in their marriage bed, terribly, but hoped he'd tread slowly with her. He'd promised.

Hannah held herself away from him. "Brice, I love you. I've been sure of it for a long time, even before I was arrested. I want to be your wife in every way, but I'm afraid, and I hate that I feel this way. I don't know what to do."

"Don't you worry about that, at all. It'll be wonderful between us when we do come together, my dearest girl." He laughed, gently taking her in his arms. "Would you mind if I shared your bed tonight? I reckon I'd hate to sleep out in the bunk house when I'm a newly married man." Hannah was speechless. "I'd never live it down," he added.

She felt his strong hands stroking gently through her hair.

"You don't have to worry," he continued. "I'll be good. I just don't want to be away from you, ever again. We were apart way too often all these months when I was workin'. We won't need to be apart again." He sighed. "I'd sleep on the floor, if you'd need that."

"Brice, I don't want to be away from you either. You won't need to sleep on that cold stone floor. It's long been a dream of mine to lie in your arms all night. You must think me confused to say that." She snuggled closer. "I love the way you are with me, taking time and all. I'll love you for that forever."

"The worst of things are over now, except for losing Jesse, and we are losing him, Hannah. I wonder about this night. Will we see him at our table in the morning?"

"I wonder that too. We're young and beginning our life. His seems done. Will it be that way for us too, Brice?" She hated to speak of sad things, but getting used to happiness might take a while.

"Probably, darling, but it'll be great fun getting there, don't you ever doubt it!" He lightly patted her bottom. "Come along, wife, I'm tired and need to turn in."

Hannah blushed in the darkness and felt the heat of it rising up her face, but she held to his arm as they entered the ranch house. She led him to her old room. "I don't even know where Thomas is sleeping. I guess I'll find out about that tomorrow." Her voice sounded dreamy to her own ears. She wondered how she sounded to Brice.

"Hannah, I'll just take off a few things, like boots. A good idea don't you think?" The room was dark, with only a shaft of moonlight by which to see.

She giggled. "Brice, of course, you must." She couldn't hide the nervous tension in her voice but looked forward to the daring idea of a night in his arms.

"Excuse me a while, I want to wash up a bit, I won't be long. We had a long trip today." She took with her some lacy item of clothing he didn't recognize.

Brice realized he could use a wash-up himself. He rushed quietly out into the ranch yard to the horse trough and did his best. *No need to scare her off smellin' like a wild critter.* He laughed at his idea but hurried back to get into the bed first. Entering the room, he looked around. It was still empty. He slipped into the bed wearing only his under drawers, hoping his bare chest wouldn't frighten her.

Hannah crept quietly into the room, smelling of soap and flowers from a cake of scented soap Leatha had given her.

Brice lay quietly in the bed. He heard her approach it cautiously. Did she wonder if he'd gone off to sleep? *Not very damned likely.* He smiled to himself.

Trying not to wake him, she slid carefully beneath the

sheets and curled herself into a ball away from him.

"Hello, darlin', you small, wonderful woman, you." His voice, soft and deep, purred into her very soul as he moved behind her and fit himself against her body. "Is this all right with you? I'm bein' about as good as humanly possible for any man."

"It's wonderful, Brice." Her voice betrayed her fear.

He felt her trembling and stroked her hair softly. "It feels real nice to me too, Hannah. I promised I'd be good and I will. Just bein' here in the same bed with you is enough for me…well, for now." He chuckled softly, tightened his hold on her, and pulled her close. "I know what heaven feels like now, darlin'." He nuzzled into her sweet smelling hair and felt the warmth of her body seep into him.

"Brice, I won't always be afraid, will I?"

He heard the tired sadness in her voice.

"No, my wonderful wife, you won't. I reckon it won't be long before we'll really be man and wife." He kissed the back of her neck, and held himself in check, though riotous thoughts raced madly through his aroused and inflamed body. He kept that part away from her as best he could.

"I love you and the kind of man you are. Good night, Brice."

She remained quiet and unmoving against him. He wondered about her thoughts, but had no idea of what they might be as they lay together in the deepening darkness.

കരുക

Dawn found them sprawled about in the bed. They had slept comfortably together, with his promise kept. Brice, awake and propped on one elbow, looked down on his sleeping wife. Her honey-colored hair flowed across the pillow, framing her soft, little face, and her hips made a wonderfully rounded contour beneath the quilts. "She's far more beautiful than she thinks, and so wonderfully a woman!" he whispered.

He rose quietly, taking his clothes and boots, and slipped out of the room, but not before taking in, once again, the sight of the sweet feminine creature who shared her bed with him. He felt his heart swelling with love and passion for Hannah.

Breakfast was called, and Jesse did not come to the table. Brice went for him but he refused. "Just give me another swig of the laudanum and let me sleep."

Brice felt heartsick at this news.

With heavy hearts, they breakfasted without Jesse and set about the day's activities. The foreman came to see Jesse, and Brice gave him his orders. There had been a subtle change of command. If Hannah wondered about that, she held her comment on it. But some subtle sense that changes had occurred in the management of Jesse's ranch were inescapable.

ఴఴ

The fiesta had been set and the Mexican people went wild with preparations and food. Near evening, the same neighbors came for the celebration who had attended Leatha's funeral.

Hannah was delighted at seeing all the people who came to celebrate their wedding. "Brice how did they know to come, and so soon?"

Quietly to herself, she wondered how much they knew of her trial. Her friend from the dance at Seligman, Bessie Morris, met her graciously along with many others.

Cautiously, she approached Hettie Bell. "Hettie, Jesse told me how you came to be married. He said, like me, you were a mail-order bride. But I see that you are happy, and I'm glad for that. I guess folks around here know what happened to me. It all went so wrong."

"Yes," Hettie replied, "we know what happened, and you should know that folks around here believe what you had to do was a terrible thing but we sided with you." She embraced Hannah. "I'd like to be good friends, my dear. You'll be all right from now on." She smiled at Hannah. "I wonder if I could have been that brave."

Hannah noted a slight shiver with her comment. "For your babies, you could," she replied. "You'd fight for any one of them."

She chatted with the women, and the men went in to see Jesse.

"I hope he'll make it out of that bed for our wedding fiesta, Brice," Hannah said. "Would you see if he'll come? He hasn't been out of his bed all day. These last days he's been so sick."

They heard a soft harrumph directly behind them as Jesse made his appearance. "I'll just set right here and watch you young folks dance," he said.

He'd gotten up from his bed, pale, but stronger at the moment. Maybe he'd be able to handle the fiesta. Hannah took it as a great honor that he'd managed to come to out of his bed for their wedding fiesta, in spite of his suffering.

"Wouldn't miss this weddin' wing ding for you young folks!" He held onto a solid chair.

Tears sprang to her eyes, and Brice leaped to aid him. "Well, Jesse, we about gave up on you. Liken' that bed too much are you?" The caring in his voice as Brice joshed the older man, touched her deeply. "Party should start soon," Brice continued. "It's getting dark, glad you're here for it, Jesse."

"How are you, Jesse?" Hannah asked. Her voice betrayed her worry at his awful fatigue. It lined his eyes and the color of his face was ashen.

"I'll be just fine, honey, don't worry about me. How's it with you and Brice?" His look told her he knew her difficulty with intimacy.

"We're fine—taking things slow. He's wonderful, Jesse. I'm a happy woman." She blushed when she told him. "I love him so much."

The fiesta began with loud and gay Mexican music. Jesse sat talking to old friends. Glad to see them, he had them meet Hannah and Brice as a married couple. "These young folks are stayin' around, might make a rancher out of him yet." He held on, staying at the fiesta, sipping frequently from his medicine flask. After several brave hours, Brice helped him to bed.

The feasting and dancing went on into the wee hours of the morning. All the cowboys who could, were there, and danced Hannah nearly off her feet. At last, she had a few dances with Brice. "You are one fine dancer, my husband!"

The floor wasn't made for dancing, but had to do, and she loved the graceful way he moved with her in his arms.

Hannah took some of the liquid refreshment, and thought she tasted more than fruit juice. After dancing and laughing most of the night, she felt a bit giddy and believed it was the gaiety of the riotous party. She didn't notice Brice quietly watching her. Suspicious that someone had added something more potent to the cider, she thought it tasted just fine and she was thirsty. It felt good sliding down her throat.

As the sun edged upward, people found their way to their wagons or rooms in the ranch house and went to sleep. The patio lay littered with plates, cups, scraps of food, and a bottle or two, empty of dubious contents.

Brice took Hannah to their bed and helped her remove her clothing. She found she was unable to protest his helpfulness. Blushing, slightly, and nearly naked, she didn't protest when he put her into the bed. Divesting himself of all of his own clothing, he joined her and she couldn't find the strength to protest his nakedness.

"Darling wife, I love you so much!" Brice whispered into her ear.

"Oh, Brice, I think I do too—Oh, I mean I love you." She giggled into his chest. She felt almost as unsteady lying down. "Brice, what are you wearing?"

"Not much, Hannah, not a whole lot." He kissed her deeply, nuzzled his way down to her breasts, and very gently took hold. Then kissed her everywhere he dared. Her protests were weak at best toward his advances as she slowly became heated in her responses.

"It'll be all right, darling. I want you. I've needed you for so long, I don't want to wait any longer. I'll be careful, dearest girl."

She felt him tasting her flesh, moving his mouth downward. She wanted to cry out, but could not as her own rising passion made her weak with desire for this man who sought her in every way.

Attempting to struggle, she failed. Then suddenly, she felt

unable to resist him and begin responding fully and completely to him. "Oh, God, Brice, what am I doing?"

"Just everything wonderful, darling girl. Meet me in this, and we'll go all the way together."

She moaned and cried out softly, as he gently turned her into a mass of burning desire and took her with him. They found their way together to a heaven of their own creation. Not once, but many times during the hazy morning hours did they make love, cementing their marriage into a solid and everlasting bond.

Late afternoon found them again sprawled in the bed, but they awoke together and looked into each other's eyes.

"I think we're really married now, Brice." She giggled softly and felt the flushing of burning heat rise in her face.

He smiled into her eyes with love. "You bet we are. You're wonderful, Hannah! I love you beyond anything I've ever imagined. I never knew it could be this way. Thank you."

"Nor did I imagine it, not real love, but this is real, Brice, so very real. It won't go away, will it?"

"Never, my love, I'd like to spend the next few days, right here in this bed with you, but we have guests, dearest. We'd best go see what's left of the fiesta."

They dressed, avoiding too much exposure before each other and, laughing happily, left their room, arm in arm.

Some of the neighbors had gathered around for breakfast or a late lunch, according to the hour.

Hannah looked about for Jesse. "He's not out here, Brice, could you see to him?"

He hurried away to Jesse's room, but quickly returned with a puzzled expression across his face. "He's not there, his room's empty."

"He was so sick, Brice, where would he have gone—Oh God!" And suddenly, she knew where to find him.

Together, they turned and ran to the graveyard out on the hill, with most of the ranch folks following, alarmed by their hosts' sudden reaction.

Coming to Leatha's burial site, they found Jesse lying across her grave—cold, motionless, and pale. His outstretched hand curled around one of the wild mountain flowers planted there.

"Oh, Jesse!" Hannah cried, sobbing as she knelt beside the old man.

"This was the way he wanted to go, Hannah," Brice told her, in sorrow.

They all knew Jesse was where he wanted to be. "He's with his Leatha now." Hannah dabbed at her tear-filled eyes. "It's all he's wanted these past weeks." Her voice was choked with tears.

Realizing the need for Jesse's final service, she said to the friends and neighbors who remained, "I'm glad we have you folks here. Jesse set a lot of store by all of you. I know he'd want you at his services. We'll take care of everyone with food, or whatever you need until we lay him beside her, if you could find a way to stay on a bit."

Bessie Morris came up to Hannah, patted her arm, and gave her a slight hug. "He set a great store by you two young folks. He spoke of you ever' time we seen 'em."

"Thank you, Bessie, he thought highly of you and your family as well." Hannah wondered how far away they lived, knowing it could be many miles. "I'm so glad you're here, and happy to know we're neighbors."

Everyone gave their condolences and waited for the laying away of this grand old man.

The next day, in the early morning, they laid Jesse beside Leatha. The Mexican craftsmen brought out a beautifully carved casket for him. It was so much like Leatha's that Hannah realized he'd had it made months ago. Jesse would have seen to that." Sobbing quietly, she pointed it out to Brice. "He's had that casket ready and waiting, all this time."

A Mexican Padre, who frequently visited the village, kindly performed the service.

Brice nodded. "Poor man, this is what he's waited for. He's with his Leatha and their boys. We'll miss him, that's for damn sure, honey."

After a good solid meal, many goodbyes, and wishes for a happy future together, the ranch folk left by wagon or horseback for their homes, leaving Hannah and Brice standing alone in the wide expanse of the ranch yard.

"What do we do now, Brice, with Jesse gone? We can't stay here if it belongs to someone else. We'd be trespassers wouldn't we?

"No, darling, we won't ever be that. I bought this ranch about three months ago, right after I knew you loved it here. I planned to raise your baby here if things went bad for you. Jesse knew he was dying and had no relatives. He made me a deal. We're to keep his and Leatha's graves as long as we live here. I promised him we would, so you're home, my darlin', for as long as you live." He nudged her. "Do you think Thomas will take to ranchin'?"

"Brice, of course, he will! You never told me! I'm happy we'll live here and never leave, but wish we could have let Jesse know."

"He knew, never fear, my darling wife, he knew." He looked at the lowering sky and drew her close. "It's comin' dark again, Hannah, we'd best get ready for bed."

Her eyes shining with happiness, she felt him pulling her close against his strong body.

The End

About the Author

Ramona Forrest is a retired RN. She keeps busy writing novels—and traveling whenever possible. Forrest has resided in the back country of Arizona, assisted in round-ups, worked in Saudi Arabia, and has had the pleasure of traveling extensively. She now resides in Phoenix and spends much time in gardening, writing, and entertaining friends and family. Her published works include *Stranger on the Tonto* (Black Opal Books 2012), *Jake's Song* (Black Opal Books 2013), *The Vigilante* (Black Opal Books 2013), *Lifting the Veil of Secrets in Saudi Arabia* (Black Opal Books 2013), *The Avenger* (Black Opal Books 2014), *A Marriage of Convenience* (Black Opal Books 2014), *Ranch Wife* (Black Opal Books 2016), and *Hannah* (Black Opal Books 2016).